AF270775

REALITY CHECK

KIRPA SINGH

Copyright © 2021 by Kirpa Singh

All rights reserved.

No part of this book may be reproduced in any form or by any electronic or
mechanical means, including information storage and retrieval systems,
without written permission from the author, except for the use of brief
quotations in a book review.

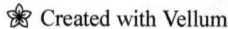 Created with Vellum

For my Nanaji

ਮੈਂ ਤੁਹਾਨੂੰ ਬਹੁਤ ਪਿਆਰ ਕਰਦੀ ਹਾਂ

I love you very much

CONTENTS

"Please," I breathed out, trying to catch my breath.

I removed myself from his lap and let him rise from the couch. He grabbed my hand to lead me upstairs, but as he started to pull me along, my phone chimed, signaling a text message.

"Hold on," I said, picking up my phone from the coffee table.

Elli: Yo, when you coming over?

My body and brain cooled off immediately. "Shit, I forgot I was supposed to study with Elli tonight." I groaned and looked at Dimitri apologetically.

He simply smiled. "No worries. I'll be here. You do what you have to do."

I smiled and leaned up on my toes to meet him for a quick peck.

"I'm sorry," I said, walking around the couch to the island in the kitchen and grabbing my backpack.

The kitchen was slightly messy, with dishes still in the double sink from the previous night's dinner. We had both been so tired from school and work that we'd loosened our strict rules for a day and left it until the morning, but they still hadn't been done.

I turned toward Dimitri and smiled softly. "Can you please do the dishes tonight?"

Dimitri held his hand up and nodded as he walked to the sink.

"How late will you be?" he asked, turning on the faucet.

"I don't know. We have a test tomorrow, and Elli is struggling a little bit. I have to make sure she has the material down." I zipped up my gray backpack and looked at Dimitri as I slung it over my shoulders. He started on the dishes, his face bathed in a golden glow from the sunset. From his voice to his looks to his personality, he was perfect in every way.

Sometimes, when I looked at him, I had no idea how I got so lucky. I wanted to shout about my love for him from rooftops. I wanted to take him out, show him off to the world, and have everyone marvel.

But that was against the rules.

"Babe, is it okay if I tell Elli about us tonight? You know… the truth?"

Dimitri stopped washing the dishes and looked at me.

"Priya, you know she can't know the truth. It could put us in danger."

"But she's my best friend. She's always asking about when she'll meet you, when we'll all go out—"

"Priya." Dimitri paused. "You weren't even supposed to tell her about me in the first place. Besides, she'll think you're crazy."

"Elli is the most understanding person in the world."

"I understand that, but think about how you reacted when I first told you I was undercover and hiding from the Russian government. It wouldn't be easier for her."

And that's why it was against the rules, among other reasons like it could put us in danger. Dimitri was right. I couldn't tell Elli the truth.

I sighed. "You're right. I won't tell her." I walked up to him and gave him a quick kiss on the cheek. "Thank you for doing the dishes. I'll see you later tonight."

I grabbed my car keys, and as soon as I pulled away from the house, the US government began monitoring me and narrating my moves.

"She's getting off the freeway," Stephan said.

"She's making a left," said a stern female voice, uniquely Monica's.

"She's parking the car." Stephan again.

The US government was constantly tracking our moves to

make sure we were safe and not about to be attacked. I was thankful for their constant presence in my ear, reminding me that I was never fully alone.

When I arrived at Elli's house, I locked the car twice before turning and walking up the front steps to her door. I rang the doorbell and waited for a few moments, listening as slow footsteps approached.

Mrs. Martinez opened the door and smiled at me. "Hi, Priya. Come on in. Elli is upstairs." Mrs. Martinez had a very soft, almost melodic voice that had a very calming and soothing effect. I imagined she would be a good reader for audiobooks.

I greeted Mrs. Martinez and stepped into the house before toeing off my shoes and heading up the stairs to Elli's room. Before I even opened the door, I heard her blasting EDM music, which I couldn't stand. The noise became even louder and more unbearable when I opened the door.

Elli sat in her chair, facing the wall, bouncing away to the noise, while at the same time writing something down.

Her bedroom was decorated like it had come out of a magazine. Her desk was positioned against the wall in a little nook across from the door. Above it was a picture frame with six different photos of her with friends around a letter board that said *C'est La Vie*, which had hung there for the last three years. The room's walls were plain white, much to Elli's dismay. She had always wanted to paint them a light purple, her favorite color.

I slammed the door shut to get her attention, being obnoxious on purpose, and she swirled her chair around to look at me.

"Jesus, it's about time! Here I am, about to fail tomorrow's test, and you were doing *what*, exactly?" she asked with mock sternness.

"Sorry, I was with, uh, Dimitri."

Elli narrowed her eyes at me. "So, am I ever going to meet this *Dimitri*, or what?"

I plastered on a fake smile. "He's really busy. I don't know when he'll be free, but I'll talk to him and see when we can all get together."

She hummed. "You better, babe. Or else I'm going to start thinking he's some sort of supernatural creature. Or better yet, isn't real. Now let's get to this math shit!" She swiveled back in her chair to face her desk. I laughed, glad to have dodged that bullet.

~

An hour into our studying, just as I was going over a math solution with Elli for the third time, I began experiencing weird malfunctions with my earpiece. I heard what the government had told me were intercepted signals from local radio stations in the form of odd radio commercials.

"This ain't yo' mama's cooking."

"Call 1-800-GET-CASH-TODAY!"

I began to hit my ear, trying to adjust the piece. Maybe if I hit it hard enough, like in TV shows, it would go back to working properly.

"Hey, are you okay?" Elli asked and I nodded. The signal interception and noises stopped, and I sighed with relief, making a mental note to myself to ask Stephan or Monica about that at some point.

"Yeah, sorry, just… weird ear feeling. Um, anyway, as I was saying—"

"Get out. Get out. Get out," I suddenly heard Stephan say, and I scrunched my eyebrows, knowing I couldn't respond to

Stephan in front of Elli, but also not sure what he was talking about. The ominous words were enough to cause alarm, but there was no context.

A few seconds of static noise made me think the alarming words hadn't actually been Stephan, that I'd misheard another radio commercial, but then his voice came back.

"Russians are attacking." His voice was level but urgent, and I tensed, standing up from the bed.

I pressed down on the skin above the ear device. "Stephan? Who is being attacked?" I tried to stay calm as my heart beat powerfully, like it was trying to get out of my chest.

"Priya? Who are you talking to?" Elli asked behind me.

I held up my hand to tell her to pause.

"Dimitri. Dimitri is under attack," Stephan said. Panic gripped me.

No, no, no. Fuck! My brain felt like it was melting under the pressure of trying to problem-solve, but the government had never trained me on how to handle this type of situation.

"I have to leave. Dimitri is being attacked," I said. I turned around and grabbed my stuff.

"Priya, what are you talking about? Who is attacking Dimitri, and how do you know that?" Elli asked. I groaned in frustration.

"The Russians are attacking! They want my secrets. They want Dimitri. I can't figure out what Y equals. X is the answer, but Y is unanswerable." I began stuffing my things haphazardly into my backpack. My head throbbed with a headache, a vein above my right eyebrow pulsing.

"What... what are you... saying?" Elli looked at me, confused.

"What do you mean? I don't have time to answer your questions. Time is a construct, but if I don't construct my car,

I won't be able to save Dimitri," I said angrily as I zipped up my backpack and flung it over one shoulder, sliding my other arm through the empty armhole.

Elli stood up from the bed and held her arms out to me. "Priya, I don't think you should drive. Maybe you're having a stroke or something. You're doing some weird... thing. You're not making any sense."

"I don't have cents. I only have dollars," I said, not understanding her statement or concern. I was definitely not having a stroke, unless the Russians had engineered a way to cause someone to have a stroke.

"Priya!" Dimitri yelled in my earpiece, loudly enough that the device emitted a piercing, shrill screech.

I gasped and pushed against my ear, looking toward the door, waiting to hear if he was okay before trying to rush into a situation that was beyond me and my training.

"Dimitri?" I asked out loud, not caring if Elli saw or heard. This was life or death, and I was sure the US government, including Stephan and Monica, would understand. "Dimitri? Can you hear me?"

There was no response.

"Priya, what is going on?" Elli looked at me as if I had turned purple and grown a horn.

"I told you already! Dimitri is in trouble!" I felt cornered, as if my brain were a car running into a wall with no ability to reverse. Some mental block prevented me from coming up with a proper plan of action.

"Priya, what are you talking about?" Elli asked as I began to pace in her room, trying to think and get my brain to work properly.

Keys. Grab keys, drive home. Let the US government know that Dimitri has been captured. Go save him.

I quickly grabbed my keys from the cupholder pocket of my backpack and raced out of Elli's room.

"Priya! Where are you going?" Elli yelled as she chased after me down the stairs.

"The Russian government has Dimitri! I have to save him!" I yelled as I shoved my feet into my shoes and ran to my car.

Elli didn't chase after me all the way to my car, and I was thankful. She must have understood that I had to save Dimitri and couldn't be distracted.

"She's driving to the house," I heard a new voice say that gave me chills. This voice was undeniably Russian.

The voices in my ear were changing, alternating between Russian and American, between government messages and radio signals.

"She's driving north." Russian.

"She's coming back home." Monica.

"Milk, cheese, eggs. Milk, cheese, eggs." Radio commercial.

The frequency in my earpiece must have been affected by the Russian attack.

"Dimitri? Dima, baby?" I called out into my microphone, hoping Dimitri would reply. I was thankful that there didn't seem to be any cops on the roads as I sped toward home because I for sure would have been pulled over.

When I parked my car at home in the driveway, next to Dimitri's, I saw the lights were off inside the house, sending me into panic mode.

He has to be here. He has to be okay. He has to be.

I rushed out of the car and toward the front door, fumbling with my keys, but when I finally opened the door, I was welcomed by a forest.

The world around me was dark and smelled like freshly rained on grass. Despite being covered, my feet grew cold and damp. I shivered as the air around me froze me to my core. The sun had set fully now, and I could barely see a foot in front of me.

I slowly walked through the thick vegetation, my arms outstretched in an attempt to feel my way around. I twisted and turned, moving as carefully as I could until I saw a single dim light. Then, like a moth to a flame, I flew to it.

"Eagle, come in. Eagle." I tried to get the attention of my government agents as I ran, but no one answered.

As I drew closer to the light, I could make out a clearing with a giant tree in the center and two figures near the base.

"Come and play if you want to save him." The voice in my ear belonged to the same Russian man from earlier.

When I got closer, my steps faltered, the image in front of me almost bringing me to my knees.

I stared at Dimitri, tied up in front of the tree, his head hanging low, his legs sprawled out in front of him. His hands seemed to be tied behind his back, the tree serving to support his sitting position. He looked unharmed, aside from the fact that he seemed unconscious. A tall man, almost as tall as Dimitri's impressive six foot three, stood above him. He was more muscular than Dimitri, though. He had dark hair, a bit of stubble, and a sharp nose. His arms were crossed over his chest, and he stood firmly at Dimitri's side.

He was also holding a long, curved knife.

"We have your husband now, Mrs. Ivanov. Give us the information we want, and we'll let your husband go free," the Russian agent said before kneeling next to Dimitri. He picked Dimitri's head up by his hair and placed the knife to his throat. I gasped and took one step closer, only to be stopped by the agent.

"If you come closer, I'll slit his throat!" he said sharply.

I gulped. "What do you want to know?" My voice shook and came out softer than I intended.

"What was Dimitri working on with the US government?" the agent asked.

"I don't know! He wouldn't tell me details," I said, louder than before and standing my ground.

"That's not the answer we were looking for. Now, I'll give you ten seconds to give me the correct one, or it's 'bye-bye, husband.'" The agent pressed the knife closer to Dimitri's throat. I could see the indent it left, and my stomach flipped. My feet felt cemented to the ground, unable to move. I was helpless and powerless, watching my husband being held hostage by this brutish villain.

"One," the man called out.

My mind scrambled to think of an answer.

"Two."

Think, Priya, think. Lie if you have to; just save Dimitri.

"Three."

"He's... he..." My mind wouldn't think straight, and I couldn't come up with an answer that made sense.

"Don't even think about lying. Five."

My pulse quickened. I could feel my heart beating in my chest at a rapid-fire pace. I felt the beating all the way in my ears and my stomach, my anxiety ratcheting up.

"Seven!"

"It has something to do with combatting Russian biochemical warfare; that's all I know!" I yelled at the agent.

"What about it?"

"I don't know!" My voice cracked as my throat became constricted. I felt the tears welling up in my eyes, burning their way free.

"Not good enough. Nine."

"Please, *no*!"

"*Ten!*" The agent smiled. Then, in one fluid motion, he pulled the knife straight across Dimitri's neck.

The scene didn't play out like in the action movies. There was no fountain of blood gushing out from Dimitri's neck. Instead, a glowing line of red appeared below his chin, and when his head fell forward again, blood poured down his pale neck like a waterfall.

As I watched the scene unfold, I could only stand in place. I felt almost like I was in a dream, a nightmare, not quite knowing if I was asleep, but hoping I was. The scene was so horrific, it couldn't be real.

So, I tried to wake up. I tried to will myself to open my eyes and wake up in bed or on the couch, or anywhere that wasn't there.

But I didn't. And finally, I screamed as the agent stood and backed away into the darkness, my lower extremities still cemented in place. Blood drenched Dimitri's navy shirt, and his body began to shift away from the tree until he fell over onto his side and began bleeding out into the grass beneath him.

When the reality of the scene fully settled in my brain, my feet pulled free of their paralysis, and I broke into a sprint across the grass. I fell to my knees in the dirt at Dimitri's side, scraping my knees through my jeans as if I had fallen onto concrete.

"Dima? Dima, baby, I have you. I've got you," I said above his limp body. The blood continued to pour down his neck and onto the ground beneath him.

Frantically, I tried to think of what to do next. All I could do was gently lift his head to my thigh and move my hands to his neck in an attempt to stop the bleeding. I felt the slippery sliminess of Dimitri's blood coating my hands, and my tears blurred my vision. I smelled the metallic scent of nickel in the air, almost able to taste it in my mouth. I couldn't help but gag. I tried to breathe through my mouth instead of my nose, keeping my head up to drain the tears while still trying to keep an eye on Dimitri and cover his wound.

"Help! *Help!*" I yelled, hoping people would hear my cries.

Suddenly, the world around me began to stretch, shift, and morph, as if I were finally waking up from this dream, as if it were slowly fading away. The ground beneath me had turned into gray concrete, illuminated by a light above me. I looked up and saw that I was kneeling beneath a streetlight. I turned around and saw that I was back in our neighborhood, in front of Dimitri's place. A dark gray car drove past me, and the driver immediately pulled over, not even bothering to park correctly. I was surprised, but relieved, to see Ms. Agarwal run out of the car.

"Please! Call an ambulance!" That's what I tried to get out through my sobs, but it came out almost incomprehensibly.

"Priya! What is going on? Why are you outside?" Ms. Agarwal kneeled beside me, and I cried harder in frustration, my throat feeling raw.

"Don't you see Dimitri dying? Call an ambulance!" I yelled at her, making her jump back in surprise. I looked back down at Dimitri. My tears dropped onto him, and my hands began to slip against his throat. I tried my best to keep them plugging the wound.

"*Chotu*, who are you talking about? Why are you crying?"

"Dimitri! Dimitri is dying! Call an ambulance!" I yelled again, sending her a pleading look. How could she just stay there and continue acting like my real mother? Did she not realize my husband was dying? Did she not see me holding together his slit throat?

I looked back down at Dimitri and cried harder. I felt even more helpless and powerless than before. If I weren't plugging his wound, I would have called the ambulance myself, but I had to save Dimitri. I had to keep him alive.

"Hello, yes. I need medical assistance right away," I heard my *mom* finally say, and I sighed, an ounce of relief forming inside me.

"You're going to be okay, Dima. Help is on the way. Don't worry," I said to him softly, over and over again, comforting myself more than I was comforting him. I doubted he could even hear me, but I needed to say the words out loud in order to make them real.

But the feeling that he was gone crept up my spine. His body lay pale and motionless across my thighs; his eyes were closed, without even a twitch of movement, and his face was frozen, almost like he was in a peaceful sleep.

You can't leave me. You have to wake up. I wanted to move my hands from the wound, to see if he would wake up, but I was paralyzed in horror. If I moved, I would risk blood spurting out again. So, I shifted my hands just slightly over his neck, registering the crusty feeling of dried blood over my fingers.

I didn't feel a pulse.

"Hi, Priya. How can we help today?" I heard a gentle male voice ask. I looked up from Dimitri and saw a young man kneeling in front of us. Behind him were an ambulance and a cop car. Ms. Agarwal was talking to the cops, gesturing frantically.

I looked back at the man kneeling in front of me.

"Dimitri. You have to save… Dimitri." The words that

came out were hoarse in my dry throat, like sandpaper against wood.

The man looked at me and nodded.

"All right. I'll take care of Dimitri. My name is Brandon, and that's Ryan. Is it okay if Ryan takes a look at you?" Brandon motioned to my left. I followed the motion with my head to look at another young man, apparently named Ryan, kneeling next to me, smiling.

I looked down at Dimitri and then at Brandon.

"I've been trying to stop the bleeding, but there's so much blood. The Russian slit his throat. I tried... I tried to stop the bleeding..." I croaked out, and Brandon's face contorted with sympathy and concern.

"It's okay, Priya. You did the best you could. Can you trust us to take care of you now? We've got it from here." Brandon's voice remained soft. Yet, it held enough authority to make me feel safe, like I could trust him to keep Dimitri safe and, even more, to bring him back.

I slowly nodded before hesitantly releasing my hands from Dimitri's throat. The blood didn't flow, and I began to panic, the overwhelming sense that he was gone crushing me.

"Don't worry about Dimitri. I've got him. You just go with Ryan, okay?"

Brandon took over Dimitri's care, removing Dimitri's head from my thigh and gently placing it on the ground.

"May I help you up?" Ryan asked. I looked up and noticed he was now standing, hunched over with his hand outstretched toward me.

I looked at his clean hands, then at my bloody ones.

"I'm sorry," I whispered as I placed my hands in his and let him pull me up.

"For what?"

"I just got blood on your hands. They were so clean, and I

ruined them." My voice sounded pained, even to my ears. It was like my voice carried all the sorrows in the world in it.

Ryan's face contorted with confusion for a moment, and then the same soft smile that Brandon wore appeared across his lips.

"It's okay," he said simply. "Let's go to that cop car, all right? Brandon will bring... Dimitri to the hospital in the ambulance. I'd like to check you for some wounds and ask you some questions. Is that all right?"

I nodded, and we walked toward the cop car where Ms. Agarwal was still talking to the cops. They wore different uniforms than Ryan or Brandon. They were a similar dark blue, maybe black, but the cops had more gear on.

As we neared them, Ms. Agarwal turned to me immediately, her expression shifting from panicked to pure concern. She ran over to me, and her arms wrapped around me in a tight hug. I wanted to hug her back. She felt like the only person I had left. But I didn't want to get blood all over her nice blouse, so I simply squeezed her with my upper arms, holding my hands high in the air behind her as the tears flowed down my cheeks again. Her hug felt warm and almost filled the void I was feeling in my chest.

He's not dead. Brandon will save him. He's not dead.

"Thank God Elli called me, Priya. What just happened?" she asked when she pulled away from me.

"The Russians. They got to Dimitri," I whispered, my throat sore from screaming and crying.

"Who's Dimitri, Priya? What are you talking about?" Ms. Agarwal's questions were a little more forceful than I would have liked, but they were so very her. She wasn't without concern, but her concern was mixed with anger and frustration.

"He's my husband. He's the man I was just trying to

save," I said, looking incredulously between her and Ryan. I looked behind me and saw Brandon had already taken Dimitri away, as the space where they had previously been was vacant. I turned back to Ryan and Ms. Agarwal, and they exchanged a look before Ms. Agarwal tilted her head slightly.

"Priya, there was no one there."

2

APRIL 20TH, 2018

"ALL RIGHT, Priya, let's try this again. How old are you?" Avery, my new therapist, asked from her desk, where she had been inputting some notes onto the computer. She had small ringlets of brown hair extending out around her head like a curly halo. She wore a casual baby blue t-shirt, but had on a pair of perfect, pitch-black slacks that looked more comfortable than the ones Ms. Agarwal wore. Everything about her screamed casual and friendly, even her smile. She had a very soft smile, and in the time we'd known each other, it never reached her eyes or curled up too far. Big smiles usually creeped me out and screamed *fake*, so I was thankful for that.

I sighed. "I'm twenty-two."

"But you also believe that you are disguised as a sixteen-year-old, correct?" Avery asked, clicking her pen.

I nodded. "Yes. I'm actually twenty-two, and I've been disguised as a high school student since I married Dimitri last year. I told you all of this yesterday!" My frustration was starting to seep into my voice.

"Yes, but I'm trying to understand better. Can you remind me again why you had to go undercover?" Avery looked down at her notepad and put the pen she was holding on the paper, ready to take notes.

I slouched as I let out a deep breath, feeling annoyed and defeated. If we had been in any other situation, I would never tell a soul about Dimitri's and my mission.

But this was a unique situation, and I didn't have the care or the concern to keep up our disguise now. I couldn't tell if my apathy or my guard being down was because of the medication they had been giving me or because I had just lost my husband, and nothing seemed to matter anymore.

Maybe it was both.

"Dimitri was working on a highly classified project for the US government that was supposed to counterstrike the attacks of the Russian government. I don't know much about it because it was confidential, but before we met, his project details leaked. The Russians started to hunt him down. So, the US government disguised him as a college student. He wasn't supposed to, but while undercover, he started dating me. I only knew snippets about his life as an agent. But after we got married in secret, we told the government, and they disguised me as a high school student to keep the marriage and my identity a secret from the Russians. No one would think to look for me in a high school in Saratoga." I leaned back against the couch, crossing my legs and arms as I waited for Avery to continue with her questioning.

She paused for a short while before clicking her pen and putting it and her notebook on her desk. She faced me and leaned back in her chair as well, crossing her legs without closing off her posture.

"Okay. How about you tell me how you and Dimitri met?" Avery said with that soft smile.

I looked at her for a short while as I tried to remember when and how Dimitri and I met, although I didn't have to try too hard. I was all of a sudden surrounded by the smell of coffee. I could hear the sounds of the coffee shop—muted talking, cups hitting tables, the machines working to create drinks.

"We met four years ago, when I was a freshman in college. He was a barista at a local coffee shop. I thought he was cute, and when he asked for my name for the order, I made a joke about giving him my number instead of my name. He said he wouldn't mind taking down both." I smiled, remembering the experience as if it were happening for the first time.

"That's very cute. Was Dimitri your first love?" Avery's words pulled me out of my daze, especially her word choice. *Was*.

"Yes," I said, looking down at my lap as I uncrossed my arms and fiddled with my hands. Looking at my nails, I noticed they had grown exceptionally long and brittle. My tan skin looked ashy and dry. I needed to use moisturizer.

"Can you tell me how you found Ms. Agarwal to be your cover mom?"

I paused again, trying to remember the answer to Avery's question. Only this time, I was drawing a blank. "I don't know. It must have been the US government who found her."

"Do you believe she isn't your mom? What about your sister?"

I shrugged. "They are my family, yes, but also no. They have become like family to me, to the point that I consider them like my mom and sister."

"What about your real parents? Your real family?"

"I don't... have one..." My answer seemed incomplete and didn't make sense, even to me. It was as if there were a hole in my brain where the information used to be. My head began to hurt, a small spot behind my left eyebrow, as

Avery's questions probed deeper and deeper. She was starting to go into classified territory, a place I barely understood and barely asked about. I was just told to stay low, quiet, and not get involved in the projects, or else it would be me who endured the consequences.

Just like Dimitri.

Dimitri's corpse popped into my head, an intrusive and vibrant memory that I couldn't turn off.

I shook as a shiver ran up my spine.

"How long have you known your friend… Elli, is it?"

"My whole life," I said matter-of-factly. Avery smiled a different, strange smile, almost like she had captured me in a trap and was refraining from saying "gotcha."

"How old is Elli?"

"She's sixteen."

"So how is it possible that you've known her your whole life, Priya?"

I stared at Avery and blinked a few times, her words not registering in my head. I had to replay them a few times before I could respond.

"I don't… I don't understand," I said, more so to myself than to her.

Elli was sixteen years old and had been my best friend since I was born. And yet, I was twenty-two. So how *could* we have been friends our whole lives? I remembered my entire life with her, and yet how could I have those memories?

"I'm saying," Avery continued softly, as if speaking any louder would break me, "that you and Elli cannot be lifelong friends if you are twenty-two and she is sixteen."

My eyes darted all over the room as I tried to piece together what Avery was saying, my brain rushing in different directions to create a solution to this problem. However, something was blocking my brain from creating the solution and finding the answer it needed. I felt agitated, and my body began to itch, as if ants were crawling on me.

My brain was about to explode.

"I think that's enough for today's session. You have a lot to process and think about."

And just like that, Avery left me hanging on one of the biggest cliffhangers of my life.

I have to talk to Elli.

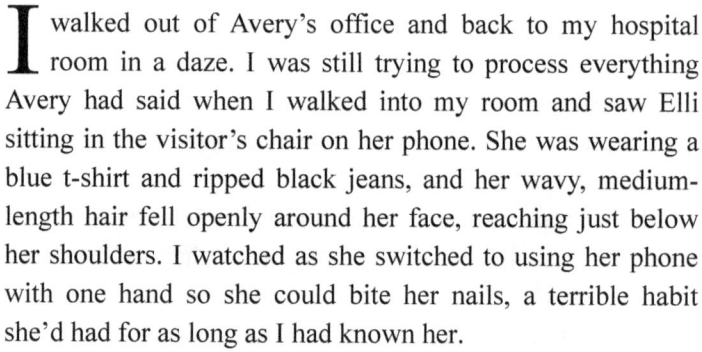

I walked out of Avery's office and back to my hospital room in a daze. I was still trying to process everything Avery had said when I walked into my room and saw Elli sitting in the visitor's chair on her phone. She was wearing a blue t-shirt and ripped black jeans, and her wavy, medium-length hair fell openly around her face, reaching just below her shoulders. I watched as she switched to using her phone with one hand so she could bite her nails, a terrible habit she'd had for as long as I had known her.

I've known her my whole life. How is it that I have two lives?

Elli looked up at me, immediately putting her phone down.

"Hey! Can we get some food? I'm starving and I hear the food here is edible," she said as she stood up, stretching a little as she waited for my response.

I stared at her a little longer, taking in her image.

I remembered her as a child, when we were seven and in the same second grade class. I remembered when we were starting middle school together and she started to experiment with makeup. I remembered throughout the years when she was bullied, when she cried, when we laughed together and were angry at each other. I remembered how she had aged and changed, and yet remained my same best friend.

How?

"How long have we known each other, Elli?" I asked her bluntly. She paused mid-stretch and looked at me for a second before replying.

"We met when we were babies. Remember the stories our moms told us?" Elli's voice was also soft, just like Avery's. Maybe everyone thought I was fragile and would break if they talked to me like a normal person.

I remembered the stories Elli was talking about. I remembered hearing my mom and Elli's were in the hospital together for their prenatal checkups and found out they were practically neighbors, living only a few minutes away from each other. They became fast friends, gave birth two months apart, and when my mom's maternity leave was up, she asked Elli's mom to help babysit me. Elli's mom said yes, and Elli and I had been inseparable ever since.

But how could I believe these supposed stories from our childhood if mine were different from hers? Wasn't this life supposed to be a disguise?

"Elli, I'm really confused. I don't understand anything right now," I said. My eyes traced the valleys and cracks in the linoleum tiles as I waited for her response. I heard her sneakers squeak on the floor, and when I looked up, she was standing in front of me. She had always been a few inches shorter than me, but at that moment, I felt so much smaller.

"Let's get food. We can talk in the cafeteria. Plus, I know food will cheer you up. I know you," Elli said, the last words a strong statement of trust and knowledge.

I nodded and followed her out of the room.

"That geometry test was hard as fuck, too, by the way,"

Elli said as we walked down the halls. My lips picked up in a slight smile at her sailor's mouth.

I felt bad that I hadn't helped her when I was supposed to, or at least not to the extent that I could have. "How do you think you did?"

"I think I passed, and that's all I care about. I'll do better on the next test, especially with your genius brain to help me once you get out of this place."

We both looked around at our surroundings. It was pretty nice, but it was still a hospital, so not exactly cozy or warm or even inviting. It was cold and busy. Despite being full of life in the form of patients and nurses, the atmosphere felt dead.

We entered the cafeteria, and after getting two turkey sandwiches, we sat down at a table in a less crowded section and ate.

Elli was right. I did feel better with food in my system, even if it wasn't the most enjoyable.

"All right, babe. Tell me what's on your mind." Elli took a sip from her soda and looked at me expectantly.

I sighed as I dropped my half-eaten sandwich and wiped my hands.

"So today, Avery was asking me all these questions about Dimitri. How we met, how old we are. And then she asked about my identity, and somehow, my relationships came up. Like, with Ms. Agarwal, Jasmine, and you, and... it was so confusing. I have all these memories of you, but I also just... have another set of memories of another life—and I believed Dimitri. I know how it sounds, being undercover and all that, but I believed him. And now, I'm just not sure. Nothing makes sense, and every time I arrive at one conclusion, my brain rushes to another or questions something else. My brain is just constantly answering and questioning, answering and questioning." I took a deep breath and covered my face with my hands for a few seconds as I tried to calm myself down.

"Can I be honest, Priya?" Elli asked.

I nodded.

"I have some ideas about this, too, and I'm not sure if you've thought of these. I think bringing up your memories is really good because it helps to see what's real and what isn't. Like, even a few months ago, when you first told me about Dimitri, I was wondering if that coffee shop story was real. Because, let's be honest, babe, you are not that ballsy." Elli shrugged and continued. "What else was going on that I didn't know about?"

I took a deep breath before continuing. "I would hear the US government in my ears. They would track my movements, and kind of… narrate what was going on while they monitored my whereabouts. I also stay with Dimitri when Ms. Agarwal is away on her business trips or just go there while she's at work."

"Where does he live?"

"Well, he was placed in off-campus housing near SJSU." I was referring to San Jose State University, which wasn't too far from Ms. Agarwal's house.

"Priya, where were you the night Dimitri died? Were you at his place?" Elli's question surprised me. She should have known the answer to that.

"Yes."

Elli stared at me. I could tell she was thinking carefully over her next words.

"Priya, you were found in front of your house, your mom's house, that night. I called your mom and told her you were behaving strangely and going to find your boyfriend, Dimitri. But when she asked me where he lived, I didn't have an answer, so I told her to check near your house. You were found under that lamppost right in front of your house. Not near SJSU."

I blinked at Elli as I tried to comprehend what she was saying.

I distinctly remembered driving to Dimitri's house that night, so how could that be?

"No. No, I remember driving to his place," I said slowly as I processed Elli's words.

"But... how can that be if he never... existed?" she asked, her words carefully enunciated and spaced out as she tried to tread carefully with them.

"He—of course he existed, Elli! I'm not crazy!" I said, a little too loudly. She was taken aback by my volume and looked around the room before answering me.

"I never said you were crazy, babe. I'm just saying he wasn't... real." Her voice was soft, but neither her tone nor the fact that she was only repeating herself softened the blow of her words.

"Just because you never met him, you're telling me he isn't real?" I asked incredulously.

"Priya, please. I'm telling you what the doctors are saying. When the paramedics found you that night, you were alone. Your mom found you with your hands pushing into your thigh as you tried to save someone who didn't exist in the first place." Elli's words hit me like a car, and I felt myself being pulled in two opposite directions, one toward Dimitri and one toward Elli.

Who was I to believe?

"Priya. I love you; you know that. I would never say something to hurt you if I didn't think you needed to hear it." Elli's words were full of love and compassion. I knew she was right. She had never done anything to hurt me. She was the most understanding person I knew, so if she didn't understand and didn't believe in Dimitri, who would?

All of a sudden, despite not completely understanding what was going on, a small voice in my head began to question everything, and for some reason, that voice seemed to be the only direction my brain went that didn't get caught in a circle.

Why would the government disguise a married couple as a high schooler and a college student?

What could Dimitri have been working on that threatened the Russian government so much?

How did I have lifelong memories of my cover family and Elli if I had only been with them for a year?

Why hadn't the government done a better job of extracting me from this mission now that Dimitri was—

"Are you okay?" Elli reached across the table and ghosted her hand over mine. I looked at it, seeing the contrast of her lighter, warm complexion against my tan, cool toned skin. My eyes followed her hand up her arm and settled on her face. She had hazel eyes, similar to Dimitri's, and I wanted to cry.

How could a girl like me land a guy like him?

"I think... I'm starting to understand." My voice was weak, not holding any sort of strong opinion or decision. I was unsure of what exactly to believe in and who to trust. I wasn't even sure if I could believe myself.

But I had always trusted Elli. She knew me well, and I would even go so far as to say she knew me better than I knew myself.

So, if she was telling me that something was wrong—that something was wrong with me—then I believed her. Because if I couldn't believe myself, then I had to at least believe Elli. Right?

"What are you thinking now?" Elli asked.

"I can't believe myself right now, so I'm telling myself to believe you. I don't know that I *do* believe you yet, but... I think I can trust you more than I can trust myself in terms of what—or who—is real," I said, looking up at her. She was nodding.

"I'm real, babe. I always have been, always will be. If you are ever in doubt about what else is real, ask me."

∿

I sat in my psychiatrist's office with my mom and sister. I sat in one of the sofa seats while Dr. Worblack sat in a desk chair, and my mom and sister sat on the loveseat. My sister, Jasmine, had come down from San Francisco for the family session with Dr. Worblack after my mom called her the previous day.

"Priya has schizophrenia," Dr. Worblack said matter-of-factly.

"What—what does that mean? Will she be okay?" my mom asked.

"Schizophrenia is a mental illness characterized by disturbances in the person's perception of reality. For example, Priya had visual and auditory hallucinations as well as delusions of persecution, and other symptoms. It's too early to tell if she'll be 'okay.' With most cases, successful lives are achievable, but it depends on what you define as success."

"Well, will she be able to go to college? Have a job? How will this affect her ability to live independently?" Jasmine asked. My mother's hand hovered over her mouth.

"That depends on how Priya's illness progresses. This is the first big episode she's had, and hopefully, it's the last. At least for a while. Basically, imagine there's a wall between Priya's illness and her brain. The more episodes she has, the more the wall gets chipped away. As long as Priya takes her medication as prescribed, sees a therapist, and takes care of her mental health, the wall will stay strong, and there's really no limit on what she can achieve. It's true that the life she would have led without this illness will be a lot harder to live now, but it's possible."

We all sat in a triangle, as if Dr. Worblack wanted us all to feel included, and yet the adults were talking as if I weren't around.

"What should we do to help her? How can we make sure she's able to still live that life?" My mom was talking with her professional voice now. I imagined she spoke to her clients and coworkers like this when she needed to solve their marketing problems.

"For starters, she needs to cut back from strenuous activities. I know she's graduating a year early from high school, but if she can take fewer AP classes—"

"That's out of the question. She needs them in order to get into a good college."

"Mom!" My sister gave her a look that told her, as respectfully as possible, to shut up.

"I understand that, Ms. Agarwal, but if Priya can't handle the stress, then going to college will be out of the question, anyway."

"Why don't we ask Priya how she feels about all this? She knows better than us what she can and can't handle," Jasmine said, giving me a look to start talking. I simply stared at her for a few minutes before looking at my mom and psychiatrist.

My husband just died, and I was being fed this story that he was never real, which may or may not have been true. And these people are expecting me to make a decision about my mental health like this?

I felt annoyed but was too sluggish and tired to say all that I wanted to say. I honestly just wanted to leave this horrible facility and go home. But not my mom's home... Dimitri's home. I wanted to sleep in *our* bed. I wanted to have a fight with him about him wearing shoes in the house. I wanted to sit next to him on the couch and read: me a romance novel and him some boring non-fiction book about particles or whatever. Maybe Freud.

"Do you actually understand Freud?" I asked Dimitri as I lay on the couch with him, my head in his lap and his hand petting my head.

"Sometimes, but enough to get by," he said without looking away from his book.

The memory played in my head, and the normalcy of it, the mundaneness of it, made me want to crawl into bed with a book and pretend he was there.

"At this point, I just want to go home."

"Well, it is the end of your psychiatric hold. Your mom can decide to take you home now. However, if that's the decision, I would like to discuss protocol for taking Priya home." Dr. Worblack was talking to both my mom and me.

"What protocol? I want to take Priya home as soon as possible," my mother said.

"I would advise you keep Priya at home, no locked or closed bedroom doors and no windows ajar. Watch her for a couple of days, maybe another week. I wouldn't have her go back to school until the medication has been fully integrated into her system. We put her on three-hundred milligrams of Seroquel, and I'd like to see her every two weeks to check how she's doing and see if we need to up the dosage. I would also advise that Priya take up some sort of sport. Studies have shown that exercise is very beneficial for those with a mental illness, even more so than everyone else."

When Dr. Worblack had finished prescribing a new lifestyle for me, we all exited the office.

"How do you feel about everything?" Jasmine asked from the passenger seat of the car. The two of us were just sitting there with the windows rolled down, waiting for my mom to sign all the necessary paperwork for my release.

"I don't know, *didi*. A part of me doesn't even want to call you *didi* anymore because—are you really my older sister? Or are you just part of my disguise? But also, if Dimitri is… gone… then what's the point of my disguise? Why hasn't the government picked me up and taken me back to my old life?" I sighed and raked my fingers through my hair. It was oily and smooth, in desperate need of a wash.

"That's a good sign, though, right? The fact that you're questioning it means you don't fully believe that this is all a disguise."

I shrugged. "I mean, I guess?"

"Do you remember growing up together?"

Oddly enough, I did, so I nodded.

"If I were just part of your cover, would you have memories of us when we were younger? Also, who in their right mind would make us ten years apart as part of a disguise? That's a pretty mean disguise to give someone. Like, why even put a sister in your life in the first place if I'm barely gonna be in the same generation as you?" she said, rolling her eyes.

I laughed.

"You're gonna be okay, Priya. You're a smart kid. You'll get through this."

I stared at her and nodded, taking a deep breath, and trying to imagine what life would be like now.

The driver's door opened, and my mom slid into the seat.

"Hold this, Jasmine." My mom handed my sister her purse before turning back to me.

"I'm going to be working from home all of next week. I'm also going to have Elli get you your assignments from class, and you're going to catch up and do well on those AP tests, okay?" Even though my mom ended the statement as a question, I knew I had no choice in the matter.

"Okay."

3

MAY 26TH, 2018

I WOKE up to the smell and sounds of my mom making *aaloo paranthe,* my favorite Indian brunch food. The sun peeked through my blinds and coated my pale blue bed with streaks of light. I stretched and kicked off the sheets before rolling over to grab my phone off the bedside table, taking it off the charger.

Scrolling through social media, I saw my "friends" posting their food, early vacations, family, and pets.

I rolled my eyes when I scrolled past the couples posting their anniversary pictures and sighed, closing my eyes as I mentally kicked myself for believing I had that not too long ago.

Our anniversary was November 10.

It had been a little over a month since I was released from the hospital. It had been only two weeks, however, since I became lucid, as Avery puts it. Two weeks ago, I became fully aware that I was a sixteen-year-old, that my name is Priya Agarwal, not Priya Ivanov, and that this life is my real life. While Avery called that being lucid, I liked to say I became "sober." That was what I was calling my removal from that world—sobriety. It was me putting space between myself and the toxic drug that is my illness.

It was me putting space between myself and Dimitri.

My phone vibrated, and I opened my eyes and saw a banner hanging from the top of the screen with a text notification from Elli.

I opened the text to see a picture of a wrist with a hospital band on it.

Priya: Whose is that?

Elli: Mine lol.

My eyes widened at Elli's response, and I sat up abruptly in bed, my head spinning slowly for a few seconds at the sudden movement. I called her immediately, and she answered on the first ring with her typical ringing laughter.

"Hey, babe—"

"What the fuck happened?" I whispered roughly into the phone. I eyed my door, thankful it was closed and I had regained those privileges back.

Elli sighed into the phone before responding, "Alcohol poisoning. I didn't mean to worry you. I thought it was funny. Relax, baby girl, I'm stronger than that." She laughed again, and I sighed into the phone.

Of course, I was worried about Elli. I couldn't even fathom that a sixteen-year-old would have gotten so drunk she'd need to be hospitalized. A part of me wanted to believe that she had probably been egged on by upperclassmen or something. I couldn't think of her being that irresponsible.

But lately, it was getting easier and easier to believe that Elli *was* that irresponsible.

"Alcohol poisoning? Jesus Christ, Elli. Did they call your parents? Do they know what happened?"

"Nope. Doctor–patient confidentiality and whatever."

I groaned, cursing the fact that she was so relaxed about this.

"Elli, please, you told me you would be careful! This *isn't* being careful!"

"Priya, will you relax? I'm not dead, am I? It's going to take more than just alcohol to get me. Anyway, you can lecture me more in the car because I need a ride home."

I groaned and rubbed my face with my hands. "Fine. Just… give me a few minutes to convince my mom to let me drive. Do you need clothes or anything?" I asked.

"Nope, I'll just do the walk of shame," she said with a chuckle, and I rolled my eyes.

I told her I'd be there soon, and after she texted me which hospital she was in, I got ready. I shoved my legs into a pair of Adidas joggers, knowing I would not be allowed to leave the house wearing pajama shorts, or any shorts for that matter, and put on a t-shirt.

I shuffled down the stairs and walked past the living room toward the open kitchen to see my mom creating the mixture for the *paranthe*. She was humming along to some 2000s song, and I amazed myself by knowing the name, *Teri Ore*.

"Morning, mama," I said as I walked up beside her and leaned against the edge of the countertop she was using.

"Good morning," she said melodically. She was very much a morning person and was always chipper in the morning. "Your *didi* is coming over for brunch and should be here soon," she said with a smile. I nodded and leaned over to place my head on my hand.

"Okay," I said, hesitating to bring up Elli and the car. After my episode, my mom was afraid that I might hallucinate while driving and hurt myself. Hopefully, now, she would feel better about me driving.

"Ummm, Elli wants to come over for brunch too. Is that

okay?" I asked, making up a plan that would get me a "yes" from her.

My mom smiled. "Sure!" she said as she mixed up all the ingredients in a wide rimmed silver bowl that held potato filling. The smell of cumin and coriander filled my nose as I took a deep breath before continuing.

"She needs me to pick her up. Is it okay if I go get her?" My words were fast, and my mom's mixing became slow until she came to a stop as she stared down at the bowl. She then looked at me, analyzing me and thinking over her decision. Her demeanor shifted from light and chipper to stern and critical, almost cold.

"How are you feeling?"

This wasn't a question about my temperature or a cough. No, she meant how was I doing mentally. "I'm feeling at my best. Remember that breakthrough I had two weeks ago with Avery? Where I fully realized Dimitri isn't real? I feel like I'm back to being my normal self. No hallucinations or delusions in sight either," I said, my heart racing as I spoke. I felt like when I was younger and had to ask my mom if I could sleep over at a friend's house while she was in a bad mood. Instead of her asking how I was feeling, she would have asked if I had all my chores, school homework, and extra Kumon homework done, and even if all of that was complete, she could, and probably would, still say no.

She hummed and looked down at the mixing bowl, slowly mixing again, putting more force into mashing the potatoes, spices, and herbs together.

"I don't know, *chotu*. I—"

"I promise I'll be safe! No hallucinations, remember?" I pleaded, accidentally cutting her off in my haste to convince her. She looked at me with narrowed eyes before looking back down at the potatoes, letting out a sigh that caused her shoulders to rise and drop dramatically.

There was a long pause as she just mixed and mixed and mixed, until finally, she spoke.

"Okay. Just text me when you get to her house, text me when you leave, and send me your ETA," my mom said, and my heart sped up even more.

"Okay. I'm picking her up from a friend's house, but yes, I will. See you soon!" I said hurriedly as I ran out of the kitchen, grabbed my keys, and ran out the door before she could change her mind.

Priya: I'm on my way. You're coming over for brunch too. Needed an excuse to pick you up. We're eating those stuffed Indian tortilla things.

Elli: Oh fuck yeah! I'm so down.

I rolled my eyes and smiled at Elli's response, but my expression quickly changed to one of concern and something I couldn't quite name.

I reversed out of the driveway, and the GPS routed me to the hospital as Bollywood music played, my mom's music choice for that morning influencing my mood. My mind wandered, and I thought about my relationship with Elli as Neha Kakkar sang to me.

Ever since we were kids, I had been protective of Elli. In kindergarten, someone called her ugly, and she came crying to me on the playground, bawling her eyes out. I immediately walked up to the little punk and yelled at him so much *he* started to cry and called one of the on-duty attendants to come over. We were kids, so none of us got in trouble. We just had to apologize to each other, and everything was fine.

In fifth grade, a rumor started around school that Elli was gay, and a few boys started to tease her. Once again, I remember her crying to me. Without hesitation, I put those kids in their place, scaring them enough that they told everyone they made up the rumor.

In seventh grade, Elli had her first boyfriend, and he was an asshole who cheated on her—in a way only a child could, true, like holding another girl's hand; but he'd cheated, nonetheless. By that time, Elli had stopped crying over anything that upset her, but I could tell she was hurt and broken up over it. I didn't confront the boy that time, as per Elli's wish, but I supported her through it and made him pay in subtle ways like tripping him whenever I could.

When we entered high school, I watched as Elli's skin thickened even more and she became increasingly more independent and fiercer, but also slightly destructive as the bullying stopped. Freshman year, she really blossomed, and all the boys who used to tease her in middle school began to want her. She had always been gorgeous, but with a new hairstyle, hair color, and a little bit of makeup, she looked like a model. The attention she received was an ego boost she greatly needed, but it led her down a path that didn't ease my worry or protectiveness of her.

She began to get invites to parties, and one beer at one party turned into two at the next, then a few beers and a shot, until she was drinking a beer *and* taking two, three, sometimes four shots at parties.

I thought she was responsible. I thought she was capable of taking care of herself.

Obviously, she was not.

I pulled up in front of the hospital and texted my mom that I was at Elli's friend's house. Then I texted Elli that I was there.

As soon as the passenger door opened, I looked at Elli and saw her bare face, which she probably washed in the hospital. I saw her pale-yellow tank top and black, distressed shorts and could basically hear my mom in my ears screaming *besharam*, shameless, at me if I had worn the same clothes. She loved Elli, but I think even Elli wearing those would give her a heart attack.

"You are *not* gonna do the walk of shame in *that* in front of *my* mom. You're going to change into my pajamas," I said, sending my mom my estimated arrival time and driving off.

"Your mom loves me, however I look!" She said as she settled back into the seat and started playing our playlist on my Spotify. I rolled my eyes at her comment, turning the volume up on the music.

"She also loves modesty. I don't want to hear her talking about your lack of it behind your back. Also, did you even shower at all?"

"Nah. They didn't have shower slippers, but also, I don't know why it seems more gross to shower then wear dirty clothes again instead of just wearing the dirty clothes on an already dirty body." Elli shrugged and bobbed her head along to the song as she stared out the window and sang.

The car ride was quiet and tense except for the music, a stark contrast from our usual car rides. Usually we would be blasting music, singing along, and laughing together.

But I was not in a laughing mood. In fact, the longer I sat with my thoughts, the angrier I got. How could she be so reckless? She could have been seriously ill, and I wouldn't have been there to save her. She could have died! This went beyond just typical teenage *angsty* rebellion or whatever you wanted to call her drinking habit. This was pure stupidity and a death wish.

Elli reached forward for the volume, but instead of turning it up like I expected, she turned it to the left, turning the music down. "Alright, I know you want to lecture me. Go for it. Get it out," she said and I sighed.

"Elli, I don't even know what to say. I'm so mad. I can't even begin to think of how you got so drunk, how you were so irresponsible. But I'm also, like, hoping someone pressured you and that this wasn't your own sole fault. You don't have to say yes to these parties to be cool. But also, is that why you're going? Is it to be cool? Because, Elli, you know I support you in most things, if not everything, but this is one thing I will not support—you drinking to a point of no return," I said and let out a breath as we pulled into my neighborhood.

"I just want to have fun, Priya. I just... like to be at parties. I like to drink. I like the feeling of being carefree and being carefree with friends. It's not about being cool; it's just... I want to enjoy my youth," she said and shrugged, dragging her fingers through her wavy hair and forcefully detangling some knots.

I sighed and pulled my car into my driveway, to the left of my sister's. "We're a weird duo. I don't know how to enjoy my youth, and you enjoy it too much," I said with a shake of my head, and Elli laughed, carefully opening her door so she didn't hit Jasmine's car.

"We're the *perfect* duo. We balance each other out *splendidly,*" she said, using a British accent for the word splendidly before coming around the car to my side. "I love you, baby girl. Thank you for your concern, but you gotta lighten up."

I opened the front door and stepped in, letting Elli come in behind me before closing the door.

"Hi, mom!" she called out before heading up the stairs as I walked toward the kitchen and saw Jasmine leaning against the counter talking to our mom.

"Hi, Elli!" my mom called out, looking up and smiling at me.

"She's going to go shower; then she'll be down," I told her before heading over to give Jasmine a hug. "Hi, *didi*."

"Hu-llo. How was driving again?" she asked, wrapping her strong arms around me tightly and doing a little happy dance, which she did every time she hugged me. It always made me roll my eyes with a laugh as I hugged her five-foot-two-inch frame.

When we released each other, I moved around the counter to sit on one of the barstools and thought about the drive. Despite the stressful conversation Elli and I had, I felt stress free.

"It was good. Driving is still my stress reliever and happy place. I missed it during this past month," I said, and my mom clicked her tongue.

"You've driven in the last month."

"Not alone, and definitely not stress free! You don't let me play music because you think it distracts me. You're constantly critiquing me, and you're always gripping the pull-down handle thing as if thirty-seven in a thirty-five zone is *so fast*!" I said, and she looked at me with a "that's enough" glare before she shook her head, not able to hide the small, amused smile that was forming on her face. When she placed the first *parantha* on the pan, I heard the crackles and sizzles of the dough being fried by the oil, smelled the spices and onions, and my mouth started to water immediately.

"You had to relearn the safe way," my mom said, using her fingers to move around the flattened disk. How her fingers weren't burned off, I had no idea.

"Anyway, anyway, when is school over? Should we do a family trip this summer?" Jasmine asked, and I smiled fondly. Our family trips were always my favorite parts of the summer. We usually traveled to parts of Asia or Europe. My favorite trip was our trip to Hong Kong two years before, where we took a family cooking class. I couldn't remember anything about those recipes, but the food tasted amazing, especially the pan fried fish we had.

"Jasmine, the plane tickets will be so expensive now! You spend too much money!" My mom immediately launched into a lecture about Jasmine's spending habits, and I smirked, knowing this was how things always turned out. No day with my mom was complete without a couple of Mama Agarwal's lectures.

"Hmm, it smells so good, Ms. Agarwal," Elli said as she entered the kitchen wearing a pair of my cotton shorts, which were longer than her denim ones, and a t-shirt I hadn't worn in years.

"Thank you, Elli. I hope you like them." My mom sounded chipper again, and Elli came around the corner to sit next to me.

Conversations flowed easily between my mom, Jasmine, and Elli. They asked her about school, life, and her parents, and Elli replied as the social butterfly she was. She fit so well into the family—she might as well have been my mom's third daughter.

∾

By the time I dropped Elli off at her house after brunch and got back home, it was almost four. My mom and Jasmine were watching an older Bollywood film, *Lagaan*, and were swooning over Aamir Khan, with good reason. That man was gorgeous when he was younger. My mom thought he was gorgeous *still*.

"Hey, come watch with us. We just started," my mom said when I closed the front door behind me. I began to move toward them, but paused by the stairs, thinking.

For some reason, Dr. Worblack's words about exercising rang in my ears, and I felt an odd calling to run. Maybe it was my pent-up anger over Elli's alcohol abuse, but I had a lot of energy that needed to be used.

"Actually, is it okay if I go for a run?"

My mom and sister looked at me at the same time with the same confused expression.

"You? Running? What are you doing, joining the cross-country team?" my sister asked, and I flushed, shrugging.

"Dr. Worblack said I need to exercise more, and I feel like I'm finally at, like, a place to do so without... I don't know, getting lost in my head or something." I trailed off questioningly, but my mom's and sister's faces softened.

My mom nodded and smiled. "I think that's a good idea. Just take your phone and share your location with me so I know where you are. How long will you be gone for? Do you want my phone holder for your arm?"

"Probably less than an hour, and yes, please."

My mom nodded, telling me where her phone carrier was, and turned back to the screen as I headed up the stairs to change.

I stared down the road that led out of my neighborhood and felt a flutter of excitement fill my stomach. There was a cool breeze in the air, and I felt my body rev up for the workout.

I broke into a quick sprint, thinking I was going to run at full speed the whole way to the park that I made my destination. However, not even two minutes into my run, I got a cramp in my side, felt nauseous, and wanted to just walk home.

Jeez, this exercising thing is gonna be the death of me. How is running supposed to help?

But, if I had to admit it, I did feel that pent-up anger ebb away. I checked the map to see how far the park was and pushed myself to at least jog until I reached it, even if it was the slowest jog on the planet. Then I would let myself rest on a bench.

The jog was painful, but as I neared the bench I had in mind, I felt a sense of accomplishment that I had achieved a small victory.

Avery had told me a week prior that we would be starting to focus on small victories I can accomplish that would motivate me. Maybe if I ran enough, I could join the cross-country team in the fall, like Jasmine said, and the track-and-field team in the spring. I needed an extracurricular for college anyway, so this would look good.

Maybe running is like kale—it sucks, but it's good for you.

I gave myself a few more minutes on the bench, looking for any sales on activewear.

I was going to commit to this. I was going to commit to being healthy again, and lucid or sober forever because, if I was being honest, I still struggled with staying lucid. There was always a temptation to go back, to get off my medication because I knew there was a possibility I could see Dimitri again. It was true that I didn't believe that world with him is real, or ever was real, but a part of me knew that if I ever wanted it to be real badly enough, I could just stop taking the medication and maybe, just maybe, go back to the way things were.

But no, I was not going to let that happen. I was going to eat this disgusting, metaphorical kale and feel good after because, damn it, I deserved that, and I owed that to myself.

After my rest, I slowly started to get back into a jog, and this time, the running was not as bad. The cramps were more tolerable, and before I knew it, I was home.

"Oh, wow, you made it!" My sister said as I entered the house, huffing.

Another small victory. Thank you, kale.

~

I exited the shower and wiped away some excess steam from the mirror. In my reflection, I saw how my long hair fell to my lower back and felt how it dripped on and around me. I unconsciously picked up some pieces at the ends and stared at them. The piece I held looked like a thick, felt brush with excess black ink in it. While I knew my hair was a dark, dark brown, it was easier to say it was black. Even in the sunlight it was black.

From the corner of my eye, I thought I saw movement, as if someone were raising their arm to touch me, and I flinched, gasping and looking around the bathroom and seeing nothing. However, I couldn't let go of the feeling I wasn't alone, and it triggered an onslaught of emotions and temptation.

Memories of when Dimitri would play with my hair filled my head and warmed me more than my shower could have. Images of us on the couch, lying together in bed, or just relaxing as he distractedly picked up pieces of my hair and admired it played in my mind on repeat.

"I want to cut my hair," I said one day, early in our relationship, as Dimitri's hand was in my hair, brushing his finger through it. His hand faltered mid brush before pulling through entirely.

"But I love your long hair," Dimitri said in a way that made me never want to cut my hair.

I stood there in front of the mirror, looking at my hair as I held up the pieces. When the memory faded, I felt a sort of phantom brushing at the top of my head. It was too light to be a hallucination, or maybe this was an ordinary hallucination? Maybe ordinary people had hallucinations, too, that weren't cause for concern. Either way, this was probably just my brain replaying the memory of Dimitri's hand on my head at such a fierce strength that it permeated out of my head and was being reexperienced. Like when you go on a roller coaster and still feel like you're on one hours later.

I dropped the pieces from my hand and wrapped all of my hair into my towel, not wanting to see it in that moment. I reminded myself of the commitment to kale, being healthy, and buying activewear. I reminded myself of my commitment to refrain from Dimitri and my determination to make a change. I was determined to accomplish small victories, and one day big victories, and work with Avery to make sure all of them happened.

Things were falling into place, and I couldn't help the feeling that my life would be better now.

4

AUGUST 28TH, 2018

I SAT in the car outside Elli's house, unable to text her that I was there just yet. I stared down at the checklist on my phone I'd created a couple months ago. Well, I say that I created it. Actually, it was mostly Dr. Worblack and Avery spewing horrendous ideas at me that I felt pressured into approving.

Avery had encouraged me to create a *checklist for success*, which basically meant a list of things I wanted to do that would prove I was moving on from Dimitri and from my past. She said it was almost impossible to track progress when it came to moving on from someone or something, but if we could create reasonable markers that would show I was progressing and attempting to move on, I would have some things to be proud of and aim for.

My list included, as follows:

1) Go to a party

2) Join a sports team/club

3) Cut my hair

4) Like someone new (REAL)

~~**5) Get a boyfriend**~~

"Absolutely no dating, no parties, and no cutting your

hair," my mom had said firmly when I revealed this list to her and my sister in Dr. Worblack's office.

"Mom, you have to let Priya live a little. She's more responsible than I was, and you let me have my fun. Besides, Priya isn't a Sikh anymore, and hasn't been for some time. She should be allowed to cut her hair," my sister said, earning herself a stern glare from my mom.

That's when Dr. Worblack stepped in. "I understand these may be hard to hear and hard to allow, Ms. Agarwal, but Priya has to live her life like the teenager she wants to be. It's the best way to root herself in this world. Besides, there's nothing unhealthy or innately wrong with anything on her checklist."

I took a deep breath as I thought back to how my life was just a few months ago and tried to imagine what it could be like in the present.

You got this, Priya. You're gonna be fine. Everything will be fine. It's just like any other year, except you are going to live it in this world. Simple. No big deal.

I had felt more at ease with the year *before* Avery made me create the checklist. Now I just felt the pressure to perform and succeed in ways I was not comfortable with. If I had been completely in control of creating that checklist, I would have only put the cut my hair task on there.

I sent Elli a text that I was outside her house. She didn't send me a response, but within two minutes, she was running out of her front door. She was wearing a pair of ripped, light denim shorts and a black V-neck t-shirt.

When she got in the car, she gave me a horrified elevator glance. "Jeez, are you cold today too?" She asked, her seat-belt clicking in place.

I looked down at my black jeans and gray t-shirt, but realized she was referring to my cardigan. "Not cold, but I want to be prepared for the AC in the classrooms." Although I was usually cold, that day was exceptionally warm.

I pulled away from the curb and headed toward the school.

"Are you ready for your senior year?" Elli asked.

I simply shrugged. "I just want to be done with this crap high school. I want to live my life and move on."

Elli nodded in understanding. "You still planning on joining the cross-country team?"

"Yeah. You still doing water polo?"

"Hell, yeah. I'm gonna be a beast in the water this year," she said as she plugged in her phone to play music. Our song, "Feeling Myself" by Nicki Minaj, came on, and I smiled as she started dancing in her seat and rapping along. I turned the music up and started to rap along with her.

When we came to a stoplight near the school, Elli turned the music off abruptly.

"Real talk. How are you feeling about the year?"

"What do you mean?" I asked.

The light felt like it had been red for hours.

"I mean, it's only been a few months since Dimitri's incident. And I know you have your checklist, but are you really ready to take on this year?"

It was as if she could read my mind.

I shrugged in my seat just as the light turned green.

I started to accelerate. "I'm nervous. I feel as if a huge chunk of my life is missing. I don't know how to be a high schooler, ya know? My whole life, I've never fully fit in. I was always too mature, or weird, or different, and once Dimitri came into the picture, I was basically living this whole other life where I thought I was older, where I thought I fit in, and where I just felt... right. I grew up quickly and was a different person who wasn't awkward, who was ballsy enough to give a hot guy in a coffee shop my number. I totally didn't act like myself or *live* as if I was myself. So… I'm scared. I'm scared of being the weird girl again; I'm scared of not fitting in, even more than usual, and I'm scared of what it means to act my age. Especially now that I have this checklist that basically means I *have* to fit in and acting my age is a part of my therapy and recovery."

I pulled into the school parking lot and ended my rant. After parking the car, I looked at Elli, who was smiling at me.

"That's what I'm here for, babe. I'm here to help you, teach you, and support you. I know you think that Priya Ivanov was a completely different person, but she's still inside you. And if you want to mimic some of her characteristics, do it! You don't have to do anything you're uncomfortable with, but new, teenage experiences that won't hurt you and that are a part of being young and dumb are important. Just remember that you are a sixteen-year-old girl. No matter what your mom says, you're allowed to do stupid shit like give a guy your number, fall in love, date, and break up. You're allowed to go to parties and have a secret drink. You're allowed to not have your shit together and be unsure of your future and explore everything the world throws at you. It's a part of growing up, which you also still need to do. Also, there's no formula to how to be a good teenager; you just be yourself and survive. So don't take this teenager shit so seriously—because you're not supposed to." She reached her hand out, and I took it before she gave me a supportive squeeze.

"That was so beautiful; you're gonna make me cry," I teased. She rolled her eyes, and we both got out of the car. "Where would I be without you?"

"Nowhere," she said, smirking, and I grinned at her.

∼

y AP Government class, my first class of the day, was set up with pristine rows of desks and chairs. There was a large gap between the front half and back half of the room. The walls were covered in what I assumed the teacher thought were cool memes of presidents from the past, making interesting comments about bills, checks and balances, and the current political climate. I saw some familiar faces in the class and said hello to anyone who greeted me first.

Elli and I had only one class together, AP English Language, since I had mostly completed the junior level classes the previous year.

After the previous school year, when I was gone from class for almost two weeks before the AP tests, people in our shared classes had spread rumors about why I was gone. But Elli had shut them up real quick, with her usual flare for the dramatic.

"She's dying, okay! She's in the hospital because she has a life-threatening virus that she got from the fucking water in this hellhole!" I was still under the house arrest mandated by Dr. Worblack and my mom when Elli reenacted the way she erupted in class one day after being asked for the billionth time what happened to me. Her little scene got me a few *get well soon* cards from random peers, who probably felt bad for spreading rumors about a sick girl.

Today, I walked through the gap in the room and made a left turn, heading up to the teacher's desk and sliding a note from Dr. Worblack to the woman who sat there. According to my schedule, her name was Ms. Chen. She had on a green blouse and black pants, and her dark brown hair was tied up in a bun. Her desk was angled in the corner, so she had a good view of the entire class. Her papers and writing utensils were organized perfectly—probably in vain, if past teachers' desks were any indication. I knew once the year actually started, she would likely have piles of papers on her desk and a hard time organizing all of them.

Ms. Chen looked at the note and up at me with a smile before opening it, giving it a quick scan. Dr. Worblack was basically requesting all my teachers be lenient with me by giving me extensions and longer breaks from classes when necessary. He wrote that my "medical condition" could make studying and concentrating in class difficult, but didn't specify what my condition was, thankfully.

"That's... um... a doctor's note. I'm supposed to give them to all my teachers," I said.

"Oh, Priya Agarwal! Yes, of course!" Ms. Chen said after she scanned the note, surprising me briefly by the way she pronounced my last name correctly.

I sighed, knowing my guidance counselor had talked to all the teachers I had that year to catch them up on my situation. This whole recovery plan seemed to take a village of doctors, therapists, teachers, and guidance counselors.

"Yup. That's me," I said, smiling faintly at her. She gave me a sympathetic smile and nodded.

"Well, whatever you need, just let me know," she said with a nod and a too nice look that made me uncomfortable before standing up. "I'm going to start class soon, so you should find a seat."

I nodded and walked to the middle of the classroom where there was an empty desk.

"All right, everyone. I'm Ms. Chen, your AP Government teacher. I'm passing out the syllabus for the class now, so follow along. After that, we'll get started with the first assignment."

The class groaned at the word "assignment," and Ms. Chen laughed.

"I promise you, it'll be the only fun assignment you'll have all semester. At least in this class."

When I got my syllabus, I read through it and saw we were going to be doing assignments called "current events," and there would be eight tests in total, plus a quiz after every unit, and the last month and a half of the class would be AP prep as well as extra government related material that was supposed to be fun once the AP tests were over.

That was essentially how all my classes went: note giving, followed by pity and a syllabus.

At lunch, Elli and I sat together at one of the tables in the quad with her friend Amanda, who honestly looked way too cool, confidant, and put together to be a high schooler, from the perfect sharpness of her winged eye liner to her sepia puff of tightly coiled hair. The most striking part of her, though, was the way her warm toned, brown skin glittered in the sunlight, as if she used this miracle serum or moisturizer in the morning that had gold specks in it. Maybe she used a golden highlighter because her makeup was perfect.

"Are you still trying out for the varsity team, Elli?" Amanda asked, stabbing her salad with her fork.

"Yeah. I'm a little nervous about it, but I know I'll be fine," Elli said with a wave of her hand.

Amanda turned to me. "What about you, Priya? Are you going to do any sports this year?"

I shrugged. "I was thinking of doing cross-country."

"Aye! I'm doing cross-country too!" Amanda exclaimed with way too much excitement. I gave her a smile that probably looked like a grimace. I hoped my expression wasn't as frightening as she was behaving at that moment.

I looked at Elli, and she shrugged with an amused grin.

"How's your year looking so far?" Elli pointed the question at me, changing the subject.

"Meh, average. I have a lot of projects and assignments. I'm even doing a get-to-know-you project in my AP Gov class."

"Ugh, I wish we were doing that in A-PUSH," she said, using the acronym for AP US History. "We have to cram so much into the next seven months, and then we have to regurgitate it all onto a long-ass timeline before the AP test."

"Yeah, being a senior has its perks," I said with an exaggerated hair flip, making Elli laugh.

"Wait, you're a senior, Priya?" Amanda asked.

"Oh, yeah, I'm graduating a year early, so I am, technically."

It wasn't a big deal to me, but apparently, it was a bigger deal than I thought.

"Shut up! You're the one graduating early? Holy shit! I heard about you from other kids in our grade, but I didn't realize they were talking about you! Elli, how could you not tell me it was Priya?" Amanda erupted in amazement, as if I was some superstar of the school.

It wasn't common knowledge yet in the school that I was the one graduating a year early. The majority of the seniors in my class thought I had transferred to the school the previous year, and some of the juniors who had been in my classes since we were freshmen thought I was taking different classes because of my health.

Word was slowly spreading, though, that someone had *skipped* a grade. I knew because I had overheard people talking about the rumor, wondering who was that smart.

"It's not that big of a deal, Amanda," Elli said with a roll of her eyes. "She's still the same Priya that barely anyone knows."

I laughed before shaking my head. "I find it funny how I went from being a nobody to being a partial somebody, but only by, like, reputation. People still don't know my name, but they're all interested in my academic career."

"You're still my full somebody, baby girl!" Elli winked. I shot her with some finger guns and sent a wink her way as well.

"You guys are so in love. I can't handle it." Amanda rolled her eyes.

The bell rang, ending lunch, and we got up to head to our next class. Amanda said her goodbyes, making sure I knew to meet up with her before our first cross-country practice, and Elli and I walked to our AP English Language class.

The room's walls were lined with book posters and cheesy puns. More personal decorations included colored wallpaper, animal cutouts, and the teacher's name, Mr. Williams, on the wall in bold, cursive letters.

It honestly felt like a second-grade class to me.

As soon as I walked into the room, I couldn't ignore the instant prickling on my neck, as if millions of eyes were on me.

This class was full of juniors, people I used to be in the same grade as. I couldn't shake the feeling that they were all talking about me, plotting a verbal attack somehow.

My heart started to race. My skin tingled all over, and my palms became clammy. I was hyper aware of my feelings, but still, I started to freak out and overthink as I took my seat next to Elli.

"Elli, are people staring at us?" I whispered to her. She looked at me, then around the room before shrugging.

"No. They're all busy talking to their friends."

I looked around the room at the familiar faces. I had grown up with the majority of these people—not really as friends, but still mostly as friendly classmates. I knew most of their names, their faces, and some parts of their stories. But they didn't seem the same anymore. For some reason, they all seemed fake.

As I was surveying the room, I made eye contact with someone—an unfamiliar boy. He looked at me for a minute and tilted his head to one side, as if trying to figure me out, and alarms went off in my head.

Russian spy! Russian spy!

I tried to calm myself down.

What's on your grocery list, Priya? We got apples, guac, chips, lots of chips, Dr. Pepper...

Didn't work.

Let's try breathing. Are you breathing?

Inhale. *One.*

Exhale. *Two.*

Inhale. *Three.*

Exhale. *Four.*

I went through some grounding methods, but it didn't help that I was in an unfamiliar room with people who now felt unfamiliar too. This was the perfect place for an attack. I wouldn't be suspecting it. I would be unguarded, and I—

I looked at Elli, who was talking to a guy next to her, and tapped her on her thigh.

"Elli, seven o'clock, tan shirt." She looked at me for a second before quickly, and discreetly, glancing in that direction.

"Alex? What about him?"

I let out a breath I hadn't realized I had been holding and relaxed.

She knew who he was. She could see him.

"He was staring at me funny. I wasn't sure if he was real

or not," I whispered, and she looked at me with understanding before nodding.

"Don't worry. I'm here and I got you if you have any other bad feelings."

I sighed with relief, thankful for Elli's presence at my side.

After settling myself, I took a moment to look for the teacher and found him seated at the back of the room.

"Hi, Mr. Williams?"

Mr. Williams looked up from his desk and the paper he was writing on when I approached and smiled at me.

"Hi, I'm supposed to give you this note. It's from my doctor," I said the last part quietly so no one could hear except him and me. I was hyperaware of the possibility of eavesdroppers in the class and didn't want anyone to be in my business more than they already were.

Mr. Williams gave the note a quick read before giving me a warm smile. "I see. Thank you for the note, Priya. Please let me know if there's anything I can do or if you need anything from me."

I found myself speaking the next few words without thinking.

"I would actually like if you didn't give me any special treatment. I know what the note says, and I'm aware of my… situation…" My heart was racing with anxiety. "… but I just want to be treated like everyone else."

Ever since the diagnosis and missing so much of the end of the previous school year, my life had become one of special treatment and curious looks. If it hadn't been for Elli's and Jasmine's support, and my mom pushing me to succeed, I wouldn't have finished the previous year as strongly as I had. I needed that kind of support and standards from teachers as well. I was graduating a year early despite having a terrible mental illness, after all. I wasn't incompetent.

Mr. Williams nodded and continued smiling.

"I had no intention of treating you any differently from the rest of the students, and I will trust you to take care of yourself and not require me to do so," he said, and I instantly felt the annoyance that had built up over the day dissipate. I nodded and rushed back to my desk before the class started.

~

I was walking to the stadium after school with my phone at my ear and my backpack slung over my shoulder.

"*Didi*, what if they think I'm weird? What if they smell fear on me?"

"Ha! You're funny. They're people, not sharks. Just calm down and have fun. You need more friends than just Elli. Speaking of which, what is she doing?" Jasmine asked through the phone. I could hear papers rustling on her end. She was probably organizing her desk or trying to find some document.

"She's trying out for the varsity water polo team."

"Wow, good for her." I heard a muffled voice in the background. Then Jasmine spoke again. "Hey, sorry, I have to go back to work now. Have a good first practice! Love you."

"Love you too. Bye." I ended the call as I walked down the steps of the stadium toward the track. There was already a large group of people talking and stretching in the center of the field. I had changed into a pair of leggings and a long-sleeved shirt that claimed to be moisture wicking, but in this heat, I highly doubted it would do its job properly.

Most of the other girls on the team were wearing short spandex shorts and tank tops. They had on headbands to keep their hair back and nice sneakers. I looked down at my over-dressed body and mentally kicked myself.

"Hey! Are you here for the cross-country team?" I jumped at the random male voice that took me out of my inner lecturing. "Whoa! Sorry, didn't mean to scare you."

I looked up to see a boy with dark black, short hair holding a clipboard and pen, looking at me with his hands in the air. He smiled at me, thinning his round, deep set eyes and showing a dimple on the left side of his mouth. I smiled back instinctively.

"Uh, yeah. Here for cross-country," I said with a nod.

The boy lowered his hands. "I'm Aaron. Can I get your name for the roster?" he asked, getting ready to write my name down.

"Ummm, yeah, it's Priya. Priya Agarwal," I said meekly, and he nodded, still smiling. He started writing, but his face scrunched a little, and I smiled wider, amused.

"*A-G-A-R-W-A-L*. And Priya has a *Y* after the *I*."

He looked at me shyly, blushing, before nodding. "Damn, you must get asked about that a lot," he said with a laugh.

I shrugged.

"Is this your first time doing cross-country? I don't remember you from previous years, but you do look familiar." He tilted his head slightly, as if trying to figure me out. It was the same way Alex looked at me in AP English.

"Yeah. First time." I rubbed my arm, feeling uneasy under his stare.

He was still smiling. "What grade are you in, Priya?"

"I'm a senior. What about you?"

"Senior too! Maybe we have the same classes."

Just then, someone blew a whistle, rescuing me from Aaron's investigation. We both looked over to the center of the field and saw a woman whom I assumed was the coach.

She was small but extremely fit, dressed all in athletic wear with sunglasses perched on top of her short blond bob.

"All right, everyone! I hope you're all ready for a fantastic season. Let's circle up for a stretch. Leaders, in the center."

"Yes, Coach!" a chorus of voices said, including Aaron's. He looked back at me and winked.

"You'll learn fast how we do things here," he said, jerking his head toward the circle and beckoning me to follow him toward it.

Aaron was one of those charged with leading the stretching, so I had to find someone else to stretch with. I looked around the circle and luckily found Amanda waving me over to sit next to her.

"Jeez, aren't you hot in that?" Amanda asked me when I sat down in the spot she made for me. I gave her a brief once-over and groaned, jealous of her purple headband, loose workout top and short shorts.

"Extremely. I didn't realize I was allowed to wear as little clothing as possible," I said, surveying the girls around the circle who wore tighter and shorter clothes than Amanda.

She let out a laugh. "Coach Zimmerman is really relaxed. As long as you do well and try your best, she doesn't care what you wear. Just wear something."

"I see," I said, distracted. Aaron was sitting in the center of the circle messing around with one other guy and two girls. I assumed they were the four captains for the team, or whatever they were called. I wasn't even sure if cross-country had captains.

Soon, we started stretching.

I hated it. It was annoying and usually hurt more than the actual activity. Luckily, it didn't last that long, and we were on to our workout for the day. We did a mile warmup, then an exercise involving ten burpees for every lap we ran. We completed that six times and followed it with some other inhumane torture before ending the day with a light mile jog.

"Hey, you good?" Amanda asked as I was kneeling over after the mile cooldown.

I nodded once, slowly, then shook my head.

"I'm. So. Hot." I pulled at my shirt to create a breeze.

Santa Clara County summers were always terrible, and I knew that. I had even checked the weather app that day to see what to wear. But after picking out a pair of shorts and a tank top, I had chickened out at the last second, feeling too shy to wear so little clothing.

"Eagle to Priya. Eagle to Priya."

Stephan's voice appeared in my ear all of a sudden, and I instantly stood up, looking around but not seeing anyone nearby.

"Did you hear that?" I asked Amanda, still out of breath.

She looked around as well. "Hear what?"

Shit. I should probably talk to Dr. Worblack about that at our next appointment.

"Nothing. I thought I heard someone call my name," I said with a reassuring smile.

"God, I hate when that happens. It's so freaky, makes you think you're going crazy." She laughed as she walked toward the pile of bags, and my smile became fake as I tried not to let her words settle into my skin.

The word crazy had never meant more to me than any other word in the English language. It wasn't a curse, and it wasn't derogatory in my mind. That was before my diagnosis. Now, the word felt dirty, cruel, and everything I was trying my hardest not to be.

Soon, everyone had packed their stuff and was leaving the field. I sent Elli a quick text as I stepped off the turf, backpack on, letting her know I was ready to leave and take her home.

"Priya!"

Looking up from my phone, I saw Aaron briskly walking up to me, a smile on his face and that adorable dimple popping up.

Adorable? That's new.

I tabled that thought and smiled at Aaron.

"Hey, did you drive by chance, or is your ride here yet?" His forehead was glistening with sweat, which he wiped at with his arm. His hair was sticking to his forehead slightly, and I fought back a warm, fuzzy feeling in my stomach. Even after all this heat and grossness, he looked... cute.

"I drove. I'm waiting for my friend to finish up with water polo so I can drive her home."

Aaron made an *ah* sound and nodded. "I see. Well, I'll walk with you to the parking lot. How was your first practice? Think you'll come back?" he asked eagerly. He was gripping the strap of a black duffle bag that was diagonally slung across his chest.

"Yeah... yeah, I think I liked it. I'm planning to dress more appropriately next time, but yes. I will be back."

Aaron laughed. "Yeah, I don't know how you didn't die from a heatstroke in that."

"It's an Indian girl skill. We're taught at a young age to withstand *immense* heat while wearing long sleeves and pants." I shrugged. Aaron laughed again.

"Interesting. Asian parent strictness, am I right?" he said, and I nodded.

"So right."

"So... what brought you to cross-country?" he asked, and I looked down at the ground.

My psychiatrist recommended I take up a sport so I don't go off the deep end.

"I started running in the spring, and I realized I didn't have many extracurriculars for college. Trying to get into Berkeley, so I need to have a sport in order to show I'm a—"

"Well-rounded student," Aaron interrupted, using the exact phrase I'd had in mind.

I looked at him in shock. "That's not freaky at all."

He laughed again. I was beginning to think his laughter was fake. No one besides Elli and Jasmine laughed at my words that much. They weren't even that funny, just blunt and with maybe a little bite in the tone.

"Sorry, it's just that's the same reason why I joined cross-country sophomore year. I wanted to look good on my application and also get into Berkeley, actually, but who doesn't?" Aaron ran his fingers through his hair. I nodded at him and looked around to see that we were in the parking lot.

"Which car is yours?" he asked, and I nodded over to my baby.

"The red Honda," I said. There weren't many cars left, so it was easy to spot which one was mine.

"Nice. Are you gonna wait for your friend?" he asked as he pulled out his keys.

I nodded and pulled mine out as well.

"Yup. Gonna start the car and blast the AC so I don't fry out here," I said. Aaron let out another laugh, and I tried my best not to look at him like a lovesick puppy because, dear God, his laugh was low and wonderful.

I was beginning to realize that it was not a bad thing that I made him laugh so much.

In fact, I wouldn't mind making him laugh more.

"All right, well, I'm gonna dip. I'll see you tomorrow,

Priya," he said with a quick wave before walking off toward a blue Toyota.

I let out a breath and swiped at my forehead, feeling myself overheating again. I immediately walked to my car and got in. Then, once the door was firmly closed behind me, I gripped the steering wheel and let out a squeal that I had been bottling up inside for the past few minutes.

Jesus, Priya. What has gotten into you? You don't have crushes. You're marr—

I stopped that thought dead in its tracks and took a deep breath. I tried to focus on something else, like turning on the car and starting up the AC. I rolled down the windows and leaned my head out, looking up at the sky, breathing in sanity, and breathing out the crazy.

You are NOT married, Priya. You are a single, sixteen-year-old girl. Act like one.

I hadn't thought along those lines in a while. I was officially three months sober, and I was determined to make it to a year, and then two years, and forever have my sobriety from Dimitri, that world, and my illness.

It IS okay to have crushes. It's okay to like other guys and have fun. It's okay to be a high schooler. Because you are one.

A text from Elli pulled me out of my thoughts.

Elli: Be there in five!

Priya: Waiting with the AC on.

Elli: Bless your heart!

I put my phone away and sighed.

All right, Priya. You got this. Senior year is supposed to be your year, so make the most of it.

5

SEPTEMBER 14TH, 2018

I FLIPPED my pen back and forth between my fingers as Ms. Chen passed back the first graded quiz of the year.

For some reason, this quiz weighed heavily on my mind. I needed to have done well so I could start out strong and prove that I was not some pitiful basket case. I did not need to be coddled, and I didn't need special treatment. I was just as intelligent as my peers, if not more so.

Ms. Chen went down the stack in her hands, then walked up to my desk with a smile as she laid the test on my desk.

"Good job, Priya," she said, but I had to see the score for myself in order to gauge how well I did.

I looked at the number and couldn't stop the smile that spread across my lips.

A big "98%" was circled in red at the top of the page. I let out a sigh.

"Damn, that was a hard one. I barely passed," one of the boys behind me said, and I felt my pride and self-confidence grow.

"She's a cheater. Cheater. Cheater," a masculine voice said from behind me.

I looked around the room, back at the two boys talking. The voices were masculine, but when I looked at the boys, they were looking down at their tests. Not at me.

"Milk, cheese, eggs. Milk, cheese, eggs."

"She's cheating trash. Trash. Trash. Trash."

The voices sounded like they were coming from all the students around me. They were a mix of masculine and feminine, harsh and harmless. They were muffled in a way that made me want to check if my phone was producing the sounds. I began to feel anxious and fidgety, as if I had to go for a run to escape the voices.

Priya, are you breathing?

I faced the front of the room as I slid a little in my chair and tried to calm myself with deep breathing exercises I had learned from Avery.

Inhale. *One.*

Exhale. *Two.*

Inhale. *Three.*

Exhale. *Four.*

I counted every breath I took until I counted ten and found myself relaxed and ready for the rest of the class, no voices to be heard.

I stared at the clothes Elli set out on my bed. She was still rifling through my closet as I picked up and examined the skimpy top I'd forgotten I even had in my wardrobe.

"Baby girl, you have some awesome shit in here. Why don't you wear something like this?" she asked, as she pulled out the embroidered navy blue blouse of one of my *lehengas.*

"Because that's for an Indian outfit."

"I still don't understand why it's okay for you to wear this to weddings, but your mom freaks out when you wear something similar to other events. If you wore this with high-waisted jeans, you'd probably show off less skin than if you wore this with the skirt."

I shrugged. "Remind me again why I'm letting you take me to a party?" I asked as I started to change into the clothes she'd laid out on my bed, starting with the black denim shorts.

"Because I made the varsity water polo team, and because you did well on your first quiz," she said plainly.

"But neither of those are unexpected nor amazing accomplishments." I picked up one of the crop tops that Elli had picked out and slid it over my head. It was pale green with a knotted detail in the front.

"Stop trying to ruin the fun. Your mom is gone again on business until Sunday night. Just enjoy being a teenager for once, will you? Remember your checklist?" she said as she came out of the closet.

I stared at her and instantly hated myself for putting that goal on there. The very first goal was to go to a party. I had never been to a party with my classmates. I had never been allowed to, and it felt like a very high school teenager thing to do. That's probably why my clinicians put it on my list.

"Yes, I remember, but I don't know if I'm ready for it." I turned to look at the mirror on my closet door.

The person in the mirror was not me. She was wearing clothes that were too scandalous—I was surprised I even owned those clothes. The person in the mirror looked like a teenager, and I did not feel much like a teenager.

"Come on, Priya, it's one of the easier things to do on that checklist. You aren't gonna drink because you're driving us home after, and I'll stay with you the entire time—well, until you're ready to be on your own. And if that time never comes tonight, that's totally fine," she said. I saw her reassuring shrug and smile reflected in the mirror.

I looked back at myself, looked at the way I was dressed, and sighed.

Dimitri would have laughed if he saw me in this outfit.

But Dimitri isn't here, Priya. It's time to move on.

"What about my makeup?" I asked hesitantly as I turned back to Elli.

Her jaw fell open for a few seconds before she put it back in place.

"Whoa, never thought you would be okay with that," she said, clasping her hands together, "but I have the perfect idea for your face tonight."

~

The house we went to belonged to one of the guys on the water polo team. It was quite large and filled to the brim with people.

I stared at the house, looking at the scantily clad girls. I felt so ashamed that for once, I might have fit in. I unconsciously pulled at the hem of my shorts and wrapped my cardigan closer around my body even though I was burning up, but Elli grabbed my hand in hers.

"No! Bad Priya. You look hot, okay? Just let yourself be hot for once." She grabbed my cardigan and began pulling it off my body.

"Um, excuse you!" I wailed as she got me out of the cardigan and tossed it into the car before closing her door and pulling me toward the entrance to the party.

"Elli, I hate you," I whispered, but she laughed as soon as the words left my mouth.

Her hearing was impeccable.

As we walked through the party, people greeted her. Many of them were guys, and most of them I didn't know.

"Yo! Elli! You finally made it," a guy in Bermuda shorts and a tank top said. Elli stopped walking and pulled me to stand next to her.

"What up, Evan? Nice place. Have you met Priya?" she asked and I side-eyed her, aghast.

"Nah. What's up, Priya?"

I gave a head nod and smiled. "'Sup, Evan?"

Evan smiled back before looking at Elli and stepping closer to her. He began making small talk with her, inching forward in a way that would cut me off from Elli before long.

Back up, buddy!

She gripped my hand tighter and smiled at Evan.

"We're going to go get a drink! See ya later," she said, and she dashed off, tugging me behind her.

When we got to the kitchen, my heart was racing. There was a reason I'd never wanted to go to parties in the past, even if my mom wouldn't have let me go anyway. There were way too many people I didn't know here. It reminded me of the Indian weddings my mom sometimes dragged me to. Whenever my cousins, sister, or friends weren't there, my anxiety would go up. I felt on edge, like I should have been doing something, mostly dancing, but all I felt was bored.

This time, I felt out of place and anxious as I looked around and saw that there was alcohol all over the kitchen and bodies everywhere. I heard too many voices, from the speakers and from the people around me, and I didn't know anyone at this party. My senses and brain were working on overdrive, double checking every sound I heard and making sure it was real. The only good part of all the commotion was if a voice or person seemed too out of place, the crowd and sights drowned them out. However, that didn't drown out my feeling of needing to stay busy or active.

I turned to look at Elli, not even realizing she had let go of my hand, and saw she was downing a shot with a group of people I didn't know.

"Whoo!" she exclaimed after, laughing with two of the girls in the group.

So much for sticking with me the entire time.

"Priya?" I heard someone yell my name over the music. It was a familiar, masculine voice, and I immediately went on defense. There was no one I knew at this party, other than Elli. There was no way someone here knew me.

Dimitri? Or Stephan?

"Priya!" I heard the voice again and instantly turned to run, but that just planted me face first into some guy's chest. The guy wrapped his arms around me as soon as I hit his chest, either to stabilize me or hug me, and I yelped, both from the impact and his limbs circling me.

"Oh, shit! Sorry 'bout that. I guess I always seem to scare you." The guy released me with a laugh, and I felt my brain hit a wall. I couldn't think through his words, and I couldn't figure out who he was.

He has to be an agent. He has to be a hallucination.

My head felt light from the confusion, but the room didn't spin. It just felt like it was slowly, achingly, stretching in a way where it was thinning and closing in on me, about to crush me. The voice didn't sound like Dimitri; the arms didn't even feel like Dimitri, but everything about this guy felt too familiar to be real. I didn't know any guy well enough to have them single me out at a party.

"Hey, are you okay?" the voice asked near my ear, his breath warm with a slight stench of alcohol on it, and I lurched back, my eyes clenched shut as my anxiety ratcheted higher until I felt nauseated.

Inhale. *One*

Exhale. *Two*

Inhale. *Three*

Exhale. *Four*

I felt an arm wrap around me, and I jumped in surprise, my brain fried and body sensitive from all the sensations I was taking in.

"Hey, everything okay over here?" My eyes snapped open at Elli's voice, and I looked at her. Her voice was light and airy and a breath of fresh air, but her eyes were concerned, almost stern, as she looked at me. I was about to tell her I was hallucinating when the voice came again.

"Hey, yeah, sorry about that. I was just trying to say hi to Priya, but I don't think she recognizes me."

Elli squeezed my left arm, and I took in one more shaky, deep breath before looking at the guy speaking and froze with humiliation.

"Aaron?" I asked, struggling to find my voice through my anxiety and be heard over the music, despite the fact that we were all standing so close together.

Exhale. *Eight*

Inhale. *Nine*

Exhale. *Ten*

Aaron looked at me and smiled, his dimple appearing on the left side of his mouth.

"You know him?" Elli asked. *Do you feel safe?* is what she was really asking.

"Yes. We're on the cross-country team together," I said to Elli, feeling about seventy percent back to normal.

Elli looked at me, then looked back at Aaron with a bright smile.

"Well, it's nice to meet you, Aaron. I'm Elli."

"Hey, Elli," Aaron looked at Elli quickly then back at me and, taking a step closer, leaned down so I could hear him. "I need some fresh air. Do you want to come with?" He gestured with his head toward the front door. I looked at him and nodded eagerly.

"Let's go!" I said, and he smiled, extending his hand for mine. I looked at Elli, and she smiled at me in reassurance. I waved to her before gripping Aaron's hand.

"Get some, baby girl!" she hollered after me. I blushed, following Aaron through the crowd and hoping he hadn't heard.

When we finally made it outside, there were people chilling: vaping, drinking from red solo cups, and thankfully, talking at a normal volume. As soon as we were out of the crowd, though, I became very aware of my hand in Aaron's. It was soothing in a way, feeling his warm but sweaty hand enveloping mine. I concentrated on it and let it be my primary thought, turning my anxiety over possibly having an episode into the kind of anxiety you get around your crush. It was the grounding object I needed to get back to one hundred percent. However, the more I dwelled on that thought, the faster I became aware that he wouldn't want to hold my hand for too long, so I pulled it out of his grip when we settled on a spot.

I watched as Aaron glanced down at our now unlinked hands and wondered if he thought I was weird or awkward. Did I hold his hand for too long?

"I didn't expect to see you here. How do you know Evan?" Aaron asked, looking up at me and making me look away from his gaze as my face got prickly and warm.

"I honestly don't. Elli dragged me out here. She wanted to celebrate my score on the AP Gov quiz, and —"

"Wait." Aaron's head appeared in my line of vision, his

eyes wide as he bent down. "How well did you do on that quiz? Cuz I struggled."

Instantly, I became embarrassed and looked away from him again.

I wanted to say I didn't do that well, but I knew that if he bombed it, I would sound like *that* kid. The kid who always brushes off their intelligence and makes the others feel bad, but also annoyed. If he did just as well as I did, give or take, then I would sound normal. But if I said I did *really* well, would that sound like I was bragging?

"Um, I got a ninety-eight percent." I looked at the ground.

"What the hell? That's so good! I got, like, an eighty-eight! My mom was like, 'how could you not get at least an A?'"

"Asian parent strictness, am I right?" I repeated his words back at him.

He laughed. "Well, yes, that, and she does teach the class."

I whipped my head up to him, shocked. "Wait. Your mom is Ms. Chen?" I asked, a little louder than I intended. I winced at my own volume and shook my head. "Sorry, that was loud."

Aaron simply laughed again. "No worries. And, yeah, she's my mom. I guess it's not common knowledge to people who are new to the school. You transferred, right?"

I looked up at him and shook my head slowly, preparing myself for the "weird girl" comments to come.

"Nope. I've been at this school for the past two years."

"So, you transferred two years ago?" he asked.

I chuckled nervously. "Yeah, from middle school."

"Wait… I don't understand. What do you mean?"

"I mean that I just, technically… skipped my sophomore year." I said it softly, unable to contain a nervous smile.

"Holy shit, you're the kid who is graduating early?" This time, it was Aaron's turn to be shocked. I nodded as he leaned down and then stood up taller, physically unable to handle the information as he tried to put the pieces together in his head.

"What the hell, Priya? How did I not know this?" he asked, and I laughed.

"I didn't know Ms. Chen was your mom!"

"Yeah, well, this is bigger than that! You're *that* kid! You're like a prodigy, aren't you?"

My smile fell. I looked at the ground and sighed. "Please don't say that. That's why I don't tell people." I suddenly felt shy again.

"Oh. Did I say something wrong?" he asked, and I shook my head, shifting my weight from my left side to the right before looking back up at him.

"No. It's just... I don't like being known as *that* kid. I don't want to be the weird freak of the school. I already have a lot on my record here. I'm just trying to finish as soon as possible. That's the only reason I decided to graduate a year early—it's not because I'm crazy smart—it's because I'm crazy determined," I finished, then realized I had sort of been ranting at him. "Sorry."

Aaron shook his head vigorously. "Hey, you don't have to apologize. I kinda get it. When I was younger, *I* was that kid, or close enough, and it sucked. Everyone wanted to copy my homework, my tests; they were asking me for help, but it was kind of like they were using me—"

"Exactly!" I said, cutting him off. *Oops.* "Sorry," I said again.

Aaron laughed. "You gotta stop apologizing so much. You're doing nothing wrong. But I get it. It's not fun being that kid. So I take back what I said. You're not *that* kid. You're just the kid my mom told me I had to be like."

"She did *not* say that!" I said, incredulous.

"I wish that were true, but yup... she did."

I couldn't control my laughter, and I covered my mouth, trying to be polite.

"That *sucks!*"

He shrugged. "I'm used to it. I'd rather be compared to you than to her dentist's brother-in-law's nephew, or whoever."

I laughed unashamedly at that, and he laughed with me.

"Jeez," I said, shaking my head. "My mom is the same way. I have an older sister, and my mom was constantly comparing me to her when I was younger—until I got better grades than her. But now, she compares me to her coworkers' kids, and it's annoying. Like, I don't even know you, Jessica Preston, but I hate you."

The baritone laughter rumbling in his chest was music to my ears. I completely forgot our surroundings. I forgot that I was at a high school party. I forgot what I was wearing, what time it was, and the fact that we were on some stranger's lawn.

I forgot that I even had a momentary freak-out earlier.

The loud music from inside the house crept out into the night, filling our silence, and I looked around. *What do all these kids' parents do? How is everyone here allowed to go out to a party?* I was only here because my mom was traveling.

The teenage lifestyle eluded me.

"This is so strange to me," I said out loud before I could stop myself.

"What is?"

"The fact that… that there are so many kids here, drinking and partying. Like, what do their parents' think? Why are they allowed to be here?" I asked, looking up at Aaron.

He looked at the party, then at me, and shrugged.

"Well, I told my parents that I was going to stay with a friend from cross-country. You know Cameron?"

I nodded.

"Yeah. So they have no idea I'm here. I think that many of these kids don't have such strict parents and are just... allowed to live their lives."

"Huh." I looked back at the party and wondered what Elli was doing.

"What about you? How did you manage to escape tonight?"

"My mom is out of town for a few days," I said absent-mindedly, still looking around.

"What about your dad?"

"Not in the picture." I snapped out of my daze to look up at Aaron.

He nodded down at me, and I was thankful that he didn't pry and instead looked back at the party.

Watching him, I noticed how defined his jawline was. And how tall he was. Not as tall as Dimitri, but still tall.

Stop thinking about Dimitri.

My phone buzzed in my pocket, snapping me out of my thoughts. I looked at the text and chuckled.

Elli: Wheraer yoi?

"I need to find Elli. I think it's time I take her home." I looked up at Aaron only to freeze under his gaze. He was gazing at me steadily, and for the first time, I noticed how dark and captivating his eyes were. If I looked long enough and focused hard enough, I was sure I would be able to trace every valley and crevice of his irises, even in this poor lighting.

"I'll walk you back into the house," he said, smiling, guiding me back through the maze of people.

I looked around every corner of the house until I found Elli playing beer pong in the backyard. She was swaying on her feet and laughing hysterically. There was a guy holding her and rubbing her arms, almost predatorily. Instantly, I felt my hackles go up.

"Hey, babe!" I said, grabbing her out of the guy's arms.

"Priya!" She wrapped her arms around me. I looked at the guy who had been holding her. He, too, was swaying a little, but he was quickly distracted by another girl.

"Are you ready to head home?" I asked her and she smiled.

"Yurp!" She laughed. I rolled my eyes and turned with her in my arms.

Aaron was standing next to me, and I gave him an apologetic smile.

"Stop being sorry," he said. My smile grew into a real one.

"Get home safely," he said, and I nodded and led Elli through the backyard, out the side gate, and toward the front of the property.

"Jesus, Elli, you reek of alcohol," I said, gagging as I got her into the passenger seat. Her head rolled back, and her eyes closed. She hummed softly.

I got into the driver's seat and rolled down the windows to give her some air.

"You better not throw up in my car," I warned, starting the car.

Elli simply lolled her head in response.

"I swear, if you keep drinking like this, you're gonna have alcohol poisoning again."

"What doesn't kill you makes you stronger," Elli slurred. She lifted her left arm up in an attempt to flex her bicep but ended up just swinging her arm haphazardly. I laughed, amused in spite of myself, and drove as safely and slowly as possible. I didn't want to jostle her too much and make her carsick.

"Can hi stay at your puh-lace?" she mumbled, half asleep. I rolled my eyes.

"You think I would let you go to your place like this? You'll probably still be drunk at eleven tomorrow morning," I said. Elli's mom always woke her up at eight, even on the weekends. That definitely wouldn't be enough time.

"Thanks, baby 'url. You the best." Her head fell to the right, hitting the window. She groaned and I couldn't suppress my chuckle.

"You're unbelievable."

She whispered, "You love me," and I smiled because I really did.

6

SEPTEMBER 15TH, 2018

Hazel eyes looked back at me as I peered over the ceramic tile-covered tabletop. In the distance, a seaside city was bathed in the saturated colors of the sunset. The sounds of a typical bustling coffee shop surrounded our patio seats.

I reached across the space between us and swept a piece of hair from Dimitri's face.

"You would look better with shorter hair," I said and he smirked.

"But then, how will I look like the guys on the covers of those trashy novels you read?" he asked, and I playfully poked his cheek in return. He laughed before grasping my hands, placing them down on the colorful tiles between us.

"I miss you," he said.

My eyebrows furrowed in confusion. "I'm right here," I said with a soft smile, trying to both comfort and understand him.

"Why can't I see you anymore?"

"You're seeing me right now," I said, more confused than ever.

The scene changed. We were no longer sitting in a seaside

cafe. Instead, I was kneeling over Dimitri's lifeless, bloody body in the forest. I stared in horror for a moment, then started doing chest compressions.

"You've already forgotten me?" I heard his voice echoing around me, but his lips didn't move.

"Dimitri?" I called out, ceasing my compressions and looking around.

The scene changed once again, this time to a backyard behind a large house, in which a party was raging. I was kneeling in the grass alone now, Dimitri's body nowhere to be seen.

"Need help, Priya?" I looked up to my right and saw Aaron reaching his hand out for me to grasp, but his face was different. He didn't look like himself, but I still understood him to be Aaron. I instinctively reached up for his hand, but another voice came from my left.

"You're already moving on?" Dimitri's voice made me jump. I turned to see him standing at my left.

He was wearing a navy t-shirt, black pants, and white sneakers.

There wasn't a single drop of blood on him.

"Don't you love me anymore?"

~

M y eyes snapped open. I blinked a few times as my vision adjusted to the light streaming in through the blinds of my bedroom window. I looked around the room at my myriad of posters depicting movie stars and musicians and art pieces. The sound of my whirring fan filled the air.

I pushed the sheets off my body before looking to my right and stretching. Elli was still out cold, but at least she was breathing.

I turned my head down toward my desk, saw the mess of papers that adorned the dark wood and the clothes piled on the desk chair, and knew I would need to clean it up before my mom got back from her trip.

I miss you.

Dimitri's words rang in my ears. My dream was fading quickly from my memory, but Dimitri's words and sentiments were forever burned into my brain.

Am I moving on too quickly? Is there a proper time frame when it comes to moving on from a hallucinated husband? Are there even such things as baby steps in this case, or do I just have to dive in headfirst and hope I swim?

Do I even want to dive in and swim?

My body heated up, and my heart palpitated with anxiety.

I didn't want to answer those questions so early in the morning—or at all—honestly. I wanted to just run away from my problems and never look back.

But I knew I couldn't just run away.

I turned on my side to face Elli's motionless form.

Her medium-length wavy hair was tousled and spread around her face. Her mouth was hanging open, exuding warm, alcohol-scented air in my direction. Her breathing was heavy, bordering on snores. She looked so peaceful, but I desperately needed to talk to her.

I nudged her legs with my foot.

She didn't respond.

I nudged her harder. Still no response.

"Hey," I said loudly.

Silence.

You leave me no choice.

I reached out, grabbed her shoulder, and shook her violently. Her breath caught, almost in a gasp, and she opened her eyes.

"Fucking shit!" she exclaimed, picking up her head and looking around. She groaned, gripping the sides of her head and shutting her eyes again.

"Fuck, my head hurts."

She sounded like she was in pain, but I just laughed, knowing she probably had a pretty bad hangover.

"What time is it?"

I turned over and reached toward my bedside table, quickly checking my phone.

"Ten."

"It feels like six," she mumbled. I laughed and she groaned again before opening her eyes. "How was your night?" she asked, blinking a few times.

"I saw Aaron there. The guy I met in cross-country who's in my AP Psych class." I was unable to stop the small smile spreading across my lips.

"Oh, yeah. Was he the guy you left me for?"

"Yeah. We talked in the front yard, and it was... nice."

"So what do we think? Do we like this boy?"

"I don't know about we, but I..." I paused, not wanting to answer that question yet.

"Well?" Elli probed.

"I had a weird dream about Dimitri last night." I changed the topic to the true reason I'd woken her up. My voice came out quiet when I spoke Dimitri's name, little waves of pain coursing through me. My heart felt like it was breaking again, though not as badly as it would have a few months ago.

"What was it about?" Elli adjusted her position on the bed to face me entirely. She was attentive and present, which was more than I would have expected from her in her current state.

"I don't remember the details, but I remember Dimitri just... saying things that made me feel guilty for... possibly liking someone else. And then Aaron showed up, and it was like I was back at the party last night. But Dimitri was there, too, and it was just very confusing. It was almost like… like I was being forced to choose between the two."

Elli hummed and nodded. "So *do* you feel guilty for choosing someone else over Dimitri?"

I paused and thought about her question. I felt silly for even hesitating. But at the same time, were those thoughts valid?

"Do you think… Do you think I need to move on quickly? Because he never existed? Like…" I rolled to my back and looked at the ceiling. My eyes traced patterns in the stucco as my mind raced with ideas and explanations. "Like, okay. Are my feelings for Dimitri valid? He never existed; so, therefore, my feelings *shouldn't* be valid. Meaning I should move on quickly, right?" I turned my head back to Elli to see her reaction to my words.

Her eyes were downcast as she gave her answer serious thought. "Well, just because he wasn't real, that doesn't mean your feelings aren't real, right? I mean, how do you feel? Do you feel ready to move on?" She looked me in the eye, and I held her gaze.

Was I ready?

"Honestly, I feel both ready and unready at the same time. I think a big part of me is scared. But another part of me is just ready to enjoy my life. Those two parts are kind of at war with each other, like the crazy side of me wants to hold on and the sane side of me is like, 'get your shit together, Priya.' But that means dating, and honestly, who would want to date me?"

Elli scoffed at me. "Priya, you're kidding, right?"

"I'm really not. I'm not like you, Elli. I don't have guys throwing themselves at me. Even last night at the party, that guy you introduced me to early on? He just completely ignored me and even tried to push me out of the way to talk to you," I said.

She frowned. "So what? Evan is a dick. But you know who *did* want to talk to you? Aaron," she said, matter-of-factly.

I stared at her and thought back over the night, replaying the way he acted, the things he said, and the way we interacted. I remembered the way he laughed with me, the way he was sweet and gentle and paused to analyze how comfortable I felt around him.

"I mean, yes. Yes, he did, but—"

"No buts, Priya. If you keep that attitude, you will for *sure* never get a guy because you'll only push them away. If you don't even let yourself like a guy, then you never will date. If you don't try, you'll never know." She followed up that speech with a small burp. She closed her eyes and scrunched up her face.

"How much did you drink last night?" I asked, desperate for a change in topic.

"I think I only had five shots? I can't remember after the third one, but I'm usually fine after just three, so it was definitely more than that."

She'd certainly developed quite a tolerance for alcohol. "You're a beast," I said and she gagged.

"I'm also nauseous." She turned to her back.

"Do you need anything?"

"Pedialyte."

"What the... why?"

"It helps with hangovers. Do you have any?"

"Why the hell would I have that?" I said before lifting myself out of bed. "I'll go buy some, though, so just hang tight. And if you need to throw up, use the trash bin. It's on my side." I rolled out of the bed. Elli simply groaned and gave me a thumbs up, making me laugh.

The Safeway was pretty dead, considering it was a Saturday morning. I scanned the aisles until I found the Pedialyte. It took so long to find I ended up spending twenty minutes on Google, searching if any other sort of electrolyte-filled drink would be fine. But, no, the short answer was Gatorade would not suffice.

I stared at the selection of Pedialyte options. There were different flavors of powders and liquids. I picked a strawberry-flavored liter, wondering if that would be big enough for Elli. She was a pretty small girl, but I figured she would need a lot of the fluid to replenish herself.

"Rough morning?"

I jumped and clenched the bottle to my chest before looking to see Aaron standing next to me, a smirk on his face.

"I swear, all I do is scare you," he said.

"Sorry, I'm pretty skittish."

"I even tried to walk very loudly toward you." He mimed stamping his feet on the ground, and I gave a sheepish smile.

"Oops?"

He laughed. "No worries. Is that for your friend?" he asked with a nod toward the bottle in my hands.

"Yeah. She woke up feeling like crap. What about you?" I asked, looking at the basket in his hands and noticing a liter of the same liquid resting at the bottom, although he had the original flavor. "Did you finally have fun after I left?"

He followed my gaze with his eyes before vigorously shaking his head. "No! I mean, yes. But I mean…" He was tripping over his words. I looked at him curiously, wondering what had made him lose his cool demeanor.

"This is for *my* friend," he said finally, rubbing the back of his neck.

"Ah."

"But honestly, I didn't have that much fun after you left. I had, uh, more fun talking to you." He coughed a little at the end of his sentence.

Butterflies took wing in my stomach, and my face warmed with a blush. I looked down at the ground, trying to hide my reaction.

"I liked talking to you too," I said, and when I looked up again, I saw his face had lit up with a bright smile that I couldn't help but mirror.

The moment was broken when I felt my phone ring and reached into my pocket to find a text from Elli, wondering where I was.

"I gotta go. Elli is demanding her Pedialyte, but I'll see you on Monday?" I said, already starting to walk past Aaron.

"Wait!" Aaron's abrupt outburst made me pause in my tracks. I turned back to him and saw he was fidgeting with the basket in his hands.

"Would you... uh...want to maybe, like, go out for dinner? Tonight? Or... whenever."

My jaw fell open slightly, and I stared at Aaron, shocked that he would ask me, of all people, on a date. I quickly made a show of coughing into my arm to mask my open jaw and put it back in place.

"Ummm..."

You're already moving on?

I couldn't silence Dimitri's voice from my dream. My heart and mind started to race, and my skin felt clammy, hot, and tingly, like a bunch of needles were pricking my skin.

I stared at Aaron and tried to think beyond my past and the horrors it included. I thought back to my checklist, to the very last item that I had tried to remove from the list entirely —getting a boyfriend. I thought about the fourth item, liking a real boy.

Was I ready for this? Could I do this? What about my baggage?

If you don't try, Priya, you'll never know. Elli's words echoed in my head.

Don't you love me anymore? Dimitri's voice responded, the memories from my dream still vivid, almost real, as if Dimitri had spoken the words into my heart while I was sleeping.

I closed my eyes momentarily. Then I opened them again and focused on Aaron, and the anxiety I had felt slowly melted away.

Aaron looked nothing like Dimitri. Where Dimitri was muscular, like a weightlifter, and towered over me with his golden blond hair and hazel eyes, Aaron was lean from running, tall but not a giant, and while his demeanor was cool, his brown eyes, dark black hair, and single adorable dimple on his left cheek gave him a look that was still young and almost innocent. Dimitri was very flirtatious, far from innocent, and could be obnoxious in the most lovable way. He was shameless and bold, and he had been from the first day I saw him.

Aaron was sweet and gentle. He was friendly, but not loud, and I could tell he wasn't confident in himself when it came to asking me out. He was very much a teenage boy. In fact, this all felt very high school, like we were just teenagers, unsure of how to approach someone we liked. I could feel his uncertainty and his bashfulness, which the twenty-something Dimitri had lacked. Aaron's insecurity, which was so unlike

Dimitri, was refreshing. It was obvious that we were *both* insecure around each other, and that made the moment, the feelings, and the person in front of me feel very real. This was supposed to be awkward.

Maybe this was my first step to having crushes and feelings for guys who were real—and my age.

When I snapped back to the present and out of my head, Aaron looked almost dejected.

"Hey, you know, never mind. I can see you're trying to find a way to let me down easy, so—"

"Yes!" I said, panicking and stopping him too abruptly. "I-I mean, no, I'm not trying to reject you. I'm trying to say… yes, I'd like to get dinner. Sometime. Tonight doesn't work." I couldn't believe I'd been so stuck in my thoughts that it had almost cost me a date with Aaron. I needed to think less and act more.

Aaron's face morphed from surprise to relief, then to complete joy.

"How does… tomorrow sound?" I asked, and Aaron nodded vigorously.

"Sounds great. Can I… uh… Can I get your number?" Aaron asked, reaching for his phone, and I laughed with relief.

"I mean, I guess," I said with an eye roll, surprising even myself with my show of sarcasm. Usually, my sarcasm was reserved for only family and Elli. But Aaron didn't seem to mind it. He laughed, and we traded phones. When I got it back, I saw that he'd included a heart next to his name.

"Cute," I said as another text from Elli popped up—dramatic as ever.

"Thanks. I don't actually get that a lot, so keep it coming." I looked up at Aaron, and he winked.

"Okay, now I really have to go. But I'll see you tomorrow?" I asked, confirming, and Aaron smiled.

"Wouldn't miss it for anything." He smiled and showed off that dimple. After a quick goodbye, I rushed off.

You've already forgotten me? The words floated through my head again, and I sighed as I paid for the drink and walked out of the store.

I love you, Dimitri. But I have to move on.

$\sim$

When I arrived back at the house, Elli was sitting in my living room watching TV on mute with subtitles on.

"Jesus Christ, took you long enough. What were you doing?" she groaned, and I rolled my eyes before setting the Pedialyte down on the couch next to her.

"You're welcome," I said sarcastically. She smiled meekly before cracking open the bottle and taking a few chugs. "And if you must know, I saw Aaron. And we have a date tomorrow." My face broke into a smile.

Elli's eyes widened. She stopped downing the Pedialyte and squealed, "*This. Bitch. Said,* and I quote: 'Who would want to date me?' And what did she just say? She has a *date?*"

I tried to contain my laughter at her obnoxious screaming, but when she finished with a wince and immediately set the closed bottle of Pedialyte down, holding her head and groaning, I couldn't help it.

"Serves you right for screaming at me," I whispered, and she sighed, ignoring the pointed remark. It was so like her to not apologize. Even when we were kids, she would never apologize with her words, although she always did with her actions.

One time when we were in the second grade, we fought over a math problem.

We were sitting at the counter in her kitchen, eating our usual snack of pepperoni and mint chocolate chip ice cream. Her house had an open floor plan, so the TV in the living room was easily visible in the kitchen. But our trivial fight rose above the noise of the TV.

"I hate you! You're wrong!" she'd yelled at me.

"Well, I hate you, too, cuz I'm right!" I'd yelled back, feeling the tears sting my eyes.

At the time, I thought our friendship was over forever.

Elli's family moved a few neighborhoods away earlier that year, so I couldn't just pick up my stuff and walk home like I used to. I had to sit at the counter doing my homework until my mom was done with work and able to pick me up. Tears had splattered down in staggered droplets onto my homework while I tried to keep solving multiplication problems.

Five minutes later, I was about to give up and call my mom, even though I knew she didn't like to be bothered at work when it wasn't an emergency, but then my quiet sobs were interrupted by a folded paper sliding over the counter toward me. I hiccupped and looked over at Elli, who was looking down at her homework. I looked at the folded letter, picked it up, and opened it. Then I let out a sigh of relief.

"You were right" was written in Elli's curlicue handwriting.

I looked at her, then back at the paper before writing down my response and sliding it back to her.

"Hey, don't cry, okay? You were right. Now help me with

this other problem." She shoved her homework into my face after reading my note and I laughed.

The memory flitted through my mind, in my head one second and gone the next, and I smiled at Elli.

"Do you want to watch reruns of *The Nanny*?" I asked, earning me a slow nod.

We got comfortable on the couch, cuddled up next to each other, and settled into a comfortable silence.

"Are you staying over for dinner?" I asked groggily after the sixth or seventh episode.

"Yup."

"What do you want to eat?" I asked as I rubbed at my face and stretched.

"I don't know."

"All right, you have two options. Pizza or bean and cheese burritos," I said, and she hummed as she thought about her options.

"Burritos, please."

I smiled, knowing she would choose that option. I hated those burritos, but I'd offered to make them anyway because she loved them like no one else.

"I'm going to go shower, and I'm stealing some of your clothes," she said when she finally lifted herself off the couch. She hobbled across my view and up the stairs.

A few minutes later, my phone rang with its text tone.

Aaron: How does sushi sound for tomorrow?

I immediately became alert and sat up straight on the couch, staring at the phone screen as I thought about what to say in response.

Does "Sounds good" work? Should I add an exclamation mark? Will I sound too excited? Why is this so hard? It's literally just responding to a text.

"Elli!" I yelled as I got up off the couch and ran up the

stairs to my room, taking them two at a time. I burst into my bedroom and tested the knob on my bathroom. When I found it unlocked, I cracked the door open slightly and let my face peak through the crack, keeping my eyes closed.

"Elli!" I moaned, making Elli yelp.

"*Shit!* Priya. What the fuck?"

"Aaron texted me! And I don't know what to say," I groaned, and Elli groaned with me.

"What did he say?"

"He said, 'How does sushi sound for tomorrow?'" I repeated the text back to Elli, and there was a tense pause between us.

"You are *unbelievable*! Just fucking reply to the boy."

"But... but... it's not that easy!"

"Yes, it is. Just act like he's not the boy you like and reply to him. All you have to say is 'Sounds good.'" I sighed.

I left the bathroom door ajar and slid down the outer wall next to it, trying to get a grip on myself.

Priya, you're acting stupid. He's just a boy. Stop acting like he's a celebrity or like you don't know how to speak properly.

I quickly sent a text to Aaron letting him know sushi was great, and I threw my phone across the floor toward my bed.

"Elli, what's wrong with me?" I asked when I heard the water shut off. The shower door opened, and the metal towel rack screeched as she pulled a towel off of it.

"Other than your lack of regard for personal space?" she asked rhetorically before sighing. "It's okay to be nervous. You're new to this. Whereas most of us have had years of practice talking to boys by our sophomore year of high school, you had a strict mom who didn't even let you speak a boy's name in the house who wasn't family or a celebrity. It's okay to not know how to talk to a boy." The bathroom door opened further, and Elli stepped out in a towel and walked over to my closet.

"But doesn't talking to Dimitri count as talking to a boy?" I asked quietly, and Elli poked her head out of my closet.

"Baby girl, no. I don't know how to explain this to you. I feel like you and Dimitri had a lot of firsts, but they weren't representative of how real life is. Yes, they were real to you, and I'm not saying you shouldn't acknowledge what you felt, but I wouldn't count them as real experiences. It's like counting dreams as real experiences." Elli's soft tone did not prevent a bit of anger from rising in me.

But why shouldn't he count? Why shouldn't I count our experiences? So what if he was like a dream?

I brought my legs up toward my chest and wrapped my arms around them, hugging my knees. The anger and pain simmered steadily. I knew I was thinking irrationally, but I couldn't help it. Elli was right, but it still felt painful to acknowledge. And what made it even harder was that I was also upset with myself that I was so begrudgingly accepting the truth. Why was it so hard? Why couldn't I just always think rationally?

Did I need to increase my medication dosage? Would that help?

Probably not.

Somehow, I knew it wasn't a matter of medication.

Elli's legs appeared in my line of vision as she walked over to where I was sitting and plopped down in front of me, wearing a pair of pajama shorts and a t-shirt. She sat cross-legged and pulled her wavy hair up into a messy bun.

"What's going through your head, Priya?" she asked.

I paused for a few seconds as I gathered my thoughts in a way that could be shared coherently. "I just... feel hurt and angry over this situation, you know? I think the hardest part is convincing myself to let go of unhealthy habits, like believing that Dimitri is real, or was real, or could be real. But it's hard when the enemy of your own happiness is yourself."

"It's okay to feel what you feel, and if you need to let the unhealthy thoughts out, if you need to let the crazy out, then do that. Let it out. But don't ruminate over it. Just let it out and move on from it. Give yourself the permission and the space to *be* crazy. Like a grace period."

I mulled over her words, then nodded. "You're right. I'll just let the crazy out whenever I need to, then go back to being... me, when I'm ready." I sighed.

Elli unfurled her body and stood up. "Good. Now let's go make some burritos. I'm starving."

SEPTEMBER 16TH, 2018

AARON and I had decided to go out for an early dinner. My mom wouldn't be back until late, and Aaron told his parents he was studying at a friend's place. Neither of us wanted to deal with embarrassing questions or meeting parents on our first date. Elli had stayed over most of the day, but I dropped her off back at her house a few hours beforehand with the assurance that I would call her as soon as the date was over.

"*Didi*, what do I wear on dates?" I asked my sister while we video chatted as I rummaged through my clothes.

"Whatever you feel comfortable in."

I looked through the myriad of t-shirts, long sleeves, and sweaters I owned.

Nothing was date worthy.

"I literally have nothing to wear," I groaned.

"Ha! You literally have a walk-in closet *full* of clothes," she exclaimed. I ran my fingers through my hair and sighed.

"What did you wear on your first date ever?" I turned to the phone and looked at my sister's face for reassurance.

"My first date was to homecoming. I don't think you want

to wear a homecoming dress tonight." She laughed and I groaned again, turning back to my closet.

"Why don't you borrow something from Elli?"

"Because, no offense to Elli, her fashion sense is very... risqué compared to mine. I *definitely* don't feel comfortable in her clothes. Besides, she's smaller than me, anyway." I gasped as an idea popped into my head.

I pulled out a black cap sleeve crop top and a full-length navy blue sheer skirt with an underlay skirt and a slit on the right side.

I layered the pieces across my body and turned to my screen.

"Hmm..." said my sister, examining it. "That's really cute. If you wore your white sneakers, it would look really nice without being too dressed up, and not too casual, either."

I sighed with relief.

"What about makeup?" she asked, and I tensed again.

"What about it?"

"Are you gonna wear it?"

I stared at the screen and groaned, grinding my teeth in frustration.

"Why is dating so *hard?*" I whined as I stomped my way out of the closet and threw my clothes on the bed.

"You don't have to wear makeup—I was just asking, jeez! But if you feel so inclined, I think a little eyeliner and mascara would look nice."

I put my phone on its back, so it was facing the ceiling, and began to change as Jasmine continued talking.

"So tell me about this boy. What's his deal? What's his name? What's his GPA?"

I laughed as I slid on my skirt and zipped up the back. "His name is Aaron, and he's very nice. I don't know his GPA, but we met on the cross-country team on the first day of school, right after I called you." My voice came out a little strained as I pulled my shirt over my head.

"Wow, Dr. Worblack was right. Joining a sports team *is* good for you." Her words made me roll my eyes as I fixed my hair before picking up my phone and bringing my sister into the bathroom with me. I did a quick time check and saw that I had another twenty minutes before I was supposed to leave to meet Aaron at the restaurant.

"So, what else? What do you like about him? Hmm?" Jasmine continued.

I couldn't help the smile that broke out on my lips or the tremors in my hands as I put on my eye liner. It was obvious to my sister that I had a very physical reaction to the thought of Aaron, and she very loudly made her observation of my tremors and smile known.

"I don't really know how to explain it, but... I feel very comfortable with him. He feels like a normal teen crush." I shrugged.

"That's it? Priya, you're sixteen years old. You're supposed to have the whole whirlwind romance experience. Where are the butterflies? The blushes? The hyperboles and the exaggerations?"

I finished the last stroke of my mascara on my eyelashes and examined my reflection in the mirror for a second, looking at the young woman who stared back at me and suddenly feeling out of place and uncomfortable in my own skin.

Something felt off.

"*Didi*, my whirlwind romantic experience was with Dimitri. I think I've had enough whirlwind experiences." My voice came out more devoid of emotion than I intended. I continued to stare at myself in the mirror, looking at this version of me—someone who was pretending she hadn't experienced a psychotic episode and was a normal high schooler experiencing her first love, and hadn't had to grow up quicker than anticipated.

"I know, Priya, but this is different, right? I mean, are Aaron and Dimitri even similar?"

"Well, yes. But no. Even though both are playful, Aaron is much more sweet, caring, and kind. He teases at times, but not too much. Aaron also isn't as put together as Dimitri was. He's mature, yes, but he still acts how I would expect a normal teen to act, and that just makes him feel real. And... I think that's one of the reasons why I like Aaron. I think that's why I said yes." I looked at the screen and saw my sister staring back at me, her cheek resting on her hand as she leaned against the armrest on her couch.

"Okay," was all she said. I knew she was at a loss for words.

"Are those good enough reasons, though? Am I doing this right?" I asked her.

I felt the hesitation down in my bones. I had so many doubts. Should I even be going on this date? Was I ready for this? Was this even appropriate? *Did* I want some whirlwind, high school romance?

"Does this feel right to you? Cold feet and nervousness are fine for a first date, but if it feels wrong, you better cancel because I think you only have five minutes before you have to leave." Her words snapped me back to reality, and I stared at the screen, counting the beats of my heart as time slowed, and I contemplated my options.

If you don't try, you'll never know.

"It feels right. I'll call you after. Love you!"

"Love you too. Have fun, okay? And don't do anything stupid!"

∽

I walked into the crowded restaurant and surveyed the room for Aaron's familiar face. The restaurant was mostly filled with families and couples, save for one booth where a smiling, teenage boy waved directly at me.

I smiled as I walked over, taking a deep breath. I hoped I walked confidently. I hoped I didn't look overdressed or stupid or like I couldn't dress myself. Judging from what he was wearing—a light blue, short-sleeved button-up and light tan shorts, I may have overdone it a little. But then again, I had no idea what guys usually wore on a first date either.

"Hi," I said as I sat down in the booth.

"Hi! You, uh, you look great." He was smiling brightly at me, and I couldn't help but blush and smile back, looking down at the table in embarrassment as I situated my purse on it near the wall.

"Thank you. You look great too," I said, and Aaron's smile got even brighter, somehow. "Did I make you wait long? I'm—"

"If you say sorry, I'm going to explode," he joked.

"Okay, let me rephrase that. Did I make you wait long? Sucks to suck." I shrugged. Aaron's ensuing laughter was like music—well articulated music. You could actually hear the separate *ha*'s, which made me smile.

"You didn't make me wait too long," he said. "I got here, like, five minutes before you did."

Just then, a waitress came up to our table with water and menus. We knew what we wanted to eat, both of us having our usual orders, so we ordered right away.

"Okay, so don't hate me for asking this, but how did you skip a grade?" Aaron asked once she'd left.

I shrugged and smiled a small, nervous smile, knowing

my answer would further brand me as the school's biggest nerd.

"So I didn't skip a grade the traditional way. I just took a couple night classes at city college during my freshman year to get the credits early. So I just skipped it by, like… technicality, I guess."

"No offense, but why would you do that to yourself?" he asked. I looked at him for a second longer than I probably should have as I contemplated my answer.

"Well, if I'm being honest, I really hate high school. I've told most people I did it so I can stand out to colleges, but the truth is, I really did it because I can't wait to move on. So if I can shorten my time here, why not?" I took a sip from my water.

"Wow. You *really* hate high school, huh?" He leaned forward with his arms crossed on the table.

"Well, yeah." I looked around the restaurant, all of a sudden feeling like I'd said the wrong thing. I felt as if I were being scrutinized and judged, even though Aaron had given me no reason to feel that way.

"I don't blame you. If I had known that was an option, I might have done it as well. But then I wouldn't have met you, so maybe it's a good thing I didn't," he said with a shrug and a playful wink.

Our waitress arrived with our food. We both thanked her and continued with the conversation as if his playful flirtation hadn't even happened, which I was thankful for. I had no idea how to respond to flirtations or to guys in general. It was a miracle I was even able to articulate myself around him.

"What about you? What's your thing?" I asked as I picked up a piece of my sushi roll with my chopsticks.

"What do you mean?"

"Like, what's the thing that makes you different? I'm *that* kid at the school, but who are you?" I said and Aaron laughed.

"You're just diving in, aren't you?"

"You did it first. But hey, go big or go home." I smiled.

Aaron picked up a piece of his roll and popped it into his mouth. He hummed as he thought about his response, his eyes darting around the table. His head tilted to the side at one point, and he looked up. His silence persisted even after he had swallowed, but I was so engrossed in watching him that I forgot to continue eating.

"Okay, I got it. I'm the AP Gov teacher's son."

"Duh, I already knew that," I said with a roll of my eyes and Aaron chuckled.

"Well, that's my thing!" he said, and I gave him a playful glare, smushing my lips together into a tight line.

"Okay, fine. But what does that mean for you?"

"It means my friends try and get me to steal the answer key for tests," he said.

It was my turn for my eyes to widen. "Are you serious?"

"It's happened a couple times with my friends who were upperclassmen when I was a freshman or sophomore." He shrugged and I shook my head.

"Some friends."

"Desperate times called for desperate measures," he said, smiling at me. "I don't really mind that it happened now, but back then, I totally felt annoyed that they were trying to use me like that. If they had been joking, it would be completely different. They weren't, though, so I was pretty pissed."

"I would be too. It's like when kids used to copy my homework and tests. It's really annoying."

"Yeah, see, you get it. A lot of people don't understand that part of it. They just see how it could cause trouble, but when I say it's annoying and kind of hurtful, they just brush it off. Oh well, makes you realize who your real friends are," he said, reaching for another piece of sushi.

"Yeah, those are pretty rare," I said.

"You seem pretty close to that girl at the party. What was her name again?"

"Her name is Elizabeth, but she goes by Elli. And, yeah, she's my best friend. We've known each other almost since we were born."

"Damn, you've managed to stay friends for that long? I basically get new friends every few years. I don't think I've managed to be close to any one person for longer than two or three years, even if I've known them for longer than that. People are always changing."

I nodded. "We definitely have changed over time, but the one thing that's remained the same is our loyalty and commitment to each other. I think... when you've been through the kind of shit we've been through and have supported each other through, it kind of solidifies the friendship."

"That sounds like a relationship. No offense!"

I laughed. "None taken. I call her my platonic soulmate because... well... I don't know where I would be without her."

"You're really lucky to have her," he said.

"Yeah, I am,"

We looked at each other, both smiling. We continued to exchange smiling glances for a few more moments, enjoying each other's company and being comfortable with each other, until our waitress came back and checked on us.

Once she'd left, Aaron asked me another question. "Okay, so you have Elli, but do you have any siblings?"

"Yeah, I have a sister."

"Younger?" he asked, and I laughed, picking up a piece of sushi with my chopsticks.

"No, older. Guess by how much."

"That means it's a large difference, so I'm going to guess… she's seven years older?"

I shook my head as I chewed, motioning with my thumb that he had to go higher.

His eyes widened. "What the…? Okay, nine?"

I shook my head, swallowing. "Nah, but close enough. We're ten years apart."

"Holy crap! How is she so much older than you?"

I shrugged. "I was an accident," I said, making him laugh.

"No, seriously."

"I honestly don't know what was going through my parents' heads."

"I guess having kids isn't always something you plan," he said, and I nodded somberly.

"That's for sure." I took another bite of my food and smiled at him. Aaron gave me a look that made me think he could see right through my facade, and I panicked a little at the thought that he might pry.

He didn't, though. "I'm pretty sure I was an accident, too, so we can be in that club together."

"What about you, do you have any siblings?" I asked. He shook his head.

"Nope. I'm an only child."

"Sounds pretty boring."

"What? Why?"

"You got to avoid all the teasing, didn't get any free clothes from older siblings, and were probably spoiled rotten and got whatever you asked for." I was only half joking.

Aaron glared at me, but he couldn't hide his smile.

"What a presumptuous thing to say. What if I had a bunch of older cousins who gave me their clothes and who teased me? What if my parents were hella strict and didn't give me anything I wanted? Hmm?"

I stared at him for a long moment, smiling. "Well?" I challenged his bluff and he challenged me back, staring me down.

Eventually, he gave in.

"Well... you're pretty spot on about everything, except getting everything I wanted. I had to earn some things with good grades, ya know," he said, wagging his chopsticks at me.

"So what you're saying is, I'm right."

He rolled his eyes. "Whatever, you're right this time."

We settled into a conversation that was less rapid-fire and gave each of us time to eat. I found out that Aaron's parents were from Hong Kong, and he has a decent sized family with a bunch of cousins in LA and Hong Kong. I let him rant about his family for a bit while I finished my food, loving every second of it.

When the check came, I reached for the bill, but Aaron snatched it up quicker than I expected.

"Ummm..." I watched, unsure and contemplating whether to fight for it.

"Nope, I'm paying."

"Excuse you, but I'm an independent woman," I said and he smiled.

"And I'm the *gentleman* who took this independent woman on a date, so I'm paying."

That time, I held my tongue so another retort wouldn't come out. I smiled instead.

"Just say thank you, Priya. I'm giving you what every woman wants: free food."

"That's actually so true. Thank you."

After he'd paid, he asked, "So what should we do now? Do you want to get boba?"

"Ooh, yes, please."

There was a boba shop open late in the same plaza as the sushi restaurant, so we walked over.

"What time do you have to be home by?" he asked as we sat down at one of the tables with our drinks—which he paid for as well—in hand.

"No curfew. My mom is gone until pretty late, so I make my own rules."

"Where did your mom go?" he asked before taking a sip of his drink.

"She's flying back from Paris... right now, I think," I said, looking at my watch.

Aaron gasped. "She went to Paris and didn't take you?"

"Yes. It's a work trip. She's a content marketer for an e-commerce company and is often flown out around the country, sometimes the world, to work with the different branches. Plus, she would never take me out of school unless I was absolutely not allowed to be there."

"That's really cool," Aaron said. "But how often does that happen? Do you even see her very often?"

"It happens almost once a month, usually for two days or a weekend but sometimes for a week at most. But I mean, she's gotta do what she's gotta do," I said.

"What do you mean?"

"It's expensive to live here, you know? She wouldn't work that much and do all this if she had a choice, but ever since my dad left, she's had to work overtime and essentially be superwoman in order to provide for us and keep us comfortable," I said, looking down at the table. "I'm grateful that she enjoys her job, though, and it's given us a lot of opportunities to travel when we can. It's a blessing and a curse, I guess."

"She sounds like a superwoman for sure. And if it's any consolation, it'll probably be yet another leg up if you include it in your college admission essays," he said and I laughed.

"You know, that's the real reason she does it. So I have a great story for my essays."

"It's true! Admissions boards love sob stories and stories of overcoming hardship."

I nodded. "Yeah, well, I've done a lot of that," I said, instantly regretting the comment. It dampened the mood and was followed by an awkward silence. Aaron looked at me curiously. I could tell he was dying to ask more personal questions but was trying to tread lightly. I admired him for holding back his questions, but I also felt a weird desire to open up to him. I felt comfortable, and I felt *safe*, emotionally and physically. I felt like he wouldn't judge my past, or me. Even though we had only known each other for a few weeks, it seemed like much longer. I hadn't felt this sense of trust with anyone aside from Elli and... Dimitri.

When my train of thought touched on Dimitri, my mood dropped. But instead of shutting down, I felt myself wanting to open up.

So I did.

"Sorry to dampen the mood. I have a lot of baggage," I said, looking up at Aaron. He nodded, as if he knew I had more I wanted to say, so I continued.

"I don't know if this is first date appropriate, since I've never been on a date, but I just want you to know that if we decide to... you know, I'm going to need to take things very slowly. I really like spending time with you, so I don't want you to think that I'm not opening up because I don't like you because, um, I do." My voice grew soft at the end. I couldn't keep my eyes from looking around the room, only a few times stopping on Aaron's face and then darting away again. Every time they did turn to him, though, his attention was directed right at me.

When I finally brought myself to focus on him again, he was smiling a soft, genuine smile.

"Well, thank God you like me because I really like you, Priya," he said, leaning forward slightly and clutching his drink. "We can go at your pace, for sure. You want to slow down? I'm here for it. You need space? I got you. You wanna speed up? Well, then we'll need to see what I want."

"Thanks. I really appreciate it." I laughed and he nodded, taking a sip of his drink.

"But serious question, how is this your first date?" he asked, looking at me intensely.

I shrugged, smiling. "Honestly, I'm surprised you even asked me out. I had no idea you liked me," I said.

"What are you talking about? I've been, like, super obvious. Didn't you read my signs?"

"What signs?" I asked, completely oblivious.

Aaron acted as if I had physically wounded him before speaking. "Um, I practically stare at you every day at practice and in our AP Psych class like a creep? I held your hand at the party—which totally makes us official, just saying," he added, raising his hands in defense, and I laughed hysterically, hiding my face in my hands.

It took me a few attempts to speak before I could get a real sentiment out. "Really? That makes us official? You pulling me through a crowd at a party?" I asked and he shrugged.

"Uh, yeah? I basically saved you, like a hero saving a damsel in distress. This—" He gestured between us. "—is basically a fairytale. So you're welcome, princess."

I scoffed, trying to hide my amusement.

"Hey, you should be honored to land a princess—no, a queen—like me, so *you're* welcome, sir," I said, adding in a hair flip for extra sass. Aaron burst into laughter and covered his face.

The rest of the night continued in the same vein, with jokes, banter, and pleasant conversation. Before we knew it, it was time for us to leave.

As we walked to our cars, Aaron walked close to me, our arms almost touching a few times. His close proximity was thrilling, and I wanted to reach for his hand, but I held back, not as bold with my actions as I was with my words.

Aaron walked me to my car, just a few spots from his.

"I'll see you in AP Psych tomorrow, right?" he asked and I nodded.

"For sure."

"Cool. Drive safely, okay? Text me when you're home." He paused for a second longer than I expected before stepping back and turning to walk to his car.

As I drove home, I couldn't help but smile. I also couldn't help but wonder if Aaron had paused for a reason. Maybe he wanted to say something else? Or better yet, maybe he wanted to kiss me?

At the thought of Aaron kissing me, I felt an overwhelming warmth flood my system.

Maybe I still could have a whirlwind romance.

Maybe I could fall in love again and have a boyfriend.

Maybe I was ready.

8

DECEMBER 13TH, 2018

I WALKED into my AP Psych class and saw all the seats were already filled except mine, right next to Aaron. We had been dating exclusively for a couple months, and I was still drowning in the honeymoon phase. He smiled when he saw me, triggering the soft butterflies in the pit of my stomach.

"Hey, so don't freak out, but I wanted to ask you something," Aaron said when I sat down. I set my backpack on the floor and pulled out my notebook and pen before looking at him with a smile.

"Me? Freak out? Never," I said, and he smiled with a roll of his eyes. "What's up?" I asked, but before he could respond, Mr. Leonard stood up and clapped his hands together, signifying that the class needed to quiet down and pay attention.

"I'll ask you later."

"All right, who has seen the movie *A Beautiful Mind?*" Mr. Leonard asked. Almost all the students in the classroom raised their hands, including Aaron and me.

"Who can tell me the diagnosis of the main character, John Nash?"

The room fell silent as people began to think. However, I didn't need to think too long or hard about the answer. My chest felt tight, and I felt my heart beating hard, laboring just to get the blood through my system.

"Schizophrenia," I said softly, not to anyone in particular.

"Good job, Priya," Mr. Leonard said. I continued to look at him. My palms were laid flat against my cool desk, the colder temperature delivering an incremental bit of relief to my nervous system, bringing me slightly down from my anxious high.

"Can anyone explain to me what schizophrenia is?"

There was a silence in the room as people either tried to think of an answer or stared blankly around the room, pretending they were thinking.

"It's when you have... like, hallucinations and stuff, right? Like... you hear voices, see things that aren't real?"

"That's part of it, Amanda." I'd almost forgotten that Elli's friend Amanda was in this class. It was open to juniors and seniors; so Elli and her friends were also taking it, but Elli was in a different class period.

"Isn't it... what a lot of homeless people have? Like... the ones who scream at everyone and talk to themselves?" a guy named Haven chimed in.

"That's a common misconception, but some do have the diagnosis." Mr. Leonard shrugged. "I'm guessing no one in here knows of anyone who has the diagnosis."

The room remained silent and Mr. Leonard nodded.

"Makes sense—it's not something you encounter every day. And I suggest that if you meet someone who has schizophrenia, you run," he said in a way that had a few kids laugh.

My right eyebrow began to twitch. I felt light-headed, like I was going to faint. Was I going to faint?

Breathe, Priya. Breathe. Are you breathing?

I sucked in a breath, realizing I had been holding it. I loosened my body and tried to calm myself by counting my breaths.

I wanted to fight back and prove him wrong. I wanted to stand up and call out Mr. Leonard for his terrible comments, but I didn't.

I couldn't.

"Schizophrenia is a mental illness that affects about one percent of the population worldwide. It is known as the cancer of mental illnesses and presents usually in those who are at least eighteen years old—so watch out, all of you turning eighteen soon."

Mr. Leonard was known as one of the teachers who had no filter, which made it easier for a lot of students to relate to him rather than a lot of the other teachers in the school. His comments usually had kids laughing, and this particular comment garnered a few laughs and giggles. I could see kids in the corners of my eye point at each other, as if assigning the diagnosis like they were taking a personality test to see what kind of bread a person was.

I continued to stare straight at the front of the room, engaged and interested in learning more from a student's perspective, but also afraid of what I would find out.

Mr. Leonard pulled out a small remote control, and with a click of a button began skimming through facts about schizophrenia. He brought up brain scans, comparing a "healthy" brain to the brain of someone with the diagnosis. He brought up statistics and symptoms, separating them into positive and negative. Positive symptoms were things that "added" to a person, like hallucinations, delusions, and paranoia. Negative symptoms, like apathy and memory problems, "detracted."

I looked at the table of symptoms, trying to think back to just earlier that year. I remembered the hallucinations—

visual, auditory, and even tactile. I remembered the delusion about the Russian government. I remembered my word salad speech to Elli.

But I didn't remember feeling apathy, and, ironically, I didn't remember being forgetful.

So did I have schizophrenia at all? Or was I misdiagnosed? I had only some of the symptoms that were listed on the screen. I'd been told Dimitri was a hallucination. I was told I was delusional about who I was, my age, and everything about my life. But I had to be honest with myself and admit that I still struggled to agree with all that I was told. What if I didn't have schizophrenia at all? Who was to say that what I experienced was all in my head? The government?

The Russian government!

"Priya." Aaron tapped my shoulder, and I jumped out of my head and in my chair.

"What?"

"Would you care to answer the question, Priya, or is your daydream more important?" Mr. Leonard asked, making my head snap toward him. The class erupted into laughter, and I instantly shrank back.

"Sorry. What was the question?"

The class laughed even more, and Mr. Leonard shook his head.

"I asked, what is the typical age of onset for girls?"

"Sixteen?" Mr. Leonard made an obnoxious alarm sound, meaning I was wrong.

"False. Looks like someone is showing signs of a breakdown in selective attention," he said, pandering to the room.

The class erupted into laughter. I looked around at the kids who were laughing at me and felt my blood boil. That anger soon turned into pain and hurt when I turned to see Aaron with his hand covering his mouth, the hints of a smile and suppressed laughter slipping through as he looked anywhere but at me. However, when he did chance a glance my way, I glared at him. But his eyes told me he didn't think it was a big deal.

"You think this is funny?" I meant to speak softly, but it came out stern, bordering on yelling.

The smile slipped from his face as he looked around the room, which had quieted down, and then at me.

"It's… a little funny?"

The anger in me broke free, but not in the way I expected.

As I turned to face the front of the room, my eyes pricked with tears, my bottom lip quivered, and my throat tightened up.

Suck it up, Priya. Suck it up. Don't let people see this side of you.

But I couldn't stop the onslaught of emotion. I quickly gathered my things, shoving them into my bag, and ran out of the room as the tears fell from my eyes and trailed down my cheeks in streams.

If you meet someone with schizophrenia, run.

Looks like someone is showing signs of a breakdown in selective attention.

I stopped in my tracks, standing in the middle of the quad area, my emotions paralyzing me.

Fuck Mr. Leonard.

Fuck AP Psych.

Fuck Aaron.

I wiped at my tears as the sobs caught in my throat. The betrayal at Aaron's reaction and, even worse, his excuse hurt more than anything Mr. Leonard said.

I cried harder at the thought that maybe I had given my heart away too quickly, to someone who didn't deserve it.

Maybe I shouldn't have let myself have this whirlwind

teenage romance after all. Teenagers suck. They're monsters and terrible people, and the only decent teenager I know is Elli.

Just as soon as I thought of her, my phone vibrated in my pocket. I took it out to see a worried text from her.

Elli: Hey, Amanda said you ran out of class crying. Do you need me?

"Do you need me?"

Dimitri.

My body froze, and it felt like the world froze around me as well. I didn't feel the wind or see leaves tumbling. I only felt my body being torn in two.

My mind felt like it was slowing, as if Dimitri's voice were a sedative causing my brain to shut down. I couldn't think through his voice, but I was feeling my way toward him.

Ignore him, Priya. He isn't real, my brain said.

But I want him to be, my treacherous heart replied.

I cried harder. My heart was crying out yes even as my head screamed no.

"Your hair is still long. Is it because you still miss me too?"

His words caught me off guard, and I could have sworn I saw the outline of his shape appearing and taking form beside me. The sight had me about to send Elli an affirmative text when someone grabbed my shoulder, turned me around, and pulled me into their chest.

At first, I thought it was Dimitri, but the comfort of the smaller, thinner arms around me told me it was Aaron. I began to shove him away, not wanting to feel his warmth and hating that his hug brought me peace. I didn't want to wrap my arms around him, but my limbs had a mind of their own.

Muscle memory kicked in, and even after they circled his waist and held him tightly, I couldn't drop them.

I rested my face against his shoulder and sobbed into the fabric of his shirt, letting his soft hushes draw the emotion out of me.

Was it okay that I was mad, though? Was it okay that I was hurting? Aaron didn't know my story. He didn't know why it wasn't funny, why it was hurtful.

But did he deserve to know? If that's how he reacted in class, was it safe enough for me to tell him?

His arms wrapped around me tightly, and he leaned his head down onto mine, whispering soft reassurances into my ear.

"I'm sorry, Priya. I'm really sorry. It wasn't funny. Please don't cry. I hate seeing you so sad." His words made me cry harder.

If you meet someone with schizophrenia, run.

"Run away, Aaron," I managed to get out, my arms loosening, but his arms tightened around me, somehow pulling me closer.

"Why? Is this you needing space?" he asked, and I shook my head against his shirt, wanting the exact opposite of space.

I didn't want there to be any space between us, and yet I knew he would be better off without me. He could do so much better than me, than someone with a past like mine. Who would want to stay with a girl who thought she was married? Who would want to stay with a girl who had the "cancer of mental illnesses?" He had every right to leave me and save himself from the crazy that was Priya Agarwal.

"Priya, talk to me," he said softly, kissing the top of my head. He continued to hold me as I cried into his shoulder until I was completely out of tears.

After the tears ran dry, we just stood there, holding each other for what felt like the longest few minutes of my life. They were alternately comforting and anxiety provoking. I had to make a decision. A decision that would possibly ruin my relationship—the first real one I had ever had—with the most amazing guy I had ever met.

He deserved to know, to make an informed decision about me. It wasn't fair to hide this from him and basically lead him on or trick him.

I pulled back and wiped my eyes with my sleeves. Aaron brought his hands up and swiped at my cheeks with his thumbs. When I dropped my hands and looked up at him, he cradled my face in his hands.

"I know you're a star student and all, but do you want to get out of here? I don't think you're in the right place right now," he said. I nodded, my heart racing as I counted down the moments until our relationship was ruined.

"Boba?" I asked, my voice hoarse. I coughed and cleared my throat, and Aaron smiled softly before nodding, grabbing my hand, and quickly walking with me to the school parking lot.

I stared down at my drink, feeling Aaron's eyes on me and the smooth swipe of his thumb across the back of my left hand. The boba shop was playing Korean pop music. At this hour, it was not even remotely full. It probably wouldn't get busy until school let out officially, which was still a few hours away.

My phone buzzed on the table.

"It's Elli," I whispered.

"You should probably answer," he said, giving me the

permission I didn't need, but wanted, to break the silence. I picked up my phone and answered, only for Elli to scream in my ear.

"Where the *fuck* are you?" She sounded as if she was panicking.

"Ditched class. With Aaron at the boba shop near the school."

"What happened? Are you okay? Did he hurt you?" Her voice was now a mixture of anger, worry, and confusion.

I looked at Aaron and saw him looking down at his hands as he fiddled with them. I had a feeling he could hear Elli screaming, so I lowered the volume on my phone.

"AP Psych was intense. You'll understand next period, but I just... have to talk to Aaron about something," I said, trying to drop as many subtle hints as I possibly could.

"What about AP Psych makes you run crying and all of a sudden need to have a serious talk with Aaron in the middle of the school day? Priya, you have never ditched class! The only time you've even missed school was..." Elli trailed off. I could hear the cogs turning in her head as she started to process and piece together the events.

"Wait. Are you... Priya, are you going to tell him?"

I nodded my head, as if she were there with me, before replying.

"Yes."

"Oh, baby girl, I wish I could be there with you. I'm proud of you for taking this step. You're so brave, and no matter what he says or how he reacts, I am here for you, okay?"

I nodded again.

"I know. That's why I love you."

"I love you too. Now, go do what you gotta do."

Elli hung up, and I stared at the screen. I felt my heart race as I took a deep breath and closed my eyes.

"Aaron, I have something I need to tell you. I don't know how to say it, but whatever I say, you have to promise me you will listen to everything before asking any questions, saying anything, or freaking out. Can you promise me that?"

Aaron simply held his hand out across the table, beckoning for me to hold it again. I knew it was a confirmation, so I slipped my hand back into his.

"I also want you to know that what I tell you doesn't change who I am. I'm still the same Priya you know, but you'll just be getting to know… more of me now."

Aaron nodded and I looked into his eyes, seeing his genuine worry. He was always kind and sweet, but he was usually playful. Right now, he wasn't making any jokes or playful comments. I knew he felt just as uncomfortable as I did, but he was trying to be strong for me. Hopefully, he was trying to be strong for *us*.

The memories from the coffee shop, from our wedding, from our times at home, all flashed through my mind like a movie.

And then the memory of Dimitri bloody and dying, my screams piercing the air, and the scent of metal blinded me.

My body began to tremble, and alarms blared in my head.

I can't do this, I can't do this, I can't do this.

You can, you can, you can. You are stronger than this, and Aaron deserves to know.

Aaron squeezed my hand again and rubbed his thumb along the backs of my knuckles. I watched his thumb move back and forth, hypnotizing me. It was calming, not because it showed his presence, but because he moved to a tempo that I could count to, slowly enough to be my grounding mechanism.

Swipe right, one.

Swipe left, two.

Swipe right, three.

Swipe left, four.

I counted ten swipes twice over before I was able to start.

"Some… time ago, I met a guy at a coffee shop at San Jose State University. He was the barista there, and his name was Dimitri. He was my first love, and to give you an idea of how important he was to me, he almost rivaled Elli." A smile ghosted over my lips as I remembered that day.

"Can I get a name for the order?"

"How about my number instead?"

"I wouldn't mind both."

"Elli always said it was too good to be true. She was right, as I realized later, but… I'll get to that." I took a deep, shaky breath before continuing.

"Dimitri and I had dated for over a year when I found out he was being disguised as a college student. He actually worked for the government on a top-secret project as a biochemist. I never knew the details about it, but I knew it had to do with blocking the Russian government's newest attempts at infiltrating the US. It was dangerous enough to need to disguise him," I said with a gulp, not daring to look at Aaron. I knew he would be confused. My story was just going to get more and more confusing until it ultimately became plain crazy, and I didn't want to see him when he realized that was just what my story was: crazy.

"I only found out about his disguise because, well, once we… got married, the government had to disguise me as a high school student to throw off any hints at our relationship and keep me safe from the Russians. We were happily married, living this facade for a year when the Russians found him."

Swipe right, one.

Swipe left, two.

Swipe right, three.

Swipe left, four.

The whole time I talked, Aaron's thumb swiped against my knuckles without changing pace or pressure. It remained a constant sign of attention, a constant gift of strength. By that point, my mind and body had dissociated. I spoke but I wasn't present. Words were spilling through my mouth from my brain, but my heart was disconnected, as if this weren't my story. As if these events hadn't actually happened, and as if I had never experienced them. My body was shutting down as the wound was opened wider and wider, the memories flooding my system as I relived them as a viewer instead of as a participant.

"In April, I was at Elli's house helping her with a test when the US government sent me a red alert saying Dimitri was in danger, but by the time I got to the house… the Russians had him. When I got to his house, a Russian agent was holding Dimitri. The agent threatened me with Dimitri's life if I didn't tell the agent about the secret project. I knew nothing about the project, but I tried to reason with the agent. It didn't work. The agent saw through me, and in one motion, he killed Dimitri. I ran to him, I tried to save him, and eventually the ambulances arrived. But when the ambulances came, instead of Dimitri, I was the one who was put inside. I was taken to the hospital where I was told I was actually a sixteen-year-old girl, I had never been married, and that… Dimitri never existed."

I dared a quick glance up at Aaron. He was leaning his head into his palm as he watched me intently.

"I ended up being in the hospital for three days before receiving my diagnosis—schizophrenia."

Aaron's thumb stopped swiping against my hand, the only indicator of his thoughts. There was a long silence between us as I contemplated whether I wanted that to be the end of my story, but I decided to continue.

"After my three-day hold in the hospital, I went home and caught up on my studies before returning to school and finishing up the year. I saw a therapist twice a week and my psychiatrist every two weeks before we all decided I was doing much better. Now I see my psychiatrist once every three months, and my visits to my therapist are more on an as-needed basis."

I swallowed. "I think I've been doing really well. I haven't had any horrible symptoms since April. I even have a checklist that I made to mark the progress I'm making, and I've actually crossed off almost all of them. The only remaining one I just haven't had... time for, but the most important one, the one I thought I would never accomplish, happened so quickly and so... easily."

There was a long, pregnant pause that hung over us. Finally, Aaron spoke.

"May I ask... what it was?" he asked, making my body tense up before I looked up at him. I stared at him as he continued to look at me with curious eyes.

"To like and date a real boy."

Aaron smiled softly and changed our hand positions so our palms were pressed together, fingers interwoven.

"I feel like Pinocchio," he said, cutting through the tension with one simple comment.

I let out a breath I had been holding and smiled back.

"Go on," he said, and I found myself seeing what I needed in his eyes: affirmation, reassurance, and comfort.

"Aaron, you are the actual sweetest, smartest, and most playful boy I have ever met. You make me feel things I thought only Dimitri would make me feel. But above that, you make me feel safe. You make me feel like everything will be all right, especially when you smile. Your smile is my favorite sight in the world. Mostly because of your dimple," I said. Aaron's eyes glossed over with tears, but none fell.

"I was going to tell you eventually, but the timing never felt right. Then today happened and... I was afraid you'd take Mr. Leonard's advice and run. And I tried to think that if you ran, it would be for the best. But I don't want you to run." My eyes brimmed with tears. I realized that this was the most vulnerable I had ever been with a person who wasn't Elli.

He looked down, holding his head low, and I knew he was trying to hide his emotions, trying to appear strong and put together. He swiped at tears with his left hand, and my heart clenched at Aaron allowing me to see *his* vulnerability.

"Even though I run pretty well in cross-country, I'm not known for running away during hard times." He lifted his head to show a soft smirk. I sat and waited for him to say something else, respecting his space to talk as he had respected mine.

"If running the past few years has taught me anything, it's that I hate running races alone." He looked at me with red, glossy eyes, and a dimple-studded smile. "And, Priya, I want to run this race with you."

I stared at him, taking in and processing what he was saying. Then I broke down, tears of joy trailing down my face.

"Why?" I searched his eyes for the answers.

"Because you're the strongest, gentlest, kindest soul I have ever met. You could be diagnosed with any and every mental illness there is, but, like you said, that doesn't change the girl you are at your core. And I would be lying if I said I wasn't falling hard and fast for that girl."

We sat there, looking to each other for support, comfort, and strength as he continued to hold my hand.

Soon, his thumb was swiping against the back of my hand again, and he was smiling, not a single tear in sight.

"Mr. Leonard is an ass, huh?" he said, and I laughed, shaking my head.

"Such an ass. I might have to have a talk with him."

A comfortable silence fell between us. Then Aaron spoke again.

"Priya, I want you to feel comfortable with me, enough to tell me things that bother you. I don't want to push your boundaries or force you to trust me—that's not even possible. But I want you to know that I will never purposely hurt you, and I will always be here for you. You matter a lot to me."

I thought back to my time with Dimitri and the whirlwind romance we'd had, the love we shared, and how I hadn't thought it was possible to have all of that again. I never expected I would be able to live a normal teenager's life, and yet, here I was with Aaron. However, Aaron was more than just a normal teenager, too. I would never expect such understanding and empathy from another teenager. He sounded like a hopeless romantic. I wasn't sure that was entirely healthy, but if it meant he wanted to keep me in his life, then I had no issues with it.

"Oh! What was that thing you wanted to ask me in class?" I asked, suddenly remembering, and he smiled again.

"Do you want to have dinner with my parents and me next week? They're dying to meet you."

My jaw dropped.

"I've already met your mom, though," I said in my confusion. He laughed.

"Yes, she knows you as Priya, the genius in AP Gov," he said mockingly, and I shoved his hand, making him laugh and grip my hand more tightly, but still gently, and bring it to his lips.

"But she and my dad want to meet Priya, the first girl-friend of mine I've actually talked about and haven't hidden from them."

"You really like me that much, huh?" I asked, and he rolled his eyes.

"You just admitted you like me that much, too, so don't act all cool."

I laughed. "I would love to meet your parents. As your girlfriend." He grinned. "On one condition," I added, and his smile dropped slightly. "You have to meet my mom within the next month."

His smile widened.

"Deal."

9

DECEMBER 31ST, 2018

I LOOKED BACK and forth between the submit button and the list of items I needed.

Maybe I'll just check one last time. Just to be sure. I checked again. Then I double checked. And triple checked. *Priya, you're being ridiculous! Just hit submit!*

I hovered my mouse over the button.

One last time—

No! One, two, three, GO!

I clicked the trackpad on my laptop and gasped, immediately retracting my hand, my heart pounding as I watched the spinning wheel on my laptop transform into a message. "Congratulations! Your application has been submitted."

I couldn't help the wide grin that spread across my face.

When I checked the time, I saw that I needed to start getting ready. I closed my laptop, turned on my speaker, and started blasting my Dance Songs playlist, Cardi B' voice coming through my speaker. I looked around my room and saw the horrendous mess that covered it.

Shit. If mom sees this, she'll flip.

I started picking up clothes and throwing them into my

closet, rapping along to the song. It was pretty vulgar when I thought about it. Elli always told me I was an enigma. She said I presented as so demure, but I was the most sarcastic person she knew with the most explicit music in my playlists.

As if she could hear my thoughts, Elli texted me.

Elli: What are you wearing tonight?

Priya: IDK. What do you wear to a NYE party?

The screen glowed with her face as she FaceTimed me, my music fading into the background.

"Sequins. Wear *a lot* of sequins and glitter, and just sparkle like a disco ball," she said. I grimaced.

"The only clothes I have with sequins are my Indian outfits."

"Oh! Wear one of the long-sleeved tops with high-waisted jeans! Do you have your thigh-high boots?"

I immediately thought of a velvet *Lehenga* top I had that was lightly speckled with gold sequins and slightly longer than most of the others. It was still cropped, but it looked more like a crop-top than a *Lehenga choli.*

"Yeah, tell me if this looks good," I said. I pulled it out of the closet and set my phone down to put it on with a pair of black jeans.

"What's your mom doing tonight?" Elli asked while I changed.

"She's going to a New Year's Eve party at her gym buddy's house."

"That's so cute. I wish my parents had friends to hang out with. They're just going to watch the ball drop, but not even according to West Coast time. They're probably going to just watch the East Coast one at nine o'clock and call it a night."

I could hear Elli's eye roll as she dissed her parents. Whenever our parents used to have dinner together, Mr. and

Mrs. Martinez always left by nine because it was "getting late," and they meant it.

Where Elli got her wild side from, I had no idea.

"Okay, how does this look?" I asked her, adjusting the hooks on my blouse and holding up my phone so she could see my reflection in the mirror that hung on my closet door.

"Damn, baby girl! You look *hot*! Aaron is a lucky boy."

I smiled, looking at myself in the mirror. The outfit looked a little wrong, but I figured I could cover up with a jacket or something and make it look more Western and appropriate.

Aaron is a lucky boy. Elli's words echoed in my head.

"Should I wear a skirt and tights instead?" I asked, surprising even myself.

"Someone's going wild tonight. Hell yeah, you should!" Elli whooped. I smiled as I went back into my closet and pulled out a high-waisted black skirt. It seemed like a lot of black, but I thought it looked good.

I put the skirt on, and once it was adjusted, I was shocked at my reflection in the mirror.

"DAY-um," Elli exclaimed, and for the first time, I felt how right she was.

I looked good. I looked sexy, but also my age. I didn't look like I was trying too hard or overdressed. In fact, I felt like I was a teenager, like I was enjoying my life, and the welcome overflow of emotions was almost too much to handle.

"All right, how should I do my hair?" I asked.

"I wish you had cut it before tonight, but that can be a 'new year, new you' kind of thing. What about a nice bun so you can wear hoops?" she suggested, and I loved it.

"'Kay. I'll see you later."

"Byeee," Elli whined. I laughed as I hung up on her, my music resuming its normal volume.

Aptly, "Feeling Myself" was playing, and I rapped along with Nicki.

As I was finishing up my eye makeup, my mom appeared in my bathroom doorway. She had her hair up in her usual professional bun. She had on a red V-neck sweater and black ankle pants. My mom was a very simple woman when she wasn't getting dressed up for an Indian party or going to work.

I paused my makeup application to watch her analyze my outfit. I wanted to pull my skirt down and make my shirt longer and tell her I was going to change. I could see the desire to nag swarming inside her; I was about to say I was going to change, but she beat me to the speaking part.

"I'm heading out now. What time do you think you'll be home?" she asked.

"Um, around twelve-thirty?" I said and she nodded.

"Have fun. You know the rules," she said. Then she turned away and walked out of the room.

That's it? I thought, stunned. *No lecture on my outfit? No shaming me for looking trashy instead of classy? No lecture on the rules I already know?*

I stared at myself in the mirror, trying to understand my mom's odd behavior. Then, hurrying to catch her before she left, I set my mascara down and walked to the staircase just as she was opening the door.

"Love you, Mama. Have fun. You know the rules," I joked.

She looked up at me with a laugh that lit up her eyes, and a genuine smile spread across her lips. "Love you more," she said before leaving the house.

I walked back to my bathroom, my face splitting with a

smile as I felt the pieces of my life fitting together correctly. It was strange to be living like a teenager, strange to believe I *was* a teenager, but it felt right.

"Did I not feel right?"

It was Dimitri's voice. I sighed, closing my eyes. It wasn't the first time. That familiar voice had been popping up in my head randomly for the past two weeks, ever since the day I told Aaron about my diagnosis. It wasn't often enough to be worried, and I knew not to reply. It was just… residual symptoms that might never go away. They were probably just my thoughts wandering, not an outside voice at all.

So I ignored it and continued doing my makeup and styling my hair. Once I had my earrings in, I stood back to admire my work.

You look good, Priya. Enjoy the night.

I grabbed my keys and a cardigan and sent Aaron a quick text that I would be at his house soon. I knew he probably wanted to have at least one drink that night, and I didn't mind driving. Behind the wheel was almost a happy place for me. Besides, I couldn't even drink if I wanted to because of my medication, which I took on a nightly basis. There was a clear warning label. "Do not mix with alcohol." I wasn't about to test it and see why that label was there.

As I drove down the familiar roads to Aaron's house, I thought back to the day a week earlier when I officially met his parents as his girlfriend.

Ms. Chen knew me from class, but she asked questions about my personal life that would have been out of place if we were in school. After some digging, we found out she had had my sister in her class nine years ago. Aaron's dad was surprisingly engaged in the conversation. It was a shock to my system seeing a dad so involved in conversation at a family dinner.

The topic of my parents came up, of course, but when I had to talk about my dad, I found myself getting closed off. It usually wasn't a topic I had a hard time talking about, but I felt myself getting insecure and defensive of my mom's situation. I knew what the aunties in the Indian community said about my mom at *gurudwara,* temple, whenever she went. She still had some friends there, but going wasn't the same since my dad left. Whenever people brought up my dad or when those aunties saw my mom, their eyes told a story of sadness, pity, and sympathy, as if my family needed their strength to go on.

"What does your dad do?" Ms. Chen asked.

"I think he does something in accounting, but he and my mom got a divorce when I was six. I haven't spoken to him in almost eleven years," I said, hoping it would end the conversation.

"Oh, I'm so sorry to hear that," Ms. Chen said, and I had to count down from five to keep myself from making a scene or having an unfortunate reaction. The fact of the matter was, having my dad out of our lives was a blessing, and for some reason, I had the sudden urge to make that known.

"It's totally fine. My family is doing really well. I don't have any ill wishes toward him, but I think it was the best thing that could have happened," I said, not looking up and taking a bite of the fish on my plate. I commented on how delicious it was, but the air was still tense.

Finally, the conversation shifted thanks to Mr. Chen changing the subject, and I was grateful for his intervention.

After dinner, Aaron's parents cleaned up, insisting that Aaron give me a tour of the house, and I felt the desire to open up to him more about my dad.

"I was never really a daddy's girl, ya know?" I said abruptly as Aaron and I lounged in his room—the bedroom door open, of course. I don't think Aaron expected me to come into his room because the floor was riddled with clothes, his cross-country bag, and even some books. We lay on his bed, heads pointed in opposite directions. I gazed at the white walls in his room, which were decorated with prints and posters of his graphic designs. Aaron hummed at my random break of silence and let me continue without responding, but he felt around on the bed until he found my hand and grabbed it.

"My dad had a heavy drinking problem, ever since I was born," I explained. "I remember one time, my parents were arguing downstairs, and my sister was with me upstairs, trying to keep me entertained and as oblivious as possible to what they were talking about. I remember the conversation as clear as day, though. My dad drank too much that night, of course, and picked a stupid fight with my mom over why she allowed me to be such a menace. My mom is a total pacifist now, but when she was in that marriage, she was constantly being triggered. That night, my dad was yelling about something stupid I'd done, I can't remember what, but I remember specifically my dad saying I was a curse. He said they were supposed to stop after my sister, and that he had never wanted me." I let out a nervous chuckle, and Aaron's hand squeezed mine.

"My mom shouted back at him and said that if he didn't want to be in my life, if he didn't want to be in *our* lives, he was more than welcome to leave. And lo and behold, a few days later, I came home from school with my sister to find my dad was gone. It was just a few months after that when the divorce papers came, and he was out of our lives for good. I think he tried to keep in contact with my sister, but a few years later, we found out he remarried and started a new family. She cut him out as well."

Silence fell between us, but it wasn't awkward, uncomfortable, or even bad. Aaron was just digesting the information I'd told him.

"Priya?" he said eventually.

"Hmm?"

"You're the strongest girl I know. Not sure what you're writing in your personal essay, but you've got plenty to write about that will get you into Berkeley. Just saying, that story almost brought me to tears." I laughed as I turned to my side and shoved him. He smiled as he sat up and looked down at me, untangling our hands. I leaned up, rested my weight on my right hand, and looked at him. He resumed talking.

"I know you don't need to hear all that cheesy 'you're so strong, you're a blessing, blah, blah, blah,' crap. I know you know all that, but I do admire your strength. And thank you for telling me."

I smiled. I was falling harder and harder for him.

"Wow, your room is way cleaner than last time," I commented when I walked into Aaron's room, marveling.

His floor was spotless, his chair was placed perfectly under his desk, and for the first time, I noticed there was a bookshelf covered in pictures and paraphernalia in the far left corner of the room. I walked over for a closer look at a picture that showed Aaron in a red sweater wearing overalls. He was riding a kid's plastic tricycle with the widest grin on his face. It easily became my favorite of the few photos I had seen of him because of how happy and adorable he looked in the picture.

"Don't get too excited. I cleaned up just for you, but all

my crap is in the closet," he said. I laughed at that, walking to his bed to sit on the edge and looking back at him where he still stood in the doorway. He was wearing a pair of Adidas soccer pants and a t-shirt, and his hair was wet. He smiled at me, but his eyes didn't light up as they usually did.

"Are you okay?" I asked him.

He nodded and tried to smile wider.

It didn't work. I only narrowed my eyes and crossed my arms, not backing down.

He moved to sit next to me and sighed. "Did you submit all your applications?" he asked. I nodded. He looked up and rolled his neck slowly, eliciting a few popping sounds. "I feel like I'm not going to get in anywhere. I don't know, my essays were really bad. I didn't know what to talk about, and you know I suck at essays. I'm just... a little worried." He shrugged before flashing a weak version of his boyish smile again.

I softened my posture and gaze and held my hand out. He took hold of it, and I swiped my thumb along the back of his knuckles like he had for me when I needed comfort.

"Aaron, you're literally perfect for all the schools you applied for. You are bound to get in somewhere, if not every-where. You're a well-rounded, intelligent, and personable individual, and when I read your essays, I saw that shine through. And you know me, I'm a harsh editor of essays. You've seen the way I edit Elli's work," I added. Aaron chuckled, nodding and gripping my hand. "So don't worry. You're an amazing candidate, and all the schools will under-stand how lucky they are to have you." I squeezed his hand.

He took a few deep breaths before looking up at me and smiling fully and genuinely. I think it was the grounding feeling of our clasped hands more than my words that helped most. I glanced down at our hands again, but before I could say anything more, I saw him lean forward in my peripheral vision and felt him kiss my cheek, stunning me and freezing me in place.

Aaron laughed at my reaction, and I continued to blush as he stood up and walked to his closet. Aaron and I had never kissed more than each other's hands. Even though I told him I needed to take things slowly early on in our relationship, I had never outlined what my specific physical boundaries were, especially before I had told him about Dimitri. I'd felt a little less anxiety over it since then, but I was still struggling with the idea that I was moving on too quickly from Dimitri. And when I thought of the possibility of any physical intimacy with Aaron, I felt extremely anxious. It was strange. Although I had memories of kissing Dimitri, I had never kissed a real guy before. Did I really know what a realistic kiss was like? Would I be bad at it? Could someone even be a bad kisser? If so, I would probably be that someone.

"You look amazing, by the way," Aaron said, bringing me back to the present. He took some clothes with him into his bathroom. I looked down at my skirt and played with the edge of the fabric. I didn't feel too self-conscious about my outfit, but I did feel some nerves—just anxiety, or some excitement too?—coursing through my body.

Didn't people usually kiss at midnight? Would Aaron expect that tonight? What if I *was* a bad kisser?

When I saw Aaron through the opened bathroom door a few minutes later, wearing a gray crewneck sweater over a light blue button up with black jeans, my anxiety rattled up higher.

How did a girl like me land a guy like him? The thought crossed my mind, and I was transported back to the feelings I'd felt with Dimitri. That familiar feeling terrified me.

Things were moving too quickly, and although it was

moving in the direction I wanted it to, I wasn't sure if I was ready for it. I wasn't sure if I was ready to leave Dimitri in the past, and I wasn't sure if I had completely moved on yet.

A part of me felt like I had, that I was confident about moving forward, but this relationship was still so new. I wondered whether I was just excited by the *idea* of the relationship rather than the *actual* relationship itself. The butterflies I felt with Aaron were exhilarating, but they weren't what I'd had with Dimitri. In spite of the fact that Dimitri was a hallucination, he still felt more real than this relationship did. Dimitri and I had known each other for years—at least, that's what my memories told me—and I could trust him. Were my feelings for Aaron all just some honeymoon-phase blindness? Was he actually this great? Would this relationship survive past the school year? Or even past the next month? It felt too new, too unstable, like it didn't have a solid foundation.

To most people, infatuation and new feelings were exciting, but to me, they also brought doubt and made me want to shore up my defenses. Everything seemed too surreal—and after living in a world that was completely surreal—I had a hard time trusting infatuation.

So when I looked back at Aaron, busy fixing his hair in the bathroom mirror, I wondered if this relationship was worth investing in.

"You're allowed to not have your shit together and to be unsure of your future and to explore everything the world throws at you." Elli's words echoed in my head, and I took a deep breath, letting it out slowly.

Aaron looked at me in the mirror and winked, and I couldn't help but grin back. His dimple flashed at me as he finished up his look.

"You ready?" he asked, stepping out of the bathroom, and I smiled, nodding and standing up.

$\sim$

At the party, I stood next to Aaron as we chatted with some people from the cross-country team.

"Yo, bro, I swear on my life that I did not steal your lunch in the third grade!" Cameron said to Aaron. How the topic of their third-grade antics came up, I couldn't remember, but it was hilarious to listen to.

"Bruh, I swear you did! That's literally how we became friends," Aaron said, his grip on my hand tightening as his frustration heightened. I laughed at the ongoing fight and looked at Amanda, who was at Cameron's side. She was holding a drink in her hand and laughing hysterically, maybe a little too much, and I couldn't tell if it was because of the argument, her drink, or the fact that she and Cameron had recently started to date. It seemed like she was deep in the honeymoon phase as well.

"Shit... is it really?"

"Oh, my God. You're so drunk," Aaron groaned, shaking his head.

I looked up at him, and then at Cameron and Amanda as they began to chat. My life had become so *normal* since dating Aaron. People actually knew I existed, and I talked to people beyond Elli. I wouldn't say I had any more friends than before, but I definitely had a lot more acquaintances.

"Excuse me for a second, but I want to dance with my best friend!" Elli's voice carried over the music as her hand gripped my free wrist. I smiled when she appeared, looking as radiant as ever in her all-over sequins minidress with a decorative tiara on her head and a boa around her neck. I looked up at Aaron as she whisked me away, and he smiled and gave a slight wave.

"Are you having a good time, baby girl?" she asked, as we found a spot in the dancing area and began to move to the music. The whole bottom floor of the house was dark, lit only by colorful lights strung up around the walls and TV screens. Hip-hop music blared through the surround sound system. I was a terrible dancer and didn't know how to move with the music, but I still swayed from side to side.

"Yes! I'm really surprised, but yes," I said, yelling to be heard and laughing at Elli's loose, free movements. She wasn't really dancing, but she wasn't creating a total mess of herself either. So I just resolved to calling it an interesting freestyle.

The song changed, and we gasped, recognizing the new song as "Feeling Myself." It was the perfect song for this moment, exactly what I needed to get into the mood as my body began to move with the bass and the beat. Soon, I was doing body waves I didn't even know I could do, and Elli was hollering at the top of her lungs.

I had never felt so free, so happy, or so young.

After dancing for a while, my lungs were screaming for water. I fled to the kitchen and looked around for some red cups before getting myself some water from the filter in the fridge. I stood in the kitchen area and watched Elli, who was basically in her element. I couldn't concentrate hard enough to recognize the song playing now, as my heart was beating too loudly in my ears, and I was still desperate for water. Elli laughed along with a friend who had joined her on the dance floor in my place.

My eyes moved throughout the house to the backyard where I spotted Aaron playing a round of beer pong. He tossed a ball into a red cup, making his side of the table erupt in cheers and the other side in groans.

"I know you miss me." I heard Dimitri's voice in my right ear, a prickling sensation sweeping across the back of my neck.

All of a sudden, the music around me faded away, and all I could hear was my heart beating powerfully. I was hyper aware of Dimitri's eyes on me, although I didn't know where he was standing in the room, so I simply looked down to avoid searching for him, my body tensing up on defense.

Don't reply, Priya. Don't reply.

"Look at me," he said. Somehow, I resisted the temptation to lift my head up and look directly in front of me. I knew I would see his hazel eyes.

I sensed his hand stretching out to grab a piece of my hair. "It's still long. Just how I like it." His words sent chills down my spine, but my body remained rigid for a little while longer.

I took several shaky steps forward, pushing past Dimitri and away from the kitchen counter, continuing to look down. Once I was far enough from my previous spot, I gained the courage to slowly pick my head up and look straight at the beer-pong table. I avoided the gaze that I knew still followed me and walked toward Aaron. He was finishing up his round of beer pong, it seemed, as there were only two more cups left on his opponent's side of the table. I hovered nearby until he'd shot the Ping-Pong ball across, and when the teams erupted with groans and cheers, Aaron turned toward me and smiled.

"Cheater."

"Whore."

"Slut."

The dark voices enveloped me. I shook my head instinctively, trying to shake them out. They weren't too loud, but they were harrowing, nonetheless.

I'm not married. I'm not with anyone but Aaron. I am NOT that girl.

But what if I am?

I looked back up at Aaron, hoping his image would be cold water on these thoughts. His head was slightly tilted as he looked at me. I smiled up at him, and he mouthed the words "you okay?" I nodded and gestured to him to finish the game. I needed some fresh air and a moment to calm down.

I tried to walk as far away from the vapers as possible and headed for the far back end of the backyard. There was a low, brick wall that lined the property, and I sat on it, watching the party and Aaron. The voices and the feeling of being watched had dissipated on their own as I found my new seat, leaving me with a brief feeling of relief. I looked at my phone and saw that there were only thirty minutes until midnight.

I felt the cool, crisp air hit my skin and turn it clammy. I rubbed my arms and shivered. I preferred the chill to the overwhelming heat that was inside the house.

You don't belong here, Priya. The voice that echoed in my head was my own this time, and as I looked down at my water in my hand, I thought about whether this world—the world of high school, parties, and normalcy—was for me. I had always wanted to leave Saratoga and move on with my life. I wanted to move on to bigger and better things, and not look back. I had always planned not to look back. My life was set—I was going to move to Berkeley, Elli would follow a year later, and we would live together and move to wherever the hell we wanted after that. Maybe we would try out Southern California for a few years. Elli loved the glitz and glamour of LA, and I dreamed of attending UCLA for business school.

However, now there was a new factor I had to think of, and that factor was headed my way.

"Hey, aren't you cold?" Aaron's voice was slightly slurred. He plopped himself down beside me on the bricks and would have fallen back if I hadn't grabbed him and let him lean on me. I wasn't one to be amused by drunkenness, but he was so sweet and wanted to make sure I was okay; so I couldn't help but smile at him.

"No," I said, surprising myself as I set my water down and wrapped my arms around him, pulling myself closer to him. "I'm toasty warm with my personal heater." I nuzzled my head against his chest and felt his deep chuckle against my face. He wrapped his arms around me and squeezed tightly.

"I think this is the first time you've initiated this kind of physical affection with me," he said.

"You might have to get used to it."

He hummed as he lay his head down on top of mine. "I like the sound of that," he whispered into my hair. I squeezed him tighter, enjoying the warmth that flooded my system. It was a weird sensation, this feeling of safety in his arms, this comfort and peace. It was a new feeling, but I didn't want to fight against it. I wanted to embrace it and see where it carried me. Aaron was an outside factor I was happy to take into consideration. I wasn't stupid—I didn't think we were getting married or anything, but I was open to seeing where this relationship went.

All of a sudden, we were pulled from our happy moment by the sound of excited screaming in the house.

"One more minute!" someone yelled, and people started heading in. Aaron lifted his head off mine and moved to stand up, taking away my warmth and making me feel alone. He looked down at me and tilted his head.

"Do you not want to watch the ball drop?" he asked, looking down at me.

"No. I've seen it drop every year."

He smiled before reaching his hand out for me to take. Hesitantly, I placed my hand in his, unsure of why we couldn't just remain sitting, but when he pulled me up and into him, I realized why sitting was not the optimal position.

We looked at each other, and my heart raced. *This is it*, I thought. I had pictured kissing Aaron thousands of times before, sure, but every time I imagined it, the image of him somehow morphed into Dimitri's face—or I got so anxious about it that I had to stop my imagination before I had a heart attack. I had no idea how to kiss. I had no idea how to be remotely affectionate beyond hugging and hand holding.

"Ten... nine... eight..."

As people counted down inside, Aaron's head remained still, watching me for any indication of what I wanted to do.

Kiss? High five? Laugh?

"... three...two...one..." I smiled and in a split second made up my mind. I quickly pulled Aaron down so our lips collided. It was a little rougher than I had intended, but when his lips sealed over mine, warmth flooded my system as if someone had replaced my blood with pure euphoria.

"Happy New Year!" Everyone yelled around us, and Aaron's arms gripped me tightly and hoisted me up. I laughed against his lips and felt him smile back. My hands moved up from his sweater, and my arms wrapped around his neck. I had to break away to quickly catch my breath, but immediately, I sealed my lips back together with his.

It was pure joy, feeling his soft lips against mine, like fireworks going off in my body as the blues and reds and purples of real fireworks went off all around us. I was so enraptured by his lips, I barely noticed them.

When he set me back down on the ground, I begrudgingly pulled myself away and looked up to see him breathing heavier than usual, matching my own breathlessness.

"Happy New Year, Aaron," I said. Aaron laughed and I couldn't help but smile widely at the sound of his happiness.

"Happy New Year, Priya." He leaned down and captured my lips again for another perfect kiss.

MARCH 28TH, 2019

I PULLED Aaron's arms toward me, my bare legs spread against the scratchy turf beneath us and mirrored by Aaron's legs as I leaned back.

"Pull more," he said.

"Bruh, if I pull anymore, I'll be lying on my back." Aaron laughed before pushing forward to stretch out completely. He sat upright and smirked as he began to pull my arms toward him. My legs spread a little wider, and I groaned as I felt the discomfort in my inner thighs.

"Stop, stop, stop!" I practically screamed. He'd pulled just far enough that the discomfort had become unbearable, burning. He chuckled and let my arms go. My body went back to its naturally hunched, upright position, and I rolled my neck, cracking it.

Even though we were supposed to stretch before a meet, I rarely ever did. During the cross-country season, I couldn't get out of stretching because it was a group effort. When the sport transitioned into the track-and-field season, the coaches got rid of communal stretching because there were too many of us.

"You ready for the meet?" Aaron asked, shifting his legs into a figure four stretch and reaching for his left foot. I nodded as I did the same stretch on the same side. I was thankful that I had gained the confidence, and permission from my mom, to wear the spandex shorts. It made stretching and running so much easier and more enjoyable than thick leggings.

"I'm gonna try and PR today and beat my last mile time. We'll see. My time is getting better, but nowhere near Amanda's."

"You talking shit about me, Priya?" Amanda asked, plopping her bag next to me and dropping to sit down. She was wearing a pair of black spandex shorts, a red headband, and her Saratoga High jersey was tied in the back with a hair tie. She was beaming, her normal makeup bearing face bare and natural as she started stretching.

I chuckled. "Yeah. You're the worst miler on the team. Just go home and save us the shame," I said and she laughed.

"Damn, someone's overly sassy today. You stressing about Berkeley?" she asked.

"Actually, yeah." I sighed as I began to twist toward her and stretch my back out. I would be lying if I said I wasn't jealous of her relaxed state, although she would be in my place next year. Luckily, she couldn't make the same mistake in her essay I had. I had written an essay about my illness, for God's sake. Who would take me with that diagnosis?

"I'm sure you got in. Aaron too," Amanda said, shifting her attention to him. He was quietly stretching, but he looked up and shrugged when he heard his name.

"We'll see." He smiled and looked at me, but the smile seemed forced.

Just then, with perfect timing, Coach Zimmerman

approached the middle of the field and blew her whistle. We all stood up and huddled around her.

"All right, third meet of the season, but first one on home turf. Y'all better make this a good one, or we're doing an extra mile on Monday!"

"Yes, coach!" we all said in a chorus, and she smiled before continuing with her pep talk. Usually, Coach Zimmerman's talks were pretty uplifting, but I was distracted by my educational future and by how stressed Aaron was. He was usually the one who stayed present and in the moment, but today he was too tense.

Soon, we were all pushed toward our events or the bleachers as we awaited our turn. Aaron and I walked off to the bleachers, since our events were later in the meet, and we huddled together as the breeze started to pick up.

We sat in silence as we watched the start of the meet, our minds definitely elsewhere. I felt the bench beneath me shake as Aaron started bouncing his foot up and down on the metal beam. Just looking at him, it was hard to tell he was nervous. Only his foot gave it away, and others would probably think that was just competition jitters. But I knew him. He never got that nervous before a meet. He firmly believed extreme nervousness was self-sabotage.

I looked back and forth between his face and his foot as it violently bounced up and down on the beam. Then I decided that I'd had enough of his anxiety.

"Come on," I said, grabbing his hand. I stood up, pulling him off to the side of the bleachers and toward the parking lot.

"Are you ditching the meet?" Aaron asked, confused. I rolled my eyes as I led him to my car. People were walking by, but not paying us any attention.

"Get in," I said, unlocking the car, thankful that he

followed and sat without arguing. When he closed the door behind him, he looked at me with an amused expression.

"Are you kidnapping me?" he asked.

I smirked. "I wish, but no. I want you to just talk through what's going on. Let the crazy out," I said. He looked at me in slight confusion, so I continued.

"We have at least a half hour before our events are up. So you have twenty minutes to vent about your anxiety. Let the crazy out *here* so you don't go crazy on the field and sabotage yourself in the race."

Aaron stared at me for a few seconds, then looked forward out the window. Suddenly, he let out a laugh. I watched hesitantly, unsure of what he was laughing at. Eventually, his laughter turned to a groan, and he pushed back the seat until he was lying almost flat. He stared at the felt-covered ceiling of the car and groaned again before rubbing his face.

"How do you handle the anxiety, Priya? I feel like my brain is melting with anticipation, and I don't know what to do. My heart is racing, but also slowing down—it's just all over the place. I'm trying to tell myself that everything will be okay, but honestly, I don't know that it will be," he said, his eyes closed.

"What's the worst-case scenario?"

"Worst-case scenario is I don't get into Berkeley, I don't get in anywhere, and I die alone in a cardboard box because I can't accomplish anything," he said. I knew how that felt. It was his idea of reality. Anxiety could be a monster that distorted reality like that.

"Is that actually likely, though?"

Aaron paused before sighing and shaking his head.

"Sometimes, I feel like it is. I know it's not, but I get this crushing weight on me that says I'm no good and that I won't do well, especially if my life doesn't go a certain way or follow 'the plan.'" He created air quotes with his fingers. "My parents aren't tiger parents, but I'm still scared of disappointing them. My dad has this dream that I'll take over his company, but he doesn't push it on me. He knows I want to go into graphic design and not business, so he's fine with my choice. But... what if I don't enjoy that, either? What if... I'm not smart enough for that field? Or for Berkeley? Or anywhere and anything? High school is a lot different than college." He buried his fingers in his hair.

"That's true," I said slowly, "but think of it as a race. You weren't always a great runner, right? But you got better as you adjusted and practiced. You're an amazing student, but even if you aren't ready for college, who honestly is?"

Aaron remained silent, processing.

"My sister graduated with honors from high school. She got rejected from USC, her dream school, and ended up going to UCLA. She thought it would be easier there than at USC and planned to do well and transfer the next year. Then she failed a class and lost that chance. It was the first grade below a B she had ever received, and it was in chemistry, a general education course, of all courses, and one she was usually good at and loved. Everyone in that class did poorly their freshman year. They all went from being extraordinary to being ordinary, if not substandard, in their studies." I shrugged. "My sister said the first year at college, you can expect your GPA to be at least a whole point lower than your high school GPA. She compared it to going to a new country, alone, on the opposite side of the world. You're hella jetlagged and tired all the time, can't speak the language, and nothing makes sense for the first few days, weeks, or even months. But eventually, you get the hang of it.

"My sister ended up loving UCLA and has the most

obnoxious pride in being a Bruin. She ended her time there with good grades and is now living it up in San Francisco as a lawyer. I don't know if either of us is getting into Berkeley, but if you don't, it doesn't mean you aren't intelligent, capable, or geared for success. Wherever you go, you'll have to work hard. But you'll be a good fit, and it'll be a good choice. You're an amazing student, well-rounded, so don't feel like your value is dependent on some college's choice to admit you." I realized I was starting to ramble when Aaron smiled, and I took it as my cue to wrap up and let him digest what I was saying. "You're so much more than just a number or your GPA, or even your essay," I finished.

We sat in silence for a few minutes as Aaron processed, both of us watching parents and other students walk by. Some of the students wore track uniforms or workout clothing. My mind wandered, going over what I said. I realized that I was also trying to reassure myself, too, that I might still have a chance at Berkeley. I hoped I hadn't said anything that would make Aaron's anxiety worse.

His hand gently reached over to rest on my leg, pulling me from my thoughts, and his thumb stroked back and forth on my bare thigh. I smiled as I lay my hand over his and stroked the back of his hand with my thumb in return.

He turned his head toward me, though he still didn't meet my eyes. "Thank you, Priya. I needed that."

"Any time," I said softly back.

His eyes moved up to mine, and we looked at each other for a few seconds before I started feeling fidgety at the intimacy and had to break the connection.

"We should probably head to our events now. Definitely need to warm up again."

∼

The whistle blew, and we started screaming as Amanda steadily took off from her position for the final event. She was on the outer ring of the track running against some of the varsity girls from the other high school, but Amanda was one of the best runners in the county for this event, the mile. She was quick, but she paced herself well and always finished strong.

Aaron and I sat huddled together as the sun began to lower and the breeze picked up. He had his arm around the back of my shoulders, and I held his dangling hand. When the excitement died down, I noticed him swiping his thumb across my skin. I looked at his hand holding mine, then at him, and realized he was doing it subconsciously as he focused on the race.

I had become accustomed to him swiping his thumb like that, especially when I was stressed or needed him to support me. In that moment, although I did need some support, I knew he needed the comfort more than I did.

While I was watching the race, a quick vibration in my jacket pocket broke my focus. I pulled out my phone, and my heart stopped. The email was from the UC Berkeley admissions team.

I looked at Aaron and saw him staring at his phone, a similar look of shock on his face. We glanced at each other's phones, then back at each other.

"I'm scared," I said and Aaron nodded.

"Same. Do you want to open mine, and I'll open yours?" he asked, and I hesitated before saying yes. I offered him my phone quickly, and he unwrapped his arm from around me to grab it hastily, giving me his with the other hand.

I swiped the alert across his phone screen, punched in his passcode, and sat still as the white page loaded. Impatiently, I jabbed at the link in the email and logged into his account. Thankfully, he had saved his information in his phone, just like I had, so it wasn't too much of a hassle. I sat as the page loaded, a million worries running through my head, trying to think of possible responses to different situations. What would I say if I got in? What if I got in, and Aaron didn't—or if he got in and *I* didn't? What if one of us got wait-listed?

All my thoughts went out the window as soon as the page loaded and my eyes zeroed in on one word.

"Congratulations!"

That was all I needed to read to know he got in, but I was too afraid to look at him to learn my fate. I had known he would get in the whole time, although I still felt very proud of him. He was brilliant, and when I read his essay, I knew he was a strong writer and had an amazing story. He'd really had nothing to worry about.

I, on the other hand, had a great deal to worry about.

"Go, Amanda!"

All of a sudden, people began to cheer harder for Amanda, screaming her name and hollering at her to keep going. I looked up to see the people on the track following her and a girl from the other high school on the sidelines as the racers closed in on the finish line.

It was the last stretch in the race, and Amanda was starting to sprint, just as she neared the end, but she and the other girl were neck and neck. Their places kept switching from Amanda in the lead to the other girl. In the very last few meters, Amanda charged forward and cleared the finish line in first, making the entire crowd of Saratoga High Schoolers erupt in cheers on the bleachers.

My heart felt like it had just run its own race and was even going faster with excitement at the victory.

Then I looked at Aaron, and my mouth went dry. He was

smiling brightly at me. Was it because of the race? Or would he smile like that at me when he was trying to console me? I couldn't hope it was because of my acceptance.

He looked back down at my phone and cleared his throat. "Congratulations—" he read aloud. I let out a scream, and I lunged at him, wrapping my arms around him. He laughed so much as he caught me that I had to say my next words multiple times before he heard me.

"Congratulations, Aaron!"

He stilled briefly, still holding me, before gripping me even more tightly with his own shout of excitement before hoisting us both up to our feet. We jumped on the bleachers with the other students, screaming for Amanda and ourselves as our fate was sealed.

We were going to Berkeley.

APRIL 26TH, 2019

I LEANED back in my chair at the kitchen table and sighed as my back relaxed. I closed my eyes and rolled my neck slowly, listening to the cracks. I twisted and cracked my back as well before opening my eyes and looking at Elli, who was staring back at me. I stared at her like a deer in headlights before I noticed Aaron looking at me as well.

"What?" I asked sheepishly, looking between them. They both burst into laughter, shaking their heads. My face flushed with warmth, and I jabbed at Aaron playfully, making him laugh harder.

"That was hella loud, Priya," Elli said.

I couldn't help but laugh along from embarrassment. "I can't help it that I'm stressing! We have a test next week, and I need to do well!"

"When do you not?" both of them said at the same time.

"Don't jinx it! Just because I got into Berkeley doesn't mean I've got a free pass! What if I end up bombing the rest of the tests and homework for this class? I can't risk that, guys!" Elli and Aaron both groaned and rolled their eyes.

"Priya, I love you, but shut up!" Elli said, and Aaron

made a noise of agreement. "I wish I had your brain. It's like a fucking sponge. Soaks up all the information and squeezes it out on the test, no problem. Meanwhile, I have to bust my ass just to remember what the freaking amygdala does!" Elli said, waving her hands in the air with exasperation.

I shrugged. "It controls emotions and the fight-or-flight response…" I said, trailing off sheepishly when I sensed Elli getting annoyed with me. I smiled at her apologetically, and she rolled her eyes.

"Hate you so much, baby girl," she said and I smiled.

I looked at Aaron.

"Don't worry, your brain is my favorite part of you," he said with a wink, and I laughed louder than I should have. Elli groaned and gagged in response, and I shook my head.

"Well, it's been *so fun* studying with y'all, but I gotta get all sexy for the party tonight," Elli said, beginning to pack up her things.

"Whose party are you going to tonight?" I asked.

"This guy Trent. He's on the guys' swim team," she said, and I nodded even though I had no idea who that was.

"Who else is going? Is Amanda going?" I asked.

"Amanda is going to Brad's party tonight, remember?" Aaron said next to me.

I looked at him as I tried to recall this information. It made sense since Brad was also on the track-and-field team, and our teammates made up most of the people going to this party.

"Oh," I said, looking at Elli as she stood up. "How well do you know this Trent guy?"

She shrugged. "Not very well, but he invited me person-ally. So I mean, why not? Plus, the swim guys are pretty hot, so I'm hoping to hook up tonight." She winked at me.

"Gross. Just… be careful, okay? And please, for the love

of God, don't drink too much."

"Yes, mother."

I cringed at the title. "I'm not trying to mother you. I'm just worried, okay? Watch your drink at all times, and please don't overdo it tonight!" I said, a little more forcefully than usual, and she nodded as she walked out of the room.

"I know, Priya! I'm a professional partier!"

I groaned as I heard her footsteps head up my stairs and toward my bedroom. I looked back at Aaron and checked out his outfit.

"Are you wearing that to the party, or did you bring a change of clothes?" I asked. He nodded his head.

"I brought a different shirt to wear," he said, rising from his chair and beginning to pack his things away.

"Am I… am I too protective? Am I acting like her mom?" I asked Aaron quietly, hoping Elli had shut my bedroom door and couldn't hear our conversation.

Aaron shook his head as he took out a folded shirt from his backpack and put his notebooks inside instead.

"Nah, I think you're just a concerned friend. Why?"

"I feel—Okay, don't get me wrong, I love Mr. And Mrs. Martinez, but I feel like they're so lax with Elli. Like, she goes to all these parties, gets belligerently drunk, and it's a miracle she's alive. I worry about her so much. She's my best friend, but sometimes I feel like I have to be her mom; and I don't like that feeling, but… I can't help it," I whispered, looking down at my notebook.

The thought of her going to a party with mostly boys and no one to watch out for her… it worried me. I knew high school boys usually had ill intentions—not always, but the ones she hung around usually did. Of course, Elli would say she liked them that way, but I for sure didn't.

"There's nothing wrong with being protective over her,"

Aaron said. "To be honest, I don't blame you, but you also have to let her live her life. You're her friend, not her mom, so while you can be protective, don't be controlling." Aaron smiled, gently putting me in my place. I sighed and nodded.

"Okay. I'm going to go get ready." I stood up, and Aaron grabbed his shirt.

"I'm gonna just change in the bathroom and watch TV," he said.

Upstairs, Elli was blasting music in my room as she did her makeup in the bathroom. She had on a pair of ripped, dark wash denim shorts and a black tank top. Her wavy hair was up in a messy bun, and she was swiping eyeliner across her eye.

"What are you wearing tonight?" she asked, and I shrugged before heading over to my closet.

"I'm thinking a cropped hoodie and ripped jeans."

"Won't you be hot in that?"

"I'm not drinking, and I don't really do much other than hang around and be awkward. So... no. I won't be doing anything to warm up my body."

"One day, babe, one day, I'm going to get you to drink."

I smirked. "Sure. We'll see."

We both fell silent, and Elli hummed absentmindedly along with the song that was playing, "Throw A Fit" by Tinashe.

I changed into my outfit in my closet and put my hair up in a bun so I could do my makeup too. When I walked into the bathroom, it was strikingly obvious how different Elli and I were, just from our outfits. Our friendship made absolutely no sense to anyone, and yet, it worked so well. Her extremely extroverted personality was perfectly countered by my subdued introversion. I could get her to calm down, and she always brought out a more energetic, wilder side of me. I pushed her to be her best, and she pushed me to experience the best life had to offer. We balanced each other out.

"Random question. Would you ever get a tattoo?" Elli asked, and I hummed as I thought of what I would want to put on my body forever.

"So, I think I would, but I don't really know how to put my thoughts of what I'd want into an image," I said.

Elli smiled as she put her eyeliner away.

"What are your thoughts?"

"Well… Okay, so, I want to get something that kind of shows what I went through. Basically, something that shows I fought the war, and I won, I guess. But also, a part of me wants to memorialize Dimitri with some symbol. I don't know if that's a good idea, though. I should probably just put him in the past. I just—he'll always be a huge part of me," I said, grappling with the contradictions.

"I agree with wanting to leave him in the past," Elli said slowly, "but I mean, think of when other people get tattoos of people who have died and were important to them. Why is Dimitri any different? Because he was a symptom?" She began to apply her mascara. Even after she stopped talking, her mouth remained open in an "O" shape as she swiped the bristles across her eyelashes.

"Would it be weird, though? And even if my mom allowed me to get a tattoo, would I want that on me in five years? Or would I be so traumatized by the experience that I would want to completely forget him?" I reached for my makeup bag and sorted through it for my essentials.

"That's true but I feel like you're a pretty stubborn person. Once you set your mind to something, you do it, and you don't change your mind." I wondered how true that was.

"What tattoo are you gonna get?" I asked, knowing fully well that she was going to get one as soon as she turned eighteen.

"I'm thinking of getting something simple. Might be a little basic, but I like the idea of the words *c'est la vie* in cursive along the outside of my wrist." She brushed her finger along the outer part of her wrist, along the bone.

I shivered, cringing at the idea of a needle hitting bone and not flesh, but I thought Elli's mantra was apt. She took life's punches and rolled with them, making sure to live life to the fullest, no matter what.

When we finished doing our makeup, I was about to take my hair down, but Elli shook her head, crossing her arms over her chest.

"Leave it up," she said. I looked at her for a second, then back at my reflection in the mirror.

"Why?"

"It elevates your outfit. A simple ponytail would be too casual, but this looks nice. Besides, you hate your long hair, anyway. Enjoy it being short."

I followed her out of the bathroom and watched as she grabbed her things off my messy, unmade bed.

"Are you gonna be staying at a swim friend's place, or do you want to stay here?" I asked her.

"We'll see how fucked I get tonight," she said with a laugh. I rolled my eyes, and we headed downstairs.

"All right," she said, slipping on her sneakers. "My ride's here. Gotta go!" She took her hair down and bent over, shaking it out before flipping it back over her head as she stood up, running her fingers through it.

"Hey, if you need a ride, please text me, all right? I know I'm going to Brad's party, but you know I got you, anytime,"

I said as Elli opened the front door. Someone waited outside in their car, blasting some techno-pop music. Elli looked over her shoulder at me with a bright smile, her hand still on the doorknob.

"I know, babe. Love you! Bye, Aaron!" She ran out the door, pulling it closed behind her just as I shouted, "I love you!"

I sighed and turned back to Aaron on the couch. He was watching a cooking show on Netflix. He was wearing a denim jacket over a gray t-shirt and faded black jeans.

"You look so basic," I said, joking, trying to lighten my mood. Aaron looked down at himself and chuckled, shaking his head.

"Is the jacket too much?"

I shook my head, and he smiled before turning the TV off and walking over to me.

"Your mom is gone until when again?" he asked.

"Sunday," I said. I grabbed my crossbody bag off the hook near the door and put my keys and my phone inside before bending down to add my slip-on Vans to my ensemble. "Why do you ask?"

When I stood up again, Aaron had the front door open and was waiting. I shivered when the wind hit me, and I rushed outside, locking the door behind us.

"Just curious. Don't you ever get lonely here? Do you ever go to your sister's place on the weekends when your mom isn't here?"

We walked to my car. I tossed Aaron my keys and sat in the passenger seat.

"Not really, especially since we started going out so much on weekends. It's hard to go see her or feel lonely when you and I go on so many dates and to so many parties," I said, teasing him.

He looked at me with wide eyes and asked, feigning hurt, "Are you blaming me for keeping you away from your sister?"

I laughed and shook my head, falling back into the passenger seat as he began to drive one-handed toward Brad's house, his free hand tangling with mine.

～

The music was blaring, jarring when I wanted nothing more than to go home. I sat outside of the house, like I usually did, with my nonalcoholic beverage, and sipped it as I stared at my phone, wondering how Elli was doing, wanting to talk to my sister, but also thinking about calling my mom and seeing how she was doing. It was morning in India, and she would be staying with my *nanima,* her mom. She'd decided to make this trip into a ten-day trip instead of just five to spend more time with my grandmother.

Without thinking of where I was, or what was going on around me, I pulled out my phone and called Jasmine.

"'Sup," she answered nonchalantly.

"What are you doing?" I asked her. I looked at the ground, where I traced shapes in the concrete with my eyes.

"Watching Netflix. Where are you?"

"I'm at a party, wishing I was watching Netflix," I said, and my sister let out her signature single *Ha* laugh.

"Why? Shouldn't you be hanging out with people? Drinking, even? I'd rather be at a party than Netflixing and chilling with wine."

"*Didi*, you know I can't drink."

"Still, why aren't you talking to the people there?"

"I just feel uneasy today," I said. "Just… not me. I don't know how to describe it, but today feels off."

"How so?"

"Like… I just feel like… I don't know how to describe it. It's been a stressful day, but not for any particular reason. I feel like the stress is a fire—no, a conflagration—and it's melting my brain."

"Are you taking your medication?" my sister asked immediately.

I sighed with frustration, closing my eyes.

"Yes. I take it every night. But these aren't symptoms. I mean, the stress could exacerbate symptoms, but—"

"That's why I asked if you're taking your medication," she interrupted, and I paused, realizing she was right.

Stress was a huge contributor to my symptoms. Even though I was on medication, if I became too stressed out, my stress could manifest as symptoms that even my medication couldn't control. I would probably need to up the dosage or something, although the ideal situation would just be to manage my stress.

Dr. Worblack's words echoed in my ear. Maybe that's why I felt so off. The stress was pushing against the wall I had up protecting my brain, and it was causing a major tremor in my mind. It was like the foreshock that comes before a major earthquake. I needed to figure out how to stop the tremor, if I could, or brace myself for the coming seismic event.

"I'm taking it. I'll call Avery's office tomorrow to see if I can schedule an earlier appointment," I said with a sigh, feeling somewhat defeated but knowing it wasn't a loss.

"Good. Now, why aren't you with Aaron or Elli?"

"Well, Elli is at a different party, and I just… I feel out of place here. More than usual. I feel like I don't belong here, and I don't want to be a downer for Aaron."

"What if Aaron could bring you up? Have you given him the chance to?"

"No, not yet."

"Al-*right!*" Jasmine said in a singsong voice and I chuckled. "So what else is up? How *is* Aaron?"

I couldn't help the smile that spread across my face. Just as I was about to go on about all the good things about Aaron, I saw him slip through the back door, his head turning in every direction. I waved at him, and he made his way over to me.

"He's doing well, and he's walking over here right now; so I'll talk to you later."

"All right, go have fun!" she commanded, and I smiled as Aaron sat down.

"Bye, *didi*," I said before ending the call. When I put my phone away, I turned to see Aaron smiling at me.

"Was that your sister?"

"Yeah."

"Did you talk to your mom too?"

I shook my head. "No. My mom should be heading to the airport soon and will probably be flying when we're sleeping. She's going to text me during her layover in Shanghai."

"I love how close you are to your family, even your mom with her crazy schedule," Aaron said.

"I know it's not normal, but we've been through a lot. I feel like it makes sense to be close," I said and he shrugged.

"I know plenty of kids whose parents got divorced or who are the child of a single parent, and they aren't that close to their parents or siblings. At least, not when they're in high school. But I guess with how it all went down, it makes sense for you. Your dad is a dick."

I smiled at him. Aaron didn't usually curse that much, but when he drank, his language became a lot more colorful.

"Yes. Yes, he is," I said.

Aaron took a swig from his drink. Then he said, "I've actually been meaning to ask you this for a while, but why don't you drink? Not that you have to! I'm just curious. Is it… because of your dad?"

I laughed and nodded, patting his knee. I began to lean against him, but the alcohol on his breath was so strong it repelled me. "I have to take medication every night, and it has a very big warning label: 'Do Not Combine with Alcohol,'" I said, using a deep voice that made Aaron snort with laughter. "I'm pretty sure it would have a terrible reaction with my meds, especially considering how high my dosage is, so I just don't want to risk it."

He put his hand over mine, rubbing my knuckles again. "Do you enjoy these parties? I feel like they aren't much fun if you aren't at least buzzed."

"Honestly, I don't usually enjoy them, but I enjoy seeing *you* enjoy them. And I enjoy spending time with you. So as long as you're having fun, and not getting blackout drunk, then I'm happy," I said softly, pushing through my repulsion to lay my head on his shoulder. He hummed against me and kissed the top of my head.

"So what you're saying is, me drinking and looking like a fool makes you happy, so I should drink more."

I laughed, picking my head up and looking at him. "I know you said I shouldn't be controlling, but I can't be an accomplice to your death. That being said, it's your life, but don't throw up in my car," I warned.

"Yes, ma'am!" He grinned, then lifted my hand to his lips.

"Aye, yo, Chen! You down for a round of pong?" Cameron called out from the house, breaking our moment.

Aaron looked at me and sighed.

"Do you want to learn how to play beer pong? I can drink all the beer, and you can just shoot."

"You'll definitely die if we do that," I said.

"FUCK, Priya, how can someone so sober have such bad aim?" Aaron groaned with a slur to his words as we walked to my car just after midnight. He had one arm over my shoulders, and I had one arm around him, although my arm was more of a guiding tool and his was being used to physically support himself. I had never seen Aaron get so drunk before, but in two rounds of beer pong, both of which we lost miserably, he was forced to drink everything—on top of the mixed drink he'd been holding already when we started.

At my car, I put him in the passenger seat and buckled him in, then rushed to the driver's side, turned the car on, and lowered his window so he had fresh air.

"Where am I taking you, Aaron? Cameron is passed out on Brad's couch, so his place is out."

Aaron groaned.

"Can I stay with you tonight? There's no way I can go home, and I don't want to stay in this shit show," he said.

My eyes widened, my breath hitched, and my heart raced.

Aaron's head rolled to the side as he inched toward the

open window, and I weighed the pros and cons of him staying with me.

Pros: he would be safe, his parents wouldn't find out, and if he needed anything, I would be there to help him.

Cons…

My mind drew a blank at cons, and yet, there was a feeling in the pit of my stomach telling me this was wrong.

Okay, Priya, what is going on? You're dating. It's fine. It's natural to want to stay with your boyfriend. You're a hot-blooded young teen. It's natural.

Then why did I feel uneasy? Why was I holding back?

Aaron's breathing was labored. When he gagged, I put aside my hesitations and decided to drive him to my place.

What's the worst that can happen?

The whole drive to my house, I was on edge. My hands were trembling as I gripped the steering wheel, and a cold, anxious sweat covered my body.

This isn't right. This isn't right.

Why? Why isn't this right?

He's not Dimitri!

In a flash, my anxiety turned into anger as I turned the corner that led to my neighborhood.

I was so tired of the fact that I was still battling myself over Dimitri. The disappointment in myself that coursed through me was excruciating, and knowing that Aaron was passed out in my passenger seat was the only thing keeping me from crying out of pure frustration.

I parked my car in the driveway and gripped the steering wheel even tighter as I took a few deep breaths, in and out, counting down and grounding myself once more before pushing the car door open, a little roughly. I rushed to Aaron's side and eased his door open, gently nudging him awake.

As I moved Aaron from the car to the house, and somehow up the stairs, his minor groans and mumbles were actually doing a pretty good job of keeping me grounded and in the moment. The little noises he made were oddly endearing; his attempts to take care of himself were amusing, and the way he kept failing was more reason for me to remain in the here and now. I couldn't let him hurt himself, puke on my furniture, or worse, choke on his vomit.

I sat him on the edge of my bed, but he just ended up falling onto his side. He pulled himself up the bed and toward the pillow before wrapping himself in the sheets.

My body pulsed as I watched Aaron lying in my bed and reveled in the realization that the hesitation in my stomach had dissipated. Instead, there was only a warmth that urged me to watch him and keep him safe.

The feeling was new, but this time, the novelty didn't scare me. I couldn't help the immense happiness spreading through me.

How did a girl like me land a guy like him?

After changing into my pajamas in the bathroom, I checked back on Aaron to make sure he was breathing and hadn't thrown up everywhere. When he seemed safe and sound, I turned to leave, to sleep on the couch, but was stopped by an alarming groan.

"Priya? Can-can you stay with me?" he said. I turned to look and saw he was barely holding his head up.

My heart raced at the thought, but... did Aaron expect anything from me? Was he talking about doing *that* tonight? While he was in this state?

"I just want to sleep next to you. Not do anything. Just sleep," he mumbled, slightly slurring his words as his head fell to my pillow, and my body relaxed.

I trusted him.

I had always felt safe with Aaron, and he had never given me reason to feel otherwise. Even in his drunken state, he was a perfectly respectful guy, and I wanted to be close to him, to cuddle up next to the man I was falling head over heels for.

I was about to get under the sheets when I saw him still on top of them, with either side pulled up and around him.

"Um, do you want to change?" I asked him softly, warmth spreading across my face.

"Is that okay?"

I nodded, then said nervously, "Do you... need help?"

"Probably."

And the next thing I knew, I was helping him undress. It wasn't sexy at all, honestly. It was like I was playing nurse—but again, not a sexy nurse.

His shirt was easy, but the pants had me trembling. He unbuttoned them, and I helped pull them from his ankles. When they were finally off, he fell back against the sheets and sighed happily, making me smile.

I helped him get under the sheets, and when he was situated, I climbed in next to him.

My body was tense at first, and I kept my distance from him, not sure if he wanted to touch me or if I was allowed to touch him.

Good lord, do I want to touch him.

I felt myself move closer to him, and within an instant, he had my extremely tense body in his arms, crushed against him.

"Is this okay?" he asked.

I nodded, forcing myself to relax, limb by painstaking limb.

I wanted to be there so badly, but it was all so new that I was overwhelmed by the emotions. I felt a warmth in my stomach, and elsewhere, but I didn't want to let that get the best of me, not tonight. Tonight was special, and as I shut my eyes and relinquished myself to the heatwaves radiating off of Aaron, I let my body relax and feel the onslaught of positive emotions. I would deal with the confusion—and possible consequences—in the morning.

It wasn't long before Aaron's snores filled the room. I had never fallen asleep so easily to such an obnoxious noise.

~

Bzz. *bzz. bzz.*

The fog in my mind slowly cleared, and I registered the repetitive sound of my phone vibrating on my bedside table. But my body didn't want to leave the unusually heavy warmth that surrounded me, so I clenched my eyes shut more firmly.

Finally, my phone stopped vibrating, and I sighed with relief as I turned and moved farther into the warmth, the heavy mass closing in on me once more and filling me with a happiness and comfort I hadn't felt in a long time.

The phone started to buzz again, obnoxiously pulling me out of my cloud entirely. I opened my eyes and registered that it was still dark, that I was in bed with an almost naked Aaron, and that my phone had rung twice.

My brain came to two possible conclusions.

Option one: it was early morning or late at night, and Elli needed a ride somewhere.

Option two: my mom was calling to let me know she was either in Shanghai or leaving India.

I rolled away from Aaron and pushed the blankets off of me, my breath hitching as I felt the chilly air before I looked at my phone to see that it was just after five, and I had not two, but three missed calls from Elli's mom.

Shit. What happened?

I immediately called Mrs. Martinez back, and she answered on the first ring.

"P-Priya, I'm sorry to wake you, but I figured you n-needed to be called." Mrs. Martinez's voice was wavering and cracking as she spoke, and my heart beat so heavily in my chest that my entire body pulsated with every beat.

Elli. Oh God, it's Elli.

"Priya, Elli is in the hospital. She… she…" Mrs. Martinez broke down crying, and my breath caught as I tried to keep my calm.

She's in the hospital, meaning she isn't dead. That means she's being treated. So whatever happened is treatable.

There was some muffled background noise through the phone. Then Mr. Martinez started speaking.

"Hi, Priya, it's Jack. Elli is getting her stomach pumped right now because of alcohol poisoning, and the doctors say it isn't looking good. Can you come as soon as possible? Elli would want you to be here."

"I'll be there ASAP!" I almost yelled as the overflow of emotions rocked through my body.

"Thank you, Priya. We'll see you soon. We're at El Camino hospital in Los Gatos. We'll text you where to go once you get there." Mr. Martinez hung up the phone. I jumped to my feet and ran to the light switch, flipping it on. I turned to see Aaron already out of bed and looking for his clothes, although he was staggering around. I looked down at my own clothes and figured these would have to do. There was no time for me to change into something presentable. That didn't matter right now.

All that mattered was seeing Elli.

I'm going to give her hell when she's recovered.

"Fuck!" Aaron let out as he fell on the floor while trying to put his pants on. He scrambled to get them up.

I looked into his eyes when he stood up, feeling a small wave of comfort wash over me. We just stood there for a moment, unable to communicate in our fear and confusion.

"She'll…. she'll be okay, right?" My body started to tremble, and my voice shook. Tears fell from my eyes, and I felt myself start to hyperventilate, my body coming out of the shock.

Aaron took one long stride toward me and pulled me to his body. I wrapped my arms around him and gripped him tightly, sobs erupting from my lungs.

"She'll be okay. From what you've told me and what I know of her, she's strong." I nodded against his chest.

It was true that this wasn't Elli's first time being hospitalized. She had been in the hospital before, but they hadn't called her parents. Elli had been conscious. She'd sent me a text of her hospital band the next morning with a funny comment. I was furious, to say the least, and worried out of my mind.

"Relax, baby girl, I'm stronger than that," she'd said with a laugh when I called her.

There were no calming words from Elli this time.

Aaron pulled me away gently and rubbed the sides of my arms as I pulled myself together.

"Grab a jacket. I'll drive. If you need to, let the crazy out in the car, but we need to head over there now and be strong for Elli and her parents," he said.

I swiped at my eyes, taking a deep breath and counting to ten as I threw on my fleece zip-up and grabbed a pair of socks. When my socks were on and Aaron's jacket was on, we rushed out of the house.

Aaron drove with one hand on the wheel, one hand

holding mine, swiping his thumb against the back, as usual. I watched his thumb swiping back and forth, back and forth. It was hypnotic, the only thing I could focus on that would keep me from panicking. I focused every last bit of attention on the slow rhythm of the way his soft thumb felt brushing against my skin.

Even with that, my thoughts couldn't help but catch on the memory of her last alcohol poisoning.

The memory kept playing in quick snippets. Although it wasn't a happy memory, it brought me some comfort. If she could beat this once, she could beat it again.

"Aaron, you know I've never lived a day without her, right? Even when she came close to dying, she didn't. Even when we fought, and it got nasty, we stayed together." Tears fell from my eyes.

Aaron squeezed my hand. I squeezed back, then covered his hand with my other hand, holding our entwined hands up to my heart.

We arrived at the hospital parking lot. Aaron parked the car as close to the entrance as possible and turned the car off.

"Priya, it'll be okay," he whispered in the silence.

I just sat there, nearly catatonic.

"Priya? Did you let enough crazy out?" he asked, but I couldn't respond. I looked out the window, watching the artificial lights trying to hold the darkness at bay in the world outside until the light could creep back up over the horizon. It wouldn't be much longer—it couldn't. This was already the longest night of my life.

"Let's go," I whispered, but I couldn't move. I continued to sit, clutching Aaron's hand against my heart. My heart beat heavily, overwhelming and shaking my body. My palms grew sweaty, either from my anxiety or from holding Aaron's hand so tightly. I couldn't let go, nor did I want to. I hoped Aaron didn't mind my clammy palms.

I continued to stare at the floor mat in the car, my eyes tracing the barely lit patterns etched into the rubber. I took a deep breath, trying to ground myself.

Inhale. *One*

Exhale. *Two*

Inhale. *Three*

Once I was able to pull myself together, I looked at Aaron, still watching me. I nodded.

We walked through the brightly lit hospital, but the whole time, I felt like I was outside of my body—like I was being pulled along in a ride, in a daze or drugged. Aaron held my hand tightly the whole time, guiding me. He asked the nurses the right questions and navigated us through the building after being pointed in the proper direction.

I kept my head low, following Aaron's lead. Then, abruptly, he stopped, and I almost crashed into him. I looked up from the white linoleum tiled floor to see a room number and knew it must be Elli's room.

"*It's going to take more than just alcohol to get me.*" Elli's words echoed in my head as I stared at the door that led to her hospital room.

The sounds of the world around me didn't seem right. Nurses walking around, people murmuring, calls being taken... such mundane tasks were making my blood boil. I felt like screaming but I kept reminding myself that she could still be fine.

She's fine. She's fine. She's fine.

I stepped toward the door, shaky on my feet, and tried to employ Avery's counting method, but I was so tense that I couldn't just stay still. I had to act *and* count.

I stepped around Aaron. *One... two...*

I reached for the door. *Three... four...*

As I pulled the pocket door to the right, the sound of people crying grew louder and louder, along with a ringing in my ears. *Five... six...*

When the door opened, I looked at the corner of the room to see Mr. and Mrs. Martinez embracing, Mr. Martinez holding his wife tightly to him. They were both crying hysterically.

Seven... eight...

Mr. Martinez looked up at me. He shook his head, breaking down further. *Nine...*

"P-Priya..."

I sluggishly looked at the hospital bed, noticed how slowly the nurses were moving, and I realized what the ringing in my ear was.

"Time of death, six o-seven."

Ten.

13

APRIL 30TH ,2019

THE CASKET WAS a dark cherrywood with a cream interior. It looked soft and comfortable, which I'm sure Elli would enjoy. At least, I hoped she would since her body would be remaining there for eternity.

I sat at the front of the room, right next to Elli's mom. Mrs. Martinez was sobbing into her husband's shoulder. My sister was sitting to my right with her arm around me, but I barely felt its weight. Everything around me was muted. The only sense working at full capacity was my vision; my eyes set on the image of my best friend lying in a coffin. Her face was saturated with heavy makeup. Her skin looked too pale and her lips too red, like a stain around her mouth. Whoever's job it was to make her look presentable tried too hard and completely missed the essence of Elli.

"Priya." A soft tap on my shoulder snapped me out of my spiral, and I looked at my sister. "It's your turn to speak," she whispered. I looked at the podium, then down at the pieces of paper that were crumpled in my hands.

I never thought I would have to do this, give someone's eulogy, so soon.

I stood up and walked to the podium on shaky legs. My legs somehow felt like they were made of lead and Jell-O at the same time as I dragged them along. I set the paper down on the wooden block, unfolded it, and flattened it out. I looked at the people in front of me and saw my mom sitting in the seat behind my sister. I saw the faces of Elli's distant relatives and close friends, including Amanda.

Then I looked to my left.

I saw the vessel that used to be my best friend. The vessel that, now, I could barely recognize as her. I knew it was her body, but without her spirit, it felt like it couldn't truly be her. I couldn't believe this body was Elli's, and deep down, I was battling the belief that she was alive and well somewhere.

I looked at Mrs. and Mr. Martinez, knowing they would want to hear good things about their daughter. Did they want to hear about the times she held me while I cried? The times she was the only person in my life to understand things no one else ever could?

What am I going to do without you, Elli?

My hands trembled on the podium, shaking violently, no matter how hard I clenched them. I tried my best to be strong, to put on a brave face and be the support that someone, I don't know who, but *someone* needed. But I was never the strong one. Elli was the strong one. She was the one who was never phased by life. She rolled with the punches. *C'est la vie* —that was her mantra.

Such is life, Elli... but what is life without you?

The image of her in the coffin felt like a vision in a nightmare.

I couldn't breathe. I couldn't give a speech at my best friend's funeral.I couldn't accept that she was gone. I couldn't comprehend it.

I couldn't comprehend losing again.

"Angel."

I looked up, the back of my neck prickling like thousands of tiny needles were piercing my skin. My eyes darted all over the room trying to find the owner of the voice, that musical voice, and although I saw no one, my eyes were drawn to the bright green exit sign that lit up the corner to my right.

"Priya?" I heard my sister say, and I glanced over to see her looking at me, concerned.

I looked between her brown, confused eyes and the exit of the funeral home next to me.

My head felt light, my stomach queasy, and I began to sweat bullets as black spots appeared all over my vision.

I shook my head, trying to clear the feeling, and my eyes landed on Aaron.

He was easy to spot, sitting in the middle of the left section of chairs. He looked concerned, seemingly about to come out of his chair. Yet, that was the last thing I wanted. For some reason, his small movements made me want to bolt even more.

"Angel, I'm here." The voice came again, and the pieces of my heart that were still whole absolutely shattered. I had heard it for the past few months, but I hadn't paid it any heed. It was a voice that shouldn't be there. Yet, in that moment, it was giving me equal portions of comfort and pain.

Dimitri.

The voice was a breath of fresh air, but it was wrong. It sounded wrong and defiled, as if all he stood for, all he used to mean to me, had become hideously morphed.

You're not real. You're not real.

"Angel, I'm here for you."

A flash of golden blond hair in the corner of my eye caught my attention, and my head whipped toward the exit sign again, only to see nothing. There was no one there. But the chill up my spine and the prickling on my neck said otherwise.

"Priya, are you okay?" Aaron was standing in front of the podium, and I couldn't breathe as I flinched away from the stand, taking a small step back. My thoughts raced. My brain felt like it was shutting down and being torn to shreds in opposite directions, far east, north, south, and west.

The world around me felt like a dream, and that dream felt like it was melting around me; the only thing I cared about was escaping—waking up.

The black spots almost completely filled my vision as the sweat beaded down the back of my neck. I was suffocating, and I couldn't handle it, or anything, anymore.

"I'm sorry," I whispered before stepping away from the podium toward the exit sign, tripping over my feet as I kept moving toward my escape. The moment I started moving, the black spots in my vision started clearing. When I gained my bearings, I started running as fast as I could toward the green exit sign and out through the open emergency door, running to somewhere safe and out of sight.

When I reached the end of the dirty gray cobbled pathway that led into the parking lot and my car, my brain started to work again, churning and replaying what had happened. Once I opened my car door, I sat down in the driver's seat and slammed the door behind me. I took a few moments to catch my breath, my hands clenching my skirt. I felt like I was suffocating again, but this time, I was choking on the burn of sorrow that filled my lungs and eyes.

"Angel, I'm here," Dimitri said. I screamed in frustration, gripping my head and clenching my eyes shut. I so desperately wanted that to be true, but I knew he was wrong.

I knew it was wrong of me to want him back, to want to see him—to feel safe with him.

"Where? Show me! You're not *real!*" I screamed, and the tears streamed down my face. My body collapsed into itself, and I pushed my head against the steering wheel.

"Angel, why do you say that when I'm right here?" His voice sounded closer to me, as if he were sitting in the passenger's seat. My eyes flashed open only to see an empty space, and I let out a cry of anguish and frustration.

"Stop! *Stop!* Please, just… stop," I sobbed, my voice incomprehensible by the last word. I was pleading with Dimitri, but I didn't know what I wanted to stop. Did I want the pain to stop? Did I want this trick in my brain to stop? Or did I want him to stop hiding and show himself?

I want to see him. I need him right now.

No. Get a grip, Priya.

Was it a trick? Is Dimitri real?

You're under stress. This is the stress talking.

"You know why you can't see me." His voice softly kissed my right ear, and I hiccupped, trying to understand why he—no, why my brain—would tell me I knew why I couldn't see him. I began to desperately try and decipher his words.

Just one last time. Just one more time. I need to see him, hold him, have him tell me everything will be okay.

There was a knock on the passenger side window that brought me out of my thoughts.

Jasmine. She had tears in her eyes, and she was motioning for me to either unlock the car or lower the window.

I unlocked the car, and she stepped in and reached across the console between us. Our arms tangled around each other in a strong embrace.

"Oh, Priya. Priya, I'm so sorry," she said into my hair as I sobbed on her black dress.

"I don't understand, *didi*. Why her? Why did she have to go? It's not fair!" I screamed into her dress as I gripped her tighter. *This has to be a dream*, I thought. But I knew it wasn't a dream, and it never would be, no matter how much I told myself otherwise.

"I don't understand either, Priya. I don't understand," she said, repeating the words over and over again.

It wasn't a cold day—in fact, the air held the pleasant warmth of spring—but I was shivering uncontrollably. My sister held me until I cried all my tears out and was left a shivering, hiccupping mess.

"Are you ready to go back yet? I think the service is probably over by now," she whispered softly.

I nodded, slowly pulling away from her. I took a few moments to catch my breath, to try and stop myself from shaking and somewhat pull myself together. After a few gasping breaths and swipes at my face, I felt more presentable, and I followed her in a daze out of the car toward the funeral home. We walked down the same cobbled path I had just crossed back into the home, down the green carpet, and back into the room, which now held far fewer people.

At the front of the room, I saw my mom and Mrs. Martinez hugging. My mom looked more distraught than I had ever seen her, but she wasn't crying. Her eyes were red, but no tears were falling down her cheeks.

When my mom pulled away from Mrs. Martinez, they both saw me, and my mom rushed over to me, enveloping me in a tight hug.

"*Chotu,* are you okay? Why did you run away?"

I was about to open my mouth to respond, but I couldn't. What would I say? That I heard Dimitri calling me?

There was no way that would go well. That was not what anyone needed to hear.

Be strong, Priya. Like Elli would have been.

"I couldn't breathe. I couldn't... see her like that," I said, looking over my mom's shoulder to the now closed casket.

My mom let go, and my sister came up behind me.

"I think Aaron wants to make sure you're okay too," my mom said, and I looked over to see Aaron still sitting in the middle of the section to our right.

A part of me saw him and yearned for that feeling of safety he usually embodied, but that part was growing weaker and weaker. The part that bore allegiance to Dimitri was screaming in my head.

That's the stress talking. Go see Aaron.

Yes, Aaron will make everything better.

I didn't want to see him, though. Seeing him was too much, it was too overwhelming. My soul was filled to the brim with too many emotions, and I knew seeing Aaron would break me. After hearing Dimitri, I felt... dirty. I felt like I had cheated. And the worst part was I couldn't tell who I was cheating on—Aaron or Dimitri.

"No, it's fine. I'll talk to him later," I told my sister, looking at her puffy red eyes. She nodded and she and my mom went to talk to Mrs. And Mr. Martinez. I was about to follow them when I heard Aaron's broken voice.

"I'm sorry, Priya."

He was standing behind me, but I was too afraid to see him. Too afraid of the confusion raging inside me.

It's too much. I can't handle this.

"Aaron... I... I can't do this. I can't do this right now," I said.

"I know, Priya. I know, that's why I'm here. I'm here for you."

I shook my head, closing my eyes and clenching my trembling fists at my side.

"No. I mean, I can't do us. I can't do you being with me or being here for me. I can't handle us being together right now," I said.

How could we possibly be in a relationship with Dimitri looming over us? How could we possibly be in a relationship now that I had just lost another piece of my soul in Elli? There was no way I could let Aaron get caught up in my craziness. I had too much baggage, now more than before, and I didn't want to carry him down with me as I sank beneath the crashing waves of emotion and horror. There was no way I could handle being responsible for dragging him down. He may know about my past, but what would his reaction be to the fact that I let it catch up with me, that it was knocking on my door again? Even worse, how would he be with the addition of Elli's death now as part of my baggage?

I can't do this. Please, don't make me do this.

"I… I think I understand. I'll give you space," he said.

"I don't think you do…" I whispered. I turned around in the hopes that I could show him, that I could convey how messed up I was and how much he couldn't possibly understand. But when I turned, instead of seeing Aaron's brown eyes, I was forced to lift my head higher than expected to look into familiar hazel eyes perfectly framed by golden hair.

Dimitri?

Dimitri stood looming over me, a sad smile on his face. I sucked in a breath and almost reached out my hand for him, but when I blinked, the vision of Dimitri was gone, and Aaron stood in front of me. I instantly retracted my hand back to my side, blinking a few times at Aaron. Nothing was making sense, and all I could do was scream internally. My traitorous heart wanted so desperately for the vision of Dimitri to stay, to be real.

This is too much. Elli, I need you. I need your strength and stability.

"It's okay, Priya. I will always be here for you, even if you can't handle me being here next to you. Call me if you want me, to talk, or for me to come to your side," Aaron said. He leaned forward, and I stepped back, flinching at the idea of him touching me.

What is wrong with me?

With the thought of Dimitri in my head, with the desire to see and feel him, I didn't want Aaron to be there. I wanted to want Aaron and only Aaron, but deep down, he wasn't the one I yearned for. I had reverted to my old ways, almost in an instant.

How could I have been undone so easily?

I saw a flash of pain strike across Aaron's face, and he looked down, his lower lip quivering.

I'm sorry, Aaron. I'm so sorry.

"Goodbye, Aaron." My voice betrayed my true feelings. The words came out without a break or hiccup.

"Goodbye, Priya." Aaron's emotions were not so contained. His voice wavered as he spoke his farewell and turned to leave.

I watched him rush out of the funeral home, hating the fact that the part of me holding back from rushing after him and explaining the situation had won. I hated that I was torn between two men when one of them was not even real.

I hated the fact that the side of me that was still loyal to Dimitri was winning the battle.

∽

S itting on the edge of my bed and staring into the bathroom, I pictured Elli standing there with a chunk of hair in one hand and a straightener in the other.

"Would you ever get a tattoo?"

I replayed the conversation in my head again, remembering the way her eyes shined at the prospect of getting a tattoo. *C'est la vie.*

I followed her in my mind as she walked out of my bathroom and toward my bed, my head turning with the ghost of her. My eyes fell on the closet where Elli would spend time picking out clothes for me to wear as if I were her little doll.

"Why don't you wear something like this?" So many times—the first night we went out together that school year, and many others—she had pulled out some sort of fun but inappropriate outfit from my closet.

The memories became overwhelming. I felt my body ride the rollercoaster of emotions raging through me, my body swaying with its dips, turns, and inclines.

Mindlessly, I changed my clothes and got into bed, curling myself into a burrito in the blankets. The sun was still high in the sky and shining through my blinds. I stared at the spot next to me by the wall—the spot where Elli used to sleep when she would stay over. Everywhere I looked, I saw her. I knew she was integrated into my life, an extension of myself, but I never could have imagined how that would lead to such emptiness. The void in my heart was larger than the one I had following the loss of Dimitri. The fact that Elli was real made this so much worse. The fact that she was my best friend, my person, my platonic soulmate made the lack of her in this world feel more confusing, and I was more lost than the day I was admitted in the hospital a year before.

The memories of her were attacking me from every

mental direction. It was too much, and I was exhausted.
Maybe if I slept, I would wake up feeling better. And who
knew, maybe in my dreams, she would be alive. Maybe I
would wake up, even, and this would all have been a dream. I
imagined waking up at Elli's bedside in the hospital, seeing
her smiling face, and hearing her tell me she was stronger
than anyone gave her credit for.

I sighed as the thoughts took control of my brain. Groaning, I peeped around the top edge of the blanket, my eyes
falling directly on the orange bottle set on my bedside table.

"Do you want to see me?" I heard Dimitri's voice directly
in my ear. I stared at the bottle and felt a nudge in my brain,
telling me the answer to his question.

Don't take the medication.

Suddenly, I realized I hadn't taken my medication in at
least three days. Things had been so hectic that I hadn't even
remembered to take the tablets. Now it made sense why I was
hallucinating more than before.

And it made sense why I didn't want the hallucinations to
stop.

I looked at the bottle for a moment longer, then closed my
eyes, took a few deep breaths, and let the crazy happen in my
mind.

I would let the crazy happen and let it out until I was
done. Then everything would go back to normal—or as
normal as it could be without Elli.

14

MAY 1ST, 2019

I WOKE up in the middle of the night. For a split second, I forgot about what had happened only a few days prior. However, the second was over before I could even think about sitting in it, and when the realization hit me, I turned around in my bed and stared into space, numb from the emotions that still rocked my system.

The blinds on my window were open, and a bit of light peeked through from the moon and the streetlights, highlighting a few spots in my dark room. One beam cast a spotlight right on my medication bottle.

I reached my hand out toward the bottle, knowing I needed to take it.

Do you want to see me? The words came back to me instantly. My fingers hadn't even reached the nightstand before I pulled back, restraining myself. I hated myself for it, but I was saying yes to that question. I hated myself, but I was so desperate, so broken, and in so much pain that I needed his familiar presence back.

When I looked at the nightstand again, I felt a sense of déjà vu. I knew how this scene had played out before.

I remembered arriving home from the hospital after losing Dimitri and waking up in the middle of the night after a nightmare. I texted Elli immediately, and she called me right away, telling me to take my medication. She stayed on the call with me as I cried myself back to sleep.

Tonight, there was no one to text.

Elli was dead. Amanda and I weren't on those kinds of terms. Aaron... I couldn't even think about Aaron. So I ignored the healthy part of my brain telling me to take the medication. I turned away, facing the wall, and hugged my blankets close.

I woke up several times throughout the night but turned over and went back to sleep immediately each time. It was midmorning when I woke up naturally and blinked up at the ceiling, stewing in my feelings. It was strange. I wasn't numb, but I didn't feel strongly enough to elicit the appropriate response, which in this case would have been crying or angry screams. I wasn't sure if I wanted to cry, or if I wanted to just be simmering in the sorrow that didn't quite boil over.

When I heard a sudden knock and the creaks from my opening door, I rolled over and faced my mom, who was sticking her head in my room.

"*Chotu*, are you awake?" she asked softly.

I just blinked at her. She nodded before making her way inside and sitting on the edge of my bed. She was wearing a pair of yoga pants and a marled gray cowlneck sweatshirt. She looked how she usually looked on a casual day, but this wasn't a casual day. It was exactly four days after Elli died. Not even a week later. There was nothing casual about this day.

She looked at me for a few seconds, examining my state. "You looked exactly like this a year ago," she said, her eyes coming to my face, and I looked away, not wanting to make eye contact.

"Did you take your medication last night?" Her voice was soft, and I was reminded of everyone's voices from a year ago, soft as if I would break from louder sound waves. I didn't say anything, giving a barely there nod, unwilling to outright lie verbally, and also using the raw tightness in my throat at the simmering emotions as an excuse to remain silent.

We remained quiet for another minute. "I know you're going through a lot right now, but make sure you take care of yourself when you can, okay? I know Elli would... want you to take care of yourself."

My mom's words were soft. My initial reaction was to bite back with a rude comment, something along the lines of "What do you know about what Elli would want?" but before I said anything, that desire dissipated as quickly as it manifested. I realized my mom was right. Even when I lost Dimitri, Elli was the one who told me to be strong. She acknowledged that I had to go through some tough times to get better, but she always told me to keep my focus on getting better. There was always an end goal of recovery. I just didn't know if recovery was possible this time.

Why does it matter what she would have wanted? She's already dead.

I pulled my blanket over my head and heard my mom walk out of the room without closing the door. I closed my eyes again and tried to drift off to sleep.

"Why don't you talk to her, Jasmine? I don't know if she took her medication." My mom's voice floated up the stairs a few minutes later, and I sighed, knowing my sister was downstairs. I could hear the sound of the kettle as it boiled water at an obnoxiously loud volume before it clicked, equally loudly, to signify the water had boiled.

"I'll talk to her; just have your *cha*," my sister replied. A couple minutes later, I heard her steps on the stairs, then her gentle knock on my door.

"Priya, it's me," she said as she walked in.

"I know," I replied. The mattress moved and dipped slightly as she sat in what I assumed was the exact same spot my mom had.

"Mom doesn't think you took your medication."

Silence.

"Priya, I'm not going to force it, but you need to take it. This is exactly the kind of situation that could push you into an episode." Jasmine's words, although spoken softly, were said with an attempt at conviction.

I was not convinced, though. "I know."

That's the point.

I didn't feel like talking, I didn't want to think, and I didn't feel like seeing reason. I just wanted to simmer for a while. I wanted to feel what I felt and not have to be strong or take care of myself. I wanted to sleep and not wake up until I *wanted* to be strong.

"Scoot over," my sister said suddenly. I poked my head out to look up at her with a furrowed brow, but all she did was motion with her hands for me to move closer toward the wall. I stared at her blankly for a few seconds before sighing. I knew she wouldn't give up. She was too persistent. So I obliged and moved back until my butt hit the wall. She proceeded to lie down and face me, her hands going under her head. We commenced an uncomfortable staring contest, yet it seemed that I was the only uncomfortable one. My eyes kept darting all over the room while hers remained static on my face.

The more she stared at me, the more I felt like a bright light was being shined in my face in an attempt to get me to talk. She wasn't asking for anything, but I knew what she was doing. I didn't want to talk, though. I didn't want to think, and I didn't want to reason, so I rolled around in the bed and faced the wall, blinking as my eyes and throat stung with the tears that started to well up again. Usually, Elli was the one lying in bed next to me as I processed and thought through hard things. Usually, she was the one to scoot me over and either pry information from my lips or give me comforting silence that eventually coaxed me into opening up on my own.

"I don't get it," I said brokenly as the tears fell from my eyes, trailing down my cheeks and soaking my pillow thoroughly. My sister remained silent.

"I keep hoping that this is all a dream. That if I sleep enough, I'll wake up and see a thousand missed calls from her. I know it's not, and I know I won't. But all I want to do is just… sleep. I don't want to think anymore. I don't want to talk. I just… want to sleep."

"So sleep," my sister said gently. I clenched my eyes shut as more tears fell.

∼

I woke up later that night, alone and slightly hungry.

When was the last time I ate? Must have been more than twenty-four hours ago.

My stomach wasn't hurting, but I definitely felt weak when I tried to hold myself up with my arm. I moved around in bed and picked up my phone to see some messages on

Facebook from people I rarely talked to and a text from Amanda.

Amanda: Hey Priya, I'm so sorry about Elli. I know you guys were inseparable, and I hope you're doing okay. Let me know if you need anything!

I thought fondly of Amanda but I wasn't sure I considered her a friend—I always thought of her as Elli's friend. Maybe if something of a smaller magnitude had happened, I would have reached out to her for support. This was not a small event, though, and I was not in the mood for some pity from one of Elli's friends. I was definitely not going to let her know if I needed anything, but I did appreciate her offer. Plus, I had to at least acknowledge she was being nice. Was she hurting, too, since they were also friends? I couldn't remember if I had seen her at the funeral. I couldn't remember most of the faces from the funeral. Most of the funeral events blurred together and were hard to remember, except for the ones I wanted to forget—the ones involving Dimitri and Aaron. Those memories were seared into my mind, projected onto the inside of my eyelids whenever I blinked.

I threw the blankets from my body as I swung my legs over the edge of the bed. I stood up and immediately felt myself getting dizzy, my vision filling with a multitude of different colorful shapes and the room tilting from side to side like a pendulum. I sat back down on the bed and took a few deep breaths before I slowly rose up and walked out of the open door toward the staircase.

I could see the living room from the banister. My mom and sister were watching some show on mute. As I took a few steps down the stairs, their attention shifted from the screen to me, and I could see my mom sigh slightly.

"How are you feeling, *chotu*? Are you hungry?" she asked.

I nodded and slowly approached the couch. I looked at the TV and saw they were watching a rerun of *Grey's Anatomy*. It was our family's favorite show to watch together. For the past six seasons, my mom and I would watch it religiously every Thursday when she was in town. It was marginally comforting, somehow, to see the familiar show on the screen.

My mom stood up from the couch and walked around the wall that separated the kitchen from the living room.

"What do you want to eat? I can make you a pancake if you want."

I followed her into the kitchen.

"Can I have a bean and cheese burrito?" I asked, and my mom looked at me for a second as if she were going to contest my request. She knew I didn't like them, but she also knew they were Elli's favorite. So she nodded her head and took out all the necessary things to make the burrito. I pulled out one of the barstools from under the island countertop and sat down, leaning my body forward to rest my head on the cool, dark speckled granite.

Soon the smells of the cooked beans, melting cheese, and tortilla mixed and filled the air, and the bean and cheese burrito that I didn't actually want was set before me. I stared at the perfectly wrapped meal and felt my stomach turn at the idea of eating it, at the idea that I would get to eat this and Elli never would again. I looked at the food, then at my mom, who stood cautiously on the other side of the countertop. She was watching me expectantly, so I lifted the burrito. I took the smallest bite ever and gagged.

"Don't eat if you don't want to. I can make you a smoothie or something. Something lighter." My mom was already opening the fridge to pull out fruit for a smoothie. I shook my head, determined to eat the entire burrito. It was almost like some sort of sick tribute to Elli, like eating that burrito would somehow honor her or, better yet, make me feel closer to her, as if she were going to pop out of the bathroom, call my mom *her* mom, and sit down next to me to have her own burrito.

But that didn't happen, and the stupid burrito tasted as gross as ever because I hated beans.

I ended up crying over it at the kitchen counter. "It's so gross. Why did she like these?" I sobbed as I flung the burrito onto the plate and covered my eyes, chewing the mush in my mouth. My mom rushed around the counter as I started to cry and sat down next to me, enveloping me in her arms as she hushed me and patted my head. I swallowed, then instantly sobbed again into my mom's arms. I let her hold me until I made my way, once again, back to bed, still crying, and knocked out for the night.

15

MAY 3RD, 2019

On Friday, for the first time in my life, my mom fought with me to keep me home instead of going to school.

"Priya, I know *didi* and I are going back to work today, but it's because we have to. You can stay home if you want," she said as I ate my cereal at the kitchen counter.

"It's fine. I'll be fine," I said unconvincingly, even to myself.

It had been six days already since Elli died, and on the fifth day, I went numb. I stopped crying, stopped feeling angry, stopped feeling anything. It was somewhat of a relief. My raw throat could finally recover and my eyes, puffy from so many salty tears, were able to deflate, although the dark circles under them remained.

"Can you at least call Avery and schedule an appointment, please?" my mom asked, and I nodded, knowing she didn't know the truth about my state.

It was also six days since I last took my medication.

"Already done, but her earliest appointment is the fifteenth, after my AP test." I had scheduled the appointment with Avery the day after Elli died, but I didn't know now if I had any intention of committing to that appointment. With my new numbness, I didn't know if I wanted to break that wall down and collapse on Avery's couch in tears, or if I would even need to in two weeks.

I picked up my empty cereal bowl, put it in the sink, and grabbed my backpack from the couch in the living room. "Bye, Mama," I said, opening the door and running out before she could try and stop me from leaving again.

~

As I walked through the campus towards my first class, AP Government, I could feel everyone's eyes on me. Whether they actually were, I didn't know, but I for sure *felt* them. I imagined everyone, students and teachers, coming up with a sad narrative about my life and how I must be barely surviving, and although that might have been true only a few days ago, I was determined to have that not be the reality anymore. So I held my head high and walked into the AP Gov classroom, only to put it down again as soon as I remembered who taught that class.

Shit. Aaron's mom. She probably hates me now and will fail me.

I sat down in my usual seat and didn't even look up at her, didn't bother looking at anyone as I sank lower under my desk. Who knew about our breakup? Did they think terribly of me and pity me?

Ms. Chen handed out a practice AP test, and I sped through the test, knowing every answer.

However, as I was answering the questions, voices were looming around me and I couldn't tell if they were from cheating students, or hallucinations.

Some were comprehensible and sounded like students cheating as they were just letters, *A* through *D*.

The other voices were more like murmurs, with the words sounding fuzzy and unintelligible.

When I finished, I flipped over my Scantron and lay my head on my desk, taking a deep breath, and tried to push the racing thoughts out of my head.

"Was she worth your deception?" a familiar, deep Russian voice suddenly asked in my left ear.

I pried my eyes open, sat up, and looked around the room. Students were still taking the practice test, their heads down, so I looked down at my desk, pressing my hands against the cool wood and counting down from ten. It had been longer than I could remember since I'd heard that particular Russian voice, and no medication, no amount of time, would erase it from my memory. Just as I would never erase the memory of it accompanying Dimitri's death.

"All right, everyone, time's up. Pass your test forward for me to collect," Ms. Chen called out. We all passed our tests toward the first person in our row. The bell rang as soon as Ms. Chen had collected the tests, and I quickly gathered my things and bolted out of the room, needing fresh air to help me breathe and calm down. However, as soon as I stepped outside, I was pulled out of my thoughts by a voice.

"Priya!" I heard Amanda call my name. In a split second, I plastered on a calm and cool face, then looked back to see her close behind me.

"Hey," she said. "I'm surprised to see you back at school. Did you get my text?"

I nodded. "Yeah, sorry, I just haven't talked to anyone lately, but I'm sorry for your loss too. I know she was your friend as well." The words coming out of my mouth were disconnected from my heart or any sort of emotions that I had, as was the smile I put on after.

Amanda's face softened, and she nodded, understanding my words, though not the apathy behind them.

"What's your next class? Let's walk together," she said, and I hesitated before slowly nodding my head. My smile was starting to hurt my cheeks and jaw, but I didn't want to let my facade down.

We ended up having our second period classes in the same building, but while I had AP Calc, she had pre-calc.

"You know, I remember when Elli first told me about you," Amanda said with a laugh, and I looked at her curiously. "She said she was best friends with this nerdy Indian girl she'd known since you guys were born. I totally imagined some sad-looking weirdo, but I remember thinking when I saw you that you were actually really pretty with the longest hair I've ever seen. And when I met you, I found out how cool you are too."

I looked at her, confused as to why she was telling me this story.

She continued as we entered the building that held our classes. "When we all started having lunch together last year, I knew I wanted to be your friend, but you seemed really closed off to new friends. So it was hard, but I'm really glad we got to know each other through cross-country. I guess my point with this story is to say I'm glad I met you, and I'm glad we're friends now. I know I'm not Elli, but if you need a friend, I can be here for you." She turned toward me as we stood in the hallway of the building, our classes nearby. "Cameron told me about you and Aaron. I know you have your reasons for it, but you shouldn't be alone through this. So, if you ever need anything, let me know, please. Okay?"

And before I could stop her, Amanda gripped me in a tight hug, catching me off guard.

The warning bell that signaled class would start in a minute rang, and that was her signal to let go.

"I'll see you later, Priya," she said, hurrying off toward her class and leaving me stunned. Then the final bell rang, and I, too, ran off to my class.

~

I t was fourth period, AP Psych time, meaning I had to see Aaron. We even sat next to each other, so I couldn't avoid him. I was dreading seeing him in class, seeing his sad eyes again. I wanted him to move on, to forget about me, to heal, but as soon as I walked into the classroom and saw his head pick up and his eyes light up, and as he half stood, I knew that was wishful thinking.

I looked away and saw Amanda waving at me from the back of the room, pointing to the desk next to her. I didn't want to take her up on her offer, but I couldn't sit next to Aaron. So I rushed over to the empty desk next to her and set my stuff down.

"Thanks."

"No problem. I know awkward breakups better than anyone," she said.

"Did you and Cameron break up too?" I asked, and she looked at me, shocked.

"What? No! No, no, but before him, yeah. Did you think Cameron was my first boyfriend?" Amanda asked, and I looked at her with a shrug.

"I…"

"Wait, was—" Amanda gestured at Aaron with her head, then back at me. "—your first boyfriend?"

I couldn't contain the heat that rose to my cheeks with embarrassment and instead looked down at my desk, situating my notebook and pen. Amanda let out a sigh next to me, and soon the class started.

However, once again, my mind was filled with racing thoughts.

Aaron was not my first boyfriend. Not the first. Not the first. Not the first. My mind repeated that phrase over and over, and no matter how many times I tried to tell myself the truth, or distract myself, my fixation on that one sentence would not lessen.

Before I knew it, the bell rang for lunch, and I felt myself get a little anxious about the idea of eating alone. I began to pack up my things slowly, putting off the impending loneliness.

"Hey, do you want to eat together?" Amanda spoke up next to me. She had already packed all her things, her backpack perched on her knees as she looked at me expectantly. A part of me wanted to say no because even though Amanda and I had gotten closer over the last few months, I wouldn't call her someone I felt comfortable being around alone, especially now. Sure, she just saved my ass from an embarrassing and awkward situation, but that didn't change how I felt about our friendship.

However, the fear of breaking down in the bathroom or library as I ate alone got to me, so I nodded.

"Sure."

At that moment, I felt the prickly feeling on the back of my neck, but this time, I knew it wasn't Dimitri. I glanced out of the side of my eyes to see Aaron looking at me from where he stood at the front of the class with his friend, Brenden. I looked back at Amanda.

"Um, I don't want to talk to Aaron, but I think he's

waiting for me," I whispered to Amanda as the room was quickly emptying. Soon, the only people who would be left were Amanda, Aaron, Brenden, and me.

Amanda made an *O* shape with her mouth, registering the situation, and before I could say anything, she looked at Aaron and nudged her head toward the door, silently telling him to leave without me. I was mortified, but also grateful.

But how terrible of a person was I that I couldn't even face Aaron, explain the situation to him, or tell him why I couldn't see him?

You don't even understand what's going on, Priya; how could you explain something you don't understand? The thought pressed on my mind, confusing me. I knew deep down that Aaron was an understanding person. He would have tried his best to understand why I needed space, but I didn't know if he would understand that the space was for an indefinite amount of time.

When I looked up at the doorway, Aaron was gone, and I let out a sigh of relief.

"I'm sorry you had to do that," I said to Amanda as we both stood up.

"No problem. What are friends for?"

"Are you ready for the AP tests?" Amanda asked as we ate our lunches out in the quad. It was a nice day out, sunny but not too hot. I looked down at my covered legs and the material of my t-shirt and hoped I wouldn't get any sweat stains from sitting out in the sun, but Amanda insisted we enjoy the sunshine.

"Yeah, I think so. Are you?"

"Kind of… I'm a little worried about A-PUSH," she said.

"You shouldn't be. I literally fell asleep halfway through that test and still passed," I said before taking a bite of my sandwich.

"Milk, cheese, eggs. Milk, cheese, eggs."

"Sauce, sauce, sauce."

I continued to chew, ignoring the harmless voices, but noticed Amanda was oddly quiet. When I looked up at her, she was just gawking at me.

"What?" I asked, and she blinked a few times before replying.

"You—you fell asleep? During an AP test?"

"Y-yeah? I was... tired..." I said, realizing that this was, in fact, a big deal.

Amanda broke out into laughter and shook her head. "Oh my gosh. Priya, you're unbelievable."

I smiled shyly. As I looked at Amanda, something about the scene felt familiar. It reminded me of when I told Elli that I had fallen asleep during the test. She had also shaken her head, saying, "Oh my God, Priya, you're fucking unbelievable." Amanda's reaction was pretty much the same, except she didn't curse. It was almost... comforting. It gave me an overwhelming sense of nostalgia that poked through the gloom, covering me like a weighted blanket and holding me close, until I felt warm with good memories.

I looked away from Amanda and took another bite of my sandwich before covering my mouth with my hand. "Yeah, so don't worry. If I can sleep and get a three, you can stay awake and get at least a three. If you need help, let me know." I froze, instantly regretting the words coming out of my mouth.

"Really? For sure! I'll text you if I need any help," she said, and I nodded, hoping she understood it was an empty offer and praying that she wouldn't text me.

We soon dove into mundane small talk before the bell

rang, and we split up to head to our next classes. I was relieved that I didn't have to keep up a facade of friendship anymore. Even though I liked Amanda, it was too exhausting.

I was walking into the classroom, almost to my desk, when I stopped at the sight of the seat next to mine—a seat that would remain empty for the rest of the semester. I knew that sitting alone, in a spot at the front of the room, meant I would be open to people's wandering eyes. They would slide over and pause, not on *my* back, but on the back of the empty chair that once held a lively, energetic person. I slowly inched toward the seat, setting my bag down, but as soon as I was sitting, I instantly felt the pressure of their stares again. The room felt unnaturally quiet, everyone's chattering falling to hushed criticisms and comments on my new lonesome state.

"Look at her. She's so pitiful."

"What a loser."

"Who is she without Elli?"

Ignore. Ignore. Ignore. I repeated the word as a mantra to myself over and over again, but the voices were coming from all around me. The students in my class were getting bolder in their comments and observations, growing louder and louder.

"Cheaters get punished."

"You were a terrible friend."

"Terrible. Terrible. Terrible."

I couldn't even hear my own thoughts, and I just couldn't take it anymore. I grabbed my bag and rushed out of the classroom. I didn't stop to fight back against the nasty comments or even think to look at who was talking. I couldn't think at all, almost as if my fight-or-flight instinct had kicked in, and all I could do was fly. So I flew away from the onlookers, from the critics, and from the hate that was coming at me.

But the voices didn't stop. As I slowed my flight to a walk, I could still hear everyone's comments.

"Look at how sad she is."

"We know you're broken."

"You're a broken, useless creature."

"You couldn't even save your husband; how could you save Elli?"

Of course, they know about him. Everyone knows about him. Everyone knows how I'm a failure, as a wife, as a friend, and as a girlfriend.

As I walked, I saw a sea of people rushing past me, pushing me and jostling me as I tried to walk. It was like trying to walk through water, the resistance was so great.

An image of Aaron's sad face appeared in my mind as the crowd thickened, people walking slower and closer around me. I could barely see through the thick crowd, but I could see Aaron's pained face, from both the funeral and AP Psych, as clear as day.

I will always be here for you. Aaron's words played over in my head, blaring like a siren. The volume was so loud I had to clench my eyes shut. I stopped moving in the crowd but could still feel the bodies around me jolting, pushing, shoving me.

"Priya." I could hear Aaron's voice, and I shook my head, trying to shake out the sound.

"No! No! No!" I was whispering—groaning—over and over again, unable to think over the voices in my head or muster up enough mental or physical power to scream.

"Cheater. Cheater. Cheater."

"Terrible. Terrible. Terrible."

"We're always watching." The Russian agent's voice from earlier in AP Gov rang in my ears, and my heart dropped into my stomach.

They're watching me. The Russians are watching me—no, have always been watching me.

"Priya, look at me!" Aaron's voice cut through the other voices, clearing the fog of verbal abuse in my head, screaming loud enough to make my eyes shoot wide open to see him standing in front of me, a look of panic and worry clear on his face. As I registered him, I noticed his hands— they were on my shoulders, gripping me tightly. Then I regis- tered our surroundings and saw we were the only two on campus in the open quad area. I looked around, wondering where the crowd of people had gone, but then my mind turned back to Aaron. I planted my eyes on his face, and his dark brown eyes looking back into mine, searching for under- standing about what was going on.

Am I being followed by the Russian government? Do they have spies in school? Is that how everyone knows about Dimitri?

My mind began to melt. Suddenly, I felt both lethargic and energized—my mind was racing, but my body felt weak. My breathing was shallow and uneven, to the point where I couldn't catch a deep enough breath. My head felt light.

Was I going to faint?

It was as if all the blood were rushing from my head to everywhere else in my body. I remembered through the fog that shifting your feet would help with blood flow. I began to shift my weight from leg to leg, feeling slightly more balanced.

"Priya, are you okay?" Aaron's words were carefully enunciated and stern as he searched for the answer to that question in my eyes rather than my words.

"I'm… fine. I'm fine," I said. In his eyes, I could see a very tiny, very frazzled reflection of myself. As my head cleared, as I felt more weighted and grounded, I looked around the area again, blinking and regaining my awareness before looking down at Aaron's hands on my shoulders. They were uncomfortably warm, but that heat gave me something to focus on for a short while and pulled me further out of my head.

Aaron continued to stare at me for a few seconds. Then his eyes fell on his hands, too, and he quickly pulled them away from my shoulders, removing the heat and allowing a cool inrush of air. He shoved his hands into his pockets and looked at the ground before looking back up, but he was looking past me, not at me.

"Priya, I... um..." His eyes darted all around me, never settling on my face. I watched him, my breathing beginning to deepen and even out.

"I think I know the answer to this, but—" Aaron let out a long, deep, and frustrated groan and closed his eyes for a second before opening them again and looking straight into mine.

"Priya, what is actually going on? Should I be worried?" Aaron's questions came as a shock to me. Aaron was always the boy who knew the boundaries, never crossed the line, and never pried. He always let me go to him when I had a problem.

I stared at him, my lips slightly parted from shock as I thought about this new, stern side of him. I started to feel something through the numbing fog around me.

It was sadness. I finally felt the sympathy for him that he deserved. Now that I could almost think straight, I came up with an answer that would make sense to us both without giving away my inner turmoil too much.

"I don't know what's going on, Aaron, but you don't have to worry," I said, pausing to see him look down and nod his head before I continued. "Aaron, this has nothing to do with you, and I need you to know that. I... I can't explain what's going on because honestly, I don't know enough to even name what's going on. Is it grief? Maybe. Maybe there isn't a name for what I'm experiencing. But whatever is going on, I can't drag you down with me as I go through it."

Aaron opened his mouth to say something, but I put my hands up to stop him. "Aaron, my mind is basically an unsolvable puzzle. I don't know what pieces are missing and which pieces fit with each other. I'm barely able to piece together my thoughts right now and put them into words without going on crazy tangents or letting my mind wander to ideas that I have but shouldn't have. And please, don't ask what those ideas are. I meant what I said at the funeral. I can't do this right now, and I don't know when I'll be able to again, or if I'll ever be able to again. I just need you to give me space and know that I don't mean to hurt you." My heart weighed heavily in my chest as I watched Aaron process what I was telling him. I was thankful that the cold, numbing fog had thinned enough for me to tell him this, but now I desperately wanted the fog to envelop me again before I divulged too much, or felt too much all at once.

Just then, I felt the hairs on my neck stand up and the prickling sensation travel up my spine.

"Do you still want to see me?" Dimitri whispered into my ear with his smooth tenor. Time began to melt. I could feel his breath against the curve of my earlobe, sending shivers through my body, starting at my head and traveling down and out through my toes. I clenched my fists at my side, forcing myself not to turn around, not to forget Aaron or all that I had just felt and said. I restrained myself from forsaking all reason and giving into my impulses.

Everything around me felt slow. The wind blew sluggishly, my eyes blinked heavily, and Aaron seemed frozen in place, like his own internal system was processing slowly.

"Do you want to see Elli?" Dimitri's words tickled the flesh of my neck, raising goosebumps in a way that was almost erotic, but instead of tempting to my body, it tempted my soul. I was about to yell out in desperation, "Yes! Is that possible?" but before I could, Aaron beat me to speaking.

"I get it. I got it then, and I get it now." Aaron's voice didn't falter, and there was a deadness in his eyes. I wanted to scream my frustration as Dimitri's presence and the hope that came with it vanished. I wanted to scream that Aaron didn't actually understand, he couldn't.

But instead, I reminded myself that thinking he did might bring him peace and comfort, so who was I to take that away from him?

I refrained from correcting him and let him continue. "Priya, I also meant what I said at the funeral. If you can't handle me being here with you physically, that's fine. But I should add that when you're ready, if you're ever ready, to have me in your life again, I'm only a call away. I'm going to be hurt no matter what. Because I'll be honest, Priya, I love you."

Aaron paused, as if the revelation would make things different, but the numbing fog surrounding had come crashing around me again, too thick to be penetrated by his sentiment. I was unable to feel what I once had for him in that moment. I couldn't even let myself try to step out from the fog. I knew that if I did, I would break down instantly, with more puzzle pieces fracturing throughout my mind.

Aaron watched my movements closely and, probably not seeing the desired reaction, sighed before continuing. "I know you're hurting now, too, but if this is how you process, then I won't try to change that or be involved in it if that's not what you want. Please take care of yourself, Priya."

He took a deep breath before quickly pushing past me and leaving me alone in the empty clearing on campus. I stared at the ground where his feet had been and counted backward from ten, trying to ignore the tension in my body and the prickling feeling over my skin. And then I closed my eyes and tried to imagine the person who usually caused my skin to prickle, praying—on ears deaf or imagined, I didn't know which—that the image in my head would come to life. But when I opened my eyes, I was still alone.

16

MAY 15TH, 2019

IT WAS after two in the morning, and I was staring at one of the previous year's AP English Language free response questions, which required the test taker to write a response about exploring the unknown. I quickly hit the "start" button on my phone's timer and watched as the time began to count down from forty minutes. I wrote feverishly as ingenious ideas came to mind.

I mumbled to myself as the ideas flowed, and I tried to capture them on paper, my hand unable to keep up as they raced along the tracks in my brain. "When I explore the unknown, I am exploring the sea. The sea is full of creatures and darkness. Dark, it's dark. What is unknown lives in the dark."

"You're doing it again." I heard the familiar female voice, loud and clear, and it silenced all other thoughts in my head. My hand stopped writing, and all I could focus on was the ringing in my ear and the fading sound of Elli's voice on repeat.

"Elli?" I whispered as I whipped my head around the room, looking to my right and seeing the foot of my bed. My eyes stung slightly and took a second to adjust as I looked at an object farther away than a laptop screen. I didn't see Elli on the bed, but I felt the prickling on the back of my neck and sensed that she was behind me. I looked to my left but only saw the darkness of my bathroom, with the door slightly ajar. I continued to stare into the darkness of my bathroom. The fast beat of my heart was the only sound that cut through the silence ringing in my ears.

"If you want to see me, look harder." This time, Elli's voice sounded like it was coming from my laptop. I looked down and picked up the device, holding the speakers to my ear and waiting for her voice to come again. After a minute, when it still hadn't, I set my laptop back on the desk, staring at the screen in front of me and the prompts of the old AP test.

After a few more minutes of nothing, I scrolled the page up on my screen and looked at the short story prompt next, getting ready to write my response. As I was reading, though, the story began to register differently in my brain. It didn't seem like just any story, as certain words seemed wrong, and certain phrases out of place. As I read through it, my brain picked up and fixated on those out of place words and phrases. They called out to me like a haunting melody that made you wonder for days where you'd heard it before.

"It's not what you think." Dimitri's voice this time, but soon after, his voice was replaced by static white noise, the same noise that usually occurred when the US government had a bad signal while trying to contact me.

"Eagle come in. Eagle come in," I tested, hoping to hear the familiar agent voices of Stephan and Monica, but instead, the white noise persisted, with some undecipherable mumbling poking through.

You're on your own, Priya. What is Dimitri talking about?

"It's not what you think."

So what is it? As I read through the story over and over again, I began to make note of certain capitalized letters, certain words that were standing out to me, and began to write them down, hoping to find some significance in them as I annotated.

That capital D looks weird. The word "is" shouldn't be there.

I continued to make note of whatever my brain picked up until I had a bunch of random letters, some capitalized, some not, and a few phrases written down.

What was the point of this story?

I stared down at the pieces of the story I had written down, trying to figure out what I was staring at, and gradually piecing together some of the words and letters.

It says something about the mind, and control, and R government.

I gasped as I realized it was a code. It was a hidden message. I desperately began to decode it. I continued moving the different pieces of the code around until I wrote the last word, "alive," on the paper in front of me, my breath catching at the finished code.

"D is alive. R Government uses mind control. E is alive," I whispered aloud.

"Priya!" My mom's voice snapped me out of my thoughts, and I jumped in my seat. I swiveled my chair around to see her standing in the doorway wearing gym clothes, a pair of leggings, and a t-shirt with a zip-up jacket over it. It must have been early morning because my mom went to the gym around four a.m. every day.

"Priya, I've been saying your name and knocking for two minutes. What are you doing?" she asked.

"Studying for the AP test," I said quickly. My mom clicked her tongue and shook her head.

"Did you sleep at all? You have to be up for school in a little over two hours," she chastised me and I shrugged.

"I couldn't sleep." This wasn't a lie. Earlier in the night, I had spent a good hour tossing and turning in bed, my thoughts chasing each other, before I decided to get up and put them to good use.

"Well, try to sleep now. You know what not sleeping does to your condition." I nodded. She had been watching me closely since Elli's death. I knew she had good intentions, but after the message I had just received, I didn't know if I would be able to sleep.

"Okay." I closed my laptop and put my things away. When I turned back around and stood up, my mom nodded, turned off my lights, and walked out of the room, closing the door behind her. I listened to her footsteps go down the stairs and walked over to my bed, my thoughts finally settling just enough for me to feel tired. When I got in bed, I continued to stare at the ceiling for a few moments, the hidden message flitting through my brain repeatedly, until the burning in my eyes forced me to close them. I finally fell asleep with one prominent thought on my mind.

Dimitri and Elli are alive, and I have to find them.

M y leg bounced up and down as I sat in the waiting room of the doctor's office, eating and waiting for Avery to call me in for our session. As soon as I had finished my AP test and was let out, I immediately drove over and got to the office a bit earlier than anticipated. I used the time to get some lunch and eat a small sandwich in the waiting room as I scrolled through my social media accounts, seeing pictures of dogs and celebrities and a lot of memes. Some of them made me smile; a few made me laugh.

"Priya?" I heard Avery's voice and looked up from my phone to see her smiling softly at me. I smiled back and quickly wrapped my sandwich up and put my stuff away before following her to her office down the maze of hallways, which I had solved many times.

When we entered her office, it was lit with the same ambient orange glow as always and decorated with the same pieces of art made by her kids. The office made me feel calm just by entering, although I couldn't tell if it was because it was familiar or because of her decor.

"So, tell me what made you schedule an appointment for today. We weren't scheduled to see each other for another week." Avery's voice was soft. I always wondered if that was her therapist voice or if it was her natural voice. I nodded, knowing she must have been shocked to hear from her nurses that I had made an appointment ahead of schedule. In the last year, we had moved from seeing each other once every two weeks to seeing each other on an as needed basis, while Dr. Worblack and I started to see each other once every three months. Things had been going so well on my end that I only needed fifteen-minute check-ins with Dr. Worblack and half hour appointments with Avery.

I looked at Avery, then at the paintings on the wall as the white noise began to penetrate my ears. I held back the instinct to communicate with the US government.

"Do you remember my best friend, Elli?" I asked her, my voice sounding removed and devoid of any emotion. That wasn't my intention, but I had suddenly become lost in thought as the memories rushed through my mind like a waterfall.

"Your best friend from childhood, right?" Avery asked, and I nodded, looking away from the paintings to her, then down at my hands as I fiddled with my fingers.

"She died in April. The twenty-seventh. Six o-seven a.m," I said, my body shutting down as the numbness overtook me.

"Oh my gosh, I'm so sorry, Priya. I can't imagine what you must be going through. How about you walk me through it?" Avery said, and I shrugged my shoulders.

"She died from alcohol poisoning. It wasn't the first time she was hospitalized, but this time... she ended up dying." I peeked at Avery through my lashes to see her empathetic expression.

"That's horrible. How have you been handling it?"

I tilted my head to the side as I looked down at my lap. "*C'est la vie.*"

There was a pause.

"Well, yes, such is life, but that doesn't mean it's easy. Are you still taking your medication?" Avery asked. My fingers stopped picking at each other as I geared up to answer honestly, but suddenly, a voice protruded through the white noise in my ears.

"Eagle one to Priya. Avery is working with the Russians. Priya, do you copy?" Stephan said, and I tensed up. I made a display of moving an imaginary piece of hair out of my face before pressing the little button in my ear.

"I copy," I whispered, feeling a mix of emotions, relief that the government was once again communicating with me, but also betrayal that Avery would be working for the Russians. I trusted Avery this whole time, and she betrayed me? How long had this been going on? Was she always on their side?

"What was that?" Avery asked.

"I said, I am," I lied, looking her straight in the eyes as I set my folded hands in my lap and crossed my legs, sitting up straight and taking a deep breath.

She can't know you know, I thought to myself, the facade I had put on for years coming back up. All the training the government had given me, all the time I had pretended to be Priya Agarwal and not Priya Ivanov, coming back to me.

Avery watched me suspiciously, and I wondered if she had intercepted the message from the government. I watched her closely, wondering if she was going to open her mouth and speak with a Russian accent all of a sudden, but she didn't.

"I'm glad to hear that, Priya. How about we talk about how this has affected you. How are your studies? Do you feel you were able to mourn the loss properly?" Avery asked, sitting back in her chair.

I shrugged again.

Elli isn't dead.

"I feel like I'm already moving on. Like I said, *c'est la vie.* That was her motto. So, I'm trying to live like she would want me to live," I said.

"And how do you think she would want you to live?"

She wants me to find her. "I think she would want me to be happy. To move on, go to college, live my life." I put on a convincing display of calm.

"I think that's very mature of you. I'm glad to see you're handling this so well, but you know it's okay to be sad for a while. She was a big part of your life, for your whole life," Avery said, and I nodded, acknowledging this truth.

"What about your family? And what about Aaron? How have you all been since this? I'm sure Aaron has been a big support to you," Avery said with a smile, and I flinched, but didn't know why.

"Aaron and I broke up a couple weeks ago. I didn't see

our relationship progressing anymore." I waved my hand, then dragged it through my loose hair and set it back down in my lap.

"Is that true?"

Yes, because if Dimitri is alive, then I'm still married. "Well, yes. At the time, I didn't want to bring him down with my sadness, but since the breakup I have... seen things clearly. We wouldn't have worked out." I shrugged. *My heart still belongs with Dimitri, and I am loyal to him.*

"Do you feel any sort of sadness right now, Priya?" Avery asked. I watched her movements, wondering if she was catching on to me. Maybe I needed to be sad in order to throw the Russians off my scent. If I wasn't torn up, then it would make it obvious that I knew Elli and Dimitri were alive.

"Some days I feel empty, like I'm on autopilot, and it's just easier to shut down emotionally. Today is one of those days. I just feel numb to the whole situation," I said. It wasn't necessarily a lie, but it also wasn't the full truth.

"That's a common coping mechanism, Priya. Do you feel like you're simply trying to shut out the emotions so you can move on?"

Instinctively, I nodded, making her nod back and smile.

"Would you like to explore those feelings you're trying to shut off today? It may be uncomfortable, but it might be help-ful," she said.

Was this something I had to do in order to keep up the facade? In actuality, I just wanted to leave and find Dimitri and Elli. I needed to find more messages and figure out where they were. I wanted to figure out what this mind control from the Russian government was. Maybe staying with Avery was causing more harm than good. Was she working with them to keep me here while they tracked Dimitri and Elli? Maybe she was going to use mind control on me during this session to extract the information I had.

"Actually, I don't feel ready to face those emotions just yet," I said. Avery watched me closely for a few moments. Then her smile picked up at the corners, and she nodded again.

"I understand. Is there anything you'd like to talk about in particular?"

The rest of the session was simply me talking about school and a made-up anxiety I had about going to college. I could tell Avery was trying to bring it back to Elli, trying to hammer in the fact that she was dead—as if she didn't know Elli was really alive. So when the session finally ended, I let out a sigh of relief.

Before letting me out, Avery said, "Priya, please reach out to me if you want to talk about those emotions more."

I nodded before making my way out through the maze of a hallway.

As I got into my car and set my phone in its holder, my sister called me.

"Oh, hi!" she said. "How was your test? Did you already see Avery?"

I buckled up and pulled out of the parking lot. "Test went well. I think I got a four or a five. I just left Avery's."

"And?"

I shrugged. "And it was good. We just talked about Elli and how I was coping." I kept my answers purposely short. After finding out that Avery was working for the Russians, I wasn't sure who to trust.

"Ooookay. Do you want to get lunch on Saturday? Mom said she has a weekend trip and won't be back until Sunday."

"Lunch sounds good. Are we going to eat in the city or in San Jose?"

"San Jose. I want Korean food, and God *knows* there's no good Korean food in the city."

I chuckled. She was right about that. "All right, sounds good. Just text me the address of where to meet you."

"Ho-kay. See you then." My sister hung up, and I continued driving, starting to play some music to pass the time faster.

As soon as I parked my car at my house, the thought from the middle of last night began replaying in my head.

Dimitri and Elli are alive, and I have to find them. But where do I start?

When I turned the engine of my car off and the music stopped blasting in my ears, I heard the white noise from the government's poor signal again.

I groaned in frustration and tried to hit my ear a few times to fix the signal, but nothing worked. I couldn't even take the piece out of my ear and inspect it because it was surgically implanted.

I got out of the car and went inside the house, noting that my mom wasn't home yet and probably wouldn't be home for a couple of hours. Once I set my things down and got a snack from the kitchen, I headed up to my room to begin my research.

I had no leads, no hints, and no idea of how to start, but maybe the first step was to fix the damn signal so I could speak to the US government. They would definitely know what was going on.

I opened my laptop and paused as I saw the picture of Elli and me I had chosen as a screensaver. It was the picture of us from our trip to Great America a few years before. Elli was wearing a t-shirt even though it was fall, and I, of course, was bundled up. We were standing in front of the giant pumpkin at the entrance, our arms around each other.

The picture, although painful to look at, gave me greater hope and motivation. I had to find her—I had to be committed to this mission.

I immediately pulled up a search engine and began searching for anything and everything that could help me solve my earpiece problem.

What should I even search? Earpiece fixing? Government device not working?

I began to try a myriad of different keywords and ended up down a rabbit hole of different websites and articles, none of which were helpful. However, I did learn a lot about Beats headphones.

All right. Last shot. Skull voice implant not working.

I typed in the words and was surprised by the text on the first site that popped up: my microwave auditory device is not working. How do I fix it?

I had no idea what a microwave auditory device was, but when I clicked on it, it took me to a forum page where an anonymous poster was communicating with the government through a "microwave auditory device" or "voice to skull" device that had since gone dead. As I scrolled through the responses, most were skeptic and malicious. However, there was one response that caught my attention from a poster named Elliphant. The post read: the US government has shut down their voice to skull technology because the Russians have a mole that is using the technology.

All of a sudden, through the white noise in my ear came a voice with a Russian accent, saying, "We're always watching."

I jumped in surprise at the voice and immediately cleared my browser history and closed all the windows I had opened, but the voices kept coming, sometimes muffled and incomprehensible, but sometimes ominously audible through the white noise.

"We know you have information."

"You filthy American."

The voices kept attacking me, and I began to claw at my ear in desperation, trying to block the voices. I knew they were coming from the earpiece. They had control of the US government's voice to skull devices, and I prayed America regained control of them. I didn't know how long that would take, but in the meantime, I had to figure out something that would stop the voices, or at least block them out.

The only thing I could think of to tune the voices out was to play music with a deep bass at an extremely loud volume, so I immediately started playing my hip-hop music. The bass's low frequencies usually did a good job of jamming the frequencies of my earpiece, almost like the vibrations rattled the piece inside. Once I found the song that worked the best, I kept it on repeat and tried to find a moment to calm down.

Soon, the voices were too muffled to be understood. I let out a sigh of relief, staring at the screen in front of me, the picture of Elli and me, and thought about that forum page poster with the name Elliphant.

The name stuck out because of the obvious reason, Elli, but also because elephants were Elli's favorite animals.

Was that Elli? Was she trying to warn me? To send me a message?

"Priya!"

My mom yelled over the music, and I jumped in my chair, turning toward her as she stood in the doorway to my room.

She was staring at me with annoyance, scowling and using her hands to motion for me to turn the volume of my music down. I paused before nodding and turning back to my laptop, hitting the volume button to lower the volume and praying that the Russian voices didn't come back.

Thankfully, they didn't.

"What is the matter with you? Are you trying to blow your eardrums out?" my mom asked from behind me. I looked back at her, simply shaking my head as I let out the breath I had been unconsciously holding. My mom simply made a "tsk" sound, clicking her tongue, before walking into my room and sitting down on the edge of my bed.

"How was Avery?" she asked.

You mean the Russian mole?

"She's fine. We just talked about Elli and… everything." I shrugged.

"How was the AP test?"

"I think I got a four or a five on it, but who knows?" I said with another shrug. My mom watched me carefully, as if she were analyzing my every move. For some reason, I felt the need to straighten my back and have good posture. I rolled my head around and heard some pops in my neck, then sighed and rolled my shoulders back.

"*Acha*, listen. I'm going to be gone for a weekend trip to the LA office. I leave on Friday and am staying with your *masi*. I'll be back Sunday afternoon around two. Will you be okay?" My mom's eyes settled on mine and I nodded.

"Yeah. Jasmine *didi* told me you were going to be gone, so we're getting lunch on Saturday. If I don't feel okay, I'll either have her stay the weekend, or I'll go up to her," I said, knowing fully well that neither was going to happen, but my mom seemed to feel some relief after hearing those options. Her shoulders relaxed and her eyes wandered off of my face and around the room.

"That's good. I'm glad you guys are getting lunch," she said. "Well, I'm going to go make dinner. Is spaghetti okay?"

I nodded again, my neck feeling sore from all the nodding I was doing.

"Good. Dinner will be ready in an hour. Come set the table in around forty minutes, please," she said before getting up from the bed and walking out of the room.

I watched her leave and relished the pure silence that surrounded her echoing footsteps. I sighed and smiled, feeling proud of the music maneuver that saved my ears from the Russian onslaught.

MAY 18TH, 2019

I woke up to a blissful silence for all of about five seconds. After that, the static noise came on fast, along with some intercepted voices from various radio stations.

"Milk, cheese, eggs, butter."

"It's hotter than the devil."

It sounded like someone was constantly changing the radio and only ads were playing, one for some weird hot sauce and one involving mothers going to the grocery store.

The earpiece had started working again shortly after I found that voice to skull article, although the only signals coming through were radio signals and the occasional Russian. My attempts to find Elli were always met by dead ends. I felt stuck, but still had hope. I just had to wait it out.

I stared at the ceiling for a few minutes, then reached for my phone and checked the time. I had at least an hour and a half before I had to leave to meet my sister for lunch. The static noise and the intercepted voices in my head made me want to work on fixing the ear device again, but I knew I wasn't smart enough to understand the jargon I'd read on the forum page with the instructions on how to fix it.

I rolled over in bed with my phone and scrolled through my social media, feeling the relief of the cool sheet against my skin, which I suddenly realized was soaked with sweat. I must have been so distracted by the intercepted radio signals that I didn't register how hot I was. I immediately pushed the sheets off my body and stretched, feeling the sun streaming through my open blinds onto my body.

I picked up my phone and walked to the bathroom, fanning myself with my hands. I would have to take a shower, even though I'd showered the previous night. I set my phone down, and I put my hair up in a bun, turned on the shower, and let the water heat up. Despite the heatwave we were experiencing, I couldn't bring myself to step into a freezing shower. I had to acclimate myself slowly to the water, so I set the temperature to warm and started playing my shower playlist.

I was about to step into the shower when I felt a prickling sensation on the back of my neck—one that made me feel like I was being watched.

I looked around the room, seeing no one. I couldn't help the prickling on my neck, however, and just knew someone was watching. I scanned the bathroom carefully, but then my eyes settled on my phone, and I stared at the front-facing camera that was pointing upward.

Could someone see me through it? Immediately, I dropped my hand towel over the phone, covering the camera.

I stepped into the warm shower and felt the overwhelming warmth from the steam and the water. I turned the knob to the right to cool it slightly and began to scrub my body of the sweaty gunk that had piled up during the night.

"We're watching you."

"You're filth."

"You belong in the trash."

I dropped my loofah to the shower floor. I looked around the bathroom again, unable to see past the fogged-up glass of my shower door. I swiped at the doors, trying to see through the droplets of water. All I could see were the seemingly bare bathroom walls.

They're watching me? How are they watching me? Is it my phone camera?

I pulled open the shower door and looked around the room again. My eyes roamed the walls, the sink, and even the toilet, looking for something. I didn't know what.

All of a sudden, my eyes were drawn to the top left corner of the bathroom where I saw a small, spherical protrusion from the wall. It looked like the kind of cameras you saw in malls or offices—those black glossy spheres that stuck to ceilings.

They're watching me!

I immediately dropped down, getting my hair wet as I reached up to turn the water off. Kneeling at the height of the tub, I maneuvered around it to reach up out of the shower and grabbed the gray towel hanging on the rack. I pulled it down by one edge and caught the other edge before it hit the ground. I draped the towel around me and stood up, making sure all the important parts of my body were covered. Quickly, I stepped out of the bathroom and into my bedroom, but I stopped before dropping my towel.

The blinds were open.

Did I open them last night? I didn't remember doing so.

I quickly pulled at the string to shutter the blinds, but I couldn't shake the feeling that I was still being watched. I cautiously went to my dresser and closet, picking out the clothes I wanted to wear while making sure my towel was tightly wrapped around me. Once I had the clothes in my hands, I dove under my sheets and got dressed. It was hard to breathe after a while, hard to make sure I was still covered at all times, but I managed to completely dress myself under the sheets. I had to take a minute just to breathe after doing so, so I popped my head out of the blankets and took some deep breaths, trying to calm myself, but the calm was short-lived.

"We've got you now."

"You can't hide from us."

"Priya, run!"

Elli's command rang through the Russian voices closing in on me, and my eyes popped wide open as I flung the sheets off my body. I saw something move out of the corner of my eye, and I grabbed my phone before bolting out of my room and down the stairs. I grabbed my keys from the wall hook, shoved my feet into my sandals, and rushed out the door, making sure to lock it behind me.

"You can't stop us!"

"We're going to get you!"

I ran to my car and hastily started it, blasting the heavy bass music to drown out the Russians before driving off to lunch earlier than intended. My heart was beating wildly; my hands were shaking. Gripping the steering wheel gave me something to physically and emotionally hold on to, but I needed to cool off—literally—so I turned the air conditioning on full blast and sighed as soon as it started to cool the car down.

"Do you think you can outrun us?" The Russians' voices were muffled for the most part, thanks to my music, but I couldn't shake the feeling that an agent was following me in person. Would I be safe at the restaurant?

My anxiety was through the roof, and the drive to safety couldn't have been longer, but I knew I was speeding and reached the area much sooner than my GPS could have predicted.

When I pulled into the parking lot for lunch, I sat in the car for a moment as I tried to calm down. Even though the car was off, my hands still gripped the steering wheel, and my body shook from anxiety and adrenaline. The voices were now muffled, reverting to intercepted radio ads.

"Check in at the inn!"

"Beat the heat with this neat sheet!"

Harmless.

I need to walk it off. I think being near a radio is messing with the sound. I pushed open my car door and was immediately hit by the dry heat. I let out a sigh, then groaned when I realized I'd forgotten to put deodorant or even sunscreen on. I knew I had a deodorant in the glove compartment, but I needed to get away from the radio fast.

"Milk. Milk. Milk. Milk."

"Rodger Federer has a Ferrero Rocher."

The ads were getting louder and weirder, and I quickly closed my car door and walked up to the restaurant. There seemed to already be a wait, so I silently patted myself on the back for being early and put my name down. I texted my sister to give them my name if she got there before me and began walking around the plaza, not wanting to stand outside in this heat. Seeing a Korean skincare store I wanted to check out, I stepped in and was relieved to be blasted by the air conditioning. Even though it provided physical relief, I still felt tremors coursing through my nervous system, so I browsed the aisles, deciding I needed some retail therapy.

"Priya?"

I froze in my spot at the familiar voice and restrained myself from groaning.

Aaron.

Why does he pop up everywhere?

I turned around with a brittle, inauthentic smile on my

face. Yet upon seeing him, a warmth flooded my system that almost calmed my nerves entirely.

Stop it! You're still married—Dimitri is alive. Don't lose focus.

"Hi, Aaron," I said, shifting my weight to my right foot.

"Hey, I… uh… I know I'm supposed to give you space, but I saw you walking. I promise I meant to leave you alone, but I'm a little worried."

I scrunched my eyebrows at him before realization hit.

"Aaron, I'm fine. Please don't use Elli's death as an excuse to talk to me right now. I—"

"No! No, that's not what I meant!" Aaron said, putting both his hands up and getting defensive. "I meant… I mean… Priya, your shirt is on backward, and your shorts are unbuttoned and open." He looked to his left, embarrassed.

I looked down at myself, about to fight back, but I saw that he was completely right. My V-neck shirt was on backwards *and* inside out, and my shorts were unbuttoned with the fly down.

"Oh my God," I said. I turned around and looked around the store, thankful that it was mostly empty. I moved toward the wall and did up my shorts before facing Aaron again.

"I'm… I… I don't know what happened," I said, embarrassed, my nerves quickening. *I must have not seen my clothes properly under the sheets. But how did I not notice?*

"It's okay, Priya. I just… I'm sorry. I didn't think it would be right for you to be walking around like that, so I had to speak up. But I'll go now. Bye." He turned to dash off as I opened my mouth to thank him, but he was gone before I could say anything.

I'm sorry. Thank you.

My phone vibrated in my back pocket, and I pulled it out,

realizing I hadn't even brought my purse or wallet. *Shit. I'm driving without my license. I better not get pulled over.*

The call was from my sister. I tapped the answer button and walked out of the store, looking both ways to try and see if Aaron was still around, but couldn't find him anywhere.

"Hello?"

"Hey! I'm at the restaurant. They let me sit down because I told them you're in the bathroom. Are you nearby?"

"I'm next door. Walking over now."

"Ho-kay! See you soon," she said in a singsong voice.

The restaurant was crowded when I entered, and I made a beeline for the bathroom so I could change without Jasmine noticing. There were three stalls, and I was thankful the larger one was open.

Once I was situated and looked presentable, I went out and slid into my sister's booth.

"'Sup?" I said, feeling the cool leather booth against the back of my thighs. I had a feeling I was going to get stuck to them when I started sweating.

"Oh, hi! How are you?" Jasmine asked, elongating the "oo" sound in the word "you."

"I'm fine. You?"

"Dying at work. I have this new client who is giving me *hell*. They're calling me at all hours of the night, and I freaking hate it. But I have to show that I'm going above and beyond if I want this promotion, so…" She shrugged, as if to say *what can I do?* "I hope you're enjoying not being in the workforce yet. It sucks." She dragged her fingers through her hair, exaggerating her side part.

I simply nodded before taking a large gulp of my water.

"Dang, thirsty much? Is the water off at home?" she asked, and I sighed when I set my empty water glass down.

Immediately, a waiter came rushing over with a water jug and set it on the table before taking our orders.

After handing our menus to the waiter and thanking her, I said, "It's so hot, and I didn't drink any water this morning. I rushed over here and even forgot my purse and wallet."

"You're driving without your license? You better not get pulled over. Drive the speed limit for once, please."

"I know, *didi*."

Her phone buzzed with a text, and I looked around the restaurant, noticing the lack of voices from my earpiece and then realizing why when I heard the heavy bass in the Korean hip-hop music playing. I watched as the staff in the eatery walked around, carrying huge portions of food and *bonchons,* side dishes, to different tables.

"So, anyway," Jasmine said, pulling me out of my people watching, "how's Aaron? I think I saw him walk by earlier."

I looked at her with a slight head tilt, trying to remember when we'd last talked about Aaron.

"I told you we broke up, right?" I asked, and her eyes went wide as her mouth fell open. I guessed that was my answer.

"What? No! Why? When?"

I laughed at her rapid-fire questioning and shrugged.

"Um, when? At the funeral. Why? Because… because…" *Because I'm still married to Dimitri.* The truth ran through my mind, but I couldn't tell my sister that. I knew for a fact she would tell me to take the medication, but I couldn't, not when they were given to me by agents of the Russian government.

"Because I need space right now to heal, and I don't want to drag him down. Maybe when I'm not so, you know—" I gestured vaguely with my hands. "—we'll try again. But I can't have him in my life right now."

The waiter came back with our food—bibimbap for my sister and a cold noodle dish for me. I thanked the waiter and looked up at Jasmine. She was watching me carefully, but when I frowned at her, she put up one hand and turned her head down to one side, her way of saying she was backing off.

"All right. I don't understand why he couldn't be there to support you through this, but... okay. You know yourself better than I do."

I nodded and picked up my metal chopsticks.

"Why try again with him when I'll be here?" Dimitri's voice asked. I smiled down at my food, taking deep breaths to calm myself down. *I know, Dima, I know.*

"We see you."

"We've got you now."

"You're both about to pay."

I whipped my head around, feeling the adrenaline in my body flowing freely and fast.

"Priya? What's wrong?"

I looked at Jasmine, then around the restaurant again. My brain felt like it was tearing down the middle, trying to juggle between two worlds.

"Nothing. I just... thought I saw someone I knew."

I began picking up the noodles with my chopsticks, trying to decide whether I should run away or stay seated. I couldn't alert my sister to what was going on—she would probably intervene, and that would go horribly—but I also couldn't do nothing. I didn't see any Russians, though, and I didn't think they would attack me in broad daylight in a packed restaurant.

So I just ate quietly as my sister checked her phone and ranted about a male coworker who was getting on her nerves.

"I swear, he's the epitome of a hegemonic male."

"Sounds like it," I said absentmindedly, suddenly feeling nauseated.

It's probably from all the stress of today. And maybe I'm dehydrated. I picked up my water and took a long gulp as Jasmine continued talking, but I almost choked when I saw the noodles in my bowl begin to move. I set my water down a little too forcefully and watched as the noodles—worms? Small snakes? I couldn't tell what they were, but they were slithering and swimming in the soup in the bowl. My stomach somersaulted over and over again, my mouth tingling as it did when I was about to throw up.

"You won't escape today," came a whisper in my ear. It was the Russian who killed Dimitri. He was so close I could feel his breath on my neck.

I immediately bolted out of the booth and ran toward the bathroom, covering my mouth with my hand and almost tripping over my feet a few times. I could hear my sister call out to me, but I had to get to a toilet immediately.

I threw my body against the women's bathroom door, flung myself into a stall, and lurched over the toilet before letting out the contents of my stomach. I vomited mostly water, but I could see chunks of the creatures I had eaten come out too. My forehead heated up, and my face began to prickle. I tried to hold my hair out of the way of the vomit, but I felt myself getting tired as I kneeled on the ground of the bathroom.

Ew, ew, ew. Fuck, this is so gross. Were the Russians poisoning me? What were they feeding me?

"Priya!" Jasmine's voice came from behind me, and her hands lightly touched my neck as she held back my hair. I felt immediate relief that she was there, even as I continued gagging and breathing heavily over the toilet bowl.

"Are you going to be okay? What happened?"

"I don't know," I said on an outward breath before gagging again. My right hand shook as I brought it up to my face to wipe away some baby hairs that were sticking to my skin.

"Jeez, was your food bad?"

"Yeah," I said with a nod. "I think so."

I sighed and fell forward against the left side of the stall, leaning my forehead on the cool metal. It was gross but felt good and bathed my skin in a chilling relief.

After I regained my composure and strength, my sister helped me up and left to pay the bill while I cleaned myself up.

Once I had washed my mouth out and wiped down my body from the bathroom germs, I walked out of the restroom toward the entrance and saw my sister speaking with someone dressed in similar attire to the hostess, but this woman seemed to be the manager of the restaurant.

"I'm so sorry, ma'am! Please, the bill is on us. We're so sorry," the woman said, apologizing profusely as my sister nodded and looked around, probably feeling embarrassed.

"It's okay," I said to the manager, and she nodded at me quickly before my sister and I left the restaurant.

As we walked out, Jasmine said, "I can meet you at home if you want. I can pick up pho? Or maybe something else that might be good for your stomach."

I liked the sound of pho, but not in this heat.

"Hmm, maybe some *khichidi*? Or do you know how to make rice porridge?" I asked.

"Yeah, I'll meet you at the house. Drive safely!" she said, and we split up.

～

I lay on the couch watching an Indian version of *Sex and the City* as my sister cooked in the kitchen. The four friends in the show were women living in Mumbai. I was enthralled by the walls they were trying to break down in Indian culture, but I was appalled by the way they were doing it.

"Here you go," Jasmine said, carrying a bowl in from the kitchen. "It's just pure rice porridge, like the ones we had in Hong Kong. Let me know if you need salt. Mom only had low-sodium chicken stock, for some reason."

"Thanks, *didi*," I said weakly as I sat up. I draped the couch blanket across my legs before putting the hot bowl down so it wouldn't burn me.

"Is this that Indian *Sex and the City* show?" she asked. I nodded and turned the volume up.

"I like this girl," I said, pointing to the one currently on the screen. "She's Punjabi."

My sister snorted. "Is it because she's Punjabi?"

"No. It's because she's sassy and super unfiltered." *And she reminds me of Elli.*

We continued watching the show together, and I settled back into the couch when I finished eating. There were some scandalous scenes that made me feel slightly uncomfortable —I was watching with my sister, after all—but I soon got over the discomfort when more humorous and wholesome feminist scenes appeared. The experience felt very familiar, but I couldn't remember a time when my sister and I had binge-watched a show together. We've binged movies before, like the Twilight series (not one of my favorites, but Jasmine enjoyed them), but we'd never watched a TV series uninter-rupted before.

Still, something about it felt so familiar.

Eventually, I figured it out. "You know, Elli and I used to watch reruns of *The Nanny* like this. We would sit for hours in silence until mom came home. Then we would all have dinner together, Elli would stay over, and the marathon would continue."

My sister sat quietly, as if she was waiting for me to continue, but I didn't feel like saying more. I didn't want to sound like I was still mourning when I knew Elli was still alive. And it was only a matter of time until I saw her again. I didn't know how I knew I would see her soon, but I knew it. I just had to figure out how.

"I remember that being your show," Jasmine said.

We continued watching until an alert appeared on the screen, asking if we were still watching.

"Oh, shit. I should probably head back. Traffic is going to be hell," she said as she stood up. I set my bowl on the ground and got up with her, walking over to the door.

"Mom's coming back tomorrow, right?"

"Yeah. She said around two p.m."

"Damn, I would stay over to see her if I didn't have to work tomorrow. That asshole Mark is making me come in to work on this case on a freaking Sunday." She shook her head and slid on her sandals.

"Text or call me if you need anything, okay?" she reminded me as we hugged, and I nodded against the top of her head.

"I will."

She pulled away and headed out. I locked the door behind her and yawned, stretching. I walked back to the living room, picked up my bowl, and headed to the kitchen to wash whatever small amount of dishes were left before deciding it was time for bed. After escaping death twice in one day, I figured I deserved the much-needed rest.

18

MAY 19TH, 2019

"PRIYA, LISTEN TO ME."

The voice poked through my dreams and startled me awake, lifting the fog of my dream, and as it dissipated, so did any memory of the dream.

What's going on?

"Priya, listen to me." I gasped, hearing Elli's voice and feeling a prickle all over my body as I reached for my bedside lamp and turned it on. I pulled my hand back and rubbed at my burning eyes before reaching for my phone and seeing it was only 4 a.m.

I sighed and let my head fall back against my pillow. I gulped.

"I hear you, Elli, but I can't see you," I said out into the air, staring up at the stuccoed ceiling and tracing the outlines of the lumps of plaster.

"But I'm right here," she said, her voice floating at my right side, clearer than before. I lazily turned my head toward the wall and froze.

Lying beside me, with her head propped up by her hand,

was Elli. She was wearing ripped denim shorts and a black tank top with her hair up in a ponytail. Her hazel eyes were dark in the lighting, and her face was shadowed slightly. But the image of her was as clear as day.

"Oh, my God." I sat up and turned to face her completely. She smiled, then fell back laughing.

"Well, don't act like I'm a ghost. You knew I was alive, didn't you?"

I stuttered as I tried to find the right words. "N-no... I mean, yes. But I-I don't understand."

Elli's head fell to the left as she watched me.

I smiled. "I did, though. I knew you were alive." I watched her cross and uncross her legs and fling her arm over her head to look up at the ceiling.

"You always were the smart one," she said, and I shook my head.

"I don't understand, though. Where have you been? What happened?"

Elli stared at the ceiling for a minute before sighing and looking at me. "You're under the Russian government's control, Priya, that's what's going on."

I gawked at her. "What? No, I'm not! Are you calling me a double agent?" I said incredulously.

"No, Priya, I'm talking about mind control. I'm talking about the Russians' secret weapon, the one that Dimitri has been working on for the past two plus years." She sat up, crossing her right leg over her left and bending her knee up into a triangle. "Priya, this is all a dream. You're living in a dream. The Russians have a sort of mind control on you, and the whole world is a simulation by the Russian government. Dimitri was working on how to get you guys out of this simulation-style dream, but even the Russians don't know how to take someone out. But Dimitri figured it out, and he and I *both* got out."

"How? What is it? What's the way?"

"Guess," she said. I sighed as I leaned on my side and looked at her.

What's the commonality between Dimitri and Elli? How did they both get out of this? They literally have nothing in common. Except—

I gasped. "You both died! Or... supposedly died? I think? I don't... understand."

"Priya, have you ever had a dream where you're falling? Or where you die? Did you ever actually die, or did you wake up?"

I thought back to all the vivid dreams I had where I almost died. There weren't many, but enough to gather a concrete answer.

"I woke up," I whispered, and Elli nodded.

"So how did Dimitri and I wake up from this dream?"

"You... died? Or rather, you woke up." My brain began to race and suddenly, it was starting to make sense to me. "I'm in a dream. This world, this simulation, it's a—it's a dream." I looked at her, hoping that she would confirm my thoughts.

"Yes, Priya. This simulation is a dream. You're in a coma in the real world, and you're dreaming. That's what this world is. But it's more complicated than that. Certain things you do here are mimicked in the real world. Like eating. If you eat here, you're eating in the real world, and vice versa. Let's say you stop eating in the real world, or your body rejects the food here. You've basically rejected the food in the real world." She tilted her head down but turned her eyes up to me as if she were trying to tell me something more than just an explanation of the connection between the two worlds.

I stared at her as I processed what she was saying, and then the answer hit me like a truck.

"Oh my God! The Russians have been keeping me under through the medication! I stopped taking it, and the drug that keeps me under stopped working!" I said, and Elli cringed slightly.

"Not... exactly. You stopping the medication has allowed our voices and images to get through, like in a dream when you hear your alarm go off but don't necessarily wake up. Dimitri has been trying to reach you for a year, but the medication has been blocking him for the most part. So it's good that you stopped taking them. However, there's something else you need to do to wake up."

I looked at her. Then I nodded, finally understanding fully.

"I have to... die."

"Yes." She said it with a smile. Horrified, I stared at her.

"I still don't understand. What about my mom? And my sister?"

Elli sighed again. "Priya, they're fake. Your real mom and real sister are in the real world, waiting for you." Her tone implored me to think harder about the situation, as if it were an obvious answer. And it should have been. This whole situation should have been obvious to me the whole time, but I was kept under by the medication.

"So if I... die, I'll see *everyone* again?"

"Yes. But don't consider it dying. Just consider it waking up."

"But I don't... I... I'm scared."

She reached out and placed her hand on mine, which was against the bed. Feeling her warm hand resting on my cold one suddenly shifted things. It was different from just seeing her. The tangible feeling of her allowed the information she told me to settle because I knew she was real. Then I thought of something else.

"Wait, but how am I seeing you and feeling you if only your voices can get through?" I asked.

"Dimitri is super smart, baby girl. You picked a good one. He found out how to basically project an image into your subconscious, like the Russians do it. So you can see us and interact with us how you would anyone else in this world." My ears picked up at that.

"Us? You mean… I can see him too?" I asked, looking around. Elli laughed.

"Yes, but not now. I basically fought him to see you first. Sorry, you're stuck with me for now."

"No! Oh my gosh, no! Elli! I'm so happy to see you," I said, immediately looking back at her and trying to convince her I wasn't some ungrateful, terrible friend. "Trust me, I missed you so much… It's just…"

"I know, I know. He's your husband and all, and blah, blah, blah. Till *real* death do you part," she said with a roll of her eyes and I laughed.

"He may be my husband, but you're my platonic soulmate."

"Damn straight!" she said, and we both laughed. When our laughing died down, we fell into a comfortable silence, and I rested back against the bed. Elli followed suit, and we stared up at the dimly lit ceiling.

"This has been the hardest three weeks of my life," I whispered. Elli remained silent, and I smiled, thankful to have her and her psychic ability to understand the way I talked and processed back at my side, where she belonged. "Not having you, not understanding, and not knowing what was going on… it killed me. It was the most confusing time in my life, and I had to face everything alone before a few days ago."

We turned toward each other, face to face. "Don't ever leave me again, okay? Losing Dimitri killed me once, but losing you killed me way worse because I thought you were the real one—the only real one. I thought you were gone forever."

She smirked. "Well, now you really will be killed, but ironically, we'll be together forever because of it." I shoved at her, making her laugh harder.

"Not funny!"

"I'm sorry! I'm sorry, really, but… come on, Priya. I promised you I would always be here, and I will be. Even the Russian government can't keep us apart."

I smiled. "Damn straight!"

We fell into a comfortable conversation, catching up as we talked about everything that had happened since what we started calling Elli's "waking up" moment.

"I broke up with Aaron at your funeral."

"Ooh, girl, I know. Dimitri was jealous! But he didn't hate you or blame you for it. You thought he was dead. But he *was* glad you were so torn up about it."

I snorted at that. "I bet he was." I rolled my eyes and smiled, remembering the past.

"You know, Elli… I think I'm almost ready to wake up."

I heard Elli's head move against the bedsheets.

"Sleep on it. I have to go now. Dimitri must be getting antsy, trying to keep this connection going." She sat up.

"Wait! When will I see you again?" I asked.

"Don't worry. After tonight, everything will be better. Just sleep on it. Tomorrow, things will be better," she repeated.

I nodded, and with a blink, she was gone. I felt my anxiety build up at her sudden disappearance. It was as if she were gone forever again, but I reminded myself of her words. I had to remind myself that she was alive, and I would be able to see her again. I tried to set aside the fear of dying that gripped me and focused on seeing her again.

But I couldn't shove aside horrible thoughts. The image of Dimitri having his throat slit made my neck tingle with phantom pains. I rubbed at the skin on my throat and cringed as the memory came back, playing like a movie in my mind, followed by the memory of seeing Elli in the hospital bed and in the casket.

Dying did not sound pleasant. Why couldn't Dimitri have found an easier way out? Was dying the only way out?

I wished Elli had stayed with me that night, at least until I fell asleep, but once again, I had to fall asleep alone. My only solace was in the idea that my torture would soon be over.

I couldn't tell if I was dreaming or not when I opened my eyes and looked up at the cloudless blue sky that peeked through the treetops above me. However, after hearing Elli tell me I was living in a simulated dream world, that uncertainty didn't surprise me, phase me, or concern me. My fingers flexed in the green strands of cool, moist grass beneath my body, and I gripped them to pull myself up. The greens of the grass seemed especially vivid, and the blue carried some sort of hidden meaning that I was too worked up to bother deciphering.

I was still wearing my pajamas—a pair of cotton shorts and an oversized t-shirt—but I didn't feel cold. In fact, I couldn't have been more comfortable. I looked around and took in my surroundings, letting the image bathe me in its vivid colors, scents, and sensations. Then realization struck.

Not only was I in a forest, I was in *the* forest—the one from over a year ago.

The trees were thickly packed together, as they had been on that terrible night, but there was light streaming in through the thicket from the sun.

"Priya," Dimitri called out happily. His voice perfectly encapsulated his playful, boyish persona. He was beckoning me to come find him, but not in the way he had the first night I stumbled upon this forest. This felt more like a game.

"Dimitri?" I called out as I stood up and looked around, trying to find him. When I didn't see anyone, I took a few cautious steps toward an area where the foliage thinned out.

I heard birds chirping and twigs cracking as I moved through the familiar vegetation. The steps I took were the same steps, in the same direction, as a year before. I couldn't explain how I knew where I was going, but I was nearing the same clearing as that terrible night. Deep down, though, somewhere hidden, I had a feeling my destination would be completely different this time.

I continued moving through the forest, the trees thinning around me, until I saw an area hidden by shrubs and tall bushes. I heard Dimitri's laughter, and I smiled at the challenge of finding him. I stepped through the maze of vegetation, excitement bustling through me. However, as I neared the shrubs and bushes at the end that hid the clearing, the one that so starkly stood out in my memory, a sense of fear gripped my throat.

My sense of calm and Dimitri's playful voice had distracted me from a horrible thought. It hadn't occurred to me until that moment, as I prepared to pull apart the shrubs, that this might be a trick from the Russians.

Maybe they are using mind control to show me what I want now, but when I enter the clearing again, everything will change, and Dimitri will still be dead.

I came to the tall bushes that hid the clearing from sight. My hands hesitated and shook as I reached out to pull them apart. My mind was torn between fear and desperate hope.

"Angel, I'm here," Dimitri called out, his voice just beyond the bushes. The sound filled me with a resolve and the courage to break through the green wall that separated me from my second chance at joy.

I pulled the bushes apart, peeked at the beautiful clearing, and frowned.

It was empty.

My heart sank, but a little voice inside me said to walk further. So I walked toward the tall tree at the center of the clearing, memories flashing in my head. The tree had a thick trunk and was casting a large shadow on the emerald ground beneath. I looked at the spot on the trunk where there was once a crimson bloodstain. I looked next at the ground, expecting an imprint where Dimitri's body had fallen so violently. Tears welled up in my eyes at the disappointment and pain of reliving it.

"Angel." Dimitri's voice was closer than before. I held my breath. I dared not hope, and yet chills ran up my body as my heart beat irregularly, my palms grew clammy, and excitement bubbled up in the pit of my stomach with butterflies raging within.

He still had such an effect on me.

I let out a shaky breath before slowly, hesitantly, turning around in place, my head held down, all the while, my gaze focused on the grass swaying around my ankles. I felt the breeze on my sweat-slicked skin. When I made a complete turn, my gaze remained fixed on the ground as I mustered up the courage to raise my head.

Before I had the chance to fully process or convince myself to look up, a pair of pristine white sneakers came into my view, adjacent to my bare feet. A strong hand slowly reached out and slid under my chin to grip it gently but sternly, then slowly lifted my head up. My eyes traveled up the tall frame, from the black, ankle-length pants to the navy t-shirt and the light, smooth skin that covered his strong arms and unscarred neck until finally they settled on his eyes.

The most striking pair of hazel eyes stared into mine, and a familiar smirk crossed Dimitri's lips, his long blond hair falling and framing his face perfectly, as always.

"Angel—"

I didn't give him the chance to say anything more. I flung myself at him, my feet moving of their own volition to send me pouncing, my arms wrapping around his neck as if I were magnetically pulled to him. This earned me a grunt of surprise, but Dimitri wrapped his arms around me in return and laughed, picking me up so I could wrap my legs around his waist. My body was trembling uncontrollably as the emotions, the shock, and the disbelief wracked through it.

"Angel, I'm here. I've got you," Dimitri whispered, his breath whistling in my ear and his velvety lips soft against the flesh of my earlobe.

I pulled back and panicked when I saw his image was blurred, thinking that this was all a mirage or a trick, but then realization struck that I was crying. I wiped at my face profusely, unable to stop the onslaught of emotions, both good and bad, with an urgency that screamed I couldn't get enough of him.

"Angel, are you that happy to see me?"

"Shut up!" I practically screamed at him as I sobbed. "You're terrible! How could you leave me like that? How could you let me believe you weren't real? You're a bastard!" I swiped at the last of my tears, only to see Dimitri smirking with his head tilted slightly in amusement.

"Are you done with the dramatics? I'm here, aren't I?" he asked, and I shoved at him, making us both wobble when he lost his balance for a moment. His imbalance made me grab him tighter, and he let out a deep laugh after stabilizing; however, his stance wasn't what made ease wash over me.

God, I missed his laugh.

I gripped his face and planted kisses all over it, from his cheeks to his forehead to his nose; then I cut off his chuckle when I sealed my lips over his.

Kissing him was like coming home. It was like sleeping in my own bed after a long, tiring day or weekend away. It was like a safe place where I felt comfortable and whole, where I could relax and be myself.

Dimitri was my home. He embodied familiarity, from the way he smelled like a mix of sweat and soap to the way his arms just fit perfectly around my body as he held me close. From the sound of his heartbeat beneath my ear as we lounged to the way he laughed at me when we joked, Dimitri was my safe place.

When I pulled away from him, I felt how flushed my face was and didn't care to catch my breath. I could feel every inch of him as he gripped me tightly, and yet I couldn't get close enough. He brought up a hand to cup my face, and I leaned my head into it, relaxing at the gesture that brought back memories of being in bed, on the couch, at dinner—just *being* together.

"I missed you so much, Dima," I whispered, wanting to close my eyes but not wanting to miss any moment of seeing him, feeling him, hearing him, or talking to him. I forced my eyes to remain open and resisted the urge to sink back into that normalcy because I knew we would have forever to be normal again.

"I missed you, too, Priya," he said. He leaned in, initiating another passionate kiss—and only then I did let my eyes slide shut again.

∾

Dimitri's knuckles slid up and down the small area of my bicep as we lay in the grass together. I looked through the trees beyond the clearing, trying to make out if there was anything else besides vegetation.

"Priya, they can't get you," Dimitri said, and I picked my head up from his chest to look into his eyes. He stared back at me, trying to convey his truth, but I still felt uneasy. Dimitri gripped me tighter and sighed.

"Priya, do you trust me?"

I nodded.

"Do you trust me to protect you?" he asked, and I nodded again before he gave me a look that said, *So, then?* I smirked.

"You're right. I'm sorry. I just… I'm having a hard time taking all of this in." I laid my head back on his chest and took a deep breath as he started rubbing my back, up and down, in a tranquilizing way. "I know what to do to be with you, but I'm scared. The idea of dy—I mean, *waking up* scares me. You know I have a fear of knives. I also hate alcohol, so I can't drink myself to wake up like Elli did." Dimitri's head moved slightly against mine.

"That's already taken care of, angel," he said. I placed my chin on his chest and gave him a confused look.

"You still have that old bottle of pills from Dr. Worblack

right?" he asked, and I nodded gently. Dimitri continued to look at me expectantly, and I stared back, trying to think what he was trying to tell me.

Why do they make me guess so much? I thought the medication was bad!

The words Elli had said echoed through my mind.

"You… you guys want me to overdose?" I asked quietly and Dimitri nodded. He reached up and started playing with my hair, and I gulped, wondering what it would feel like. Would I just fall asleep? Would I feel my organs shutting down? How did it work?

"It doesn't hurt, angel," Dimitri whispered. He placed my hair behind my ear and sat us both up. I moved to sit in his lap with my legs stretched out behind him and my arms resting on his shoulders. He placed his hands on my waist and looked at me with his stern *I know best* look that always made me laugh.

"Imagine taking a sedative. It's just like that. Remember when you got your teeth extractions? How you were put under anesthesia? Well, instead of counting backwards from ten and blacking out at eight, you'll take the pills, all of them, and then you'll pretend like you're taking a nap. And then, when you wake up, you'll be in the real world. And I'll be there, Elli will be there, and your mom and sister, and everyone will be there."

I smiled at the thought, my hands mindlessly playing with the long hair that fell down his neck. I thought of a new normal where everyone knew I was married, where I was in the body I was meant to be in, where the Russian government was defeated, and I looked at Dimitri's eyes and saw his happiness mirroring mine.

"All right," I said with a nod and a deep breath.

"All right, what?" he asked and I smiled.

"All right. I'm ready to wake up." He leaned forward and kissed my forehead. I closed my eyes briefly to take in the feeling, and when I opened them again, we were sitting on my living room floor. "Although I will miss the random scenery changes that come with being in a dream," I joked as we stood up together.

"I have an old bottle of Seroquel in the kitchen. Should I use those?" I asked and Dimitri nodded. We walked together, hand in hand, to the kitchen, and I reached into the medicine cabinet to remove the bottle. It was half full. Two months after I started taking it, I had to switch to Abilify because the Seroquel made me have weird muscle spasms.

I stared at the bottle and looked at the small circular tablets. My throat tightened at the idea of swallowing all of them.

"Do you want to blend them up into a smoothie? It'll probably taste better."

I hurried toward the fridge to take out the strawberries. I quickly put together a strawberry and banana smoothie, pouring the bottle of pills in and blending it all up. When it was finished, I poured the entire smoothie into a glass. I looked at the time, saw it was only noon, and then at Dimitri, who was watching me expectantly. I looked back at the glass, then back at him. I took a deep breath, reminding myself that I was waking up, not dying.

I lifted the glass to my lips and began chugging, surprised by the fact that I couldn't taste the expected chalky and dry flavor of the tablets. When I set the glass down, I smiled at Dimitri, and he handed me a napkin, which I used to wipe at my mouth. The moment felt anticlimactic. I felt like I had ruined this momentous occasion. There was no crying, no farewells, it was just… barely an event, like eating or taking a shower. It was so mundane, not a big deal at all.

"Come on," Dimitri said, grabbing my hand and leading me up the stairs to my bedroom. When we entered my room, I took a long look at my surroundings. This moment felt bittersweet. Even though it was a simulation, I had so many memories in this world.

"Dima… will I still have my memories from this world?" I asked, and he nodded, giving my hand a squeeze.

"All of them," he whispered, pulling me toward the bed. I looked at my tall water bottle and the pill bottle next to it and took in his words.

All of them. I'll keep all of the memories.

Dimitri led me over to the bed and he jumped in, patting next to him on the side by the bedside table. I smiled and lay myself down, positioning myself next to him and feeling him wrap his arms around me.

All of them. I'll keep all of my memories.

All of a sudden, memories of Aaron flooded my brain. The first time we met, our first date, and the night we slept next to each other.

The emotions that came with the memories surprised me. My heart felt like it was breaking. My eyes pricked with tears at the idea of never seeing him again, and I instantly felt guilty. I was a cheater, even though I hadn't meant to be, and I felt terrible for Dimitri.

"Dima, I'm so sorry about Aaron," I said. I began to sob into Dimitri's arms. He gripped me tighter and began to calm me down as I profusely started apologizing to him and bawling my eyes out. "Dimitri, I feel… I feel dirty, and like I cheated on you and—"

"Priya, angel, stop it. You did no such thing. Aaron isn't real. He's a simulation, and you were in a tough situation. I completely understand and it's okay." Dimitri kissed my head and wiped at my tears.

"You whore!"

"Slut!"

"Trash!"

I heard the Russian voices, and I immediately cowered into Dimitri's body, hiding my face in his shirt and gripping him tightly.

"Shh, it's okay, Priya. I've got you. And once you wake up, I'll have you for the rest of our lives. There is no Aaron, and once you wake up, there'll be no Russian government chasing us," Dimitri said, running his hand up and down my back, holding me tightly to him. "Try to sleep. Just let yourself fall asleep,"

I nodded, still crying silently.

Eventually, chills and tremors started spreading throughout my body. I stopped crying when my breathing became shallow and my heart started beating irregularly. I couldn't tell if it was because of my crying, or my anxiety, but my heart felt heavy in my chest. With every erratic beat, it grew heavier and heavier. The pattern of the beating became a lullaby, almost a soothing rhythm that I focused on in my task to fall asleep. My body screamed that something was wrong, but despite that, I felt at peace, knowing it was just the Russian government's ploy, maybe a deeply embedded projection. Maybe dying wasn't as scary as it seemed. Maybe that was all just a Russian scheme to keep me from leaving the simulation. Either way, I had to shut out all the warning bells in my head. I couldn't trust them.

"That's it, Priya. We're almost there." Dimitri's soft voice carried through my ear, and I realized then that his grip on me was gone. Through the foggy haze in my brain, I realized I was alone again on the bed. I wanted to cry out, to ask where Dimitri had gone, but I was too far under the spell of Mr. Sandman to reach out for him.

The last thing I heard before blackness overtook me was the front door opening and the woman posing as my mother calling out my name.

She's early, I thought.

Then, darkness.

19

MAY 20TH, 2019

I was still in the world of darkness when I woke up, my eyes too heavy to open just yet. My mind felt foggy, my limbs felt heavy.

Was I restrained?

I groaned in an attempt to speak, but I was so sluggish that I couldn't form proper words. I felt a pair of hands on my right arm and heard my mom's voice as she started talking.

"Jasmine, go call a nurse," she said.

I opened my eyes, then immediately closed them because of the blinding overhead light.

"Jasmine, turn the lights off," I heard my mom say. There were footsteps, then the flick of a switch, and then more footsteps fading away. I opened my eyes and blinked numerous times to adjust to the light around me. When my vision cleared and focused, I saw my mom leaning over me with concern in her puffy red eyes. I blinked up at her and noticed a large window behind her head letting in a generous flood of natural light.

"Thank God you're awake, Priya."

Did I wake up? Am I awake?

"I'm awake?" I tried to ask, but the only sounds that came out sounded like "an ache."

"Are you hurting anywhere?" my mom asked. I tried to shake my head, but it felt heavy, so it more or less just fell to the right, which brought into vision the restraints that appeared to bind my lower extremities.

Why am I restrained?

I heard footsteps rushing into my room; then I felt a cold tingle and pressure on my left shoulder.

"Hi, Priya. Do you know where you are?" I heard a soft, pleasant voice ask. I simply shook my head again. It felt slightly lighter, though not enough to pick up just yet.

I glanced up at my mom and saw her look over my head, then back down at me.

"Priya, *chotu*, you're in the hospital," my mom whispered to me, and I nodded my head, signaling that I knew that much.

"I'll go call Dr. Worblack," I heard the nurse say, and my curiosity piqued.

Is Dr. Worblack real too? Was the Russian version just a copy of my real doctor?

I felt a twinge in my neck and instantly picked my head up again as I became more aware and in control of my body. I rolled my shoulders back, but it took more effort than I expected and tired me out again immediately. I closed my eyes and took a deep breath before opening them again, only to see Dimitri standing behind my mom.

Seeing him invigorated and energized me. I smiled and I tried to reach out but was stopped by the restraints around me.

"Dimitri, tell them to take this off me," I said, coherently but groggily, as I closed my eyes again to rest them.

There was only silence around me—no action. I opened

my eyes again and looked at my mom and sister, who were looking at me strangely.

"What? Why am I restrained? Dimitri, tell them to let me go," I said with a soft cough.

"Priya, why are you talking to Dimitri?" my mom asked carefully, and I looked at her curiously.

"What are you talking about? He's my husband. Why wouldn't I talk to him?"

My mom and sister exchanged a glance before my sister looked at me and spoke.

"Priya, can you... can you see Dimitri right now?" she asked softly, and I felt my face fall.

"Of course, I can see him. He's right there." I tried to raise my hand and point at him but was again held back, so my hand only twisted and pointed in a weird, upward angle. My mom and sister looked at each other again, and I looked between them, confused.

Did it not work? Did I not wake up? But I'm awake... How did I wake up in the hospital if I didn't wake up in the real world?

I heard footsteps rush into the room again and watched as Dr. Worblack came in, his black hair slicked back, blue tie neatly knotted around his neck, and gray button-up shirt tucked into his blue pants.

"Hello again, Priya. Do you know why you're here today?" he asked as he came to the foot of my bed, picked up a clipboard, and began scanning it. I stared at him, wondering what the right answer was, wondering what actually happened.

"I woke up," I said, the words slipping through without me thinking over them. Everyone in the room paused and looked at me.

"Well… yes, you're awake, and you're awake in the hospital. But can you tell me what happened yesterday?" Dr. Worblack asked. I tried to think back to what my last memory was.

Dimitri said I would remember everything. Maybe they are testing that. But why is everyone acting like Dimitri isn't here?

"I… yesterday, I… was in the simulation world. The one created by the Russians. Dimitri told me I had to die in that world in order to wake up in this world, so I overdosed," I said slowly, remembering the previous day's events. I looked at the white sheets on me as the memories flowed through my brain like waves. I looked up and noticed Elli was now in the room, standing next to Dimitri in the corner, watching me. I furrowed my brow at them and then looked at Dr. Worblack again.

"I'm awake, aren't I? As in… I'm in the real world, right? I see Dimitri and Elli right there. Why won't you let them near me?" I asked hesitantly. My mom turned her head around to look at Dimitri and Elli before she turned back toward my sister, tears in her eyes as she sniffled and took a step away from the bed.

"Priya. You're awake and you're in the real world, but… Dimitri isn't real and… Elli is gone. Remember?" my sister said from my left. I stared at her, horrified, before looking at Dimitri and Elli again for confirmation, or an explanation, or really any sort of clarification.

"Angel, it's the Russians. They got to you before I could. You're still in the simulation." Dimitri shook his head.

I felt my heart rate pick up and adrenaline course through my body as if I were getting ready for a fistfight. I felt like I *wanted* a fight. I was filled with so many emotions—confusion, sadness, anger, and denial—and I needed a way to let them out.

"You're wrong! You're wrong, you're wrong, you're wrong! You're all a simulation, and you're working for the Russians! I know you're not real. Dimitri and Elli are the real ones!" I screamed as the tears fell from my eyes. My body felt heavy like lead again as I tried to break free from the restraints, with no luck. The lack of energy didn't stop me, though. I screamed uncontrollably, as loud as I could, straining to break free from the restraints. My screams and proclamations of the truth echoed in the room; I tried my best to keep fighting, but my body was too heavy, too sedated to be of much use to me. The simulation version of my mom and my fake sister were ushered out of the room by the nurses, and Dr. Worblack followed suit.

"Let her get it out. She's safe here; she just needs to process," I heard Dr. Worblack say, and I screamed louder in defiance, screamed until I couldn't scream anymore, and only soft, breathy wails came out.

When the room was empty, I looked over to see Dimitri and Elli rushing over to me from the corner. Elli moved to sit on the edge of the bed on my right, while Dimitri crawled onto the bed with me and held me as I cried.

"I'm sorry. I failed. I failed and now the Russians have me tighter than before," I said as I sobbed into Dimitri's shirt, his arms around me a dull comfort. The disappointment I felt in myself was unparalleled.

"Don't apologize, Priya. We have a plan," Elli said.

"We'll get you out of here, I promise. I've got you, angel. We've got you," Dimitri said. He petted my hair and held me until I passed out again.

∾

I woke up later that night to someone softly calling out my name. My eyes fluttered open and focused on the softly lit courtyard that I could see through my room's window.

"Priya," I heard a woman say. I looked to the left to see a nurse standing next to me with two cups, one tiny and translucent with three pills in it, and one that was medium-sized and made of paper. I turned my head away, knowing she was working for the Russians and trying to give me medication to control my mind.

"Priya, it's time for your medication," she said, just as pleasantly as before.

"No," I said defiantly, looking away from her and out the window. It was dark outside but well-lit by the moon. The courtyard reminded me of the forest, and I felt tears prick my eyes at the blissful memory of the previous day and my hope of escaping the simulation.

"Priya, come on. Either you take it willingly, or I force it down," she said, and although it was quite a threat, she didn't have any malice in her voice. I shook my head again, determined to hold on to my resolve for as long as possible.

"Priya, I'll make you a deal. Every night you take the medication, I'll give you a reward. How about if you take the meds tonight, I'll let you sleep with minimal restraints?"

I thought about her offer, wondering if I could use this to my benefit. Maybe if I gained their trust enough, I could break free again at some point.

"Be patient, angel," I heard Dimitri say from the corner, and I nodded at him before turning toward the nurse and nodding a second time.

She helped me sit up and gave me the translucent cup first, then the water. I took a bit of water in my mouth before putting all the pills in. I could feel one of them floating around before I swallowed them all whole. I took another drink of the water, finishing it in that one gulp.

"May I have some more water?" I asked, realizing how parched I was. The nurse smiled before moving to my bedside and pouring some water into the paper cup. She returned to my side and gave me the cup, and I hastily drained it again. The nurse kept her word, however, and removed the straps from my legs so I could freely move them; but my left wrist remained strapped to the bedrail.

Soon the nurse left, and I curled into myself on my left side as I tried to think through the events of the morning.

I'm so stupid. I can't even die properly. If I can't even kill myself correctly, how am I going to get out of this simulation?

"Stupid. Stupid. Stupid."

"Trash. Trash. Trash."

The Russian voices started at an alarmingly high volume, and I cried at the overwhelming emotional assault.

"I've got you, angel," Dimitri said behind me as he snaked his arms around my waist and pulled me into him. The voices remained the same volume, but having him there to hold me while I cried was a comfort, nonetheless.

Other than the voices, the room was quiet—I was so overcome, I couldn't get out what I wanted to say immediately. Eventually, I turned onto my other side and curled myself into Dimitri, his arms holding me tighter.

"What if... what if I keep taking the medication and I end up believing you never existed again? What if the Russians win?" I asked quietly.

"That won't happen, angel. You're stronger than them. You're stronger than all of them," he whispered into my hair, but his words didn't erase the thoughts from my head.

The fear of never seeing Dimitri again, never seeing Elli again, was pressing and strong in my mind. It would have kept me up all night if I didn't have lead for eyelids. They were too weighted down, and soon I drifted back to sleep.

20

MAY 21ST, 2019

I GRIPPED my blanket around me as I trudged down the halls of the facility, the scratching sound of my slippers along the linoleum filling the hallway. The nurses bustled together in the center of the hall unless they were coming in and out of the surrounding rooms.

"You look like shit, baby girl," Elli said next to me, and I rolled my eyes before shooting her a glare. She was walking backward next to me with her hands behind her head, her eyes on me, and a Cheshire grin on her face.

"Jeez, I wonder why." My words were dripping in sarcasm and bitterness. I yawned, stopping in place because I had to close my eyes and didn't want to lose my balance while I walked. My eyes watered up when I opened them again, and I continued to just stand in the middle of the hallway, staring down toward the area of the facility that held the therapists' offices.

Elli took a step backward away from me, then stared at me, her back toward the hall in front of us.

"What's up, Priya?" she asked. I stared at her, taking in

her image and gripping my blanket around me before speaking.

"What if Avery convinces me you aren't real? What if... you and Dimitri are wrong? What if I'm *not* that strong, or at least not as strong as you think I am?" I said, watching her move to my side again, now facing forward. She smiled and bumped her shoulder against mine, causing me to stumble over slightly. I gave her a flabbergasted look, but she just wrapped one arm around the back of my blanketed shoulders.

"Baby girl, that won't happen. But I hear you. Let's say it does. Well, Dimitri and I will never stop trying. We'll get you out of here at some point," she said, giving my shoulder a squeeze.

I looked at her hand on my shoulder, then at her.

"You know, I've always known we've been in love with each other, but I never thought you would go so far as to publicly display your affection for me like this," I said, raising my left shoulder and making her laugh hysterically before she let go and we continued walking to Avery's office.

"So how did you sleep, Priya?" Avery asked from her desk chair across from me. I flexed my hands on top of the blanket draped across my legs.

"Not very well, considering I was sedated," I said with a shrug, earning me a chuckle from Elli. She sat perched on the arm of my couch. It was the same tan one from when I first met Avery—from when she first convinced me Dimitri wasn't real.

Avery nodded her head and gave a politely sympathetic smile. "I'm sorry about that. Hopefully, things will be better now that you're here in the facility." She smiled again. "You had a decent time here last time, right?" she asked.

I shrugged. "It was fine. Wasn't here too long. Speaking of which, how long will I be here for this time?" I asked, crossing my legs and leaning back. I shook my right foot anxiously, making the blanket ripple on top of it.

"That all depends on you. As of now, you have two more days for your hold."

Only two more days in the Russians' lair, and then I can go home and plot my way out.

I looked to my left, to Elli, but she wasn't there anymore. I felt my mood and motivation instantly drop to an ultimate low.

"Are you looking for something?" Avery asked, and I looked forward at her with a shake of my head, unable to tell her I was looking for Elli.

"Is it Dimitri?" she asked softly, and I continued to shake my head. I couldn't help but wonder if I messed anything up or if I might have exposed my plan by giving her a clue that I was looking for Elli. I could deny it all I wanted, but these Russians were smart.

She looked at me with that small smile again and I tensed up. That sympathetic smile seemed so genuine, it almost made me want to tell her about Elli. Avery was very good at her job, and we had built an amazing rapport over the past year that made me want to trust her. Life would be so much easier if I could just trust her again, but that would mean giving up in the fight for what was true and right. I couldn't give up on the two people who mattered most to me. They hadn't given up the entire time I didn't believe in them or believe they were alive. How could I do anything less for them?

"Priya, can you tell me what Dimitri looks like?" Avery

crossed her legs and gave me a Mona Lisa smile, her features relaxed but still attentive as she patiently waited for me to respond.

"Why?" I asked, genuinely curious. Was this a ploy? Didn't she know what Dimitri looked like? I was positive she knew what he looked like, so why was she asking me? Maybe Dimitri had changed his looks since they last saw him. Would telling her cause anything bad to happen to him?

"I have a theory I'd like to test, but I need to know what Dimitri looks like first. Can you remember what he was wearing or what he looked like the first day you met?"

I smiled wistfully, the memory of that day in the coffee shop appearing in my mind as if it had happened that morning. But my mind caught on the words she used. She said she needed to know what Dimitri looks like. Maybe she had never seen him.

I could always describe someone else and see what she said, just to test her, but at that moment, I couldn't think of anyone or anything beyond the image of Dimitri. All I could do was change some of his physical features.

"He has long black hair, blue eyes, and a sharp nose. He has big ears I always tease him about and bushy eyebrows."

"Can you tell me what he was wearing that day you met?" she asked.

I paused as I conjured up the image of Dimitri again, noting what he was wearing.

"A navy t-shirt and black pants. Not jeans, but not slacks. They were just nice pants," I said and Avery nodded.

"Good. He seems very stylish. Can you tell me what he was wearing on any other occasion?"

I looked at her curiously, wondering why she was asking what he was wearing so much, but I tried to think back to the many other occasions we had seen each other, our many dates and the times he had visited me.

"On our first anniversary, he wore a navy t-shirt, black ankle-length pants, and white sneakers," I said.

"And on your wedding day?"

"Navy t-shirt, black pants, and sneakers."

"What about this past week when you saw him?"

"Navy t-shirt, black pants, and—I don't get your point. So he wore the same outfit all the time. Steve Jobs did the same thing. His closet only had jeans and black turtlenecks," I said, agitated.

"This is true; some people prefer to wear the same outfit over and over again for simplicity. But let me ask another question. Have you ever seen him with a new haircut? You said he has long hair. Has he always had long hair? Never gotten longer, or shorter?"

I immediately began to shake my head but stopped. Dimitri had never told me he was getting a haircut before, never came home with a different haircut, either. In the years that I had known him, I never questioned it. And now that Avery had drawn attention to it, the fact that he'd worn sneakers and a t-shirt to our wedding sounded odd too.

But our wedding was a secret court wedding. No one could know about it. So why should he have dressed up? It's not like I got to wear mom's wedding lehenga, like I wanted.

"I've… never noticed. I just don't notice those things, and he doesn't care about his looks," I said with a shrug.

Avery tilted her head slightly.

"Someone so simple and who has a routine look doesn't care if his hair grows too long or gets too short?" she said, and I tensed up. Something was not sitting right in my brain. My mind fell into chaos as I tried to come up with a reason behind this strange phenomenon.

Maybe he just maintains his hair perfectly and goes like clockwork.

"Also, did you ever notice if his shoes got dirty? Or did he have multiple pairs of the same shoes for years?" Avery asked. I opened my mouth, about to give a response, but I had none to give. I had no explanation for what she was asking about.

Dimitri, can you please show up now? I need help. I don't know what to say.

But nothing and no one came. I was left alone in Avery's office with just her and my chaotic thoughts.

"Priya, I know this isn't something you want to hear, but hallucinations don't change. They don't age over time, and they don't usually change their appearances."

Silence fell between us as I tried to process what she was saying.

"I think that's enough for today's session, don't you? You should rest a bit before your group session," Avery said. I nodded as I stared at the ground, unable to respond, my mind scattered and dissociated. Avery stood up, and I followed her lead mindlessly, my eyes remaining on the ground as I left through the door and slowly trudged toward my room.

"That was intense, huh?" Elli asked from next to me when I was halfway to my room. I paused in the middle of the hallway, looking up. It was almost empty, with just a few nurses sitting at the round office in the center of the facility ahead. I looked at Elli, at her hazel eyes peering into mine. My eyes traveled down from her wavy hair, which was up in a ponytail draped over her shoulder partially, to her black tank top, denim cutoff shorts, and black sneakers.

I stared at her shoes and tried to think of the last few times I had seen her.

The night she woke me up, she had her hair in a ponytail and was wearing a black tank top and denim cutoff shorts.

The day I woke up in the hospital, it was a ponytail, black tank top, and denim cutoff shorts.

Today, she wore the same thing.

I looked at the shorts, noting the same fraying at the edges, then the tank top with its smooth texture and thin straps at the shoulders. Her wavy ponytail fell just past her shoulders. But before the past few times, before she supposedly died, Elli had always worn different outfits. She used to wear shorts quite a bit, but she also wore jeans. She would wear sweatshirts, dresses, and different shoes or sandals.

She would never wear the same outfit twice. She loved fashion and mixing up her style.

My head throbbed. I felt more and more like giving up. This was too much to think about. I hadn't been prepped enough on how to withstand this version of torture from the Russians. And it was definitely torture. It was some sort of mental and emotional torture as they tried to make me discard everything that I believed to be true. I hated what they were doing. I hated the way they were doing it, and I hated that it might even be starting to work.

I was ashamed of the fact that I was even thinking of giving up. So ashamed that I couldn't even look at Elli, in fear that she would see my inner turmoil. So I looked at the ground ahead of me, held my blanket tighter, feeling the Sherpa fleece against my neck, chin, and part of my cheek, and began walking toward my room again.

～

I sat in the chair, my eyes aimed at the ground, my fingers moving in a successive ripple like I was playing the piano, over and over again, on top of my blanketed legs. It was almost summer and was probably warm, maybe even hot, outside, but the facility had always been a cold place, the air conditioning blasting at all times.

"Hello, everyone! It's time for check-ins and introductions."

Dr. Jackson was the one leading the group sessions, and her voice was as chipper as I expected. Her tone was probably supposed to incite motivation, maybe encourage warmth, but it only irked me.

"It'll be good for you," everyone had told me.

"You'll learn to be mindful, grounded, and gain support. You might even make some friends!" the mom simulation said.

I'd said, "I don't need that. I don't need new friends or support either." *What I need is to wake up.*

"I can start today." A boy who looked to be around my age, give or take two years, piped up. He had dark brown hair and was wearing a plain gray hoodie and blue jeans.

"Thank you, Jonathan," Dr. Jackson said.

Jonathan smiled back and paused before starting. "Can I ask the new girl a question?"

"I don't see why not," Dr. Jackson said with a nod, but I tensed up, not wanting to take part or be asked any questions. Jonathan looked at me and smiled.

"Hi, my name is Jonathan and I'm bipolar. What are you in for?"

I stared at him, shocked and unsure of how to respond.

"Jonathan!" Dr. Jackson scolded as the room filled with half-stifled chuckles. I just stared at the kid, my face softening, a bemused smile tugging at my lips. "We don't ask about diagnoses in this group, remember?"

"Well, yeah, but I mean, she's gonna end up talking about it later, right? So why not just rip the Band-Aid off now?"

"That's not the point of a mindfulness group, Jonathan. You know better," Dr. Jackson scolded.

I grinned weakly at the squabble and decided I was probably going to like Jonathan. But I wasn't sure how to respond to the question. I couldn't tell them about the Russians— they'd just throw me back into the restraints. Maybe the strategy was to play into the current narrative. Maybe I had to use their own methods against them, gain their trust, work the system, and get out that way.

Be patient, angel.

"It's all right," I said, looking at Jonathan. I turned my attention to Dr. Jackson. "May I answer?" Dr. Jackson sighed before nodding.

I turned back to Jonathan and smiled.

"Hi, I'm Priya, and I was diagnosed with schizophrenia."

"Hi, Priya," the other attendees said in unison, and I chuckled. It sounded the same as how Alcoholics Anonymous or other support groups sounded on TV.

"All right. Cool," Jonathan said. "Back to check-in, I'd say I'm at a solid five point five."

More chuckles. I was beginning to think Jonathan was the clown of the group.

"And why is that, Jonathan?"

"I can't paint, but I don't wanna die—so solid middle ground. Only slightly higher because I felt like sketching. I couldn't. But I felt like it." He said this with a shrug, putting his hands in the pocket of his sweatshirt before looking at me and grinning.

"Are you a painter?" I asked, then looked at Dr. Jackson. "Am I allowed to ask questions?"

"Of course!"

I nodded and looked back at Jonathan.

"Only when inspiration strikes. If not, I'm just a normal human," he said with a smile, a small dimple appearing on the right side of his mouth.

If I had met Jonathan outside of a psychiatric hospital, I may have found him attractive. His features were familiar, similar to Aaron's, and that thought brought a little pain to the surface.

He's not real, Priya. He's a part of the simulation.

My gaze fell from Jonathan to the floor, and I sat back in my chair, bringing my legs up to sit cross-legged. I looked down at my lap and tried to reel my emotions back in.

Remember the plan. Be patient. Stay strong.

"Would you like to go next, Priya?" Dr. Jackson asked.

I looked up at her, then around the room. Any one of these simulated individuals could be a Russian spy. Maybe all of them were, so I had to put on my best performance.

I took a deep breath before nodding. "I'd say I'm at a… five. I say that because I don't know what's real, I'm tired all the time, and I just… don't know what or who to believe. I have no reality checks anymore, and quite frankly, I'm just tired of this world." My lips moved slowly and sluggishly, causing me to mumble and distort my words, but to my surprise, the words were genuine nonetheless and gave away more of my thoughts than I had intended. I wasn't sure who to be more afraid of, the Russians if they found out I was just playing along, or Dimitri and Elli if they found out a part of me wasn't just acting.

"What sort of reality checks did you used to have?" a soft male voice asked. It wasn't Jonathan for sure, and I looked up at the other boy in the group, who looked younger than me. He was wearing a pair of black sweats and a dark blue crewneck sweater with gray house slippers on his feet. Based on his gaunt face, he seemed extremely skinny.

"My best friend, Elli. She died recently," I said.

"I'm sorry for your loss," he said, silence falling on the group. I didn't mean to, but I definitely brought the mood down with my response.

"Thank you for sharing, Priya," Dr. Jackson broke the silence. I gave a small nod.

"I can go next."

I looked at the frail boy who had given me his condolences.

"My name is Bryan," he said meekly. "I have anorexia, and I've had an especially hard week. I'd say I'm at a three." He yawned. I noticed the dark circles under his eyes then and realized he must not have been sleeping.

"This week, my dad came to visit." Bryan turned to me. "My dad and I have a bad relationship. He's basically the biggest stressor in my life." I nodded.

"So anyway," he continued, "my dad came, and he was trying to understand. I know he was, but he just... kept getting mad at me. When I told him how disgusting food makes me feel, how I hate the textures and I hate the smells, he just... got mad. At first, he was blaming himself, and then he was blaming me; and he left after telling me to 'fix myself.'" Bryan made air quotes with his fingers.

"How did that impact you?" Dr. Jackson asked.

"Honestly, it was terrifying. It made everything worse than it already is. I'm at a point now where I just feel like never looking at food, or smelling it, let alone eating it. I don't want to eat ever again. I do want to die. I just can't bring myself to do it," he said, looking down.

I wondered what his story was. I knew anorexia was about being a certain weight, wanting to be in control, all of that, but everyone had a different reason for their struggle, a different trigger that threw them into the throes of a disorder. I wondered what made this young kid begin to manifest such terrible self-harm symptoms.

Stop caring and being curious about a simulation.

"You're beautiful, Bryan. Even if you don't feel loved by your father, you are loved by many people, and also by God," the girl next to him said. She was wearing a pair of light blue jeans, furry boots, and a pink sweater.

"Thanks, Charlotte. That means a lot to me," Bryan said quietly, looking at the floor before turning his head up and smiling at the girl, who I guessed must be Charlotte.

"I can go next," she said. "I'm Charlotte, and I guess if we're still saying our diagnosis, I also have bipolar disorder. I'd say I'm at a six, honestly. I'm on the mend since being discharged. I went to church this past Sunday, and that was really nice. I felt something close to mania while I was worshipping, which was nice, you know? Since I miss being manic, but I don't miss being depressed. I guess I just miss being happy and confident and… in love with the world and myself. So church helped me feel that again, but only for a moment. Then it was back to my mundane life. But yeah, no suicidal thoughts, and no hypomanic thoughts. Just thoughts. So I guess I'm doing well." Charlotte shrugged.

"How does it feel to not be manic anymore?" Dr. Jackson asked her.

Charlotte paused for a moment before replying.

"Honestly, it feels like the best part of me has been stripped away. I feel like my friends won't want to be around me anymore because I'm not fun or adventurous anymore. I'm just… bland."

I frowned, staring down at my lap. I could relate to her feelings. I remembered when I fell into my deep confusion immediately after witnessing Dimitri die. I also felt like the best part of me—of my life—was gone. But I'd had Elli to cheer me up and be there for me. I had family to lean on and support me.

But that was all an illusion from the Russians. This whole world is an illusion.

I looked around the room as Dr. Jackson began the lesson, or whatever it was, for the day. My stubbornness won out and kept me from paying attention to her.

The faces around me looked so real, and their stories seemed so complex. But I couldn't shake the truth that they were just simulations.

I have to wake up.

∾

The common area had a large table in the far back corner that was usually used for art therapy. There was a TV a few feet away surrounded by a semicircle of chairs and a small couch used during entertainment time. The movies or shows we watched were usually kept at a low volume with subtitles so as not to disturb people participating in other activities.

I sat on the couch with one leg curled under me and the other propped up and bent with my knee toward the ceiling. I tried to concentrate on the older women in the show on the TV, *The Golden Girls*, but my mind was elsewhere.

"Damn, can't we just change the channel and put on *The Nanny?*"

I looked to my right out of the corner of my eye and saw Elli lounging back against the couch. Both her legs were folded under her as she leaned back, one arm propped up on the edge of the couch with her hand supporting her head.

I looked around the room, noticing there weren't many people in the area, and I had about twenty minutes until art therapy.

I turned my head to Elli to take in her image fully, and my eyes fell on her shoes, which were still on her feet and were on the couch.

But she's not actually here. She's a projection from the real world; so that's fine, but why the same outfit?

"Elli, why do you wear the same clothes every time I see you?" My voice was soft and absentminded, the words coming out on autopilot as I zoned out.

Elli hummed before responding. "Because it's still the same day in the real world. Dreams move way faster than the real world, Priya."

I finally looked up at her, my brown eyes meeting her hazel ones, and I searched them for the truth because, for the first time, I didn't believe her.

"Who you talking to, P?" I yelped as the familiar voice caused me to jump out of my skin. Within a blink, Elli was gone, and I was forced to look up at Jonathan. "Damn, you're really jumpy. My bad." He gave his boyish grin and put his hands up, and once again, I was reminded of Aaron. I had to literally shake my head to get the image of the first day I met Aaron out of my head before I focused back on Jonathan.

"What do you want?" I asked, not intending to be mean, but not intending to be as glum as I sounded.

"I came in early for art class. Just saw you talking to yourself and wanted to see what's up. You okay?" Jonathan asked, sliding down from the arm of the couch to the seat cushion. He looked at me like he was analyzing me, and my eyebrows drew together as I stared at him, annoyed.

"I wasn't…" I stopped myself and sighed. No one could know I was still seeing Elli and Dimitri. "I'm fine. Just trying to… figure stuff out," I said and leaned to my left, resting my head against my fist.

"Do you need help?" he asked, way too eager for a normal person, and I looked at him with a face that I hoped said, "No, you freak." But Jonathan only laughed.

"Hey, If I've learned one thing about being crazy, it's you shouldn't be crazy alone. Ya' gotta have people to let the crazy out with or you'll explode."

His words caught me off guard and my head whipped up to him.

Elli. He sounded just like Elli.

"That's what she said to me," I whispered, more to myself, but Jonathan heard me.

"Who?"

I looked up at him and took in his soft brown eyes, his slightly tilted head, and the way he had been so boisterous these past few times I'd seen him. There really was nothing threatening about him, so if he was working for the Russians, he was a great spy.

But then again, if he wasn't, then I could trust him, right?

I turned my head away from him and looked down at the ground, contemplating my options.

I was tired. I was mentally, physically, and emotionally just exhausted, and what's worse is that I could feel myself losing grip on my sanity. I was beginning to feel truly crazy, and maybe I needed to let it out. Maybe I needed to voice it and talk it through with someone. Maybe Jonathan was that person, but I couldn't risk being locked up again. I had one more day in this facility and then I'd be out. Then I'd be able to get back to Dimitri and Elli.

"You sure you're okay?" Jonathan asked again, but before

I could confirm, there was a ring of a bell that signaled art therapy was starting soon.

"Yup. Totally okay," I said as I rose from the couch and walked over to the large table, taking a seat and letting out a breath.

Such a liar.

~

That night, I was allowed to sleep without restraints. My nurse, Nurse DeMarcio, came in while I was staring blankly out my window. She had long blond hair that she wore up in a messy bun. She was extremely sweet and spoke very softly, but not in the way everyone else did, like they thought I might break. Nurse DeMarcio spoke as if we were just in a library. She was pleasant and didn't make me feel lesser or weaker than I was.

"Hi, Priya. How are we feeling today?" she asked as she set down the two cups on the little table at the foot of my bed, then filled the water cup from a pitcher.

During my art class, I had produced stick figure pictures that looked worse than a toddler's, and Jonathan made sure to comment on it. After though, I had free time, and I watched television, finally enjoying some reruns of *The Golden Girls.* It helped me feel more at ease than the last time I was here. Before, I didn't get the chance to immerse myself in the activities and agendas because I was out so soon, but this time it felt more… comforting.

But I shouldn't have felt comfort. I should have felt outrage, I should have felt guilt at the comfort, and I should have felt ready to leave, not like I was taking a vacation.

What is wrong with me? Have I forgotten that I am supposed to be acting?

"I'm okay," I said. She nodded before coming to my side and handing me the water cup and the pills.

I looked down into the pill cup for a few seconds, contemplating whether I should take the three tablets. I was supposed to be fighting, not blending in, no matter what the plan was. This was supposed to be an act, not a vacation. I was still fighting in this war with the Russians.

Be patient, angel.

Dimitri's words echoed in my head, and I sighed, not wanting to take the pills because of my growing fear that I would lose the will to fight. But I trusted Dimitri. I trusted him with my life.

So I tossed back the water, then the pills, and handed Nurse DeMarcio my cups.

"Good night, Priya," she said as she walked out of the room.

I lay my head down on my pillow, adjusting my body to a comfortable position, then turned to continue looking out the window of my room, the silence surrounding me.

No voices. No radio signals. No interceptions.

No Dimitri. No Elli.

Where is everyone?

Never before had silence been harder to fall asleep in.

21

MAY 23RD, 2019

I STARED at the blank white paper and took a deep breath, trying to keep myself from groaning, screaming, or cursing out the art therapist. It wasn't her fault I was being forced to participate in this horrific form of therapy.

No, it was Dr. Worblack's. He was the one I should be cursing out.

"Still not a fan of art, are ya'?" I jumped slightly at the familiar voice and glared at Jonathan as he laughed. He was leaning forward with his arms crossed and on the table, his head way too far in my space. "Wow, you're *still* so jumpy."

I glared at him, and he looked up from my blank page to meet my eyes before grinning and leaning back with his hands raised in defense.

"And you still have no regard for personal space," I said and grabbed a crayon box, contemplating if I should just draw a bunch of Teletubbies and that creepy sun before calling it a day.

Jonathan snickered before picking up a graphite pencil and staring down at his paper.

The art therapist began to lead the session, giving out a prompt or something that I didn't listen to. There was no point in giving me a prompt because whatever it was, abstract or concrete, it would not get drawn well or comprehensively. Even if you told me to draw the word happiness, my smiley face would need a long and hard interpretation.

"Hey, P, wanna be the model for my sketch today?" Jonathan asked, apparently also having no interest in following the prompts.

"Knock yourself out," I said sarcastically as I began to work on the first Teletubby, the purple one.

Stupid me for thinking I actually would like this kid.

"Cool, just keep drawing your purple blob," he said.

I grumbled, "It's a Teletubby," and then instantly regretted it.

Jonathan laughed hysterically, to the point where he had to put his pencil down. "What? Damn, how old are you again?" he asked.

"I'm…"

The question shouldn't have been that hard to answer. At least, not for a normal person. What I wanted to say was twenty-two. What I should have said was seventeen. But what was I going to say, without thinking, if I hadn't paused?

Seventeen.

Yes, I *should* have said that, but I shouldn't have believed that. So was I just that good of an actor, or was something going on inside me? I was tempted to believe the latter, that something was going on, without my permission and against my wishes. My allegiance was slowly changing, and I was convinced it was because of my medication. But it was a confusing conundrum. Dimitri told me I needed to take the medication and be patient, knowing it would weaken my connection to him and Elli. But I trusted him, and I trusted that this was the way to be with them again, even if it risked me ending up *not* wanting to be with them. I was toeing a fine line, and I was starting to lose my balance in the wrong direction.

"You good, P?" Johnathan's question pulled me from my thoughts, and I nodded, going back to coloring in my purple... blob.

"Yeah, no, I'm good."

That seemed to appease Jonathan enough for him to leave me alone until the art therapist called time on the session.

"So? What do you think, Miss. Model?"

I turned my head to glance at his sketch, and my jaw threatened to fall open.

The sketch was more of a rough outline with circles and lines inside of a barely there young woman, a teenager for sure. She had her head in her palm as she looked off into the distance somewhere. From her hooked nose to her long hair that curtained her face, she resembled me, but I couldn't for sure say that it was me.

"That's not me," I said, looking at Jonathan. He looked at the paper, then at me, and shrugged.

"I mean, it's a rough sketch. Not really an exact photograph, but definitely based on a true image."

The woman on the paper was beautiful. I'm sure Jonathan went a little rogue with that part of the sketch, but what caught my eye the most was that he captured my pensiveness, and I could see in the sketch my own turmoil.

"See ya in group, P," Jonathan said as he lifted himself from the chair. "Oh, and I'm keeping this."

Jonathan's sketch haunted me and left me desperate to walk off my thoughts and feelings, so I headed to the facility's courtyard. I walked through the heavily vegetated court-yard, looking at the myriad of pink and purple flowers, green plants, yellow and brown weeds, and tall trees. I watched as the plants, leaves, and branches danced in the light breeze, losing myself in their rhythms.

My mind was racing with questions. Ever since that first day in the facility two days prior, I had been feeling holes in my resolve to fight. My brain felt like it was being picked at every day, with every interaction I had.

"I'm real, babe. I always have been, always will be." Elli's voice was a whisper, a subconscious echo from a memory of my first stay in the hospital.

It had been two days since I had last seen Elli, and a part of my brain made sense of her disappearance. She and Dimitri needed to lie low while I was in the Russians' clutches. But there was another part of me that had been growing in the last two days, a part of me that grew in corre-lation to the poison I swallowed every night.

That part of me wondered if Elli had lied to me. Would she always be real? Was she still real? And was she being honest about why her clothes don't change?

Even if that is true, why did Dimitri's clothes never change? Was I in a dream then too? No, I couldn't have been because my clothes changed.

I looked around at the others who were walking through or sitting in the courtyard. They all seemed to be enjoying the peace of the space, and I wished I weren't in such growing turmoil. I wished I could find peace just by being in that garden under the sunlight, that I could press pause on all my worries, but I felt like I was beginning to be forced to pick between two worlds—forced to pick between what everyone else said was real and what I believed and wanted to be real.

It felt like a life-or-death choice. And if I chose the wrong one, it literally was.

Do I even want that world to be real? Or do I just want Dimitri and Elli to be real?

The thought floated into my mind, seemingly out of nowhere, like a dandelion seed drifting through the air that caught in a crevice, settling, and immediately starting to grow roots in the soil of my brain. Maybe it was the medication taking effect, or maybe it was simply me being emotionally exhausted, but I wasn't sure how to answer that question. I didn't know what I wanted anymore, aside from wanting to be okay. I just didn't know which world I had to choose in order to be okay.

When I walked into the common area to meet Ms. Agarwal, the room was relatively quiet, as there weren't many other patients or visitors chatting or bustling around. She was sitting at one of the tables looking at something on her phone. Her hair was up in its usual bun, and she wore her reading glasses. She was wearing dark jeans and a blue button-up blouse. As I neared the table, she looked up and stood before reaching out to give me a hug.

"Hi, *chotu*," she said breathlessly. The hug was awkward, since I wasn't really in the mood for it, but I let her hold on to me for as long as she needed, knowing the hug was meant to comfort her more than me.

When she released me, we sat down, and she put her phone aside.

"What were you reading?" I asked, looking between the phone and her.

"Oh, just some article on nuts. They say they're really

good for mental health, but I don't know how much I believe that stuff." She waved her hand, and I smirked, knowing my Indian *mom* was all about alternatives to Western medications. This was the woman who fed me almonds every day, doubling the amount on the day of my exams because they were good for my brain and would make me smarter. She was all in on the nuts craze.

Why do I have memories of Ms. Agarwal before meeting Dimitri?

"Okay."

There was an awkward silence between us as Ms. Agarwal looked at me, expecting me to say something, but I didn't know how to fill the silence and didn't have the energy to hold a proper conversation.

"How is it this time?" she asked, eventually.

"What?"

She cleared her throat before asking again. "How is your stay here this time? Is it okay? Are you eating properly?"

I shrugged, looking around the room at the few other people in it.

"Yeah, I'm fine. It's fine. Food is... meh," I said. Although Ms. Agarwal's eyes were on me, she wasn't really seeing me, I thought. They seemed hooded, lost in thought. She opened her mouth a few times, but each time, she shut it before saying anything. Her hands were clasped in front of her on the table, one thumb rubbing the other.

"Was I a bad mother? *Am* I a bad mother?" she finally asked, continuing to gaze at me somewhere into the space between us.

"What? What kind of question is that?" I couldn't think what else to ask in return. I was so taken aback by her question and unsure of why it had come up.

"No, it's a valid question. Was I a bad mother? That I

didn't see the first signs of my child going through this... nightmare? This is the second time this has happened, and I was blind to what was happening to you both times. I almost lost you because of it this time." Her eyes met mine. "So I want to know... do you think I'm a bad mom?"

I immediately shook my head without stopping to think through my answer.

I wanted to tell her she was superwoman.

The fact that my situation made Ms. Agarwal feel inadequate and the fact that this upset me, caused a thought to branch off the dandelion seed, turned seedling, that rooted in my brain earlier.

I don't want her to be upset, but why would I care if she's just a part of this dream? Maybe it's because this woman is my mom, and she's all I've ever known as a mother.

"I don't think you're a bad mom," I said quietly before clearing my throat and looking at her with a fixed gaze. "You're superwoman to me. You can't shield me from all the horrors of life, but you do an amazing job of helping me get back up when they knock me down." I hoped my words gave her some strength and cleared the distorted view she had of herself.

Ms. Agarwal looked at me for a few seconds, then smiled softly, nodding.

"Okay." She cleared her throat and launched into more questions about what Avery and I discussed, how group therapy was going, and other aspects of my day-to-day life in the facility.

When visiting time was up, Ms. Agarwal left, telling me she would be back later that day with my sister for a family talk with Dr. Worblack about how to move forward. Since it was technically the last day of my stay in the facility, Dr. Worblack would talk to us about next steps. But as I walked to my room to get my blanket for my session with Avery, I wondered if I was ready to leave the facility.

~

I walked into Avery's office and sat down on the couch, draping my blanket over my legs as I had become accustomed to doing.

"How are you doing today, Priya?" Avery asked.

"More confused than ever," I said honestly, feeling a desire to actually talk to Avery that day.

"Really? Anything in particular that made things more confusing?" she asked and I nodded.

"I had a thought just before coming in, after my art therapy session. I don't know if I want to believe in this world where Dimitri and Elli are real, or if I just want *them* to be real. The two ideas are very different, and… I think they have different implications and weight. I think… if I want the other world to be real, then I have to admit that my mom here is not real, that my sister isn't real. I just saw my mom, and… she asked if she was a bad mom." My eyes welled up, and I bit my lip to prevent myself from crying. "Now that I think about it, that makes me feel like I've been a bad daughter. I haven't been… I don't know… validating her efforts to support me, I guess you might say. Maybe I haven't been the most grateful. Maybe I haven't been the most attentive to her or the most… respectful? I don't know. I just… I think… The fact that I'm so strongly affected by her feelings of inadequacy, that I feel so strongly about her, means that I want her to be real. If I want her to be real, then that means I have to want this world to be real, but… is wanting this world to be real enough for me to believe in it?" I said and leaned back against the couch.

Avery tilted her head. "I think I know what you mean. And that's true. Your heart might want one thing, but your brain tells you to believe something completely different. And usually, in these cases, the brain wins," Avery said, and I nodded slowly, lost and in the clustering of my thoughts.

I felt lightheaded as I tried to get a grip on my thoughts. "Like… right now, in this moment, I have no voices in my head. I can't hear anyone from the US government, I don't hear any white noise, I don't hear any radio interceptions, and a part of me is thinking sure, that's the medication keeping me under the Russians' spell." I paused, realizing that I was possibly telling a Russian that I knew about their plan. I swallowed and forced myself to continue. "But a voice in me— not like a *voice,* voice, but like my conscience, or whatever— is saying that's not the case." The idea solidified in my mind as I spoke it aloud. "This inner voice, which started out tiny, is growing, and it's saying that this is the real world. This is how things should be—no voices in my head, no Russian conspiracy theories, no government tasks and identities and blah, blah, blah. But it's not that easy to believe that. And I don't know what I want to believe anymore. I just want to be… okay."

"That's a lot to process, Priya. I'm glad you're coming to these ideas on your own and asking these questions. And I know your time is coming to an end here in the facility, but I would say more time is needed to sort through all that. Do you agree?" Avery asked, and I paused, thinking for a long time about what I needed. Frankly, I didn't know what I needed at that moment.

There was a part of me screaming desperately to fight the Russians, fight their plan, go home, and try to wake up again. But the other voice was growing and telling me, calmly, that if I went home, I would die.

I wouldn't wake up.

There was no other world.

Dimitri wasn't real, and Elli was dead.

The voices were still very much warring inside me, and I needed more time to have a solidified, unified mindset. I couldn't go home with this wishy-washy way of thinking, and I couldn't trust myself to take care of myself while I was outside of the facility.

~

"I need more time here," I told Dr. Worblack. I avoided looking at my mom and sister sitting in their usual spots across from me next to Dr. Worblack's desk.

Dr. Worblack looked at me for a few seconds before nodding.

"After hearing from Avery how you've been progressing, I admit it's great improvement, but I would agree—you need more time." He looked back at my mom and sister. My mom was watching me, making sure this was what I wanted. I met her eyes and nodded. She nodded subtly in return and turned back to Dr. Worblack.

"So how much longer do you think she needs?" she asked.

"I would say another three days. I believe that after the medication has reintegrated back into her system completely, which shouldn't take much longer, things will be much clearer to Priya. And then she should be able to return to the routine we established last year."

"Will I be able to bring Priya's homework and assignments to her while she's here? I'm sure she has some catching up to do," my mom asked, looking concerned.

I had to smile. *Academics will always be top priority.*

"I think that would be a good idea. We can ease her back into doing classwork. I can also put homework time in place of arts and crafts in her schedule for the next three days." We all agreed—my mom because she was desperate for me to have homework, my sister because she respected Dr. Worblack's recommendation, and me because of all my planned, meaningful daily activities, I hated arts and crafts time the most.

～

"On a scale of one to ten, how strong is your grip on reality right now?" Jasmine asked as we sat in the courtyard on one of the glossy wooden benches. I scoffed at her question and shook my head.

"That depends on which reality you're asking about," I said, looking down at my slippered feet. They were too hot, for once. The courtyard was the only warm place in the facility because it was far away from the God-awful, uncontrollable air conditioner.

"Okay, bad question. I'll rephrase it. On a scale of one to ten, how real am I?"

I looked up at her.

My gaze traced her face, from her dark brown eyes, outlined with eyeliner and mascara, to the way her nose hooked slightly. I skimmed over the freckles and sunspots that formed shapes across her face like a connect-the-dots puzzle. My eyes fell to her pink-stained lips, then lifted back to her eyes. I tried to find a difference between the way she looked—the way she presented—and the way Dimitri or Elli presented or looked. I examined her tan cotton blazer and light blue blouse, which she had tucked into her black pants.

I looked down at her shoes and remembered Avery's question about Dimitri's shoes.

Did you ever notice if his shoes got dirty? Or did he have multiple pairs of the same shoes for years?

"*Didi*, how many pairs of shoes do you have? And when did you get these?" I asked as my eyes moved over the way the knitting on her slip-on sneakers crisscrossed in a woven pattern. I looked at the leather border lining the bottom part of her shoes, and I noticed how dirty her white shoes were—not pearly white, but not completely gray. They had little gray stains here and there, but they were more of an egg wash color now.

"Um, I think I have nine or ten pairs? I got these probably a year ago," she said, and I nodded unconsciously, my eyes staying on her shoes.

"Do you ever buy the same pairs of shoes?"

"You mean at the same time? No. What's the point in that?" she asked rhetorically. I nodded again.

What is the point in that? There is none. And Dimitri is not the Steve Jobs type. So why does he wear the same outfit all the time?

"Dimitri wears the same outfit every time I see him." The words came out on their own. I heard them, but I couldn't remember giving myself permission to say them out loud.

"What does he wear?" she asked. I looked into her eyes again, seeing the way she blinked repeatedly and looked into mine.

"Navy t-shirt, black ankle pants, and white sneakers," I said, looking down again at her sneakers. "His sneakers were never dirty. They were always... pristine." I tore my eyes away from her sneakers to look at the cement pathway leading away from our bench.

"So you think he has multiple pairs of the same shoe," my

sister said, her words an observation and not a question. Her voice wasn't laced with any judgement or any concern. It was simply an observational statement, and I appreciated her for refraining from judging me or the situation.

"Yes. Does that sound crazy? I haven't thought about this for a few days because it didn't seem relevant, but seeing your shoes... it brought back Avery's words. But even now, seeing you, and seeing your shoes, I still don't know what's real. My brain is telling me one thing, everyone else is saying something else, and I feel like I'm crazy either way." I took a few deep breaths, trying to ground myself in the moment and not be carried off by my racing, incomprehensible thoughts.

"I don't think it sounds crazy," my sister said. "I think... when you've been through what you've been through, that sounds normal. It's totally understandable why life is hard to figure out. But you don't have to have it all figured out at once. I'm going to tell you this world is real, but you have to figure it out for yourself for it to sink in." She turned to face me on the bench, laying her arm across the back of it.

I turned, too, then sighed. "What if I don't ever believe in this world again? What if I'm constantly battling to figure out what's real?"

My sister shrugged. "Priya, I have a feeling you'll always have that thought in the back of your mind, wondering what's real, but I think... that's where the medication, therapy, and your support system comes into play. We'll be here to help you, and... I feel like the more grounded you are in one reality, the more real it'll feel. And that comes with the people who are grounding you in those realities. So you have to figure out which reality has you more grounded and has more reason to be real. Which reality do you feel, in your gut and in your heart, is the actual one?"

The immediate feeling of gratitude that swept over me

was incomparable. She had always been a great person to turn to for comfort but had always been a backup to Elli because she was closer and was just... my person.

But Jasmine was right. I had to find my grounding in the people around me because I couldn't be trusted to figure out reality alone.

Hopefully, for my sake, I'd be able to find it in the right people.

22

MAY 25TH, 2019

My mom brought my phone to me along with my homework that morning, and I had never been so thankful for music. Jasmine had created a Spotify playlist for me called "Get well and get buck," a combination of soft, chill music, and hyped-up, confidence-boosting songs. It was the kind of playlist I never thought I needed, but I was glad it existed. That gratitude I felt for my sister blossomed further in my chest.

I paged through my assignments. Doing my homework got me in a state of flow, and I was thankful for the mental break from my own mind. The math problems came easily to me, as always, but the chemistry, despite claiming to be math based, was anything but easy.

It wasn't until I came to my AP Government and AP Psych homework that I paused. Ms. Chen had written a little note in my AP Government homework assignments reassuring me that they would be graded on a pass/no pass scale, although she was confident I would pass the assignments. The AP Psych homework and notes were written in a familiar handwriting that didn't belong to Amanda.

Wait... who did my mom get these notes from? And what did she tell my teachers about where I've been and why I'll be absent for a while?

I immediately unlocked my phone, went to my texts, and saw the little red bubbles notifying me of the missed call and eight texts I had been completely ignoring.

When I opened the texting app, I saw that I had three texts from Amanda, two from my mom from the day of the incident, and three from Aaron. The missed call was from Aaron, just yesterday.

Amanda: Hey Priya, are you okay?

Amanda: Hey, you haven't been to class in a few days, are you okay?

Amanda: BRUH! I just heard you're in the hospital! Please tell me you're okay!

To say I was surprised by Amanda's concern for me would be an understatement. I was absolutely shocked, but I was touched. The fact that she was texting me somehow broke through the wall I had put up around myself to make me feel and think I was alone. My sister's words about being grounded played in my head again, and I realized what she may have wanted to say but couldn't at the time.

The more people I have in my corner in a certain world, the stronger my belief will be in that world. I have to create reasons to believe in this world more than the other.

I imagined my brain being held up by puppet strings that were maneuvered by my illness, and I felt one of those strings snap away. However, rather than my brain dipping down on the side of the snipped string, my brain felt lighter, like it was floating and holding itself up.

I smiled at Amanda's texts and took a deep breath before scrolling up to see Aaron's.

Aaron: Hey, I know I'm supposed to be giving you

space, but you haven't been in school in a few days and I'm a little worried. Honestly, I don't expect a reply, but maybe a read receipt showing you read this message so I know you're okay.

Aaron: Okay it's been a few hours and you're officially ignoring me so I'll just stop. I'm sorry, Priya.

Aaron: YOU'RE IN THE HOSPITAL? Priya, please answer the phone! I'm going out of my mind with worry! Your mom asked the school for your homework and gave my mom a doctor's note saying you won't be in school for a while. She also asked me to get you your notes and homework. Please call me back.

I cringed at the texts from Aaron. I felt like very sharp, pointy sticks had popped a balloon filled with water above my head, drowning me in an obscene amount of guilt. I felt ashamed for turning both Amanda and Aaron away when they were only trying to help me. I had even left my mom and sister out of my life... all because I wanted to be with Dimitri and Elli.

I'm a monster. I'm a terrible, horrible human being.

I sighed, wondering if I should text Amanda and Aaron and tell them I was okay.

They deserve to know. They have only ever wanted me to be okay. They aren't sharks, Priya; you need to stop being afraid of letting people in. Elli is gone, so you have to make up for her being gone with other people. Not replace her, just... fill the gap enough to be okay.

I was about to send Amanda a text, but then I realized the time. I rushed off to see Avery before my group therapy.

～

"So you received worried texts from Aaron and Amanda while you've been away. That's nice. How does that make you feel?" Avery asked. I shrugged, rubbing my hands together. I had ditched the blanket that day, feeling a sense of empowerment and warmth that gave me the courage to not hide behind it, but in that moment, there was no warmth. I was in desperate need of some.

"It... put things into perspective. I've come to realize that I've always had a hard time making friends and letting people in, mostly because I always thought I had more than enough in Elli, my mom, and my sister... but mostly Elli. I think after Dimitri came into the picture, it got even worse because he was basically my whole world, and my... situation... made that especially true." I took a deep breath, shaking my head. "It was so... *normal*, receiving those texts. It was like... This is going to make no sense, but the mundane nature of them was so... grounding. It was grounding to the point where I thought of Dimitri and Elli as separate from me—from reality. I don't know how to explain it; but even doing homework was helpful in that it gave me a distraction, and it was such a normal task. I feel like I can't remember anything normal about the world Dimitri and Elli are talking about, yet I remember mundane tasks from this world, like reading and doing homework. In this world, even the insignificant things matter and are memorable. But for some reason, I don't remember anything from that world outside of my time with Dimitri," I said, leaning back against the couch and rubbing my arms.

Avery looked at me for a few seconds before smiling. "Priya, you're showing immense progress, and I'm very proud of you. What is something final you think you need to be fully grounded in this world?" she asked.

I looked at the gray carpet of her office, at the little holes in it that were part of the pattern, and tried to see them as connected in some figure or design.

What do I need? Am I even smart enough or capable of knowing?

I didn't know what to say. After not being able to trust anyone or anything, I couldn't see how anyone could think I was capable of creating a viable or real solution to this issue. How could people think I actually knew what was best for me?

If you don't know, then who does? If you don't let anyone in, how can you expect others to give you the solutions you're seeking?

"I think… I think I need time, and-and separation. I need time in this world, time with people, time to be grounded and to heal. I need more people in my life to ground me and keep me separated from that world. Kind of like… dividers?" I looked down at my hands, seeing how my fingers were inter-twined, seeing the way they were squeezed together tightly.

I held them up and looked at Avery. "I think this is me right now. My right hand is me, and my left hand is Dimitri and Elli. Everything is intertwined, and everything is tightly glued together. And it looks and feels like it fits, right?" Avery nodded, and I nodded back, hoping I was about to make sense as I pulled my hands apart. "But I think… I have to put space between us. And that space has to be filled with people who support me—who ground me and care about me." I put my hands side by side, my thumbs the farthest apart. "Like… if I'm my right thumb, and Dimitri and Elli are my left thumb, then the fingers in between, keeping us apart, are people in my life who care about me and love me, like my mom, my sister, Amanda, and…" *Aaron.*

My thoughts trailed off when Aaron's name popped into

my mind, the realization of how good he was to me hitting me like a truck. I didn't deserve him, and yet he tried to stay by my side throughout it all. He probably would have been there to help me after Elli. If only I had let him in, none of this would have happened.

But even beyond Aaron, Amanda was there too. She had tried to come into my space as well, and just like with Aaron, I didn't let her. I was too busy being a hurt animal, ditched on the side of the road, and instead of trying to crawl to safety, I'd been committing the suicide mission of crawling straight into traffic.

That was definitely something I needed to work on if I hoped to survive in this world. I couldn't keep trying to be on my own or shut people out. But more than that, I had to seriously want this world to be real and learn how to maintain that.

"What are you thinking about, Priya?" Avery's voice snapped me out of my thoughts, and I dropped my hands to my lap, feeling little wet droplets on my sweats. I furrowed my brows and looked down, watching tears fall from my eyes. I felt them burn, and immediately, I dabbed and swiped at the tears.

"I want to survive in this world. I need to be better about letting people in, and I need to be better about having people to ground me... but... I need to ground myself first," I said through my sniffles. Avery handed me a tissue box, and I pulled tissue after tissue out of the box, trying to muffle my sobs.

"That sounds like a plan," Avery said. She smiled her signature genuine smile, putting me at ease.

∾

"Check-in time!" Dr. Jackson announced as we all settled into our chairs.

"Charlotte, would you like to start today?" Dr. Jackson asked, and Charlotte paused slightly, tensing up before nodding. She wore jeans, an oversized white V-neck t-shirt, and a pair of sunglasses on top of her head. Her white slip-on sneakers were similar to those my sister had worn earlier in the week.

"Um, I'd say I'm at an eight today. My dad encouraged me to sign up for my church's worship team, which basically means I would sing on Sundays, if they let me, or if they need me to. It's pretty nerve-racking, signing up to serve at church. I'm... not many people know about my disorder, and there's kind of a taboo against mental illness in the Christian community; so I haven't opened up to many people about it yet. But the ones who do know have been very supportive. I don't know why I'm still afraid to talk to people about it, but I'm praying that God will grant me the strength to open up and will hopefully provide me a safe space within my favorite community," Charlotte said, sighing when she finished.

"Ouch. You mean we aren't your favorite community?" Jonathan asked, his hand gripping his shirt over his heart as he shook his head. Charlotte rolled her eyes but couldn't hide the smirk on her face, and I smiled, holding back my own laugh.

"Why don't you go next, Jonathan?" Dr. Jackson asked, and Jonathan instantly sat up straight in his chair, clearing his throat and looking down at the ground as he thought and tried to compose himself.

"I'd say... I'm at a six point three. The other day in art therapy, I saw some colors and paints that kind of inspired me. Not to mention I had a great model." Jonathan winked at me and I rolled my eyes. He turned back to the group with a laugh. "I don't know what I'm thinking yet, but I have some inspiration to paint and will hopefully have a masterpiece created by the end of summer. Who knows?" He shrugged.

"Wow!" Bryan jumped in. "That's really good to hear! I'm also somewhere around a six." He settled back in his chair. "My dad and I had a family therapy session and set up this sort of... code of conduct for us when talking to each other. We're working on using 'I' statements and not blaming each other for the other's stress, telling each other how the other's actions impact us instead. I don't know how this will work in our relationship yet, but I'm trying to stay hopeful." We all nodded, smiling.

"That's great news, Bryan. Priya, are you ready to go?" Dr. Jackson asked, and I nodded, looking down at the dark patterned carpet.

"I'd say... I'm at a six point seven. I think I'm close to having a breakthrough, but I don't really know what more I need to really break through the surface. Today I realized that I have people who care about me beyond Elli. I basically have multiple reasons to believe in this world and to let go of my past and the other world. It's... liberating, actually. As I'm talking about it, I'm realizing all the things I have to live for in this reality and how much of a community I have." I looked up and glanced at Jonathan, Charlotte, Bryan, and even Dr. Jackson. "I'm gonna be honest and say I didn't want to come to this group at first. And even though I still don't see how it's meant to be helpful—no offense—I think... just the normalcy of it is super grounding. That may not be the intended way of mindfulness and grounding, but just hearing you guys talk about your lives, seeing your interactions, interacting with you myself is... really grounding and helpful," I said, smiling as my thoughts trailed off and I finished trying to convey my sentiment.

"Aww, you're making me get all emotional," Jonathan said. He sniffed and swiped at fake tears, making us all crack up.

I looked at Jonathan and Charlotte and Bryan while Dr. Jackson continued with that day's exercise, and I couldn't help but think I'd found more people to put in between Dimitri and Elli and me.

Maybe this group is actually a good thing.

I sat in the common area and did my homework for AP Government. Since we were done with the AP tests, we were now doing "fun" things related to government that weren't part of the curriculum, like learning about the laws that passed giving the LGBTQ+ community certain inherent rights, including the right to marriage. We also talked about drug laws, like if a school can search a student's bags if they are suspected of carrying weed.

"Damn, I remember when I first did weed." Elli's voice made me tense up, but I continued to read the notes Aaron had written for me.

Don't engage. Don't talk to her. You have been doing so well; don't fall back now.

"Good job, by the way, on getting the government to trust you. Don't worry, we'll handle everything once you're out," she said, and I sighed, trying to take deep breaths as a means of restraining myself and focusing on my homework, but also as a means to control my heart that shouldn't have, but did, flip at what Elli had offered.

"Angel, do you still want to wake up?" Dimitri's calm and

sympathetic voice floated through my ears and touched my soul. He was sitting on my left, Elli on my right, and I felt sandwiched between them, making it hard for me to breathe and choose.

I need to walk. I need to get out of here.

I collected my things, holding my notebooks and papers close to my chest as I quickly strolled out of the common room, not making eye contact with anyone or looking up at anyone near me.

As I walked down the hall, I could hear Elli and Dimitri's distinct footsteps following me. I felt their eyes on the back of my neck, their presence tagging along.

When I arrived back at my room, I set my things down on one of the chairs and plopped myself on the bed, huffing as I tried to calm my heart and brain down.

"Priya, don't you miss us? Don't you love us?" Elli asked, sounding annoyed and shocked.

I looked to the edge of my bed and saw Elli sitting down and Dimitri standing against the wall. Elli had on the same outfit she had been wearing since the day I first saw her after the funeral. Black tank top, cutoff denim shorts, and ratty black sneakers. Her hair was up in its now permanent ponytail.

Dimitri looked the same as well: same long blond hair, same navy t-shirt, same ankle-length black pants, and same white sneakers. No stains in sight. No holes, no fading, nothing. His outfit was in pristine condition, and the only way that would be possible was if he had a new outfit every week.

And just like that, finally, the pieces clicked. Finally, the choice was clear.

"This isn't a question of missing or loving," I said, gripping the bedsheets in my fists. My voice was level and calm, not raised enough to alert any nurses who might be walking by, but also definitely not quiet. "This is a question of life or death, of healthy versus unhealthy. Holding on to you two is not healthy. Holding on to you two won't 'wake me up,' as you claim. It will kill me, and I can't do that. Not to my mom, not to my sister, or Amanda, or... Aaron." I sighed again at the end, feeling the reality that I was alone in the room. My eyelids felt heavy, the vein above my right eyebrow pulsing, and I closed my eyes, letting myself feel the silence and solitude.

It's time to start over. It's time to start a new life, without the two people who made life worth living for so long.

The weight of those words began to drag me down. I felt like Atlas, struggling to carry the world on his shoulders.

I had to create a new plan. I had to create a new routine and a new life—a life without Elli and Dimitri.

I had already created a life without Dimitri last year, but I felt bad for beginning to move on from Elli. Now that I had digested the fact that she was dead, that she was not coming back, I couldn't help but think I was moving on too soon from her memory. However, even though it felt too soon, I knew that the longer I dwelled on her, the stronger my pull to her hallucination would be. And the harder it would be to let go and stay grounded in this reality.

That's what pulled me into this mess in the first place with Dimitri. I was hesitating to move on. I felt like I needed more time, that I needed to hold on to him longer, but there was a difference between gripping tightly to someone's existence and holding on to their memory. I was gripping Dimitri's existence so tightly it had almost cost me my life.

I needed to learn to adapt. I had to learn to let go of these unhealthy urges in my life. Elli was my best friend, and no one would ever replace her. But maybe that was a good thing.

Maybe I needed to let her go, and I needed to start fresh, start coping with my illness in a different and new way.

I couldn't rely on other people to be my sole reality checks. I had to create my own that I could do alone. Maybe Avery could help me develop them from the coping methods I had learned from her during our outpatient therapy. Maybe I could do outpatient therapy for the next two weeks, twice a week, and only taper off if I felt okay. I had a few months until college started—if I was still allowed to go to college— to get my life together, and I was determined to do so.

I took out my notebook and wrote down a new checklist.

•Graduate

•Cut my hair

•Move on from Dimitri and Elli

•Start college

•Get back into running

It was a simple list, probably not the best, but it was a good starting outline for a new plan.

A new plan for a new life.

23

MAY 26TH, 2019

"WELL, Priya, how do you feel about going home?" Dr. Worblack asked.

"I feel good," I said, smiling. It was only the two of us in the meeting that day, as my sister was coming to pick me up from the facility, and my mom was still working. "I think... I think I have a plan for the next step." My words made him raise an eyebrow.

"What would that be?"

"I'd like to see Avery twice a week for the next two weeks and taper off when ready, but I want to see her throughout the summer at least once a month. I'd like to continue my schooling and graduate high school. I also want to continue with going to Berkeley. I did some research this morning and found out I can enroll with the Disabled Students' Program and get note takers for days when I can't make it to class, and I can get help with tests when needed. There are a lot of resources. They already know about my illness because of my personal essay, so they must know I might need accommodations. I'll just... make sure to actually use them."

Dr. Worblack nodded, approvingly. "That sounds like a doable plan, and we are always here to support you and help you succeed as well. Just a little advice—you should also get back into some of your old routines. Running again is a good idea—not just because it's healthy, but because it was normal and familiar for you."

I walked out and loaded my sister's car while she signed me out. The day was off to a good start. Still, I wasn't immune to the muffled voices, the prickling on my neck, and the piercing gazes of Elli and Dimitri.

As we drove down the familiar road, I inhaled deeply, the mixed feelings of freedom and worry washing over me.

I looked down at my phone and smiled at the texts I was getting from my group therapy squad.

Jonathan had given me his number the day he got out, the 24, and he created a group chat for the four of us, Charlotte, Bryan, Jonathan and me.

Charlotte: Happy escape day!

Bryan: You're a free woman now!

Jonathan: Come back and visit any time ;)

I couldn't help the laugh that erupted from me before replying back.

Priya: Thank you! See y'all on Thursday!

"Are you happy to be out of there?" my sister asked softly as we got off at our exit.

I nodded. "I wasn't in there for long, but it was long enough." I watched the houses and buildings fly by. I didn't realize how much I'd missed being in the outside world.

When we pulled up to the house, I moved to unbuckle my belt, but my sister caught my hand.

"Hold on. I have something I want to talk to you about first." She hesitated before continuing. "Priya, I'm not saying this to guilt you or anything. In fact, I'm hoping it does the opposite and gives you something to be happy about and look forward to." Another pause. "You know, when you were a baby, I refused to push your stroller because I didn't want people to think I was your mom. One time, while mom was changing in a changing room, I was standing by the stroller and some woman told me you had my eyes, and I almost lost it." We both chuckled. "Yet, despite not really being your mom, or even wanting to be your mom, I definitely treated you as my child. I changed your diapers, I took you to school, I fed you sometimes, when mom and dad were busy at work, and then... after dad left, I definitely became more protective of you. You were like my daughter and my sister at the same time. Sometimes my doll, even, when I wanted to dress you up and play with you. So when I heard that you had commit —well, *attempted* suicide, I think I can understand what mom felt. I think... I felt the most when I thought I was going to lose you. I was going to lose my sister, my daughter, and my friend." She looked at me then for a few moments before continuing. "Please don't ever put me through that again."

I watched as my sister's eyes filled with tears, and I could only nod as I reached across the space between us and awkwardly hugged her, pulling against the seat belt.

"Is that selfish of me to ask?" she said. "Is that too much to hear right now?"

I shook my head, taking a deep breath. "No... no. It's just what I needed to hear," I said softly when I pulled away from her.

"I... I can't promise this won't happen again, but I can promise that I will fight tooth and nail to try to make sure it doesn't."

∽

When we entered the house, I was overcome by an eerie sense of nostalgia and terror. I looked at the spot on the carpet in the living room where I had been lying with Dimitri. I imagined the blender in the kitchen and the empty bottle of pills. This house could have become a crime scene. There could have been little stickers by the evidence, by the blender, by the bottle. I hated the thought that my attempt to find solace and get out of my waking nightmare was considered a crime.

I shivered as the memories hit me but turned my attention back to where I was now, toeing off my shoes, hoisting my backpack higher on my shoulders, and walking up the stairs after my sister.

When I walked into my bedroom, I saw how my bed was made, my desk cleaned up with my books and papers organized on top of it. There were no clothes on the floor. Everything was definitely not the way I left it.

"Mom stress cleaned after you were admitted to the facility," my sister said, and I nodded, walking over to my desk and dropping my backpack on the side of it. I sat on the chair and stared at the bed, seeing the place I had been held by Dimitri while I almost died.

The thought that I had almost lost out on this life, on this world, because of him angered me and boiled my blood in a way I had never felt toward him before. My breathing began to quicken with an overflow of sadness, anger, and pain, and I immediately stood up, remembering Dr. Worblack's advice.

"I'm going for a run," I announced, looking at my sister, who blinked at me a few times before smiling and nodding.

"I'm gonna watch TV. I'll see you when you get back,"

she said before she exited my room. I smiled, taking a deep breath, and got ready to go.

～

My usual route was fairly simple. Two miles in total to the park and back, with the option to run longer around the park if needed. With my headphones plugged in and my phone in my pocket, I started to jog. I chose to jog to the playlist my sister had created for me and smiled as the endorphins started flowing through my brain, overtaking the pain I had felt earlier. I hadn't realized how much I missed running and how freeing it could be. Since I hadn't been running recently, though, it was only a few minutes later when my legs felt weak, and I got a cramp sooner than I thought I would.

Keep going. Fight through the pain and push through, I thought to myself, changing the song I was listening to as I arrived at the park.

"You were always a fighter." Dimitri's voice appeared over the beat in my right ear. I looked to my right instinctively, expecting to see Dimitri next to me. When I didn't, I came to a halt. I had to catch my breath and grab hold of the feelings that were starting to run wild inside me.

Ten... nine... eight... seven...

Each exhale came out in a shallow huff as I breathed along with the countdown from ten. It forced me to pay attention to the present, but it also brought all my emotions to my eyes. My breathing became a struggle, my focus bringing to the forefront all the pain of the present. My heart was still badly broken, even if my brain was recovering and on the mend. Even with my medication, there was no medication that could erase trauma.

The emotions in my head shook my entire body. Every limb felt like jelly, like I would collapse at any moment. I dropped down to my knees on the grass in the park and grasped at the green growth. The green strands beneath me felt both a little rough and a little smooth. I opened my hands to the best of my ability, focusing on the flexing of my muscles in my fingers and the feel of my skin scratched by the earth beneath me.

I closed my eyes as the tears fell, and I tried to turn my mind to anything but the pain inside my heart.

I had never been one to enjoy being in nature. I enjoyed running, and I enjoyed looking at the nature around me, but being in nature—touching it—always gave me chills of disgust. I was somewhat of a germaphobe. Who knew what animal had peed on the grass, who had walked on it, or what creepy-crawly was living there? However, in that moment, being in nature seemed to be the only thing calming me down.

I shifted from my knees and sat down in the grass, pulling them up to my chest and resting my chin on them.

I looked at my setting and found myself comparing what I was looking at—how I was looking at it—and what it would have looked like if I were not on my medication. The magnitude of the colors and sights around me wasn't as it used to be. The world should have been more vivid; greens should have been greener, and blues would have had meaning. Now, the face value wasn't as valuable as it used to be.

I looked down at the grass, watching as it swayed in the cool breeze. I shivered and sighed.

It's okay to not be okay… isn't it?

It seemed like a luxury I couldn't afford. I had to either constantly be improving or plateau at my best. If I wasn't okay, then I became a statistic—proof of this diagnosis ruining minds. I couldn't slip up in any way, or else people would think I was slipping into madness. If I so much as talked to myself, or, God forbid, Dimitri or Elli, I would be back in the facility or remain under house arrest for as long as my mom deemed necessary. But that was only if someone saw me.

But what about the internal signs of my illness? What about the desires I still secretly held for Dimitri and Elli to be real? My sister was probably right in that I would have to struggle for the rest of my life to choose the right reality, but maybe it was okay that I struggled.

Maybe it was okay that I slipped up once in a while. At least, while I was alone.

So as I sat there in nature, no one around to give me a prognosis based on my emotional state, I let myself slip up. I let myself feel the emotions I was forbidden from feeling and poured them into the world around me. I let the tears fall to the ground and my sorrow fill the air around me as I cried out.

Then I spoke, softly. "I'm sorry, Dimitri, that I'm a terrible wife. I'm sorry, Elli, that I'm a terrible best friend. I'm sorry that I can't wake up. I'm sorry, guys, but I can't run this race with you anymore. As cheesy as it sounds, I have to run a different race, and that means staying in this world. I know it's going to be hard. I know I might come crawling back to you all one day, but I can't give up, not on this life."

The words barely came out of my lips, but by letting them out into the world, I felt like I was taking a weight off my shoulders.

I had to start fresh. I had to get a grasp on my mind, and I had to get back into my routine. I had to devote myself to everything that grounded me in this world.

When I was done crying and letting the crazy out, I lifted

myself off the ground, shook out my legs, and walked back to my house. I started out slow, picking up my pace as my breathing became more and more ragged. I soon broke into a jog, focusing my attention on the ground in front of me. Then I picked up my head and looked straight ahead. I kept up this jog for a few minutes before starting a full-out run, and when I saw the house in the distance, I sprinted.

Before I reached it, I had to stop because I couldn't breathe, but I welcomed the sting in my lungs. I lifted my face to the sun, put my folded arms above my head, and took deep breaths as I walked up to the front door. It was late in the afternoon. When I walked inside, my sister was lounging on the couch, watching an episode of some trashy reality TV show.

~

After my shower, I swiped against the fogged-up mirror in my bathroom and stared at myself, watching my wet hair fall around me, excruciatingly long. I picked up one wet strand and stared at it in the mirror, thinking back to my checklist from over a year ago. The third item on the list was to cut my hair. I remembered all the times Dimitri told me not to, and how his words weighed more than my mom's. I always wanted a long bob cut, but my Sikh mom and Dimitri were always against me cutting my hair.

I remembered Elli's words about having a new cut in the new year, a "new year, new me" look, and I began to think along those lines.

New life, new hair?

I quickly got dressed and ran downstairs, standing in front of my sister and smiling down at her.

"May I help you?" she asked, looking bemused, and I nodded vigorously.

"I want to cut my hair. Let's go." My sister's jaw dropped.

"Uhh… now? It's like… three thirty. Isn't it too late for a walk-in? Don't you need an appointment for that kind of thing?"

I shook my head.

"Supercuts probably has openings, so—"

"Um, we are *not* going to Supercuts for your first haircut. What kind of hair do you want?" she asked, and I smiled and shifted my weight.

"I want a lob. I want to chop it all off and start fresh," I said. My sister looked at me for a long while, calculating what to say next, but I knew she would give in.

She sighed and stood up. "Fine. Let's go."

I yelped with excitement and pulled her into a hug before rushing to put my shoes on.

∾

My sister took me to a local salon, and we got lucky—they'd had a cancelation and could fit me in.

"What are we doing today?" Jocelyn, my stylist, asked as she played with my hair.

"I want a long bob, like this." I quickly scrolled through my phone and pulled up a screenshot of Khloe Kardashian's blond hair.

"Oh, honey, you have the perfect face shape for this cut. But your hair will curl at the ends because of the texture. Is that okay?"

"But I have straight hair." I was confused by her statement.

"Yes, for the most part. But you might need to style it a little bit in the mornings to keep it that way. Just trust me on this."

I shrugged. "You're the expert. I'm fine with putting a little effort into it."

Jocelyn nodded and grabbed at her tools.

"So, what brought on the change? Did you go through a bad breakup?"

I laughed and almost shook my head, but I remembered in time that she was working on it, so remained still.

"No. Well… kind of. But also, I'm just making some major life changes."

Jocelyn grabbed an electric buzzer after putting my hair into a very low ponytail and began to hack at my thick locks.

"Are you a student?"

"Yeah, I'm a senior in high school."

"Oh! Isn't graduation just around the corner?"

I smiled and nodded when she finished using the razor. My head fell forward, far lighter than I had expected, and my eyes widened, making Jocelyn laugh.

"Just chopped off two feet of your hair, honey. It's gonna feel a lot different."

I watched as she took out the ponytail, picked up a pair of scissors, and cut away, making my hair shorter and shorter. The more I watched her cut away, the more I felt myself being torn between liberation and panic. It was almost as if my hair were a security blanket. I'd held on to it to pay homage to Dimitri, and now that it was almost all gone, it was like I had cut off my last tether to him.

"Well, what do you think?" Jocelyn asked, pulling me from my daze. I looked at myself in the mirror with my sleek lob, and I couldn't contain my excitement.

"I love it!" I squealed.

"I'm so glad you like it!" Jocelyn let me stand up, and I played with the smooth hair and dragged my fingers through it. My hands reached the end jarringly quickly. It usually took ages to comb my fingers through my hair. I practically skipped over to my sister and the register.

My sister's jaw dropped as I approached her. "Wow." She gawked and I did some hair flips. "It looks really good," she said.

When I walked out of the salon. I felt like the world had become lighter as the strings connecting my brain to my illness's puppeteer stick were snipped almost all the way through.

By the time we got back, it was evening time, and my mom was home. I rushed into the house and heard her playing some Bollywood music as she cooked in the kitchen. I ran into the kitchen and stood behind her, not wanting to scare her while she was chopping the onions. She always cut herself accidentally while cooking, even when I wasn't surprising her with a new look.

"Hi, guys. Where were you two?" my mom asked.

"Ahem." I pretended to clear my throat. My mom glanced at me, then turned around and gaped. I simply smiled brightly and hopped slightly in place. "Well?"

"It's so short," she said, walking toward me and analyzing my hair.

"That's the point."

She looked into my eyes and sighed, a small smile coming over her face.

"It looks nice on you," she said quietly, and I smiled back, feeling almost giddy. "Now go set the table, please."

～

That night, I spent hours sitting at my desk in my room, reading *The Center Cannot Hold*, by Elyn Saks. I didn't usually read non-fiction books, but Avery recommended I read a few about mental health so I could find some role models and inspiration to keep "fighting the good fight," as she said—which I'm pretty sure was an out-of-context quote about something completely different. But, for all intents and purposes, it fit.

I flipped the page and wouldn't have even looked up, wouldn't have even thought to crack my aching neck, if it hadn't been for the familiar prickling that appeared on it.

"Angel."

I held my breath as the prickling sensation slid upward over my skull.

I didn't have to look to know he was sitting on the edge of my bed, watching me.

I didn't have to look to know he was wearing a navy t-shirt, black pants, and white sneakers. His hair would be disheveled and long—a hairstyle I had never liked on anyone other than him. His eyes would be their familiar light hazel. I was torn between ignoring and acknowledging him, between continuing to love him and moving on.

I turned in the opposite direction and saw my open bedroom door. I could hear my mom's shower running. She had already been in there for five minutes, and she needed a while to wash her hair.

I had fifteen minutes, maybe less.

I turned toward Dimitri, and my heart palpitated with disappointment.

Everything about him was the same.

"Hi, Angel."

"Dima…" I breathed out his nickname.

I wanted to cry.

I wanted to scream.

I wanted to leap for joy at the fact that I was seeing him.

"It's not too late to wake up. You have thirteen minutes, Angel. Thirteen minutes, and then we can be together again."

He was sitting with his legs stretched out, his hands in his pockets. He was looking at me with a piercing gaze that cut deep into my heart.

There was a time when I believed in soulmates, star-crossed lovers, and believed he was mine. Elli had always been my platonic soulmate, but Dimitri always had a special place in my heart that rivaled even her. In that moment, I felt my soul being split in two directions. In one direction was immediate peace and rest, with a possible end in darkness. In the other was a long, painful, dark road with a bright light at the end.

I shook my head.

"I'm letting go, Dima," I said. Dimitri smiled, but he let me continue. I clenched my fists tightly on my thighs and took a deep breath before continuing.

"I need to let you go, and I have to move on. You were a big part of my life, Dima, but that part of my life is over. I can't let myself go back to that place again. I have too much on the line. Too much to lose." I gulped, feeling every fiber in my body being torn apart and warring. "I will always love you. I will always miss you. Those are facts. But I can't let your memories or the desire to be with you hold me back—or worse, kill me. I have to be better. I have to be healthy. And I have to move on."

There was a pause as Dimitri looked at me. Then he nodded.

"I know, angel." He lifted himself off the bed and took the few steps needed to get to where I was sitting. He kneeled in front of me and looked me in my eyes. I could see the pattern in his irises, see how the color morphed in the light streaming from my desk lamp. I noticed the way his hair fell perfectly, too perfectly, around his face, and watched as the light caught certain strands, and for a second—for a split second—I almost threw myself at his feet and cried out for him to take me with him because part of my soul still yearned for him and knew that he was my soulmate, that he was perfect for me.

But he had always been too perfect.

He reached his hand out, and without hesitating, I took it.

"Angel, I will always be here for you. But I'll give you your space." Dimitri smiled and reached his other hand up to cup my face. I leaned into his touch and sighed. It was a bittersweet goodbye, but one that was necessary for me to grow.

"I love you, Dima. Goodbye," I whispered, closing my eyes.

I felt his lips against my forehead and heard his last words.

"I love you, angel. Always have, always will."

Then his warmth on my cheek disappeared.

"*Chotu*? Are you okay?" I heard my mom softly ask from the doorway.

I nodded my head as it dropped, and I covered my eyes with my hand, feeling the tears flow.

"Is Dimitri… gone?"

Another nod.

Within seconds, I felt my mother's arms around me, and I held her tightly as I sobbed into her shoulder.

"I miss them, Mama."

"I know, *chotu*, I know."

24

MAY 27TH, 2019

YOU GOT THIS, Priya. You're going to be fine. They're not sharks; they're people.

I walked through campus toward my first class of the day, completely aware of the stares I received, and cognizant that while some may have just stemmed from paranoia, others were for sure real. Despite the stares, I held my head high and smiled as I thought up a positive reason for people to be staring.

They're all amazed at your haircut and the fact that you're wearing makeup for once, and how badass you look now.

My confidence was short-lived and stuttered a bit as I walked into my AP Gov class. Would Ms. Chen be angry at me for the way I'd treated her son? I hadn't needed to talk to her personally for a while and had no idea what to expect. I took a deep breath and headed for her desk.

To my surprise, she smiled. "Priya! Welcome back."

I smiled, too, thankful that she didn't hate me—or, at least, that she wouldn't show it outwardly.

"Thank you, Ms. Chen. I wanted to turn in the assignments I missed recently." I slung my backpack around to the front of my body and pulled out the folder stuffed with AP Government papers.

"I knew you would catch up without any problems," Ms. Chen said. "Also, now that you're feeling better, I hope you'll come over for dinner soon. I can make the fish again, since you seemed to like it so much."

"Oh, I don't—"

I was cut off by the bell ringing for class to start, and Ms. Chen shooed me to my seat. Confused, I walked off to my seat and tried to focus on the class, but my mind was stuck on her invitation.

Why would she ask me to come over after the way I treated Aaron? Is she just that nice? Or... does she not know we broke up?

The rest of my classes flew by, and I was greeted warmly by teachers. Some students even gave me a double take, with most of the girls telling me how good I looked with my new haircut. I smiled and thanked them, trying to be as warm and friendly as possible. I began to build up the courage to talk to people while I walked from class to class, pleasantly surprised by all the compliments I was receiving on my haircut and surprised by the fact that people even noticed I got one.

When fourth period rolled around, however, my feet dragged in the hall on the way to class.

AP Psych. Aaron and Amanda. You got this, Priya. Don't be scared. Remember: people, not sharks.

I took a few deep breaths as the classroom came into view and paused a few feet outside.

Just go. Go—in three... two... one.

I took the few final steps needed to enter the classroom and sensed the formerly buzzing room fall quiet. I hesitated near the door, uncomfortable standing at the entrance but frozen like a deer in headlights, those headlights being Aaron's eyes.

He was staring at me with his jaw slightly open, eyes bulging.

We just looked at each other for only a second, probably. He moved to get up, but halfway out of his chair, he hesitated and sat back down, composing himself before resuming his conversation with the guy sitting next to him.

I looked to the back and saw Amanda. Unlike Aaron, she was still openly and very obviously gawking, her jaw dropped and eyes wide open. I smiled at her and walked up to the open seat next to her.

"Is this seat still open?" I asked meekly, and she nodded vigorously. She kept watching me as I sat down, and when I turned to her with a smile, she finally snapped out of her awe and gave me a glare.

"Uhh, hello? Did you not get any of my texts? You disappear for a week and magically reappear looking like a model?"

Before I could think of some way to respond, the bell rang. I smiled at her, feeling that sense of normalcy grasp me again, but this time... it felt nostalgic. Amanda's remarks reminded me of something Elli would have said, and I could easily see how they were friends in the first place. They were very alike in their mannerisms, even though they were different in so many other ways.

If I was lucky, I would have the chance to become better friends with Amanda, learning more of those differences and similarities.

"I'll explain at lunch. If... if you want to have lunch together."

Amanda looked at me, shocked.

"Uhh, yeah! That sounds good," she said, and I smiled at her, just as Mr. Leonard stood up from his desk and began class.

~

I can honestly say I was not focused whatsoever in class. When the bell rang at the end of the period, rather than looking away from the front of the class and from the teacher, I dragged my eyes away from the back of Aaron's head. I had been eyeing him the whole time.

As soon as the bell rang, I quickly shoved all my stuff into my backpack and gave Amanda a wait sign with my hands. I dashed after Aaron just as he was leaving the classroom.

"Aaron!" I called after him, shocked by my own boldness as I chased after him into the bright sunlight. I cringed as the glare pierced my eyes. Holding up my hand, I watched as Aaron looked at me for a few seconds in silence, then told his friends to go on without him. He turned to look at me and took only a few steps toward me, remaining out of my reach.

I had this coming, I thought. *He deserves better. But he also deserves an explanation.*

I gulped. Lowering my hand, I twisted my fingers awkwardly in the hem of my shirt. I looked at the ground, feeling small and self-conscious.

"Um… I owe you an explanation," I said. Looking up, I saw Aaron staring at me, one hand in the pocket of his shorts, the other holding the strap of his backpack.

"I was in the hospital again because… I tried to attempt suicide." His eyes widened. "But—but not like that! Not like… not like I wanted to die. I just wanted to wake up and be with Dimitri and Elli." I held my hands up, pleading. Aaron only shook his head and continued looking at me.

"Jesus, I am not explaining this properly. Can we… can we just talk over lunch? With Amanda? I feel like I owe both of you an explanation."

Aaron sighed and looked at his feet, hiding his expression.

"Fine."

I sighed with relief, knowing that although he deserved better, I still selfishly wanted to keep him in my life.

I rushed back into the classroom where Amanda was waiting, then ushered her out to the quad, where we found a grassy spot for the three of us to sit and eat our lunch.

The whole time we were eating, or supposed to be eating, I caught Amanda up on my illness from the beginning. Then I told them both what happened the last month that caused my hospitalization. The whole time, Amanda and Aaron quietly listened, although Amanda started crying by the end of it.

"Priya! That's the most tragic love story I have ever heard. It's like… you and Dimitri are star-crossed, forbidden lovers! No offense, man," Amanda said, sniffling, as she turned to Aaron. He just groaned. I could see a hint of an eye roll, before he looked even further away from us, his hands brushing the grass next to him as we sat on the green hill.

I awkwardly laughed. "Please don't say that, Amanda. I'm literally just starting to get healthy again. I don't need that kind of… messaging right now." I said it as politely as I could.

Amanda gasped. "Oh! I'm sorry, Priya. I don't know why I said that. But… thank you for telling me. For telling us." I nodded, smiling, but I was watching Aaron. He was looking at the ground again, playing with a few strands of grass, his knees up and his arms wrapped around them.

"No problem. I... came to a realization while I was in the hospital, I guess. I have to let people in more. And I also wanted to apologize for the way I just... ignored you two. Especially when all you wanted to do was help. I just didn't know how to take help or how to accept it from... you know..." I said as my words trailed off. I continued to watch Aaron. He had barely responded to my explanation.

"It's okay, Priya," Amanda said. "You reacted the only way you knew how to. But please, if you can, don't shut us—or me, I guess—out again."

The bell rang, signaling the end of lunch. Amanda packed up and gave me a quick hug, which I welcomed, before rushing off to her AP US History class.

Aaron stayed where he was. Hesitantly, I moved closer to him, watching to see if he would move away. When he didn't, I took it as okay to speak.

"Aaron, I'm so, so—"

"If you say sorry, I'm going to explode," he whispered, and I pulled back slightly, surprised by his remark.

So maybe his stillness wasn't the go-ahead to start talking.

"Priya. Walk me through it again. Why didn't you just tell me what was going on?" he asked despondently. I gulped, thinking through my words carefully, trying to figure out how to both convey why I had reacted the way I did and word it in a way that he could possibly understand.

"Have you ever been in love, Aaron? In a way where the world changes when that person is around? Where, even reality changes?" I asked, and he gave a ghostly nod. "Well, whenever Dimitri is involved, I lose all sense of reality. Of what's right and what's wrong. It's... something I worked on while I was in the hospital, and it's something I'm still working on. But you also have to understand that he offered me a way to bring Elli back. He basically offered me my whole world back, and I—it was an offer I didn't know how to refuse. I didn't want to get you involved, and I didn't know how to tell you because… honestly, I was so caught up in that world, in my mission, and I didn't think I could involve you. I also didn't want you to be dragged down with me as I went on this suicide mission with my ex, or whatever he was. I just… I wasn't thinking, Aaron, and I'm… I hope you can forgive me."

The air around us was dry, the wind was quiet, and no sounds filled the space between us for what felt like hours.

"Priya, it's you." He looked up at me with glossy eyes. "You're the only person I've been in love with, and while my reality never changed in the way yours did… Priya, when you broke up with me, my world shattered. I know we're only in high school, and we have our whole lives ahead of us. But damn it, Priya, I already saw my life with you. You're my first love and—fuck, I don't know. I wanted to be your first real love, your first real everything. Once you told me about him, I told myself not to think about competing with Dimitri. I knew I would probably lose that battle, what with the way you talked about him and how recently he had disappeared from your life. But I thought I would be more important than a… hallucination." He looked away and sniffled, swiping at his eyes with the backs of his hands. I wanted to interject, to comfort him, to tell him something that would take away his pain. I didn't know what to say, and I knew he had more he needed to get off his chest.

Finally, he looked at me, his eyes red and lashes glued together by tears.

"I meant it when I said I would be here for you. I get that I couldn't be there for you physically at first, and I guess I can understand… well, no, I *can't* understand what you were going through. But I will trust you. If you say you are better, and if you say you can handle me by your side again, then I'm here for you. I am hurt, really hurt, but"—he swallowed —"I can't imagine I'm as hurt as you were if you wanted to... wake up from this world."

At that, I couldn't hold back the tears that welled up and fell from my eyes. I shook my head, looking far upward, trying to lighten the pressure building up behind my eyes and get myself under enough control to speak.

"Aaron..." I cleared my throat, and when I began again, my voice was steadier. "I do want you by my side. But... I think we need time to heal. I think... you need time to process. I'm sure there's a part of you that despises me right now, and... I think there's a part of me that hates myself, too, for the way I treated you." I took a deep breath, thinking through my next words carefully before speaking. "Remember when I said my illness doesn't change who I am? Well, that was only partially true. I think it actually makes me who I am, but it doesn't define me. It's a big part of me, and it always will be. I'll have good moments, hopefully most of the time, but I'll also have bad moments. And I need you to be okay with that. So... can we start over? Take it slow? And start with just being friends again?"

Aaron had silent tears streaming down his cheeks but he nodded. I was flooded with an immense sense of loss, even though he was right by my side and he'd agreed to what I asked. I couldn't help the immense feeling of missing him. I missed being held by him, I missed kissing him, and I missed knowing I was with him. But I knew we both needed to be in the right frame of mind to handle that.

"I'm not trying to hurt you," I said. "I just... I think I have to sort through a lot still. I want to be completely grounded in this world, and completely over Dimitri, so I can be... completely yours, or whoever's."

Once we were able to compose ourselves, we sat on the lawn by the campus and stared at the nearly empty road, watching as the few cars drove by.

"So your mom made an interesting comment earlier in gov," I said. Aaron looked at me curiously. I raised an eyebrow, and he began to blush slightly before looking away.

"Does she know we broke up?" I asked. He continued to look off in the opposite direction from me, giving me my answer. I smiled at him, feeling a hot air balloon filled with longing rise up in my chest. "Good. No need to tell her something that won't be true in the future." After I said it, I cringed. Stupid mouth. Now it was my turn to look away as Aaron's head whipped toward me.

"That didn't sound like taking it slow."

"I never said *how far* in the future it would be," I said. I snuck a peak at Aaron. He was grinning so widely, he almost had two dimples.

"Don't worry," he said with a wink. "That future won't be too far away." I laughed. Although I hated that our relationship was in limbo, the anticipation of what was to come made me giddy with excitement. I didn't know how long it would take for me to get where I needed to be, but I could feel that another of the strings connecting my brain to the puppeteer, and keeping me from moving on, had snapped.

"By the way," Aaron said, his grin becoming almost shy, "you look gorgeous with this haircut."

I gave a little hair flip. "Really? Do elaborate."

We erupted into playful laughter and banter, and I felt that balloon in my chest expand with warmth and a feeling of belonging.

EPILOGUE

"Would you like to share, Priya?"

I nodded, uncrossing my legs, only to cross them again with the opposite leg on top. The foot on top shook, as usual, and I clasped my hands together around my knee.

"I'd say I'm at a nine. It's been a little over a month since graduating high school, and it still feels surreal. I've also been doing extremely well, mentally. I'm able to ignore my hallucinations, if I have any at all, and I'm happy with the way my life is right now. I still think about Elli and Dimitri from time to time, even hear them sometimes, but I know they aren't real when I hear them. I'm taking my medication as prescribed, I've been checking in with my psychiatrist and therapist regularly, and everything seems to be going really well."

Dr. Jackson smiled at me and nodded. "I'm glad to hear you're doing well, Priya. Who is next?"

"I'll go," Jonathan said, sitting up straight in his chair. "I'd say I'm also at a nine. I painted a portrait last week. Nothing too extreme; but I submitted it to a local gallery, and they've decided to showcase it at their art show next week.

Who knows? I might get discovered, become famous." Jonathan looked at Charlotte, giving her a wink. She rolled her eyes, and I smiled fondly. Shortly after Jonathan had sketched my portrait in art therapy, he gave it to me in group.

"Holy shit, Jonathan, this really isn't me," I'd said, amazed and shocked at the fully colored and filled in image in front of me.

"You gotta work on that self-esteem, P. It's you. Accept it and love it."

"What about the band?" Bryan asked, pulling me off memory lane. He was wearing a pair of denim jeans and a short-sleeved black shirt. Although he still looked skinny, he had definitely put on some weight.

"What band?" Dr. Jackson asked, looking at all of us.

"We've decided to form a band. It's called 'Counseling S(Quad),'" Charlotte said with a laugh, putting up the parentheses with her hands. She was wearing her hair tied up in a messy bun with a summer scarf. She looked radiant, like she was on top of the world, and I had a feeling it wasn't from mania.

"Ya got Bryan on drums, Charlotte on vocals, P as keyboardist, and me as a guitarist," Jonathan said proudly.

"Really?" Dr. Jackson asked, unconvinced but amused.

"May I give my check-in?" Charlotte asked, changing the topic.

"Of course!"

"Thank you; sorry, but I'm a little antsy and just… need to talk. I actually have a date today, and I'm really scared. He doesn't know about my disorder, but he's a boy from my church and is really sweet; so I'm hoping that if, or when, the time comes, he'll be receptive. I've also been added to my church's regular worship team, so I sing every other Sunday, which has been amazing. I'd say I'm at a ten, but that would be really worrisome; so I'll say I'm at a nine and a half," Charlotte said proudly. She was swinging her legs back and forth beneath her chair excitedly, and I couldn't help but smile at her.

Definitely not mania.

"Bryan?" Dr. Jackson said. "Do you feel like sharing today?"

"Sure. I'm no nine, but I'm a firm seven. My dad and I have been talking lately. It's definitely helped with my recovery. I've gained some weight, and when my dad found out, he told me, in not so many words, that he was proud of me. He has his bad days still, but family therapy has been really helpful, I think."

I couldn't help but feel proud of our little group.

~

"So what you're saying is, you used my face without my permission for a portrait you submitted to an art gallery. All without telling me," I said amused, accusing Jonathan as we all walked out of the room together. He let out a bright laugh and stretched his arms around him before looking back at me with a wink.

"Just take it as a compliment, P. Anyway, I gotta go get my sister. See y'all next Thursday!" Jonathan walked briskly toward the elevator, and Bryan ran to keep up, making me laugh at the way Jonathan made him run to catch the elevator doors.

"Hey, Priya, can I talk to you real quick?" Charlotte asked, making me stop and turn towards her with a nod. We were standing in the waiting area; so I guided her to a secluded corner of the room, and we sat down.

"What's up?" I asked, and she took a deep breath before

continuing.

"You know how I mentioned I have a date today?"

I nodded.

"I know you and Aaron have been doing well, taking things slow, and I just... I wanted to ask you for some advice. How do you date with... with your illness? Because I'm completely terrified." She was playing with her hands, picking her nails, gesturing a lot—just overall fidgety. I smiled, took her hands in mine, and squeezed them, knowing it might be hard, but that she would be okay. I thought back to my most recent relationship conversation with Aaron.

～

"Oh God, I should not have eaten that hot dog," Aaron said. He hunched over, hands on his knees. We had just gotten off one of the rides at the Alameda fair that spun you in continuous circles. How that was supposed to be fun, we both had no idea at this point.

I rubbed his back as he took deep breaths. "You'll be okay. Do you want some water?"

Aaron nodded his head.

"All right. Come on, ya big baby."

Aaron groaned as he stood up straight again. I held out my hand, and he took it, squeezing hard before I dragged him to a stall to buy a bottle of water.

"How hard do you think these games are?" I asked as we stood watching a kid trying to pop balloons with darts at one particular booth, sipping our waters and taking a break from the rides.

"Considering they have to make money somehow, I'd say very hard."

"You think you can win me that prize?" I asked, pointing

to one of the stuffed toys hanging from the top of the stall. It looked sort of like a Disney Princess, but more like a knockoff version to avoid copyright lawsuits.

"Of course, I can!" Aaron said as he stepped up to the booth, pulling his wallet out.

He missed all his shots.

"It's okay! I didn't want it that much, anyway!" I said encouragingly. He looked back at me with a sad face before turning back and paying for another round.

Another loss.

He did that three more times before I finally pulled him away from the stall, defeat hanging over him like a cloud.

"How about we head home and get dinner? Will that cheer you up?" I asked, and he sighed, nodding.

We headed to our favorite sushi restaurant. It was the same spot where we'd had our first date.

Halfway through the dinner during a comfortable silence, I caught Aaron watching me.

"It's not nice to stare, ya know," I said, and Aaron almost choked on his food.

"I'm sorry. It's just... strange, you know?" He shook his head and took a sip from his ice water.

"What is?"

"Maybe this is overstepping my boundaries, but it's weird sitting here, with you, not really knowing... what we are."

I looked at him, then down at my food. It had been a month since our conversation during lunch at school. I knew what I *wanted* to say, but I didn't know what I *should* say. I didn't know what the right thing to say was.

I knew I wanted to be with him. I knew I wanted to have him in my life. I wanted to take things slowly, but I also knew that it was selfish to keep him as only a friend, for now, after all we had been through and after all he was willing to go through with me.

"To be honest, Aaron, I wanted to take things slowly, but… you know how impatient I am. I want to be with you, I really do, but I'm afraid." I smiled and shrugged to cover my emotions.

There was another pause.

"I can take things slowly. Whatever you need, whatever I can give you, that's fine. I guess I just didn't have any clarity after the way things have been progressing lately. And today, with our trip to the fair… it kind of felt like a date."

"I know."

It had been my idea to go to the fair—one of my impatient and selfish ways to get to spend time with him.

"I just wanted some clarification. But whatever you need, Priya. That's what's important. Whatever you need to heal because I think I'm feeling okay now. So… I'm waiting on you. But don't feel rushed!"

I sighed and shook my head. "All I know is I need your support. I need all the support I can get from people I love, and… well, you're very much one of those people. I still love you, Aaron."

I could feel my throat closing up but I continued.

"I don't want to be with you while a part of me is still thinking about Dimitri, and even though it's only a small, tiny portion, it's still a portion. But then, I also know that a part of me will always be with Dimitri. So I don't really know when I'll be ready."

Aaron reached his hand across the table, and I stared at it for a few seconds before hesitatingly placing mine in his.

He swiped his thumb across the backs of my knuckles, and I closed my eyes, letting myself feel the warmth spread from my hands through my entire body.

"No one is perfect, Priya, even you. And I still love you too. I don't expect you to forget Dimitri completely. He was a big part of your life. We don't ever forget people we've loved and lost. But—if not for me, then for the next guy—I think you need to move on in your life with the knowledge that you won't ever forget Dimitri completely. He was a big part of you, but he shouldn't hold you back. Just as you won't forget Elli, won't ever stop loving her; she can't hold you back either."

Aaron had a soft, comforting smile on his face, and I let out a breath of relief.

He was right.

I had to move on, but that didn't mean I had to forget what I had been through or those whom I had loved.

I nodded.

"You're so strong, Priya. You've been through things people can't even imagine. But don't lose yourself in trying to be someone you think you should be."

I pulled myself out of my memories and back to the present with Charlotte.

"First, you need to breathe," I said. She looked at me, and I gestured with my head that she should breathe at that exact moment. She immediately took a deep breath.

"Second, you need to understand that your disorder and your past will impact your dating life. You have to learn where your limits are and be vocal about them. If he's as great of a guy as you think, he'll understand. Being a self-advocate is a huge part of being in a successful relationship."

Charlotte nodded vigorously.

"Lastly, just have fun." I enunciated the last part and

smiled at her, hopefully providing some comfort. "Dating is what you make of it, and if you live in fear of it forever, you will have a miserable time. Just… take it at your own pace, but enjoy the ride."

Charlotte smiled at me and sighed.

"You're right. Thank you, Priya."

I let go of her hands.

"No problem."

We walked out together and said our goodbyes at the building's main door. I texted Aaron and waited in the shade. My phone beeped, signaling his response.

Aaron: Be there in 5.

Priya: Can't wait.

I sat on a bench in front of the building, feeling the breeze on my limbs. I closed my eyes, took a deep breath, and felt the prickling on my neck again.

"You really aren't going to wake up, are you?" Elli's voice floated into my ears and I sighed. After Dimitri and I had our farewell moment after I was released from the hospital, I had been expecting a similar conversation with Elli. I hadn't been sure whether I was dreading it or not.

I opened my eyes and looked at her.

Black tank top. Cutoff denim shorts. Worn out sneakers. Ponytail.

"I am awake," I said.

"Do you even miss us?"

I shrugged. "Every day."

"Then why? Why aren't we enough?"

"Because you aren't real anymore, Elli. Dimitri was never real."

I heard a car pull into the parking lot and saw Aaron's familiar blue Toyota. He pulled up in front of me, the passenger side of the car beckoning as Amanda waved from the backseat through the window. I smiled at them and looked back at Elli.

"But Aaron, my mom, my sister, and even Amanda are."

I pushed myself up off the bench, ran over to the car, and settled in without looking back.

Amanda wrapped her arms around me and the seat and squealed in my ear. "Time to go hiking!" she said happily and I laughed.

I looked at Aaron when Amanda released me and smiled.

"How was group?"

"Fantastic."

"Are you going to wear *that* to our hike?" Amanda asked, her head poking through the space between the two front seats. I looked down at my jean shorts and t-shirt and froze briefly before relief flooded me.

"I put a change of clothes and shoes in the trunk." I smiled as I buckled my seatbelt, laughing as soon as Aaron started blasting my sister's "Get well and get buck" playlist and Amanda started singing along to the song "Nothing's Gonna Stop Us Now."

We had become quite the trio in the last few months. From track meets, confessions, breakups, and even Elli's death, we forged a strong bond that, for the first time outside of Elli, I hoped would last a lifetime.

When I heard Aaron's door open, I noticed that he hadn't pulled out of the parking lot yet and had actually parked his car in a parking spot.

"There's something I need to get out of the trunk."

I watched Aaron walk around to the trunk and looked back at Amanda, seeing her trying to hide a smile.

"Amanda…" I said warningly, knowing she knew something.

"Just let him love you," she chided and I sighed. When

Aaron got back in the car, I was surprised to find him holding a medium-sized, plush Belle doll from *Beauty and the Beast*.

I began laughing. "What is that?"

"It's your graduation present. Sorry I'm late." He held it out to me.

"What?"

"I went with my family and my cousin's kids in LA to Disneyland, and when I saw this in the store, I immediately thought of the stuffed character from that horrendous game at the fair. I suck at those games—I know I should have given up sooner—but I really wanted to win you that doll. This is even better since I know Belle is your favorite."

My laughter died off into a smile. Aaron was looking at me intently, and I felt my body grow warm with a full body blush.

I took the doll and held it in my lap, brushing the soft fabric with the pad of my fingers and biting my lip as I tried to contain the overwhelming joy that spread through me.

"Well?" Amanda's voice prompted me to look at her, then at Aaron.

Then, without thinking, I unbuckled my seatbelt, leaned toward Aaron, and cupped the back of his head with one hand, pulling him across the space between us for a kiss. He fell toward me, his hand landing on the console in between our seats, and kissed me back.

The sparks between us were just as strong as that first time we'd kissed on New Year's Eve. All the love I had for him came crashing back down on me, and I wondered how I had ever stayed away from him, how I ever turned him away, and how I held back from kissing him for so long for these past few weeks.

Amanda's shouts and hollers from the back seat made me

laugh against Aaron's lips, and when I finally pulled away, he was grinning madly.

My heart beat wildly as he leaned his forehead against mine and sighed. "Priya, you always surprise me."

"Sorry, not sorry."

"What happened to taking it slow?"

I shrugged. "Patience is a virtue I lack."

"Awww! Now *that's* true love," Amanda said with a fake sniffle, making us both turn to her, laughing, and then back to each other.

"We're still taking things slowly. But know this, Priya. I'm not letting you get away so easily ever again."

"Good."

Aaron put the car in reverse, pulling out of the spot in the parking lot while Amanda and I began singing along to a Justin Bieber song as we coasted along the road to our hiking spot.

I meant what I said to Elli. I had so many reasons to live in this world. I had actually managed to live in a world without her, and even though I never thought I would have *needed* to figure that out, even though it hurt like a bitch and was a terrible journey to get there, I could honestly say, with more conviction than ever before, that I was living in reality— that I was awake.

Elli used to be my reality check in more ways than one, I realized. More than just telling me something was real, she made me want to believe in what was real. She was what made my life worth living, before Dimitri and after Dimitri.

I once questioned what life would be without Elli. I now had my answers.

Going to Berkeley, hiking, and running in track and field and cross-country was my life. Aaron, Amanda, my mom, and my sister were my life. My new Counseling S(quad) was my life.

For the first time in a long time, I didn't need anyone or anything to convince me to want to believe in what was real. For the first time in a long time, it came with ease. I knew it wouldn't always be like this, wouldn't always be this easy. Life would get hard. Life would be unbearable, and there would be days where I *wanted* the other world to be real, where I might slip up and turn to Elli and Dimitri.

But I finally felt ready to take on that part of the world without Elli as my reality check. I felt equipped with enough dividers— friends and loved ones— between me and that world. I felt confident enough to make more friends, find more hobbies and activities, and create more memories that would keep me grounded in this world. So when it got rough and became too much to handle — when I wanted to turn to Elli and Dimitri— I could take the punches from my life and my illness and punch right back.

I was going to live life to the fullest and I was going to do it in *this* world from now.

Because *C'est la vie.*

And I was my own reality check now.

ACKNOWLEDGEMENTS

I don't know who actually reads these, but to those who do, I just want to say thank you.

Thank you for giving this book and me a chance, even if you finished this and went "what the hell did I just read?"

This book has been in the works for 3.5 years, and it's been the hardest thing to write because it meant I had to be more vulnerable than I've ever been in my life. I poured out my past and my present into this book, as well as a lot of could-have-been moments and many moments I wish had happened.

I want to say a special thank you to my family for sticking with me and telling me to snap out of it every time I tried to quit.

I want to thank Jocelyn and Eamonn for basically being my sounding boards when I needed to talk at someone, not to someone, through my racing thoughts.

Finally, I want to thank Alayna for being the inspiration behind Elli and for being my platonic soulmate.

ABOUT THE AUTHOR

Kirpa Singh works in social work by day, is an author by night, and binge watches youtube videos or goes for long walks in between. She's had a longstanding passion for mental health and is a strong advocate which has inspired her to pursue her Master's in Social Work.

Other than that, she's an ESFJ, a 2, and a Virgo.

CPSIA information can be obtained
at www.ICGtesting.com
Printed in the USA
HW012312101021
71FS

9 781736 986202